IRIS HAS
FREE TIME

IRIS HAS
FREE TIME

BY IRIS SMYLES

SOFT SKULL PRESS

AN IMPRINT OF COUNTERPOINT | BERKELEY

Iris Has Free Time

Copyright © 2013 Iris Smyles

Library of Congress Cataloging-in-Publication Data

Smyles, Iris.
  Iris has free time : a novel / Iris Smyles.
     pages cm
  ISBN 978-1-59376-519-4
  1. Smyles, Iris--Fiction. 2. Young women--New York (State)--New York--Fiction. 3. Self-realization in women--Fiction. 4. Bildungsromans. 5. Autobiographical fiction. I. Title.
  PS3619.M95I75 2013
  813'.6--dc23
                            2013000711

Cover design by Iris Smyles, Neil Russo, and Debbie Berne
Interior design by meganjonesdesign.com
Cover photo of Iris Smyles by Chris Stein

A different version of "Autumn in New York" appeared previously in *Splice Today*.

A different version of "Iris's Movie Corner" appeared previously in *Nerve*.

Soft Skull Press
An imprint of COUNTERPOINT
1919 Fifth Street
Berkeley, CA 94710
www.softskull.com

Distributed by Publishers Group West

10 9 8 7 6 5 4 3 2 1

Printed in the United States of America

To my parents, Arthur and Popy Smyles

+

To Frederic Tuten, my Virgil, for seeing me through the fire

Because Dante the character is a fictional creation of Dante the poet, the reader should remember that the character's feelings do not always correspond to those of the poet. . . . Indeed, on a general level, the kindness and compassion of Dante the character often contrasts with the feelings of Dante the poet, who, after all, has devised excruciating torments with which to punish his characters, many of whom are historical individuals with whom Dante was acquainted in life.

SPARKNOTES: THE INFERNO

PROLOGUE: AT SEA · 1

BOOK I

1 ▌ THE BASTARD FELIX · 53

2 ▌ THE CAPTAIN · 105

3 ▌ AUTUMN IN NEW YORK · 137

BOOK II

4 ▌ DISPATCHES FROM MY OFFICE · 151

5 ▌ CHINESE FINGER CUFFS · 197

BOOK III

6 ▌ EUROPE · 215

7 ▌ "IRIS'S MOVIE CORNER" · 251

8 ▌ SCIENCE FICTION · 263

9 ▌ SMYLES' GAMES: A COMPLETE HANDBOOK · 291

10 ▌ OUT OF HELL'S KITCHEN · 317

OVERTURE · 369

PROLOGUE
AT SEA

To be an old man and finished at twenty-three . . .

STÉPHANE MALLARMÉ, LETTER 1864

I

1

Looking back, the vintage 1930s red and green tartan suit may have been a touch too much. But it was the most conservative thing I owned. And I *did* look great in it, I noted, crouching down on the ledge of the bathtub to check myself in the medicine cabinet mirror. Just like Rosalind Russell at the news desk in *His Girl Friday*. There was no way they wouldn't hire me!

I skipped out the door, walking briskly to generate my own heat. I'd not worn a jacket for fear of corrupting my look and the sun was all but ignoring me. In the corner of the sky there it stood, aloof and cold, as if the lavish heat of summer were suddenly an embarrassment. Everywhere there is heartbreak, I thought, looking up at a thin tree, its leaves clinging desperately to branches that wanted no more to do with them. What a cad the fall is.

At the corner, I opened my newspaper. A reporter had solicited job-seeking advice from human resources personnel all over Manhattan. "Confidence is everything. You need to sell yourself!" one said. "The biggest mistake job-seekers make is not adequately preparing for the interview," said another. "Ask yourself before you get there, 'Would I hire me?' If the answer is 'Yes' you've dramatically increased your chances." The light changed. I turned the page to see what advice they gave if the answer was "No," but the article was over.

I arrived at the convention center, at the head of a long line of applicants dressed somberly in gray and blue. I lifted my mesh veil. "Is this whole line for the job fair?"

"It starts around the corner," a gray and blue man answered, in a voice that was also gray and blue. He motioned far behind him.

"I'm on the list," I said, biting my lip. This is code in Manhattan: That you're not on the list doesn't matter; you should be.

He looked at me blankly. "What list?"

I walked the whole block and half the next one before finding the end, then took out my résumé and began looking it over. Four years in the city only to end up out in the cold. . . . I sighed and unpinned my pillbox hat; it was pulling my hair too tightly and the bobby pins were giving me a headache.

Two hours later, I was ushered into a great bustling hall. Booths! Banners! Balloons! "Free Gifts!" The Hearst table was doling out York Peppermint Patties. Hachette Filipacchi Media, pencils etched with the company's name. *Star* was offering back issues, pencils etched with the company's name, *and* York Peppermint Patties. I dug my hand into a bowl of caramels at *Us Weekly*, popped one into my mouth, and surveyed the room—always my first move when attending a party.

I got on line for the men's magazine *Maxim,* behind a slightly nerdy yet well-put-together Yale grad. I knew he'd gone to Yale because the reporter who was interviewing people for a story on the current recession and its effect on recent college graduates, asked him.

The summer after Yale, he interned at a local newspaper in Connecticut, he told her, and went on to explain how difficult his job search had been even with his three languages and two internships at distinguished publishing houses here in New York and in Shanghai— he said something in Chinese, they both laughed—because the job market was just that bad right now, and so he was willing to try anything. This fair seemed like a good opportunity. He sighed. Perhaps talking to someone face-to-face, rather than just blindly sending out his résumé and performing millions of follow-up phone calls, would make the difference.

"And what about you?" the reporter asked, turning her attention to me. "What brings you to the job fair?"

"My mom," I said, rolling my eyes. "She saw the ad in the *Times* and suggested I come. Parents, you know?" I began to laugh and waited for the two of them to join in.

The reporter stared, then thanked the Yale grad and disappeared into the crowd. The Yale grad turned away, too. Nervously, I worked to straighten the seams on my stockings. What *had* I been thinking when I put this on?

When my turn came fifteen minutes later, I removed my kidskin glove and gave the HR rep a firm hand. "Etiquette guides don't require women to remove their gloves prior to shaking hands, but if women and men are to share the workplace, I believe they should be held to the same standards. I'm Iris."

A pale, bespectacled boy a few years my senior, looked back. "How modern."

He rattled off a list of stock questions, which I answered the same I would any man asking to buy me a drink. The key is not to appear too interested, while not suggesting complete indifference either. I flashed him a look that said, *We both know what you want,* a look that said, *No, I'm not that kind of girl—how dare you!—but I'd be happy to exchange a little witty banter while I down the whiskey you've so generously provided.*

He looked down at my résumé. "Wow, you interned at *The New Yorker.* Did you apply there?"

"Nope."

He looked up.

I gave the line a tug.

"I just felt like, 'been there, done that,' you know? Also, I dated a few guys in the office so it would've been awkward."

He adjusted his glasses.

"This is actually my first interview," I added, and flashed a reassuring smile. I could tell he was nervous.

"What have you been doing since graduation?"

"I was in Greece. My mom is Greek and I have family there so I go every summer. I stayed longer this year though, figuring I probably wouldn't be able to get away much once I get a job. What did you do for the summer?"

"I worked."

"Cool. Where at?"

"*Maxim*," he said, looking down. "It says you went to NYU."

"Yes, I started out studying Acting at The Tisch School of the Arts, but then in my junior year decided I wanted something more practical, so I transferred to the Gallatin School for Individualized Study and designed an interdisciplinary concentration in Literature and Philosophy. Also, I write poetry. Mostly free verse." I guided him to that line on my résumé and to the three directly below it: "make my own paper," "Reiki massage," "fourteen years tap dancing."

"Wow."

"I also play the saxophone, but had to cut a few things in order to keep my résumé under three pages." I directed him to the list of plays from which I'd performed scenes and monologues while still at Tisch.

"*Ma Rainey's Black Bottom*," he read aloud. "What's 'Alexander Technique?'"

"Theory of standing."

"Sense Memory, Voice . . ." he went on, reading the names of NYU's most competitive, invitation-only drama workshops, classes I'd had to audition for, classes that cost my parents upwards of twenty thousand dollars a year, classes that suddenly sounded preposterous. "Advanced

Movement, Speech. . . ." Apparently, in order to master the basic skills most humans pick up during infancy—walking and talking—I had had to undergo elaborate and expensive training while at college. I blushed.

"Do you type?"

"Not well," I said, trying to smile. I had lied before, but in this context where a little white lying was expected, my desire always to defy expectations prevented me.

"Do you know Excel?"

"No."

"Could you learn?"

"Probably not. I find it very difficult to learn things I don't already know." Then, remembering the advice that I try to sell myself, I added, "But I'm sure I'd pick it up *eventually*."

At last he lowered my résumé. "So, tell me. Why do *you* think we should hire you?"

Here was the big question. The one I'd worried about the whole walk over. I summoned all of what remained of my confidence and did my best to answer without crying.

"You shouldn't," I said. Perhaps he might hire me for my refreshing honesty? I laughed faintly, then added, "Just kidding," and gave him jazz hands.

"Fair enough. So why do you want to work for *Maxim*?"

I played it cool. "I just went to the booth with the shortest line."

"Is there anything you *like* about the magazine?"

"Couldn't say as I've never read it. To be honest I don't really read magazines. They're expensive, and for the same price I'd much rather read a classic like *Madame Bovary*."

"Yes, that's a good book," he answered politely. "Given your interests, Iris, I'm wondering why you want to work at a magazine at all."

"That's a good question . . ." I heard myself say, for at some point during the conversation, I'd lost control of the vehicle. It was like the way survivors of car crashes describe the moments leading up to impact. Everything slows down, your senses become keen, and while you are completely aware of the impending collision, you are also unable to stop it. ". . . I suppose I feel about working the way Thomas Paine felt about government, 'at its best, being but a necessary evil; at its worst, an intolerable one.'" I paused. "A magazine job just seemed like the least bad. I'm actually working on a novel right now. That's my main thing. Also, I draw cartoons. Does *Maxim* publish cartoons?"

He thanked me for coming and moved to file my résumé. Then he invited me to arm-wrestle The *Maxim* Man. "That's our little gimmick for the fair," he said smiling, and motioned to a small card table set up just next to his booth, behind which stood a man, six-foot-two, covered in red and blue lycra.

2

The *Maxim* Man's superhero costume stretched over his whole face and body, so I couldn't actually see him, though I was able to make out the contour of his nose and cast of his eyes. He held out his hand. I raised mine to say, "I'll pass," but he grabbed it firmly and wouldn't let go. "Okay, okay," I sighed and, like a good sport, planted my elbow on the table.

There, dressed like a 1939 career-gal and struggling arm-to-arm with a superhero, I reviewed the details of my disastrous interview, consoling myself that at least no one I knew had witnessed it. *Forget it, Iris!* I told myself, blinking back tears and gazing up into the shady hollows behind The *Maxim* Man's lycra-covered eyes. I was looking directly into them, wondering what I was going to do with my life, now that it had officially started, when it hit me: The *Maxim* Man was Donald.

Donald, the boy I had loved all through college. Donald—my Beatrice!—about whom I'd written so many of my free-verse poems. Donald, whom I still always hoped I'd run into somewhere—he'd see me first, across the room; I'd be drinking a martini and chatting with a handsome man in my thrall. . . .

By the time the back of my wrist hit the table, I was all but convinced that I was arm-wrestling the then love-of-my-life Donald and that those were his all-seeing eyes staring out at me from behind the mask. And what disturbed me most about this revelation was that I couldn't decide for whom the situation was more humiliating. I cringed thinking Donald had just witnessed my interview, but then, if he had, he'd done so covered in red and blue lycra. Of course, he at least had a job, which was more than I could say. Though it wasn't quite the job in publishing he'd bragged about last I saw him.

He let go of my hand and offered a theatrical salute.

I looked up, smiled, and staggered away.

It was all so confusing. Only five months earlier, I was being congratulated—"It is my great pleasure to present the Class of 2000!" I'd stood up to a round of applause.

I floated among the crowd of applicants, their conversations merging into a boisterous hum. I looked around, visited a few more booths, and filled the free laminated folder I got from *Scholastic* with pencil erasers and tiny Kit Kats. Heavy with "gifts," I decided to head home.

3

Where do ideas come from? The ancient Greeks believed inspiration to be divine, that one of nine muses whispered into the ear of the artist, who was not himself a genius but a conduit. "Sing in me, Muse, and through me tell the story of that man skilled in all ways of contending, the wanderer, harried for years on end," Homer begins *The Odyssey*.

I was almost home when I realized I didn't want to be. My roommate May and her boyfriend Felix would be there—they were always there—and I wanted to be alone. So when I saw the subway entrance on Fifty-third and Seventh, I decided to head downtown.

I got out at West Fourth and walked toward NYU but veered south when I came upon Washington Square. I'd spent so much time in the park during college; to go there now would mean a retreat. I continued around it, past NYU's administrative buildings, where I imagined committees busily deciding whom to admit next year, whom to give my freshly vacant spot.

I walked down into Soho, past bars I'd frequented as a freshman, past plain, unmarked doors, which at midnight opened onto chic nightclubs, past phone booths decorated with ads for the upcoming season of *Sex and the City*—a glamorous photo of Carrie Bradshaw in a black T-shirt covered with rhinestones spelling her name.

I headed east toward Broadway and then down again, bobbing along the rushing river of shoppers, past windows behind which mannequins stood silently, posed in body-hugging T-shirts—"Hottie," "Fabulous," "Sexy," written across the bust.

I turned east again wandering deeper into the Lower East Side, looking in at the displays of small designer boutiques along the way. A $150 T-shirt with the words, "Gold Digger," hung in one window. Another, "Page Six Six Six." Another, "Thank You Thank You

Thank You," written three times vertically the way it appears on plastic shopping bags.

I walked on, past a walled-up construction site plastered with ads for new albums, new movies, new stores, and past a newsstand where I paused, recognizing the faces of Justin, Shawn, and Richie staring out from the cover of *New York Magazine*.

I went in. A bell rang as I entered. A middle-aged Pakistani, with three long hairs combed across the top of his head, looked up. He followed me with his eyes as I walked the length of the store, which was covered floor to ceiling with new issues of popular glossies. Giving up, I returned to the front and asked about the magazine in the window.

He hopped down from his perch behind the register and, cutting in front, beckoned me to follow. Scanning the wall quickly, he handed me a different issue.

"No. The one in the window," I repeated.

"Is old. This one you want," he said, pressing it into my hand.

"No," I said, handing it back. "That one. I know the guys on the cover!"

He sighed and went outside to have a look, then came back in and knelt down to untape it from the display.

"Two dollar," he said, as he handed it to me.

The three had been profiled for "Models Suck," the logo decorating their popular line of T-shirts. I hadn't known about their fashion venture. I flipped back to the cover to see the date. August 24, 1998, a year before I met them in Atlantic City with Lex.

"This is not a library," the clerk announced.

I paid for the magazine and left.

I walked a few more blocks—aimless, adrift—when, looking into another window, I was startled by my own image reflected back. The late-afternoon light had cast a mirror-like glare, so I could not see in but only myself trying to. There I was, the whole of me, paused in a Depression-era suit—a woman lost in time.

What do you know about PowerPoint? About Excel spreadsheets? About answering the phone? I interviewed my reflection. And what do you care? I went on, as a song in my head started up, grew louder, and was backed by a beat to which I could dance. The song my muse was singing was clear:

Forget corporate America, Iris! Selling T-shirts! That's your game! Why worry over all the things you don't know, when there are obviously so many more important things that you do? That a T-shirt with the words, "Second Base" would be capital! That underwear featuring the words, "Bad Ass" could go with it! And the great thing about T-shirts is you don't even need to know how to sew! The really great thing is you don't need to know anything! All you need is one good idea. . . . Staring into the window, at a T-shirt just visible behind my own reflection, I discovered I had many.

4

T-shirts were just the beginning. Justin, Shawn, and Richie wanted to do music, film, to build a hip-hop empire! "It's all about who you know," they had told the reporter in the *New York Magazine* article, which I read half of later that night, after I finally arrived home.

May and Felix were there when I walked in. Felix was on the couch, using my copy of *This Side of Paradise* to roll a joint, while May was at the stereo, turning up the volume and yelling over it. I sat down on the other end of the sofa and took out my magazine, but after a few pages, I gave in to the sway of them. Accepting the joint from

Felix, I stuck the magazine, most of it unread, under the cushion of our collapsing couch. I took a long drag. *Who you know, who you know* . . . How I knew Justin, Shawn, and Richie, as Rudyard Kipling might say, is another story. . . .

I confess I haven't actually read any Rudyard Kipling, but I did read this book of Edwardian erotica by Anonymous, which featured a narrator—a perverted "uncle"—who invited two curious schoolgirls he'd met onboard a transatlantic steamer to a French brothel where he was a regular, who used this phrase to great effect. But what has Rudyard Kipling or the prolific Anonymous to do with me? Absolutely nothing! Which is why I'm going to tell *my* story, with all its twists and turns, right now.

II

1

Some say New York in summer is a wonderful town and cite the many free activities available all season. Film festivals in Bryant Park! Opera on the Great Lawn!

"There's also a truck in the East Village that gives free food to the homeless every Sunday. Maybe we should go there for brunch," Lex said over the hum of the air conditioner.

"What about Tuesday? They're showing *La Traviata* in Central Park," I said, looking up from *The Voice*.

"If I want to see the opera, I'll buy a ticket. Summer Stage is for poor people. It's the rich man's concession to the worker who can't afford to leave town. They think if they distract us with free shit, we're less likely to rob them while they're away. Direct the poor man's attention toward the stage, so he doesn't notice the darkened windows of the apartments lining Central Park. Give us opera so we don't go mad, throw a brick through the window, and haul off with their tea settings. It's insulting."

"But it's fun to picnic in Bryant Park. They're showing *His Girl Friday* next week!"

"You know who else picnics? Homeless people. They love picnics. During the Depression, people picnicked in the park all year round; they called it Tent City."

"Fine," I sighed. "What do you want to do then?"

It was June of 1999, the summer before my senior year. Classes had ended in late May and within a week all my friends disappeared, leaving the city suddenly quiet. Quiet in that noisy way, when you look around and see crowds of people talking, just none of them to you.

Up until then, I'd enjoyed a full schedule of dates and parties; college was turning out to be an education more sentimental than academic. Lectures and seminars were few and far between, leaving plenty of time to go out. And I did, constantly, working at my social life the way others worked at their résumés. To leave Manhattan then, to trade in my hard-won glamour for over a month in the suburbs, was out of the question.

"*You Can't Go Home Again*," I'd said, during my father's birthday dinner weeks earlier. We were at our favorite Red Lobster in Long Island, where I'm from. My parents looked at me quizzically. "It's a novel by Thomas Wolfe," I explained, as a means of broaching the subject.

And so, with my parents' permission, instead of returning home that June, I signed up for drawing classes at the School of Visual Arts. Since my classes only met once a week, however, I had little to do.

I took a lot of walks in the beginning. I lingered in bookstores, read novels in the park, and went frequently to the movies. I'd walk to Lincoln Center, which wasn't far from my apartment, or else, if it were a Saturday, I'd walk the fifty or so blocks down to Angelika on Houston. On the street again after, alone in the warm summer night, I'd stroll the whole way back up to my apartment in Hell's Kitchen, past lively restaurants and bars with crowds of young people spilling out, hoping that by the time I got home I'd be tired enough to sleep.

I looked forward to the free film every Monday in Bryant Park. I'd spend the whole afternoon flipping through magazines in the Mid-Manhattan Library and then at dusk, wander over. Though the park always filled up hours ahead of time—people would come early and spread blankets to reserve space for friends—I went just at the last minute. The great thing about going alone, I considered, watching *Psycho* between groups of screaming friends, was how easy it was to find a single seat.

I worked on my drawing a lot, too. At the end of every session of animation class, the teacher would gather everyone around for a critique. When it was my turn, I showed a fifteen-second cartoon adapted from my comic strip, "The Naked Woman," about the boozy misadventures of its title character, The Naked Woman: Against a flat expanse of white, a naked woman runs, trips, and falls every fifth step. Above her head, a thought bubble reads, "Open bar!" I looped it to go on forever. In silence, we watched her run, trip, fall, get up . . . run, trip, fall, get up. . . . The other students in the class, mostly middle-aged men interested in superhero comics, called it "odd."

I didn't go out much. I didn't have anyone to go out much with. There was Caroline, whom I'd met that winter when my party life was in full swing. We went out occasionally—to the karaoke night where we'd met and were both regulars, or the Tikki Room at Niagara where we'd put our cigarettes on the bar and I'd say, "Let's smoke cigarettes and act cool," before lighting up. But since she didn't drink and had an actual job to go to in the morning, she often went home early.

Mostly, I looked forward to Thursdays, to Lex's '80s party. I'd met Lex at the same karaoke party where I'd met Caroline. He was part of the celebrity set—musicians who covered their own songs, B-actors and indie-darlings who pretended they didn't want to be recognized but bristled when they weren't—that had made the party famous. "I liked your song," I told him one night. "It reminded me of my youth," I said earnestly. This made him laugh and he began inviting me to all his parties—"Soul Sucka!" a '70s night at Twilo that served chicken wings and forties, "Soft Sundays," an evening of easy listening upstairs at Moomba. I always dressed up with a nod to the era or style he was referencing. He liked that about me, he said.

Thursday would arrive. I'd compose a fresh eighties outfit—acid washed jeans maybe and a T-shirt cut to fall off one shoulder—and suck down a few beers while I got ready. Then, with my courage duly fortified, I'd make my way downtown. Usually, I'd bring something with me—a funny article I'd cut out from the *Weekly World News* ("Oldest Man in the World's Secret to a Long Life Is Drinking a Quart of Whiskey and Smoking Two Packs a Day!"), or a vintage Garbage Pail Kid I'd found at the Salvation Army ("Messy Tessy")—and turning up beside the DJ booth, I'd shyly stick out my hand. "For you."

Lex would receive my gift with a laugh and welcome me with a kiss on the cheek, while pressing a few drink tickets discreetly into my palm. Then he'd pull back to get a good look at me. "I love the acid wash." After that, I'd go to the bar and try to make friends, returning to him throughout the night to request songs.

"Do you have 'Word Up'?" "'Self Control' by Laura Branigan?" "'All Night Passion' by Alisha?" My requests were a code: I'm wiser than my years and I know what you know, Lex. All the songs from the 1980s that are closest to your heart; they are close to mine, too.

From the outset, we'd bonded over eighties music and trivia; this had been his heyday and it had been mine, too. As a kid in Greece, I'd tagged along to discos with my older cousin, who was just a few years younger than Lex; I'd danced to the same music at nine that he'd danced to at twenty-five. Couldn't he see? I was not like these other girls who came to his party ready to dance to whatever he happened to play. They didn't know what I knew, what we knew together.

By July, I was spending less time alone and more time with Lex, who'd also been left behind for the summer. The way people without family feel about the winter holidays, Lex told me, New Yorkers without summer homes feel about July and August. I commiserated, leaving out the fact that it had been my choice to stay, that I was as thrilled by our condition as he was unhappy, that I loved the terrible heat, and that I always feel lonely no matter who I'm with or what the season, and that I felt lucky to be lonely in New York City with him.

We'd meet up for brunch, for a movie, for a birthday party his friend was throwing on his roof. Lex would call and say, "I hate parties. Wanna come?" Or I'd hang out with him in the DJ booth at Lot 61 or Life or Veruka. And then, Thursday again. I'd say hello before setting up at the bar, dance by myself to Billy Idol's "Dancing with Myself," and then when I got tired, rest by sitting in the coin-operated toy car machine in the corner of the club.

There, practicing loneliness, I'd watch the crowd until Lex came to fetch me, pulling me up to dance with him until the song ended and the record cut off. Everyone looked around, waiting for Lex to set up the next one. Lex had to work, so I'd return to the bar alone to pick up guys, which is an art as much as bullfighting. This was my Hemingway moment:

They'd buy me good drinks, and with dignity we'd lean on the bar of this dirty, poorly lighted place, before a song came on, a song I could not resist, and I'd run to the dance floor to perform my high-kicks dance.

Certain songs were anthems that brought everyone to their feet. The beat would find you chatting, sipping a beer, worrying, and you'd rise up, as if called. There, dancing under the swirling multi-colored lights, the song lyrics echoing in your ears like a Greek chorus, it felt as if you were part of something, as if youth were a revolution, and your drinking, your dancing, your laughing, even your tears, were a sacred duty.

I'd get fantastically drunk and smoke cigarette after cigarette and talk and talk until I had no voice left, until the lights came on and it was 4:00 AM.

The staff would start to close up, and I'd help Lex gather his records into the trunk of his vintage Buick parked out front. With me in the passenger side, we'd speed off into the night, stopping at our favorite diner to get cheeseburgers, or at the deli to get cigarettes and a six-pack—"my fuel." And then we'd go to Atlantic City, or if we were feeling responsible, one of the illegal card rooms right here in Manhattan. Lex knew all of them. Lex knew everything.

An empty catering hall with one table occupied: A fifty-five-year-old dealer whom everyone called "The Greek," two DJ's Lex knew from Gambler's Anonymous, a truck driver, a soldier on leave, a public school teacher who said very little, Lex, and me. I'd look on quietly, drink my beer, smoke my cigarettes, and occasionally write things in my notebook—poems or snatches of prose for a novel I planned to write about desolation and how much fun it was.

Settled in with my grilled cheese sandwich and beer, I'd watch Lex gamble away the morning, study the faces of the other players, and flirt innocently with the older man who ran the room. He liked me and gave me menthol cigarettes when I ran out of my regular ones, and then took me aside to a table next to the big one in order to share his stash of hard candy. He pulled my chair out and asked me to tell him all about myself, but then didn't pause for me to speak and began telling me all about myself instead: I was a nice girl, he said, and I shouldn't be hanging around all night with a bum like Lex in a place like this.

"She likes it," Lex yelled over, without looking up from his cards.

I smiled and shrugged and chose a pink candy from the dish.

After a while I'd return to Lex's side where I'd dream about the wonderful novel that might contain us, the sordid romance of Lex and me in the underworld. Wasn't I bored just to sit there? the others asked, not understanding how busy I was in my mind, polishing the night until it gleamed like a rare fiction. Bored? How could I be? I was the heroine of a great book.

I'd pass out at Lex's place, and in the morning or the afternoon or early evening, depending on when we woke up, hungover and tired, we'd go for breakfast around the corner. We'd eat pancakes and eggs and then, tired still, would return to his apartment to escape the heat and watch TV.

In his living room filled with records, four vintage televisions sets, and his very own pinball machine, the air conditioner wheezed loudly as we sat on his stylish mod couch, ridiculing Ruthie of MTV's *The Real World*.

Ruthie always got too drunk. The camera followed her as she crawled on her hands and knees through a crowded bar. We cracked up laughing at her expense, before I asked seriously, cringing as I recalled my own actions the night before, "Am I that bad when I drink, Lex?"

"Sometimes," he said. "Not all the time, though," he smiled.

We'd walk his dog, a melancholic ridgeback named Lola. We'd walk her around the block but never over to the river, though it was only five blocks away. "What's there to do at the river?" Lex asked, when I suggested it. "As soon as you get there, all you do is start walking back!"

Walking to the river was not essential. What was essential was the invention and perpetuation of the good time. What was essential was yesterday—"In the '80s, you could go to a party and meet anyone. Basquiat, Warhol . . . People were interesting then; creativity mattered!"

Lex would frown and complain, but even his bitterness was not without style. "I went to the video store and there were all these videos. Too many! I didn't know what to get. What's the point of all that selection? If I owned a video store, I'd only stock *Caddy Shack*. Every video in there would be *Caddy Shack*. This way you'd never be confused about what to rent again. . . ."

We'd run into his friends—B-movie actors, indie-directors, musicians and designers, or party promoters like him. In the middle of what for anybody else would be a workday, they'd stand on the corner, chatting about what to do next. No one ever had any place to be.

"We're going to go buy more mint-flavored toothpicks," Bernie and her boyfriend told Lex, but not me. They twirled the ones already in their mouths.

"We're running out," her boyfriend added, looking out across Sixth Avenue and blinking slowly.

"She wants to be a DJ now," Lex began, after they left. "She called me up the other night, and she's like, 'Lex, I'm deejaying at Veruka tomorrow. Can I come over and borrow some records?' I'm like, 'Get your own fucking records!' The whole thing of being a DJ is building up a record collection, and she just expects me to loan her mine? If a club wants my records, let them hire me! I'm gonna give them to her so she can play DJ and make money she doesn't even need?" We walked a few more steps in silence. I'd learned to keep silent until his anger passed. Then he added, "It's a joke that they're dating. He's just dating her because of who her father is."

"Who's her father?"

"Bax Stubbs."

"Who's that?"

"The guitarist of Xenophobe," he snapped.

I shrugged. "I didn't know he was married."

"He's not."

"How chic. I'd love to have a little bastard myself some day. Name him Edwin . . . make him sleep in the stables . . . ask the servants, 'Where's that little bastard Edwin got to?'"

"When did everyone get to be so fucking fake?" Lex said, kicking at the ground.

2

Though Lex was thirty-six and I was twenty, in just a few years I would be too old for him. He'd had many "good friends" like me already, girls who eventually grew up and left him behind. Lex, always and forever, the boy behind the DJ booth.

Some people said he was living in the past, that he didn't revive the '80s, but had never let it go. And sometimes, behind his back, I called him "the denim gargoyle." He had lines on his face and thick skin from too much sun, too much partying and, finally, too much time. One of his tattoos, a thorn of roses circling his forearm, was fading to blue. In the mornings, before we'd head out for breakfast, I'd trace my fingers over it. I love you, Lex, I'd think, which is perhaps why I invented the cruel nickname.

"If I met you back then," I said, looking up from a photo, "if we were the same age, I don't think you'd like me." It was a Saturday night, and we were at his apartment, looking through a box of old pictures taken in the early '80s when he first moved to New York. In each, he looked so young and handsome, he and his friends so effortlessly cool. I dropped the stack onto the bed. "I think you'd be mean," I said, going into the kitchen.

Lex and his friends dated models, fresh-faced movie stars, and the daughters of the rich and famous. Seeing him among them, I felt rough and embarrassed, as if my body were sewn from a cheaper material. I returned with a beer.

Lex was laughing and handed me another photo. One of his friends, the preppy one, had gotten the Lacoste alligator tattooed onto his chest. He pointed him out.

"That's funny because I've been thinking about getting a one-legged alligator tattooed on mine," I said frowning, "the insignia for the Lacoste knockoff on sale at JCPenney."

"What about the Polo symbol without the mallet?" he ribbed back. "We could get matching ones. You get the mallet, and I'll get the rest of him."

"I don't want the mallet," I said, flopping down on the bed. I stared at the ceiling, at Lex's face as it came over mine, as he kissed me.

I would never be cool. And I wouldn't have cared finally, if I knew that Lex didn't. Still, I couldn't blame him for being shallow; his life depended on it. Cool people, cool places, cool things. As a DJ and party promoter, being cool was how he made a living. And with no distinction between his personal and professional life, Lex, quite simply, couldn't afford to date me.

That said, I don't think he really wanted to. Though he'd pursued me in the beginning, I didn't know how to hold the interest of a veteran playboy of his caliber. He'd had hundreds of "relationships," while I'd had two. Playing aloof at first, I managed for a while to excite his curiosity—I'd stand near him at the bar and then talk to someone else. But then, once I got him close, I let down my guard, began looking at him too often and too long, and the whole dynamic between us quickly shifted. He knew he had me, which was not nearly as exciting as wanting me.

We had sex for the first time in a suite at the Sands Casino, then ordered cheeseburgers from room service and went down to the floor to gamble.

After, things cooled down almost immediately. I was disappointed, but found a broken heart was not so hard to bear, provided you didn't know it was broken until after it had been fixed. Lex let me down easy by skillfully not bothering to let me down at all. Instead, he simply began referring to the fact of our friendship, as if from the start there had been nothing more. Since nothing was changing, nothing need change, was the message—no need to stop sleeping together. And because he was older, because he knew everything, I figured he must know about this, too. Not wanting to appear foolish, I didn't ask any questions but just rushed to adjust my perspective to his.

And I was happy to be his friend finally. That I was the one he talked to about girls made me feel special. More special than if we'd been dating, because if we'd been dating, I'd be his adversary, not his confidante. When you're dating, we agreed, during one of our marathon phone calls, you're basically just strangers trying to trick each other, opponents trying to win. Dating, we decided, is more about what you don't share than what you do. Lex and I, on the other hand, that summer, shared everything.

Including our secret. Because Lex had a reputation for seducing young girls—a habit I teased him for, as if identifying the others proved I was not one of them—I made him promise not to tell anyone about us. "Wouldn't it be fun to keep you and me a secret?" I whispered feverishly, after our first kiss. With nothing to gain from publicizing our relationship, Lex pulled me close, agreeing it would make for a terrific time.

Because of all this then, because I really liked Lex and was afraid of anyone finding out, I made jokes about him, told my friend Caroline that his close-cut hair made his head look like it was made of felt, told her that I wanted to stick felt animals on it and felt continents, called him "felt-head."

And catching sight of him scowling at karaoke one night, annoyed as usual, this time because his song hadn't come up yet, I tapped Caroline on the shoulder and pointed. "Look, the denim gargoyle!" And when I spied him flirting with yet another young girl at the bar, I'd say, look how old and sad Lex is, how pathetic his chasing girls half his age. I'd remark how he was getting older but not growing up, how ten years from now he'd be wearing the same Converse sneakers and Eddie Grant T-shirt and whispering the same words he was whispering just then to someone else.

4

That August, as I did every summer, I left for Greece to visit my family. Day after day, I'd lie on the beach, sweating under the sun with my eyes closed, my face covered by a straw hat, imagining what it might be like were Lex to visit. I'd pick him up from the airport in our old limping Mercedes, and after passing through the brush and pulling into our gravel driveway, presided over by clay replicas of Grecian statues, I'd introduce him to my parents.

My father wouldn't like him at first. He'd be put off by his tattoos and would hate him as a matter of course—clearly a disc jockey wasn't good enough for his only daughter. But then, convinced by the strength of Lex's love for me, my father's disapproval would melt away and the two men would eventually shake hands and laugh. Looking out at the sea in front of our house, they'd go on talking wisely about life, about the future, about Lex's with me, both of them agreeing solemnly that I ought to be treated with care.

When I returned to New York a month later, Lex finally confessed his love. For *that* girl—he pointed her out. The girl he loved was seventeen, a soon-to-be senior in high school, and because of her age, because she had school the next morning, harder to get than I ever could be. Lex had mentioned his crush on her before I left, but I had assumed it was like his crush on so many others.

It didn't bother me when he'd spoken about them or her, because *they* were passing fancies, while *I* was the one that stuck. Because his feelings for me ran so much deeper, I had been promoted from crush to best friend. I understood: Lex was a lifelong playboy who could never love only one girl. But as he enumerated all the ways in which she was different from the rest, I realized I had understood nothing. He just didn't love me.

5

In autumn I began dating someone, too. It was the start of my senior year at NYU, and I had taken an internship at *The New Yorker* where I met Jed, with whom I thought I was falling in love (again), and about whom I began, in detail, to tell Lex.

Lex was much less receptive to discussions of my relationships than he had been about his. Indeed, the sophisticatedly comprehensive terms of our friendship, which had always included frank conversations about *his* intrigues, seemed to come apart on the occasion that I had my own. "I think I'm falling in love," I told him, on the drive down to Atlantic City. Lex said Jed sounded like a loser, popped a cassette into the stereo, and turned up the volume.

Since Lex dropped so much money in the casinos, he was regularly sent comps to all sorts of casino events. And since his girlfriend couldn't go on account of her having school in the morning, Lex regularly took me with him. Together we saw Don Rickles, *Tony Danza Live!* and watched Bob Dylan from the comfort of our own private booth.

We'd get a big suite, order milkshakes and grilled cheese sandwiches and French fries to eat in our room, before going downstairs to gamble before the show. "What do the Caribbeans know about poker?" I said supportively, after he lost a few hands. We moved on to the roulette table, his favorite, where he sometimes asked me to pick his numbers.

I'd think hard about what numbers were important to me. "Sixteen," I'd say, because I had been that age once, and according to the Sinatra song I'd sometimes sing at karaoke, "It was a very good year." Or I'd calculate the difference of years between us: "Fifteen!" Or I'd choose the age at which I wanted to be married: "Thirty! No, twenty-eight . . . I'm not sure." "Fourteen!"—how old I was for my first kiss. Or I'd think hard and choose a number based purely on a feeling. Why not? It was the same way I chose my boyfriends. I'd close my eyes tightly and ask myself, "Which number do I love?"

After the show, Lex would continue gambling and I'd sit beside him happily, playing with his chips, ordering screwdrivers from the Caesar's Palace waitresses clad in their short white gold-trimmed skirts. The drinks were free, but Lex would slip me chips to tip them. Smoking my cigarettes and cheering him on, I'd pray for him to win so the fun could continue, so I could be hailed as his good luck charm. On the other side of that prayer was the fear that he'd lose and, hating me by association, would scowl as he asked me to pay for our chicken tenders at the Burger King near the highway leading back to New York.

It was on one of these trips to Atlantic City that I first met Justin, Shawn, and Richie. Lex and I were on the boardwalk on our way to the beach one Saturday morning when Richie and his model girlfriend flew past us on a rickshaw. They stopped after a few feet, having recognized Lex. They were going to see Stevie Wonder that night, Richie said.

"Cool. We're going to the Alfonso Ribeiro convention," I interjected.

"This is Iris," Lex said. "She's really into *Silver Spoons*."

I smiled and offered my hand.

Later that night, they found us at the roulette table. Wearing anti-wack baggy pants and baseball caps pulled low in order to fend off the bright glare of wackness in others, they approached with their entourage of models in tow. They'd just come from the Wonder show they said, frowning. "It was incredible."

"Hi," I said, brightly.

Justin began telling Lex about all the big names they'd met backstage and went on to show him the hundred-dollar bills he'd gotten each music legend to autograph. I stood on my tiptoes to see over their shoulders, to see the fan of ten or so hundreds he'd ruined with celebrity signatures.

"But now you can't use them."

Justin turned and ran his eyes over me quickly.

"You should have gotten a Wite-Out pen," I continued, "and asked them to sign some pennies."

No one but Lex said anything to me for the rest of the night.

6

If an internship is a way of getting one's foot in the door, I used mine to wedge my whole body in before passing out drunk inside.

Often, after discovering I'd locked myself out of my apartment, I went to the new Condé Nast building in Times Square, where *The New Yorker*'s offices had just moved, and where I'd been given my very own electronic key. I knew better than to waste another half hour knocking on my apartment door. My roommate May was inside, but in her deep, pill-induced sleep (her father, a doctor, mailed her a pharmaceutical care package every month), she never heard my knocks.

The first time this happened, I tried crashing in the lobby of the nearby Holiday Inn. I had just begun to fall asleep when a security guard, rousing me, informed me I had to leave. I explained that I lived next door, that I'd locked myself out, but he gave me the boot anyway, confusing my winter jacket with its fashion-statement safety pins for the shabby coverings of a teenage-runaway-hooker.

I went next into a nearby twenty-four-hour diner, where I slept upright with a chicken finger in my hand. The waiters said I could stay only so long as I was eating, which is why at 5:00 AM, having accidentally loosened my grip on the chicken finger—it fell to the floor; the waiters served me the bill—I was forced to make my way to 4 Times Square.

Wandering into the cartoon lounge—where Bob Mankoff, the cartoon editor, met with the magazine's regular contributors every Tuesday—I slipped off my shoes, stretched out on the sofa, and settled in for a brief nap.

Responsible to a fault, I first left a note on Jed's desk (he was editorial assistant to the photo editor), requesting he wake me in time for work. And in case Jed came in late, I also left a note for Emily.

Emily was the assistant to Bob Mankoff, and I was the assistant to Emily, who seemed to like me despite my poor work performance. I was no good as an assistant but made a wonderful office-friend, I decided. "I'm trying to make taffeta work-appropriate," I told her, smoothing the ruffles on my dress—it was the morning after Lex's Bar Mitzvah theme party. "I'm exhausted," I confessed. "I was up all night doing the Horah."

Taking my cues from Charles Bukowski and various romantic comedies in which career girls discuss their love lives at the watercooler, I spent most of the workday nursing a hangover and regaling Emily of my adventures with the men in the office, specifically Jed before he became my boyfriend.

I first met Jed in the copy room. He said, "Hi," and I jumped nervously because I'd been busy copying my own cartoons for my *Naked Woman* zine instead of whatever it was I was supposed to be doing. I shook his hand and scuttled away. Then I ran into him again in the magazine's archives while I was retrieving old cartoons to photocopy for my personal scrapbook. His hello startled me just as it had the first time, and I raced back to my cubicle. The next time he caught up with me was in the kitchen; I was wedged between the refrigerator and the coffee machine, trying inconspicuously to transfer the contents of a Colt 45 into a paper cup. He said, "Hi," and I began to sweat profusely, terrified the jig was up, when he asked me out. I said okay just to get him off my back, finished pouring my "coffee," and left to hand out the faxes.

Later that day, Emily charged me with the difficult task of handwriting the addresses on a whole pile of outgoing mail. As I drank more "coffee," my voice grew louder and my handwriting larger and loopier. After laughing at my description of Jed's "proposal" in the kitchen earlier, she gently suggested that I write a little smaller.

"Perhaps you could write the address on only the middle of the envelope," she said sweetly, "rather than using all 8 x 11 inches."

"No problem!" I said, scrutinizing her envelope, the one she'd just addressed to serve as a model. It looked much different then my previous twenty-five, which, when I looked again, well resembled the crumpled bar napkins ruined with poems that always turned up in purse and pocket after a night out. "If that's how you like it," I said, as if it were a discrepancy in taste and not sanity.

7

Most students take on internships as a means of gaining professional experience while making a good impression on a prospective boss, hoping to leave with the promise of a future job, if not a recommendation for a comparable job elsewhere. During *my* brief time at *The New Yorker*, I was careful to aquire no new skills and stealthily avoided all of my superiors, behaving instead as if I were crashing a party.

Though I'd worked really hard to *get* my internship at *The New Yorker,* I'm not sure what my purpose was once I actually got there. I had no interest in publishing, really. It just seemed like a cool place to hang out for a semester, an interesting alternative to another literature or philosophy class, maybe a new spot to meet guys.

Though I thought often about the future—spinning fantasies, my favorite pastime—it was never something I planned. I would be a great writer, a famous actress, a cartoonist on the side. . . . I didn't need to worry about how, because destiny would take care of that for me.

"Fate is character," the ancient Greeks said, and people were always remarking on what a character I was.

In the meantime, I enjoyed drawing cartoons—what I did in class while everyone else took notes—so I figured the cartoon department would be a fun place to kill time. I did not try to get the attention of Bob Mankoff, the cartoon editor who, had he liked me, might have offered me a job upon graduation, or at least offered to glance at my cartoons. Instead, I avoided him.

Though he seemed a genial man, he was solid while I was all shadow. And when he entered the room, it was as if someone had cut in front of the light or removed the screen on which I had been casting my fabulous sillhouette. He'd come in, and my illusions would vanish, my useless hands curling into knots at my sides. Reduced to who I was, I was nothing like who I would be. I was not great, not noteworthy. I was just Iris, the shy intern, sneaking around the office in gold lamé.

When not drinking or cavorting in nightclubs and at parties, my self-esteem—so prodigious, so grand—all but evaporated. Indeed, my daytime self—the one who'd made it home the night before, got dressed in the morning, and was not still drunk—stood in such stark contrast to my nightlife persona that one afternoon, going up the elevator at 4 Times Square, an employee from one of the women's magazines could not stop staring. "Excuse me," she said at last, "but do you know you have an evil twin running around Manhattan singing karaoke?"

I blushed violently before I managed to get out, "Actually, that's me. I'm my evil twin."

III

1

All of *this* is why, freshly graduated from college a year later, applying to *The New Yorker* was not even a consideration. What should I do? I asked myself, during my long walk following the disastrous job fair. I wanted to be a writer. Of that I was certain. But in the meantime, I needed a job.

I did briefly consider becoming a movie star to support myself. I had met enough of them to know it couldn't be that hard. And I still had the five hundred headshots I'd had printed in my sophomore year of college just before I dropped out of acting school. But ultimately, I decided against it. First, I liked my privacy too much to put it on sale the way an actor must. Projecting myself into a future filled with screaming fans and cold French fries (at restaurants, they'd drop by, insisting I pose for a "quick" photo); car chases with paparazzi; secret affairs with my driver/bodyguard/ping-pong partner/masseur/amanuensis; I saw great sadness behind my sunglass-covered eyes, a great weariness of spirit that even my heavily insured smile could not mask. I saw bottle upon bottle of prescription painkillers mixed up in my purse. I saw endless afternoons of shoplifting and Pilates; it wasn't a life I wanted.

Plus, there were no roles I really wanted to play. What I had disliked most about acting, during my brief time studying it—aside from the other actors, the directors, the set designers, the composers, the playwrights, the stage-hands, the ushers, the box office salesmen, the audiences, the critics, and the drafty theaters themselves—was always having to play someone else. I didn't want to be a chameleon, but a great personality photographed in black and white, my face framed by long thin fingers wilting gracefully around a cigarette, my hair hidden beneath a marvelous silk turban, my cruel lips—what are cruel lips? I'm always reading novels about characters who have them—on the verge of some pronouncement as quotable as inscrutable: "Where people go wrong is when they *sell* their soul to the devil; *leasing* is the thing. This way you'll have a steady stream of income pouring in annually and can regularly renegotiate a competitive price based on market fluctuations." To transform, yes. But into myself! Whoever that was.

And then, after being turned away from an open call for extra work in a Russell Crowe film, I realized I was just too sensitive a creature to handle so much rejection—one. As a result, the other 499 headshots remain untouched in a tightly packed box on a high shelf all the way in the back of my closet. On the same shelf, incidentally, as my stock of unsold T-shirts.

2

To begin, I had a few hundred printed at a silk-screen lab downtown where a number of the workers said they absolutely loved my "Crapola" baby-T. "It's a conversation starter," one noted. Indeed, all my designs featured similarly charming inducements. "BRAINS" in big capital letters across the bust. "Second Base" on a form-fitting baseball jersey. "Somewhat Attractive" in a flaming script. And on a pair of black underwear—I dabbled in lingerie, too—"Bad Ass" in hot pink across the seat.

I threw myself into it and a few months later, my apartment—where I was at last living alone; May had moved out—had become my "design studio." I used the bathtub for dying. With scissors, I slashed the backs open on child-size Hanes—they were cheaper than the American Apparel women's baby-T and fit roughly the same. I visited the Salvation Army—buying used was cheaper than buying new, and this way, I could call one of my lines "vintage" and have each one be completely unique—and picked up a whole variety of shirts on which I printed, "HUBRIS."

"Prozac Whore," "Free Crazy Eddie," "Spinster," "Save the Sluts"—I was coming up with great ideas every day and would dream about my imminent success for the entire shift of the minimum-wage hostessing job I had taken in the meantime.

Standing there, almost a full year after graduation, I'd remove a pad and pen from my pocket to make notes about new design ideas and all the different ways I might market them. My fantasies, like an intricate tapestry, unfurled before my mind's eye in a long perfect weave only now and then getting snagged on the jarring call of customers wanting a table for four, or the Mexican cooks caroling, "Hey, mommy," as I dreamily swept past.

I could start a website, like a magazine or something, and get everyone I know to write for it. Eventually, I could put out a print edition and publish my cartoons! I could build a merchandising and media empire and strike it rich before I turn twenty-five. At parties, no one would ever again ask me what I do, because they'd already know. And those who didn't love me for my riches would hate me for them. Strangers would talk about how undeserving I was of so much early success. How unfair it is that I should be so young and beautiful and smart and rich! And all my ex-boyfriends would regret my getting away, especially after seeing me on the cover of New York Magazine *in the nude—a clever allusion to my cartoon, for which I'll have just signed a book deal for an unheard-of advance, and which was already syndicated in newspapers all over the country, next to Marmaduke.*

I'd be like those guys on the cover of New York Magazine, Justin, Shawn, and Richie, who came up with "Models Suck," but better, because I'd be nice to people when they came up to me at parties and suggested I use a fan instead of wads of hundreds to keep cool. And this uncommon niceness, for which I would be so well known, would only make my enemies hate me more. Websites would be created just to tear me apart: www.IrisSucks.com. There would be stickers and pins. People would think I had it all. And I would.

Until all the hate would start to wear on me. And feelings of loneliness would start to close in. Tired of people talking to who they think I am, rather than who I really am, I'd start to question everything I once felt I knew, everything I ever cared about. I'd move to Europe to be with the artists and writers I admired as a child, to cultivate my still nascent talents, which I'd abandoned after my early business success. What had become of my novel?

But none of these artists or writers would take me seriously because, in their eyes, I was a sellout. Because they'd seen pictures of me at grand parties wearing my extra-large, extra-dark sunglasses purchased from Duane Reade. So I'd keep moving, spending my money in casinos all over Europe and becoming dissolute, and in so doing, letting my stateside businesses go to hell. And when it was time to make important decisions, my accountants would not be able to reach me.

I'd lose all my money. I'd return to New York penniless and with syphilis, caught from my bounder husband who cheated on me constantly and stole my jewelry to give to his mistresses. I'd divorce him; it would be expensive. The lawyers would take everything. The disease would progress. I'd begin suffering hallucinations. Past, present, and future would all exist simultaneously, and I'd watch as distorted visions of my life played out on the disintegrating plaster walls of the women's rooming house in midtown, Manhattan, where I'd be forced to take residence.

I'd take my breakfast in the dusty parlor, with its windows choked by coarse polyester curtains, in the company of other aged ladies whose lives, whose worlds, had somehow forgotten them. We'd each sit at our own tables across from no one. We'd each dress for dinner in our best jewels and Chanel suits—whatever we had left—trying our best to ignore the fact that our fine clothes were far superior to our shabby surroundings. We'd struggle to keep our backs straight, to keep our dignity in the sneering face of time.

I'd work mightily to keep a sunny outlook, and I'd say to the concierge, "Good morning, Mr. Paul" (an address we'd settled on by way of a compromise—he asked that I call him by his first name, Paul, as he insisted was common among young people in this day and age, while I insisted that some level of formality be maintained). "Looks like it's going to be a fine day," I'd say. And he'd tip his hat, as I'd instructed him. "A good day indeed, Ms. Smyles."

I'd grow older. And feeling the desperation of my situation too much to bear, one morning, while going for my ritual walk around the block following breakfast, I'd purchase a small vial of poison and retreat to my room where I'd be found elegantly dressed the next day, or even the next one, or the one after that, by Paul the concierge, "Mr. Paul" as I knew him, who'd ordered housekeeping to unlock my door after I failed to show up, yet again, to breakfast. There I'd lie—my hat pinned artfully, my white gloves pristine, clutching an almost beautiful empty vial in my long hand, a hand too delicate for toil, too delicate for this world and all its corruptions—dead at twenty-three and a half.

I took out a vendor's license from New York State and named my company "The Emperor's New Shirt" because all was image and image was all. And then I tried to sell them.

I visited two stores where I was told my price point was too high. Because I had printed only a few hundred, the cost of production had been steep. The fewer you printed, the more they cost to make. If I'd printed more, I could have paid less per shirt, but I couldn't afford to print more on spec when there was no guarantee I'd be able to sell them in the first place. I was in a bind—I couldn't lower my price without losing money and yet, I couldn't sell them to stores without lowering my price.

I decided to rent a table at the Noho flea market on Broadway and West Fourth, where one of my former professors wandered by. "I made them myself," I said, before he noticed me. "I was in your class. This shirt with the subway graffiti," I pointed, "was inspired by your 'Walker in the City' seminar. I've been rereading Alfred Kazin," I added. He nodded and asked me what I'd been doing since graduation. "This!" I said too brightly. He looked down, avoiding my eyes, and said the shirts were nice. "Very clever," he said, before moving on without buying anything. Before, blushing, I began refolding what he'd touched.

My shirts sold like day-old hot cakes: I sold twelve—pretty good. But after factoring in the fee for the table I'd had to rent, I barely broke even. Dejected and exhausted at 7:00 PM, I piled the remainder of my stock into a rolling suitcase and started home.

I was walking up Broadway, staring into nothing, when I found myself staring directly into a pair of eyes. There was Donald, coming from the opposite direction. There were those eyes—like Doctor T. J. Eckleburg's advertising contacts.

"Of course it's you. I was just thinking about you!" he said.

"Really?" I pushed my hair out of my face ("It is a truth universally acknowledged that one only ever runs into the person one most wants to see when one looks crappy."— Jane Austen). "What were you thinking?" I asked hopefully, forgetting that Donald never answered questions. He'd just act as if he hadn't heard you and then go on with whatever he felt like talking about.

"The world traveler's returned!" he exclaimed. "Where you coming from, Kid Smyles?"

"What?"

"Your suitcase."

"Oh, that! No, I'm coming from nowhere," I mumbled.

"Sounds suspicious. What's in the bag?"

"A body," I said, stiffening, deciding murder was less shameful than the truth. "I'm interning for a very prestigious hit man, if you must know."

He tipped his head back as if to size me up. I tipped mine back further so that I could not even see him.

"Hey," he said, waving his hand between my eyes and the sky. "Where'd you go?"

"I'm right here," I said, facing him again. "God!" I sighed, frustrated by my consistent failure to impress. I looked down at his shoes and then up into his eyes, and then over the whole rest of him, swapping in the identical silhouette of the towering *Maxim* Man. *Was it you, Donald? And if it was, do you know that I know that you know?* "How's publishing?" I stammered.

He looked across the street, as if he'd already lost interest in the conversation, then back at me. He squinted. "You still writing your poems?"

I shook my head, as if the notion were laughable. "I'm working on a novel now."

I carried my heavy load down into the subway steps and took the train to Grand Central, where I walked underground toward the cross-town shuttle.

There, I came across a cluster of NYU graduates standing in cap and gown. They were laughing and posing for photos. Was it June again already? Their voices echoed through the tunnel. "Congratulations!" "Congratulations," their parents sang. And I wanted to yell, "Don't do it! Go back! You don't know what it's like!" Instead, I just watched them, and like a ghost haunting my old life, passed by unnoticed, the wheels of my suitcase whizzing in tow.

I planned to try again the next weekend but never made it. The weather was iffy, I was getting a cold, my alarm didn't go off . . . I can't remember the reason. It was the same reason, I guess, that I never finished those art classes at SVA or the two writing courses I started taking at night in The New School's continuing education program. Always, I planned to go back, but then something would happen, and then, after that, nothing would happen, which made it all the more difficult to explain, which made it that much more difficult to return.

It was just like in college when, after seeing a lot of Woody Allen movies and reading a little of Freud, I decided to start seeing one of NYU's staff psychologists. It was free as part of the university's health services, so why not take advantage? Why not lie on a couch for a while and plumb the depths?

3

A wood-lined room stocked with old books, a doctor in tweed with a beard and pipe, a leather chaise on which I lay face up, my eyes trained absently on the ceiling's crown moldings as I describe in detail my most recent dream: "Last night I dreamt I went to Manderlay again, which is weird because I've never *been* to Manderlay. . . ."

Instead I was shown into a small gray windowless cubicle where the "counselor" had me sit in a plastic and metal hard-backed chair directly across from her, leaving a space of just a few feet between our knees. She looked into my eyes and after a pause asked me why I'd sought "counseling."

Counseling? I'd come to be analyzed!

I began scrambling for something, anything to tell her, scrolling through the highs and lows of my life thus far, when the whole of it, suddenly, struck me as so unimportant, so completely lacking in tragedy. Where was the pathos? The tortured soul that foretold genius in all the really good biographies?

Compelled to tell her something, I finally told her I felt pressure to have sex with my forty-two-year-old boyfriend, some alcoholic from the dive bars in Hell's Kitchen where I'd lately been spending a lot of time. (It was a lie. I'd been leading him on for the last month, but was perfectly happy to lead him on another month to boot.) "My roommate and I call him 'Uncle Craig,'" I told the counselor, thinking this might shock her, before wishing I hadn't said it, for it had shocked me more. "As a joke," I added with a laugh, though the room seemed to suck the air right out of it. Her eyes remained steadily on mine.

What would I have said if I had ventured the truth? That I'd never had any problems I could not manage on my own, that I enjoyed good health and was basically an optimist? That I'd taken a class called Madness and Genius and learned that neither Virginia Woolf nor Ernest Hemingway had been captain of their varsity swim team, president of their student body, debate team founder, ballet dancer, or member of the honor society? That I was afraid that everything good about me was just more proof that there would never be anything great? I hadn't come to therapy for a solution, but with the hope of acquiring a problem!

How was I to know, lucky as I'd been, that illness and grief find everyone eventually, that I wouldn't have to work so hard to usher them in? How was I to know that the sickness for which I'd sought treatment was youth?

4

During that first session, my NYU-assigned psychologist and I had a big blow-up/break-through. In tears, I ran to the door, yelling, "I can't do this!" I meant continue to lie to her; finding my own life inadequate, I'd begun to make up all sorts of whoppers. She yelled back, "You can walk out that door right now and give up, or you can face your fears!" Holding the doorknob in my hand, I paused; I'm not sure if it was to consider what she'd said or just act like I was considering what she'd said, but either way, it was all very dramatic, and after a suitable beat, I sat back down. I apologized for my outburst and made a follow-up appointment for the next week.

I had every intention of returning the next week, too, but then, when our appointment rolled around, I wanted to smoke pot with my roommate, so I phoned and said I was sick and would be in the week after. She called the day before our next appointment, leaving a message on my machine to remind me. I was lying in my loft bed, listening to her concerned voice, imagining myself seated across from her in that small room—her eyes boring into me, her knowing that I was a fraud—when I started to wonder if maybe therapy wasn't for me.

I didn't return to the street fair the following weekend either, nor any weekend ever again. But this time, with the T-shirts, my quitting was tangible—my apartment was filled with hundreds of my unsold stock. And to make matters worse, I began receiving notices from the federal government. Something about there being a warrant out for my arrest regarding the "company" of which I'd named myself president. Since I hadn't bothered to file a 1099—what's a 1099?—"The Emperor's New Shirt" owed roughly two thousand dollars in estimated back taxes.

Not knowing what to do, I ignored it. And not long after that, I moved. I broke my lease and moved into a new apartment located just above the Midtown Tunnel. Though I had decided by this time that I wanted to go to graduate school for English Literature, I still needed time to apply, which put me right back where I started: I needed a job. So when I saw an ad in the subway regarding a citywide teacher shortage, I figured since I couldn't do, perhaps I might teach.

I got a job at a South Bronx public school so troubled that all the Teach for America recruits quit within the first month. Though I lacked the credentials, I was hired on the proviso that I enroll in education courses concurrently. And so I found myself all grown-up and firmly ensconced in a life that had nothing to do with any one of my very intricately designed daydreams.

I was a teacher by day, a student by night, and the serious girlfriend of a soon-to-be lawyer named Martin, whom I'd met one evening at Lex's '80s party. On the bright side, my new apartment, the one above the tunnel, had good closets, so I was able to stuff my T-shirts all the way in the back on a shelf behind the linens where, for a while, I never had to see them.

I finished out the year in the Bronx (the school, it was announced in spring, would be taken over by the state and restaffed), exaggerated my way into another job at a private school on the Upper West Side and, loading up on summer courses, earned my teaching certificate after two years. And then, just as things began to settle, just as it seemed the only thing left to do was get married and die, I broke it off with Martin, quit my job at the school, and moved again.

Packing all my things, the T-shirts were the last thing I found. Hundreds of them, stuffed in black garbage bags, evidence of a crime I could not forget. I couldn't throw them out; I took them with me.

IV

My current apartment on West Tenth Street has a small walk-in closet. For the last year, I've been storing the T-shirts on a high shelf in the back. When I run out of clean underwear, I'll pull out a pair of Bad Ass panties.

After pulling on one of fifty left-over Second Base T-shirts, I gather up my dirty clothes and head to the Laundromat. Around my neck, the cotton hangs heavy. I mean, they're great shirts, don't get me wrong, but they're conversation starters, like the guy at the print shop said, and I don't want to talk about it. But there lies my punishment.

Forthwith this frame of mine was wrenched
With a woeful agony,
Which forced me to begin my tale;
And then it left me free.

Since then, at an uncertain hour,
That agony returns;
And till my ghastly tale is told,
This heart within me burns.

I pass, like night, from land to land;
I have strange power of speech;
That moment that his face I see,
I know the man that must hear me:
To him my tale I teach.

What is there to say? I shot the albatross and now I must wear it.

On my way out, I pick up a book of Coleridge poems. It's for a course I'm taking on Romanticism in the graduate Humanities department at NYU, the only program that accepted me. With an undergraduate major in "Individualized Study," my transcript—Fate and Free Will, Tai Chi, Voyages of Identity, Sense Memory, Poetry Writing, Tap—reads like the afternoon agenda at a posh mental health facility. Lacking the true English credits PhD programs require just to apply, I've had to enroll in this Humanities division. If college leaves most graduates unprepared for the real world, my degree, more ambitiously, has left me unprepared for academia to boot.

Anyway, I like being a student again, whiling away the hours in libraries and cafés, reading books I was supposed to have read back in college (*Madame Bovary*: I confess I·only read the CliffsNotes.). "Youth is wasted on the young," Shaw wrote. This is equally true of college. Certainly it's the *raison d'être* of graduate students. But what does it matter what I study finally, when time is really what I've bought? Like I told the guy at the job fair, I'm working on a novel, that's my main thing.

In addition to Romanticism, I'm taking a class called History of the Novel, which, it turns out, has been a controversial art since its inception. We've been reading all about Anthony Comstock's banned books and yesterday had a long discussion about the growing fear in the eighteenth and nineteenth centuries that novels were perverting the minds of the young, particularly the minds of very young girls. The professor distributed this text from an 1815 almanac:

> *The indiscriminate reading of Novels and Romances is to young females of the most dangerous tendency . . . it agitates their fancy to delirium of pleasure never to be realized . . . and opens to their view the Elysium fields which exist only in the imagination . . . fields which will involve them in wretchedness and inconsolable*

sorrow. Such reading converts them into a bundle of acutely feeling nerves and makes them "ready to expire of a rose in aromatic pain" . . . The most profligate villain, bent on the infernal purpose of seducing a woman, could not wish a symptom more favorable to his purpose than a strong imagination inflamed with the rhapsodies of artful and corrupting novels.

—*T. E. C., JR., MD*

After he finished reading it aloud, everyone was excited and a wonderfully interesting conversation ensued. Instead of leaping into the fray as I usually do, however, for a while I just listened. Looking around that safe, warm, wood-lined classroom, out the window of an old brownstone situated comfortably at the edge of Washington Square, and then back across the conference table, at the animated faces of my impassioned peers—eager full-time Humanities students like me, young, unemployed, would-be writers and poets, possessed by literature to the point of total incompetence—it hit me: The real danger of the novel is that it might make you want to write one yourself.

BOOK I

BOOK 4

CHAPTER 1

THE BASTARD FELIX

That winter I was in the grip of abstract furies.

ELIO VITTORINI, *CONVERSATIONS IN SICILY*

I

It goes like this: Felix will call from a noisy bar and tell me he's in town, or from a mutual friend's apartment telling me to come over, or from his car while en route to a party telling me to be downstairs in five minutes; he's picking me up. If I decline, he'll tell me it's going to be so much fun that I can't afford to miss it, and if I come and hang out with him and his friends for a few hours, it *will* be so much fun, I *couldn't* have afforded to miss it. And then the night will wind down, and everyone will take off to their respective apartments, and Felix will give me a lift back to mine and end up staying for the next three or four days.

"Wake and bake!" he sings, when I find him in the kitchen watching *Soul Train*, making breakfast, and smoking what's left of a joint. "It'll help with your hangover," he says, passing it to me. I exhale in a chain of rueful coughs. He pours me a glass of water from the tap. The Bastard Felix—my shame, my solace.

Like a child born out of wedlock, Felix is a roommate born without a lease, a bastard roommate whose origins are illegitimate. Under a mess of broken crackers, he just appeared on my couch one morning. Swaddled in my throw blanket, there was Felix gently snoring, the ignominious offspring of another long night of terrible fun.

I don't much mind having a bastard, and Felix for his part is quite happy with the arrangement. I have a pretty decent apartment, what he calls my dukedom. There are certain records of mine he likes to play, certain cheeses I keep in the fridge that he enjoys, and I'm okay with him leaving a few things, too. After he's gone I'll discover a pair of fresh socks he's stuffed discreetly between the wall and the sofa; a T-shirt stuck in with my books, folded up small between *The House*

---

of Mirth and *Martin Eden*; or some very expensive volumizing hair conditioner that one of his girlfriends gave him hidden beneath the sink, behind the toilet-bowl cleanser. "She works for a cosmetics company," he explained when I asked him about it. "She suggests I play up my curls."

It's not an uneven trade either, lest you think he's taking advantage of me. We have a lot of fun together for one thing. And for another, if I get drunk and pass out somewhere, he'll wake me up, help me home, and then in the morning take care of breakfast. Felix can make a meal out of anything—a lonely onion, a packet of mustard, salad croutons. . . . This is partially how he earns his keep. He'll tell high-spirited jokes to ameliorate your hangover while finally putting to use that two-year-old can of olives you thought you'd never eat, that weird jar of pickled mushrooms that came with the apartment, and an unopened container of paprika.

Since the host wherever Felix is staying is usually too much crippled by the excruciating hangover that almost always results from a night out with Felix to prepare any food himself, Felix's bizarre meals come as a sweet relief. Only very rarely are his dishes inedible. Once, for example, he made these deviled eggs using chocolate syrup, and another time he made tuna salad with cocktail olives and some other odd ingredients I wasn't able to identify.

Inspired after one of his better breakfasts, Felix and I came up with an idea for a TV show. We'd call it, *The Wandering Chef*, and it would follow Felix as he wakes up on strangers' couches and makes breakfast out of whatever they happen to have in their kitchen. The first segment would show him coming to in a room where a party was recently held:

Felix sits up, yawns, stretches and then, delighted to find a roach lying in a nearby ashtray, pulls a lighter from his pocket. Relighting the joint, he inhales deeply until there is nothing left but air between his fingertips. After a moment, the person whose home he passed out in wanders through and, surprised to find Felix (with a whole camera crew) on his couch, awkwardly says, "Hey, man. I didn't know anybody was still here." Whereupon, groggily but cheerfully, Felix replies, "Mind if I cook up some breakfast?"

"Nah," the host answers, "but my kitchen's completely empty." To which Felix responds, "I'll just have a look." He opens one cupboard after another before, wild-eyed, he cries out, "Waddya mean 'empty,' you got baking soda and dried parsley! Let me see what I can do."

Cut to twenty minutes later, and we see Felix serving what he calls "an egg substitute." The host digs in, "Hmmmmm," and shakes his head. "How did he do it?" the host asks the camera now. Cut back to the kitchen twenty minutes earlier, and the audience gets to watch Felix create his meal from scratch and cook along with him at home.

The credits roll as the host and Felix enjoy their breakfast. "Just like Pellegrino!" the host exclaims, following a sip of his Alka-Seltzer water. Then Felix takes a sip of his own glass filled with watered-down ketchup. "Hmmm, just like tomato juice!" he says, raising his glass for a toast.

We have lots of ideas, Felix and I. Since he's around so often, we get to talking and come up with all sorts of stuff. I try to write down the ideas as they come to us, in order that we return to them once we've finished the joint, that round of backgammon, or "The Hokey Pokey" (I have it on record; mostly I play it at parties, but one time Felix decided we should get some exercise). We've got some pretty good ideas for screenplays, too. My favorite right now is *City Squirrels!*, in which New York City in the not-so-distant future is overrun by vindictive squirrels. It's like *The Birds* meets *Escape from New York* but with squirrels instead of birds.

I'm more of a scheduler than Felix is, so I'll say, "Felix, here's what we're gonna do. At 1:00, we're gonna work on *City Squirrels!* Then at 2:00, we'll have a fifteen-minute dance break. Then we'll do an hour's worth of revision on whatever we've come up with." We've never actually gotten to the revision stage though. Usually, we get stuck arguing over details. For example, Felix thinks the squirrels should be noticeably demonic looking with extra-red eyes, while I think it would be much scarier if the squirrels looked completely normal.

"It begins in Tompkins Square Park, where the squirrels have gotten into some hypodermic needles left over from the '80s when the park was overrun with junkies, which causes them to mutate and become extra aggressive," he says.

"No way! No one should know why it's happening. It should be an existential apocalypse, a scourge open to interpretation!"

We're never able to resolve these disputes so usually after arguing awhile, we'll just move on to a different project. I'll get out my crayons and coals and suggest we clear our heads by drawing and return to the script later. I have a drawing table in my apartment, so friends are always making things when they come over. I usually draw The Naked Woman—the heroine of my comic book, which is on sale at St. Mark's right now; I've sold three copies. I'd started out trying to draw classical da Vinci–style nudes, but my nudes tended to look more cartoonish than Vitruvian, so I figured why not go with it, and gave her a drink and cigarette and began adding speech bubbles.

Felix likes to make drawings of hungry monsters eating their spectacles and the spectacles of others, or hungry spectacles eating monsters. He's very creative. All of our friends are aware of how creative and talented Felix is—though he's primarily an actor/comedian, he also paints and draws—which is one of the reasons we let him stay on our couches. We're like patrons of the arts, sponsoring him, until he makes it. The other reason, I think, is loneliness. Sometimes it's just nicer to wake up to Felix's antics than to the terrible sadness that tends to come on huge after a night of furious drinking. Felix will tell jokes and goof around, and you'll just be too busy laughing or trying not to laugh to review your own foolishness from the night before. Breakfasting with Felix allows you to put off that moment of reckoning, at least for a little while. Though lately I've been putting mine off for too long.

Felix has been here nearly a week. He's on the couch right now trying to assemble four roaches into a pinner, while I'm at my computer with my feet up on my desk, ready to write but feeling overwhelmingly, unidentifiably sad. How can I write with Felix here? I type out an idea, something I decide I'll have to get back to later because I can't concentrate now what with Felix around. I close the document and update the "about me" section of my Friendster profile. I delete what I had before and type, "60% cotton, 40% acrylic." *Save.*

I don't share all of my ideas with Felix. Sometimes I won't say anything but just write it down and make a note to implement the idea later, after Felix leaves. For example, the idea I just had is to create adult coloring books. Why not color in some porn or some scenes of East Village squatters sharing needles? Or romantic restaurant dinners between two consenting French adulterers feeding their dogs at the table directly from their spoons? Or scenes of coworkers gossiping around the watercooler about the intern's terrible behavior at the holiday party, or a panel of you getting high with your college roommate in your parents' backyard before Thanksgiving dinner, or a scene of you introducing your boyfriend to your parents, him awkwardly shaking your father's hand in the garage, or a scene of the two of you at a diner two years later, you crying into your ice cream after deciding it's best to split up, another of you in bed that night, trying to hide your tears from the man you just had sex with, whom you only just met and don't love, or another of you cyber-stalking your ex on Friendster—a light blue crayon could fill in the light reflected off your face as you stare at the picture you've been cropped out of, the one he's now using as his profile photo. Color it pink, where it says "single."

Oh, I come up with lots of ideas and I start to wish Felix would leave in order that I get to them. And then I start to worry that he might leave and that I might have to get to them, and then I just get quiet and overwhelmingly, unidentifiably sad.

Usually Felix can sense these moments and he'll rush to tell me a joke so as to curb me away from asking him to leave. I'll resist for a while and then, eventually, I'll laugh. But it won't feel good because it's terrible to laugh when you're not happy. It feels like hell, which I imagine as a great party where everyone appears to be having a wonderful time. So I'll mope around, trying to keep my face solemn in line with my mood while Felix blows straws from his nose.

Then he'll decide to cook if he hasn't already. While Felix gets into it in the kitchenette, I deal with my hangover by staring at the wall and smoking cigarettes. I'll drink a can of warm beer that I opened last night before falling asleep, or I'll put my feet up next to the computer and check my email again. I'm on all of these mailing lists so I get all sorts of junk. It's kind of annoying, but I don't take myself off the lists because I enjoy all the notifications telling me I have six new messages. If I didn't get the junk mail, I would rarely get any mail and that would just be too depressing. This way, when I go online I'm never disappointed, but have all this stuff to do. All these Words of the Day to learn. All these ads for penis enlargement pills to delete.

I learn the definition of *gallimaufry*—"a hodgepodge; jumble; confused medley." I select five spam emails and move them to the trash. I press *Delete Trash*. Felix begins to sing the *Growing Pains* theme song. I join him in the kitchenette for harmonies. When we're finished, I ask him what he thinks I should do about so and so, if he thinks he's going to call me, or if I should call him first and then just pretend he called me, pretend to want to get off the phone already because I'm so busy, and then ask him to please stop calling all the time. Felix says, "Breakfast is served."

I help him bring the plates into the living room, and we eat on top of the open backgammon board. Then Felix searches the ashtray for a roach. We get high, play a round of backgammon, and go for a walk. If Felix can't find any weed in the ashtray though, then we'll take his parents' car—if he's come directly from his mom's place upstate, he'll usually have her PT Cruiser with the seat warmers parked around the block—to his dealer's apartment in Brooklyn, this guy named Forrest who also went to NYU.

I hate showing up to someone's home empty-handed, so before we go I'll take some stale cookies out of an Entenmann's box and wrap them in aluminum foil and ribbon as if I baked them myself. Or, if I haven't any cookies, I'll make a card for him on my drawing table, with a little drawing of me naked holding out flowers and saying, "I love your shirt!" You'd be surprised how much Forrest appreciates it. He basically loves me, but only because I'm always leaving just as soon as I arrive. He always insists on kissing me on the cheek or hand just before I go, as if I were some delicate thing. I get into it, too, and bat my eyelashes and say, "Oh, Forrest!" Almost everybody loves to be addressed by their name, I find. It's such a simple thing, and yet most people neglect to do it.

I love the drive over the bridge on the way there. There's a great fullness that occurs when crossing city bridges, like you're pressed right up against the surface of your life and can feel all its varying textures. For a few minutes everything comes into a strange focus and you just know it's one of those moments that would be pivotal if a movie were made about you. One of those moments that would be featured in previews—you looking out the window, thinking about something or other.

Just as often, Felix won't have any money to buy weed, and it'll be too early to go over to a friend's place to smoke theirs—if they're not at work, they're still sleeping or doing who knows what—so we'll just go downstairs and hang out in his mom's car for a change of atmosphere while we wait for someone to call us back.

We sit in his parked car, listen to music, fiddle with our individual seat heaters, and comment on the people walking by and their suitability for potential romantic encounters. Felix says the toothless bum on the corner outside the Tasti D-Lite is my type. I tell Felix I had thought so too, but it didn't work out. Then we change parking spaces if alternate side of the street parking is in effect and go back upstairs to my dukedom and dance to "Macho Duck."

II

1

I first met The Bastard at a dorm party in college. He was drunk and people were saying things like, "Who's that?" and "Oh, that's Felix" and rolling their eyes while he fell down, broke things, and danced to the sounds of traffic coming through the window. Apparently he got that drunk at lots of dorm parties and was getting something of a reputation for it. People thought he got too drunk. Regardless, he was unquestionably having more fun than anyone else, and when he got tangled in the Christmas lights and began quoting *Tron,* I said as much.

Later that night, my roommate May and I smoked a joint with him in the bathroom, and when the joint was close to finished and we both declined a last drag for fear of burning our fingertips, Felix demonstrated how to smoke a roach into nothing but ash. It was almost magical the way he just let his fingers go, like a magician making a whole rabbit disappear. . . . He doesn't remember any of it.

The first time we met that he *does* remember was a couple of years later. May and I were at Three of Cups for a birthday party. With red Christmas lights, crummy sofas, and skulls punctuating the liquor bottles behind the bar, Three of Cups was at that time very popular among the NYU crowd. Though Felix had graduated a year earlier, he had been scene-partners with the birthday boy, so he was there, too.

Relatively sober this time, Felix immediately took a shine to May and went ahead and introduced himself, as if for the first time. May is very pretty—she's petite, wears her dark straight hair in a bob, has big blue eyes like fishbowls without fish, and looks like a film star from another time, beautiful in a way that women aren't anymore. When she first got to school, she didn't think so though. She thought she was fat and talked all the time about how she wasn't fat but just healthy. I told her she looked like Mae West. She told me Mae West was fat.

May is from Alabama and has down pat that Southern Belle sweet-and-cruel-way-of-being that just accidentally tears men apart. The way it works is that she never seems to know she's being cruel, which is what enables her to be sweet at the same time, which makes the boys she's cruel to like her even more. She doesn't like them though is the thing, so she's unaware of her power.

For most of college May didn't have a boyfriend. She dated now and then, nice looking boys a little soft in the arms with fine manners whom she'd accidentally destroy before finding their pleading remnants too disgusting to tolerate—they'd save flowers that fell from her hair and months later, commemorating the day of their meeting, present them to her inside jewelry boxes cupped repulsively in shivering hands. No wonder she was still a virgin. Or, she'd date guys with way too much game, handsome men who'd cast her off right away because now it was she who liked them too much, her hands that shivered repulsively, because she was not cruel at all, but looked at them too long with her terrible, pleading, fishbowl-without-fish eyes.

Felix, on the other hand, isn't handsome at all. He *is* striking, maybe even ugly, but the kind of ugly that in the eye of certain beholders (May's, it turns out) could be taken for beautiful. Extraordinary-looking is the best way to describe him. He has a giant nose, a sort of monument to noses, a parody of a nose really, right in the middle of his face, which is where a nose should be, I guess, and then all this wild curly brown hair—now there's some gray in it—sprouting from his head like a set of disordered but brilliant ideas.

He was standing under his hair at the bar that night—much more composed than when we saw him at the party two years earlier—

performing an elegant lean with a look of half-seriousness, as if in his mind he were telling a very cool joke and were taking his sweet time with it. May was ordering her second Amaretto sour, when Felix said, "Hi," or something similar, and gave her a look like he was really about something, so says May.

Then, channeling Mae West, May looked him up and down and asked, "Is that *Deadeye Dick* in your pants, or are you just happy to see me?" He had a Kurt Vonnegut novel tucked into the front of his jeans where a pistol would have been if this were an action movie. After that, May began to lean too and they talked for a while about their shared love of Vonnegut. May didn't know what came over her, she told me later, just that all of a sudden she found herself possessed of a wit and self-assurance she never imagined she had. She fell for him that night.

I liked them as a couple, I told her at home after, mostly because I could draw caricatures of them together pretty easily. I had just started to draw, mostly when I was stoned or in class, or both as it often happened, and I would practice by drawing people I knew. I found my ability to draw people increased with the amount of time I spent with them and so got to know which of their features were the most telling. I particularly enjoyed drawing May because I knew her so well and also because she sort of looked like a cartoon already, which made it easy.

Just like May, Felix looked completely unrealistic in person. I mean I was able to draw him perfectly on my first try, that very night, while they stood chatting at the bar. When May introduced me a few minutes after, I showed them the napkin on which I'd drawn their joint portrait. Felix, leaning in, his hair a third party; May, looking away, glamorous, aloof.

They agreed with me that it looked much more like them than they did, and I ordered my third whiskey while they continued to eye each other. Finding little else to do—I wasn't attracted to anyone at the party myself—I decided to spend the night brokering their first date, negotiating the exchange of phone numbers so May could play it cool, as if his calling were a matter quite beyond her concern.

I was only returning the favor. I often asked May to field phone calls from my own boyfriends, arrange with them the particulars of my dates, or else provide them with small talk until I was ready to talk myself. "Hand me the phone once you've tired him out," I'd sigh, lying in my bed as she chatted them up. Sometimes I wouldn't bother talking to them at all. We'd call it a "science experiment," and I'd just ask her to pretend she was me. "Like a placebo Iris."

Hanging up the phone, she'd submit her report, describing to me in detail how the conversation went. "Fascinating," I'd remark. And then, analyzing his response, I'd try to determine whether his feelings for me, "his symptoms," as I called them, were real or psychosomatic. "Love is a disease," I told May. "The question is whether it's viral or bacterial."

I'd roll a joint, we'd get high, and then I'd record the results of the "experiment" in a chemistry ledger I'd purchased from the college bookstore for just this purpose. I'd draw up elaborate tables and charts in the rigorous fashion of the lab reports I'd submitted in high school— I got very good marks in science incidentally—and then we'd discuss my findings over margaritas.

Seeing as May and I pretty much shared everything, I figured why not share this, too. I went on my dates alone, of course, but found the reporting of them after to be much more fun. Whether or not it worked out with each guy, after a while, hardly mattered. How paltry love and heartbreak began to seem in the face of so much cold hard science.

Thus I began setting up for the experiment of May and Felix. Donning my imaginary lab coat that night at the Three of Cups bar, I told Felix that he could pursue May provided he honor certain protocol. "I'm going to give you May's phone number along with this brief list of rules. Be sure to identify yourself politely when you call, or I *won't* put her on with you."

2

"319!" Felix said, raising a hand to high-five us both. We were sitting on our couch—well, they were. I was bouncing a few feet away on our mini-trampoline. Felix high-fived May and then got up off the couch to high-five me and also pass the joint.

It was around 4:00 AM, and we'd just gotten back from karaoke where May had introduced her new boyfriend to our group. It was the first time May had brought a guy—usually she came alone, that is, with me—which made it that much worse when each of our friends, one at a time, said, "You do realize you're dating a male version of Iris." "My nose isn't that big," I protested drunkenly. May protested, too, though vaguely with a "No, he's not." The likeness became intolerable when The Bastard went on stage and sang "Just a Gigolo," not knowing it was my signature song.

I hadn't noticed the resemblance before that, but after everyone said it, I began to see it, too. It was, I suppose, a big reason why Felix and I got along so well and yet never felt even the remotest physical attraction—it was as if we were each other's long-lost brother and sister. We *both* have big noses, wild curly hair, and a tendency to become the life of the party, or its death, depending on how heavily we've been drinking.

In fact, when I first saw Felix at that dorm party—the one he doesn't remember—tripping over things and carrying on badly, I'd cringed with recognition. Comparatively sober for the moment, I'd felt as if I were watching myself on a different day. So much so that when the guy next to me passed a mean remark about Felix, without even knowing him, I'd rushed to his defense, not because I'm heroic, but because I was defending myself.

May and I, on the other hand, are nothing alike. Though we do share a tendency toward excess, the respective outcomes of our indulgences are quite different—while May might get too drunk and fall asleep, I might get too drunk and set something on fire. Further, while May is petite and shapely, I am tall and rangy. I'm more Laverne than Shirley, you might say, less pretty if more likely to sport a large embroidered *I*. I raise all this only to supply some possible reason why May, at that time, was regarded by all who knew us as "Iris's sidekick."

Certainly neither she nor I defined our relationship this way. Quite the contrary, we saw ourselves as partners, equal halves of a dynamic duo always in complete accord. Indeed, were we sold a motorcycle with a sidecar, there would have been no argument about who would sit where. She'd choose the motorcycle, happy to take charge at the wheel, while I'd choose the sidecar, preferring the role of passenger as if it were a limo.

My point is that though others may have defined her in relationship to me, she did not. So when she finally found a boyfriend, The Bastard moreover, I think she was excited to shed her old role. It was naturally upsetting to her then, to have this new relationship defined as just an echo of her relationship to me, as if being my sidekick were a fate she could not escape: May, a bizarro Oedipus, running from 319 and choosing Felix, only to discover that in choosing Felix, she'd in fact chosen her roommate once more.

"319!" Felix said again. "It's fate!" he went on as I passed the joint back to him.

We'd been talking about NYU and the dorms, and had stumbled onto the uncanny fact that Felix had lived in the same Fifth Avenue dormitory that May and I shared two years prior when we'd been randomly assigned to each other as roommates. Not just the same fifteen-story building, but the same floor, and not just the same floor, but the same room—319. And which bed did Felix occupy? Mine.

"My eyes!" May cried, after some ash from the joint flew up into them. Blinking in pain, blind for the moment and leading with her arms, she ran to the bathroom screaming, in order to splash some water on her face.

How bizarre it was to reflect back four years, to recall the many conversations May and I had before falling asleep. How bizarre to think of Felix lying exactly where I'd lain two years before, to think that if you could dial back time on one side of that room, it would have been Felix and she that were randomly assigned to each other. It would have been Felix with whom she would have shared so many secrets.

3

Felix and May were soon a couple. They spent the normal amount of time any couple might spend alone, but then, seeing as we all got along so well, they also spent time with me. And so, for a while, the three of us became something of a gang. Then when I had a date, the gang expanded to four. Then once when I didn't have a date, Felix asked if he could bring his friend Reggie, who had just graduated from a college down South and who was in New York for a temporary consulting job. Then, after a while, Reggie and I started dating, too. Sort of.

Here's a little lesson in Physics: While celestial bodies are governed by the laws of attraction, some other kinds of bodies—mine and Reggie's, for example—are governed by the laws of boredom. Imagine for a moment a satellite orbiting Earth for no other reason than that it has nothing better to do. An orbit only aping paths defined by known physical laws but fundamentally free of any actual gravitational attraction. This was my relationship to Reggie, one of those attempted flirtations where you try to manufacture pull, but finally feel nothing and after a while just give up and turn on the TV.

More bored to Reggie than attracted to anyone else, every now and then we'd find ourselves alone—he was there, I was there, and for a little while, there we were—and kiss. But sharing a joint with May and Felix a little later, the kiss would be forgotten. That is until the next time Reggie and I found ourselves alone, thrust against each other once again, unable to resist the physical equations of the bored state.

And another little lesson, this time in Biology: After graduation, I left for Greece, where I remained for the next four months. By the time I returned to Manhattan in the fall, things between May and Felix had gotten serious. The symptoms of their relationship had progressed and like a chronic condition, Felix was flaring up daily; he'd practically moved in with us.

You know how Lyme disease makes you not want to do the things you used to want to do? May's relationship with Felix was sort of like that. She rarely wanted to hang out with me anymore and after a while, I hardly ever even saw her without him by her side. May and Felix were, "like, best friends," May told me privately, during one of the few lucid moments that very occasionally punctuated her fever.

Outside of that, she'd completely stopped reporting on their relationship to me, but had actually begun reporting on *ours* to him.

She'd slip out to the corner deli to buy crackers or crazy straws for Felix—"he likes the ones shaped like flamingos"—and Felix would come up to me and say, "Maybe you should clean your hair out of the shower drain after you're done, Iris. It's not fair when May and I end up doing it." I contemplated reminding him that May was my roommate, not he, and considering the fact that he was an unpaying tenant, it was actually *quite* fair that he not only clean the shower drain but also sweep and mop the living room. Instead I apologized. Though Felix was out of line, May had a point. But I had a point, too, which was this: Judging by the seriousness with which your illness is progressing, perhaps it's time you two seek quarantine—I'm paraphrasing. "Maybe you guys should get your own place."

May did eventually move out. And then I met Martin and came down with the fever, too. We got pretty serious and then, you know how it goes. How many close relationships can a single person juggle? In the beginning, May and I still saw each other; we went on a few double dates. But gradually, we saw each other less and less until eventually we did not see each other at all. It was the exact opposite of a big deal. It was more like the end of the world.

Just another word or two about Physics and the Second Law of Thermodynamics in particular: When I was a kid I thought often about what the end of the world would look like. I mean, the edge of the universe, how does that work? What exactly is the border between something and nothing? But now I see I was thinking about it all wrong, that there is no edge, no hard and fast end of the world, just like there is no end to certain friendships. People, like stars and planets and everything else, just drift apart.

May and I were like space. We didn't end our friendship as much as let it go. Things got cold, the universe expanded between us, disorder replaced order, chaos and entropy and all that. Cosmic stuff. Until I didn't even know her phone number anymore, until the next thing I knew about her was coming from Reggie's mouth two years later after I ran into him downtown, on line outside The Halloween Store.

I looked up from my book—*The Elegant Universe*—and there he was cued up right behind me, the laws of boredom thrusting us together once again. He'd ended up settling permanently in New York and was renting an apartment in the East Village, he told me. And hadn't I heard? May and Felix had gone out to L. A. about a year ago and were living together over there, trying to break into movies.

I told Reggie my idea about the end of the world, about expansion and cooling and increasingly entropic conditions resulting in a state of perpetual California—I'm paraphrasing.

"Yeah, L. A. sucks," he replied, before craning his neck to see inside the costume shop window. "So what are you going to be for Halloween?"

"Oh, I have my costume already squared away. I'm just here to buy a mustache for Martin's costume. Martin's my boyfriend," I explained.

4

Martin and I were going as "The Damsel in Distress" and "The Villain," archetypes from the silent film era. I'd built a stretch of train tracks extending five feet, out of some balsa wood, nails, and silver spray paint, and planned to tie myself to them. My idea was to carry them around on my back, as if I'd been freed by cutting the tracks instead of the ropes. The rest of my costume was an old-fashioned, damsel-like lace dress.

The idea was born out of Martin's unwillingness to participate altogether. Martin said he hated Halloween and never ever dressed for it, so I had to come up with a couple's costume that wouldn't require much on his end. It was a battle just to get him to don the mustache and black hat—barely a costume at all—and he refused "on principle" to take part in any of the preparations, which is how I ended up at The Halloween Store alone.

We'd had an argument before I left. I asked him why he couldn't just dress up because *I* wanted to and not make such a big deal about it. Martin said he was being civilly disobedient as a way of defying my increasingly totalitarian reign over his life. I said that he was the dictator, and why couldn't he just compromise? I told him that Halloween was important to me, that it would be fun—I said this while crying.

I pointed out that I'd attended multiple Seders and Yom Kippur suppers for his religion, and he said Halloween was not my religion and my comparing it to his religion was further evidence of my being an anti-Semite. Somehow all our arguments, which were increasingly frequent, ended up with his declaring me an anti-Semite. I said that was unfair, and he said my resorting to tears was unfair. Then he said he'd wear the mustache if I got it for him, but that's it.

So I got all the stuff—including the mustache—and was very excited. I hadn't observed Halloween in two whole years, not since I met Martin because I'd been too tired and depressed about my new life as a school-teacher to make the effort. That, coupled with the fact that I'd recently stopped flying in my dreams, suggested a significant psychological shift about which I was deeply concerned. I felt my soul was dying and I didn't know what to do. Martin said this was called "growing up."

When I arrived at his place with the supplies, Martin was in a miserable mood and made a big show of it; it was like he put himself in that mood just to get back at me. I persevered. I handed Martin the black hat and mustache and offered to help him prepare the rest of his look.

He took the mustache with him into the bathroom and swatted me away. "I'll do it."

From the open door, I watched him apply a thin line of spirit gum above his upper lip before carefully pressing the mustache into place.

I smiled.

He scowled.

"You make a perfect villain," I said.

"Because I'm so cruel to you, right? You're just the innocent victim, I suppose."

"Damsel," I corrected him, twirling my hair.

He rolled his eyes.

Fred, Martin's friend, was having a costume party downtown, so Martin's other friend Zach, and Zach's girlfriend, Michelle—both of whom lived on the Upper East Side—had decided to come over to smoke pot and have a drink before heading down all together. Zach and Michelle arrived as a wounded hockey player and a witch, respectively.

"Last-minute costumes," Zach explained, heading directly to the kitchen.

"I would have loved to do something creative like you," Michelle told me sweetly, as we waited for our drinks, "but I had no time and couldn't think of anything anyway." We sat on the couch where Martin was packing his bong. "I'm boring," she said.

"No, you're not. Witches are classic!" I said.

"Relax, Iris. She's just trying to make you feel better because your costume's so ridiculous."

"I can't believe you got him to dress up," Zach broke in, handing us glasses. "Martin, what's happening to you?"

"I'm whipped," he said. "I'm her slave."

"Woe is you," I said.

"Zach already had the hockey jersey, and I just put some of my eye shadow around his eye to make a bruise," Michelle said. "I used glittery shadow though, so he just sort of looks dressed up or something." She shrugged, as if to give up.

"I think we should go," Martin said. "Before Iris gets impatient. Halloween's her religion, you know."

Because my tracks, when attached, made me five feet wide, I wouldn't be able to put them on until we got to the party, so I brought the rope with me and told Martin he could tie me up once we got there. A taxi stopped for us at Park and Eighty-second. I put the tracks in the trunk while everyone else got in.

The cab dropped us just north of Union Square and I was excited to see the streets filled with people in costume. On the walk over, we started talking to a couple our age that were dressed as contestants from TV's *Double Dare*, the popular kids game show from the '80s and '90s. Their costume was pretty impressive, and I nudged Martin as if to say, you see how much fun this is, everyone is doing it, not just us. He said, "Ow," as if I'd jabbed him in the ribs.

"Martin, can you tie me up now?" I asked, stopping on the sidewalk.

"I'll do it when we get there."

"It'll be too late then. I want to be in costume when we walk in or the effect will be lost."

"I'll do it in the lobby."

We got into an elevator filled with vampires, sexy witches, pimps, and white trash. When we got out, Martin kept going.

"Wait, you said you'd tie me up!"

He sighed. "Is this really necessary?"

"Yes!" I said. "It's our whole costume!"

Zach and Michelle stood by.

"You guys go ahead," Martin said. "*I'm* not allowed."

They went in, and Martin and I got to work. I had already figured out how best to secure the tracks and tried explaining to Martin, but he got mad and said he knew what he was doing and that I should just "keep quiet for a change."

"You keep quiet," I whispered, as he circled the rope around my arms and torso, weaving it through the tracks until I couldn't move my upper arms. "Circle it more times," I said, when he stopped after only two loops. "You have to do it more times or it won't look good."

He circled it a few more times and then, walking on ahead without me, said, "I don't know how you're going to move around, but you got what you wanted. Happy?"

Since I was now attached to the tracks and the hallway was so narrow, I couldn't walk straight but had to walk sort of sideways, like Gloria Swanson entering stage left. "This is part of the fun," I said, flanking in behind him.

Past the front door was another long, even narrower hallway that led into a large loft-like living room packed with costumed guests. Martin and I stood at the edge with Zach and Michelle. I smiled excitedly and, maneuvering just the bottom of my right arm, handed Zach my disposable camera.

"Would you take a picture of us? Martin, could you please wear your hat?" He'd taken it off again. "At least for the picture?"

Martin put his hat back on and stood beside me. I leaned over for a second to brush a hair from my face, which caused my tracks to bump Martin in the back. He flashed me a mean look.

"What?" I asked.

"Your stupid tracks hit me. Can you try to be a little more aware of yourself, please!" he yelled, shaking my tracks angrily, and in so doing shaking me.

"Guys," said Zach, a few feet in front of us, holding up the camera. "You ready?"

My eyes filled with tears. I tried to smile but found my mouth muscles doing all sorts of weird things. "No, umm, I have to go to the bathroom," I said and flanked off down the long narrow hallway, trying not to cry until I made it outside.

I just needed a moment alone to collect myself, but the hallway was filled with pimps and white trash—investment bankers in costume—coming off the elevator, so I climbed the staircase half a flight to get some privacy. Standing on the next landing, my arms tied down to my sides, tracks on my back, I let my tears flow.

After a minute, a sexy witch spotted my feet and ducked her head up the stairs. She smiled, then frowned. "Are you okay?" My costume was a success; I looked like I was in trouble. Her boyfriend, wearing a tuxedo and an Afro wig, poked his head in next to hers and looked up at me with concern. I tried to smile back. "Fine," I said. "Great," I sniffled, as if I had no idea why they'd even asked.

After my face air-dried—I couldn't reach my eyes to wipe the tears away—I went downstairs and flanked back into the party, to the edge of the large room where our group had stood moments earlier. Martin was nowhere to be seen. A few different guys came up to me while I waited, each of them telling me how much they liked my costume before asking if I needed rescuing. I said no, told them I had a boyfriend somewhere inside, but thanks anyway. Then, after a few minutes, The Villain returned.

"There you are!" Martin said. "Look, I'm going to get a drink, you want anything?"

"A screwdriver would be nice," I said quietly.

He looked me up and down and then back at the crowd. "Well, obviously you can't come inside with your tracks on," he said.

"Yes, I can."

"So I'll come back in a few minutes." He rubbed the skin above his upper lip, pulling at the remaining glue so that it looked like he was twirling an imaginary mustache; he'd already removed the real one. "It was falling off anyway," he volunteered. "It's too hot in here," he sighed. He took off his hat and jacket and studied me. "You might as well make yourself useful," he said. And then, as if I were a coat rack, he hung his jacket and hat on my tracks and disappeared into the crowd.

5

This is almost everything that happened since I last saw May in New York:

I got *even more* serious with Martin; took a job teaching sixth grade in a public school in the South Bronx; moved to a new apartment at the mouth of the Midtown Tunnel; took a new job teaching at a private school on the Upper West Side; earned my teaching certificate; applied to graduate school; discovered Reggie on line behind me outside the Halloween store on Fourth Avenue—"I'm going to be 'white trash,'" he said; broke up with Martin after nearly three years (Not right after Halloween, but pretty soon after. He was surprised; he loved me, he explained, and figured we were in it for the long haul, which was why he resented me so much); moved to a new apartment in the West Village; accepted the third invitation sent by Caroline to join Friendster; quit my teaching job; began a master's program in Humanities after every other graduate school rejected me; tried to write another novel; updated my Friendster profile to include under Favorite Films all three Amy Fisher movies (*Casualties of Love: The Long Island Lolita Story*; *The Amy Fisher Story*; and *Amy Fisher: My Story*) and summarily accepted one hundred or so "friend requests" from former college and high school acquaintances I hadn't seen or spoken to in years; read up on "lucid dreaming" and began first by just trying to hover low, still pretty close to the ground; cried when I told Martin I didn't want to get back together though I definitely still loved him, that I'd really only come over to collect my Tupperware containers and my train tracks; took to crying sporadically on the subway when I thought about how much I missed him; and learned to live an otherwise quiet, fairly responsible life that included veggie burgers (to make sure I was getting at least one serving of vegetables daily) prepared on my George Foreman Grill (a Christmas present from my parents), the occasional jog along the Hudson river, and hanging framed reproductions of Bruegels and Manets, or whatever I could find on sale at The Salvation Army, up and down the walls of my new West Village one-bedroom apartment in an ongoing effort to make the place look more like how I felt, which was, increasingly, like having a party, before I decided to throw one in celebration of my twenty-fifth birthday.

6

I invited all my friends. But because I'd been living wholly within Martin's world for the last three years, I had only a few. So I asked my old friend Jacob to throw the party with me, to invite his friends and then ask his friends to invite theirs. Reggie, who'd found me on Friendster after our run-in at the Halloween store, wrote back that he was definitely coming and also, would I mind if he brought Felix?

Finding me within the large crowd of strangers huddled noisily inside my small one-bedroom apartment, Felix handed me a beer and also his cell phone. On the other end was May, calling from the edge of oblivion—California. And so, just as I had brokered May and Felix's first date a few years earlier, Felix brokered a reunion between me and May.

It was as if we were a movie being played in rewind. First there was May and me, then May and Felix and me, then May and Felix and Reggie and me, then May and Felix, then me and Martin, then me. Then Reggie and me, then Reggie and Felix and me, then Reggie and Felix and May and me. See what I mean?

When May came to New York for a week's visit a few months later, the four of us all went out together. Now Reggie and I were dating while May and Felix were negotiating a friendship/romance. She explained this to me by confessing that though she and Felix had kissed the other night, it was more out of boredom than out of attraction. Did I understand?

It was like a rubber band snapped back. Or rather, like a ship returning from the furthest reaches of space. Proof that the universe is just like a game of Pac-Man—I read this recently in *Scientific American*. The universe is not infinite, some scientists suppose, but shaped like a donut giving off the appearance of infinity while actually just looping.

So there we were—rounding the other side of the universe, returning through the act of departing—a chain of acquaintances made, broken, and reassembled in reverse. Pac-Man exiting on one side of the screen only to reappear on the other.

After May's visit, we began emailing each other pretty often. We were both single again—she and Felix were over, while Reggie and I had re-started only to re-stop—so we had a lot to discuss. We'd write to each other about our dating adventures, exchange advice, and occasionally even implement a new "science experiment" via correspondence.

I'd send her an email that I planned to send to some guy, and she'd hypothesize his response, laying down a small wager with it: "Twenty bucks says he'll call you Tuesday but not Monday, and if you don't call him back within three hours, he'll follow up with a text referencing the theme song to *Knight Rider*." "You're on!"

That Valentine's Day it hardly mattered that I had no boyfriend. I wrote an email that included the address of a local flower shop along with the window of time during which I'd be home to receive presents, and cc'd it to a list of guys I'd recently dated or was still dating. May enjoyed this experiment particularly and called me in a peel of laughter.

"The bitch is crazy is about me!" she said in a man's voice. "Hey, wait—" she trailed off, pretending to notice only then the long list of names hugging theirs in the cc.

I wasn't trying to be cruel. It's just, with all the waiting-by-the-phone stuff that happens when you're twenty-five—the headgames, the guys never being honest, or their acting like you're trying to do something awful to them just by caring—a girl's got to take her power back. I got five valentines following that stunt, incidentally. An unexpected result that made us both a little sad.

"It's horrible the way men will fall in love just because you won't," I wrote in my next email.

May agreed. "Even when you're winning, hard-to-get is a lousy game."

Around that same time, I began to see more of Felix and Reggie. Felix had decided to resettle in New York, which meant that for a while he would cruise the couches of the North East. And so, the three of *us* now became a gang.

It was just like in *Sex and the City*. Every Sunday, we'd meet for brunch to discuss our love lives, only, instead of four fabulous women in their thirties, it was four slovenly guys in their twenties; Felix, Reggie, Reggie's two roommates, and me. "That chick I met on Friendster tossed my salad last night," Felix told us.

Then, because Felix and I were both unemployed—me because I'd just started grad school, and Felix because he's Felix—we began hanging out more and more just the two of us, and as it turned out, we made an excellent team. When you're in your twenties, and the battle of the sexes is raging, its casualty rate increasing every day, a platonic boy-girl alliance can be a great asset. With me by his side, women were much more amenable to his advances, and for my part, Felix was an excellent ally, too. While a girl alone might look desperate, and two together, way too intimidating, a girl with a guy who is not her boyfriend eases tensions. Together, we hit the bars, "befriend and conquer!" our new motto.

Having spent so much time in the trenches with Felix, it was only natural that eventually I began to confide in him, too, asking for relationship advice as if he were a surrogate May. "It's funny," I told him one day, "how in bringing you to my party, Reggie had been like a surrogate you when you brought Reggie; and when you put me on the phone with May, you were like a surrogate me putting me on the phone with a surrogate you; and then when May visited New York a while back and you guys sort of kissed, she'd been like a surrogate Reggie; and then Reggie, in dating me for a few weeks, was like a surrogate you; while I, in dating Reggie, the surrogate you, had become a surrogate May; which in turn made you, Felix, my bastard roommate, a surrogate me."

How strange life is, I marveled, as we stood together in the kitchen, this ongoing exchange of one role for another. You're a roommate, a friend, a girlfriend, a student, a teacher, a daughter, maybe even one day a mother, and on and on, I guess, depending on how long you live. But if you eventually become all these different people, what exactly is it that makes you still you? Do *you* change, or does the *game* just change all around you, you know what I mean?—I'm paraphrasing.

"Yeah, that's why I used chocolate syrup to make the deviled eggs this time," Felix replied. "You didn't have any mayo. Go 'head and try one."

III

1

"It makes no sense," I said.

The Bastard and I were walking along Tenth Street. It was late fall or early winter depending on how you see things and the morning after another long night of terrible fun.

"Jess likes you, but you freak him out a little. He's not looking for a serious relationship and can probably tell that it would be hard to keep things casual with you, which is why he's backing off now."

"But I don't want a relationship either. I just got out of a three-year relationship. Another relationship is the *last* thing I want!"

We walked a bit in silence. Felix began whistling the Daft Punk song, "One More Time." I hummed the choruses.

After a minute, he stopped, looked around, and nodded. "It's officially a dry spell," he announced.

"Nonsense! What about all those girls from Craigslist?"

That morning he'd posted an ad on Missed Connections describing a woman he'd not actually seen but only hoped to—his ideal girl—and then picked a random subway line and related an imaginary scenario in which he spotted her and felt an instant connection though regrettably he'd not said hello. "Did you feel it, too?" he wrote. He got the idea from *Oprah*, from an episode he watched recently with his mom about "the law of attraction." "You're supposed to ask the universe for what you want—blonde, brunette, Asian, etc.—and then just wait for her to come to you," he explained before posting it.

"I think I miss May," he sighed. "I just want to meet someone nice, you know?" We passed a girl in ripped jeans and motorcycle boots. "Hey, can I borrow your torso for twelve minutes?"

The girl ignored him.

"She's clearly into you, Felix, but shy. When talking to a girl, try to avoid yes or no questions, like, 'Can I borrow your torso?' or 'May I put my penis in your mouth?' It leaves her with only two possible responses rather than opening the territory for conversation. What about that nice young lady you met last week on Friendster? The one who tossed your salad?"

"Cara?"

I shrugged.

"I'm not into her. She has weird gums."

"That's not nice, Felix."

"She's too skanky. I mean who does that on a first date? I can't take her to dinner now even if I wanted to. She's a savage!" He leaned into another girl passing on the right. "Ooh, I'd like to butternut your squash," he said in a lewd voice. The girl giggled and kept walking.

"Gross, Felix."

A shy-looking Asian girl passed in front of us. "And what do we have here?" Felix asked, sidling up beside her.

I fell back a few paces to give him room to operate. They talked for two or three minutes and then, stopping at the corner, she wrote down her phone number.

The odd thing about Felix is that he routinely says the most offensive things you can imagine, and it almost always works. Women find him adorable. The only reason I can figure is that they think he must be kidding. I mean he is, partially. It's like he knows what he's saying is gross and ridiculous, but he still means every word of it. What's even weirder is that if he goes out with these girls, if they start to date, they inevitably fall for him with the rough result that Felix has to sit them down—in their own apartments, naturally—and give them the hard talk about his not being ready for a relationship.

Meanwhile, Reggie, who is polite, good-looking, a moderately successful computer programmer at a cool downtown start-up, has none of Felix's success. Felix is crude; basically homeless; drinks and smokes way too much; and has been unemployed for the last four years save for the occasional acting gig here and there, a brief stint selling Christmas trees last winter, this one time when he got a job handing out comedy club flyers in Times Square, and another time in 2000, when he and May had just started up, when he worked a few weeks as a census taker. He has pretty much nothing to offer a girl, and yet, women want whatever he's got.

How he scored May and kept her as long as he did remains a mystery to his friends. How it ended was much less of a puzzle. Reggie told me the whole story that day on line at the Halloween store. Felix told me, too, during a game of backgammon months later. And then May gave me her version when she was visiting New York a few weeks ago and crashed on my couch, ousting Felix to Reggie's for a few days.

Apparently the whole thing fell apart a few months after her older sister's wedding. After her very Christian parents found out she and Felix were living together, they began a long-term cold war against the couple. In the three months leading up to her sister's wedding, May and her parents did not exchange a word. Then, all together in Mountain Brook, on the night before the big day, a huge argument erupted between May and her mother, with the result that May felt she'd finally gained ground on Felix's behalf.

She'd told her parents firmly, "If you love me, you must love Felix, because I love Felix and he is going to be in my life whether you accept him or not!" Exhausted by their estrangement, her parents reluctantly

---

IRIS HAS FREE TIME

agreed, and the three of them reconciled with a tearful hug. Then, at the reception the following day, Felix got drunk, and using one of the disposable cameras set out on all the tables for wedding guests to document the joyous occasion, he took a photo of his penis.

After the pictures came back from the developers, the whole family—still at the house celebrating—gathered in the family room to pass them around. May's father was the first to see the penis. He laughed uncomfortably and then, in a kind of shock-induced automatic response, passed it over to his wife, who also laughed before passing it to grandpa, who hooted and held his sides, and then passed it to grandma, who bellowed, "Get a load of that," in a strange cowgirl accent. . . .

After his penis finished making the rounds, May and Felix, who had been present for the photo-share, repaired to the patio. May, seething, inquired, "Felix, what the fuck?" Felix responded that it was a joke, and then pointed out how everyone had laughed, motioning through the glass door to May's mother, who'd laughed so hard she was now crying.

Eventually the two reconciled and returned to L. A. where they remained together a few more months, until, on the heels of a minor disagreement over where Felix left his skateboard, May ended things once and for all, thus catalyzing Felix's journey back East.

Felix was shocked by the breakup and maintains that May overreacted, that the whole photo episode was actually quite hilarious, and reminds whomever he's telling this story to that her father's initial response was laughter. May contends that her father's laughter was nervous and that, anyway, it wasn't just the photo of Felix's penis that did it, but a whole bunch of other things, too, which the photo of his penis had only made clear. "It just got to be too hard," she told me.

Felix and I rounded Bleecker. Since we had no place to go and very little money, we decided to walk over to the large Picasso statue below Washington Square Park.

"That's weird," Felix said when we got there, looking at me and then at the statue ten feet away. "It looks just like you."

"Most of the work from his cubist period does," I answered. "It's my broken nose. It creates the illusion that I can be viewed from all angles at once. I also look a lot like Mondrian's color block paintings, though the reason for that is less clear."

"My balls are cold. I hate winter," Felix said.

"I mean, fine. We're not exclusive, I get that," I exploded, thinking about Jess again, about what happened last night. "But did he really have to grab her ass right in front of me? That's just rude."

"If I had the money, I'd buy one of those chemical hand-warmers and put it in my underwear," Felix went on dreamily.

2

Jess was a friend of Felix on whom I'd developed a small crush. Two weeks ago, we ended up alone in his apartment—he was having a barbeque and all his guests were up on the roof. Though there was no music playing, we'd started to slow dance. Then he kissed me. It was all very romantic until he told me he wasn't ready for a relationship. I said that was good because I'd just gotten out of a long one. "I hate relationships," I said, spinning away and out of his arms.

Then last night, a whole bunch of us were supposed to meet up at this bar on Delancey where someone's friend's band was playing. Jess had been there awhile before Felix and I arrived, and I was excited to see him because Felix had told me he was excited to see me. He'd been asking about me, he said. "A lot."

"What's up?" Jess yelled, over the music.

I gave him a kiss on the cheek and explained why we were late. "Poor Felix," I shouted and looked over at him.

Felix nodded weakly, before sinking into a stool at the bar.

"We stopped at Matt's on the way over and Matt had this really really strong weed, which made Felix sick. We were playing Awakenings but then had to stop in order to minister to his health. He's mostly better now, just tired I think. Have you ever played Awakenings?"

Jess shook his head.

I knew he hadn't because I invented the game myself; I suppose I was showing off. I have a pretty good track record when it comes to inventing games: Turbo Sculpture, The Water Game, Let's-Throw-Magic-Markers-at-My-Ceiling-Fan. . . . Unlike conventional games, however, mine have no winners or losers; you just play to exhaustion.

Before Felix got sick, he'd been sitting on Matt's couch, feigning catatonia, like in the movie *Awakenings* with Robin Williams and Robert De Niro. "I'm the doctor," I explained, and threw a head of lettuce at him. Without looking up or in anyway changing position, Felix caught the lettuce in one hand.

I went on to Jess, describing the game's few rules, thinking he would be impressed, maybe say to himself, "Wow! Iris is not like the other girls." "That's basically it," I said, smiling at him expectantly.

A bullet leaving a smoking gun, or a truck bearing down on the love interest as the hero mouths, "NOOOOOO," one quarter of the way through the summer's hottest blockbuster—these types of things always occur in slow motion: A girl arrived at Jess's side and greeted him with a kiss on the cheek. He greeted her with his hand on her behind. They laughed. Then . . . her hand against his chest . . . his mouth beside her ear . . . his arm around her waist . . . his eyes to her eyes . . . and then back on mine and with that time resumed its normal flow, as if they were a movie and my face were a Play button.

I kept talking, searching for the conclusion to some stupid thing I'd gone on blabbing about, while he continued to whisper in her ear. Lifting her chin, she let out a musical little laugh before flipping her hair—straight and shiny—a taut sail catching the gale-force wind of their joyous rapport.

I finished my sentence—"You know what I mean?" I asked desperately, looking back and forth between them.

"Totally," the girl said.

"Totally," Jess agreed.

I mumbled and looked down at my feet.

Shipwrecked. Washed ashore. The crew's lone survivor, I spot a lighthouse, crawl my way to it, and knock on the door. A man opens it; warmth and firelight spill out into the cold dark night from which I've just emerged. Dripping in the doorway, I motion dumbly to the storming sea at my back, before a woman joins him to see what's the matter. He puts his arm around her waist and I understand I've interrupted something. Offering an apology for not having drowned along with my crew, I begin, "What's that? I couldn't hear you over the music."

"This is my friend Jenny," Jess repeated.

I touched my chest, squeezed the front of my shirt to ring out the damp.

"I'm Iris," I said and offered my wet hand.

"Oh, *you're* Iris," she said looking at him. "Jess has told me so much about you."

"He has?"

"I was getting off work when I called you the other night," he said abruptly. "Jen and I tend bar together on Thursdays."

I nodded. "Great band," I said, stretching my neck to see around them. And then, pointing at nothing in particular, "Excuse me," I said, following the line of it to the back of the bar.

He had called last Thursday "just to talk." That's what he said. I asked him what he wanted to talk about. He said he'd been thinking about me. He said he got my number from Felix. He said, as if referring to the newly discovered scientific fact of us, "Iris, Iris, Iris . . . what are we going to do about you and me?"

3

"That's it!"

Felix was miming a creepy hand gesture to three girls passing by in NYU sweatshirts.

"I'm done playing games! One minute he likes me, and the next—"

"Maybe you guys should see other people," Felix laughed.

"Yeah, I should tell him that."

"Text him."

"It would be pretty funny," I said.

"Break up with him," Felix smiled. "I dare you."

"A text saying we're through, even though we were never actually together."

"Exactly."

I took out my phone and smiling, began to type. I read aloud, "'Jess: I'm breaking up with you. I hope we can still be friends.' How's that?" I looked at Felix.

"Perfect," he said, distracted by a blonde woman in pinstripes.

"Send!"

We circled the statue once more, laughing as we imagined Jess receiving my message. Then we started back to my place in silence.

"You think he knows I'm kidding?" I asked after ten minutes.

4

Regardless of however negatively "the experiment" might affect my relationship, regardless of however much I might actually like the guy on whom I was "experimenting," I had to go through with it, "because," May and I agreed, "it's too funny not to!" Showing up to a date in a pink ski mask, mailing an autographed photograph of myself in a heart-shaped frame, calling a guy and saying, "I'm in prison; bail me out!" just had to be done if not for the laugh then "for science," my faithful lab assistant reminded me.

"Ours is an age of enlightenment," I noted solemnly, "and it is toward this noble end that I sacrifice myself." Because we smoked so much pot back in college, pretty much everything struck us as hilarious, too, with the rough result that if something were even whispered, if the words "wouldn't it be funny . . ." even left our mouths, I ended up having to go ahead and do it. We'd laugh and laugh, imagining the outcome of each new scheme, and then, on the crest of this hilarity, I'd sadly take up my mission, compelled to follow through like some martyr to the joke.

Felix and I eventually made it back to my apartment where, immediately, he began checking the responses to his last Craigslist post. I fixed us drinks—orange juice with some vodka I'd gotten on sale—and washed a few dishes to get my mind off Jess and the fact of his not texting back.

I had sent the message with the vague idea that this would be the last word, a "joke" to cap the whole stupid non-affair. But in the silence that followed, none of it felt very funny. I didn't really want a laugh, I realized. I wanted him to win me back.

An hour later my phone beeped, and I rushed from the kitchenette.

I'M SORRY YOU FEEL THAT WAY.

Felix looked up from the computer. "What'd he say?"

"He didn't get it," I said and showed Felix the text.

"There are better guys for you, Iris," he said and looked back at the computer.

I read the text over again, the words becoming blurry. I missed Martin.

"All I ever do is break up with people," I said, laughing thinly. "Every time it ends faster and faster. Pretty soon I'll be able to skip dating all together and just start right at the end. Why wait, when I know where it's going? I could post an ad on Craigslist:

'It's Not You, It's Me—W4M:

I saw you on the subway. You had your hands in your pockets when I walked by and smiled. If you are reading this, I don't think we should see each other anymore.'"

Felix was silent.

I flopped onto the couch and lit a cigarette. I thought of the time May and I decided it would be too hilarious for me to call this guy I'd been seeing and pretend to cry into his answering machine while recounting the plot of a particularly moving episode of *Alf*. It had been so funny when we smoked a joint and talked about it over Mac and Cheese. But then, when I was sniffling into his answering machine and there was no laugh track provided by May—she was standing beside me holding her breath in order not to corrupt the conditions of the experiment—all the humor dried up, and I knew I didn't sound funny at all, just nuts.

I hung up and May burst into laughter. "How'd it go?" she asked.

"Yeah. So that's over," I said. I told May he wouldn't be calling anymore and entered my prognosis into my chemistry ledger to make it official.

What did all my experiments prove?

"Is humor my tragic flaw?" I'd asked her later that afternoon, after closing the ledger and putting it aside. In addition to Physics and Quantum Philosophy, I was taking a class called Fate and Free Will in the Epic Tradition and had begun to project myself into the role of tragic hero. "Your comic flaw," May replied, passing the joint back.

5

That afternoon, Felix continued to troll the Internet for girls while I retired to my bedroom. I turned on the TV and fiddled with the antenna, changing the channel before settling on the only one that came in with decent reception.

I watched *Oprah*. Tom Cruise was on, promoting his new movie *War of the Worlds* and talking about his burgeoning relationship with Katie Holmes. He jumped on the couch, threw his head back and bared his teeth. He was thrilled and smiling and took Oprah's hands and shook her. He jumped on the couch, then to the ground again. "I love her," he said, so sincerely it seemed he had to be kidding. And then it was time to bring out his new girlfriend.

The studio audience rose in a frenzy. "Ka-tie, Ka-tie," they began chanting, as if preparing a virgin for ritual sacrifice. When the sacrifice wouldn't come out, he had to go backstage and get her. The cameras followed as he found her, got hold of her arms, pulled them behind her back, and marched her onto the soundstage and up toward the mouth of the volcano. The gods were angry and required a gift. Everyone was screaming, Oprah leading them. I lowered the volume and turned over on my side.

A white cat sat in the windowsill across the street. I watched him for a while and tried to catch his eye; he wouldn't look at me. I gave up and shut my eyes, pretending that the sound of the restaurant doors slamming downstairs was soporific, pretending that the sound of the Tenth Street bus screeching to a halt and growling as it pulled away was peaceful. I pretended that I was tired and numb and couldn't feel anything anymore, and eventually I fell into a quasi-sleep.

Drifting in and out of consciousness, I thought about my future now that I'm single again. I thought about my almost-something with Jess, a bad movie with a script full of problems. Our romantic comedy would never get made, because nothing much happened, because we disagreed on the details, because we couldn't agree on how to move the story forward. Scenes from our unmade movie passed before my closed eyes:

Our running into each other on East Tenth Street, how he saw me from behind a fence in Tompkins Square Park and called my name. How we passed the rest of the day together on a bench, how it got cold and he put his arm around me, how I told him not to kiss me and then he did, how I told him to call me later and then he didn't. The way he called me last Sunday, depressed about his lack of career, asking if we could meet up for milkshakes. He was thinking about moving, maybe to L. A. "What do you think?" "I think you should go if you think you should," I answered. "I could visit you if you want. Or not," I added, when he looked away. Or when the three of us, Jess, Felix, and I, had been walking together on our way to Matt's. Felix had found a large piece of wood left out on the curb among the trash. He was excited, he said; he could use it for a painting. He was excited because it had six sides and six was his lucky number. "My lucky pentagon!" he exclaimed.

"Actually, a pentagon has five sides," I interrupted. "A hexagon has six. Ask me anything!" I joked, before Jess, a step or two behind me, asked, "What about your heart? How many sides does that have?"

A thin sleep, punctuated by the Bacchanalian screams issuing out from the *Oprah* program. I imagined Jess and me running into each other months from now. I wouldn't expect to see him. He'd be the furthest thing from my mind. But then there he'd be on the sidewalk and, naturally, we'd stop to talk. I'd be beautiful and stoic, and with a look we'd say everything and nothing; we wouldn't laugh at all.

6

I emerged from my bedroom at 6:00 PM and found The Bastard watching the baseball game on the small kitchen TV with the foil crunched around its antenna. He was eating spaghettied lettuce with jam instead of sauce. He had cut the lettuce into long thin strands and then boiled it.

He said he'd heard about an office party of a friend of a friend's and we could head over to midtown at around 8:00 PM. I went to the fridge and retrieved a couple beers from what was left of an eighteen pack. I handed one to The Bastard.

"Wanna play backgammon?" he said, turning the sound off on the TV and heading over to the stereo to put on his favorite CD, *Felix's Cool Hits Volume IV*. He'd made it upstate at his mom's and brought it with him. It included Daft Punk's "One More Time."

"Sure," I said, cracking a beer. "But then I need to figure out what to wear. You have to help me." Back in college, I tested my outfits on May. Now I have The Bastard.

We played a round of backgammon and then Felix watched baseball and danced, while I tried on dresses and asked his opinion. Then we danced together, and after that we were ready to go. We played one more round of backgammon for the road and chugged our beers. I lit a cigarette and regretted it while smoking it. "I like everything about smoking except for the actual smoking," I said, puzzled, putting it out halfway through.

We took the subway uptown and played a word game. I said, "Sh," and Felix said, "ishkebob." I said, "Sh," and Felix said, "atner comma William."

We made it to Thirty-third Street and walked down the wrong side of the block three times before we found the address and walked in behind some girls. "Well, what do we have here?" The Bastard cooed when we got on the elevator. The girls giggled.

The elevator doors opened and a rush of music flooded in. We stepped out into a large wood-lined loft with great windows framing the night on all sides. We followed the music past a maze of cubicles before arriving in an open space—a makeshift dance floor lined with clusters of office personel, a DJ booth, a bar, and a young man tinkering with a multi-colored light fixture as a woman looked on, holding his drink.

I went to the bar and got a beer but couldn't finish it. I took a seat on the side somewhere and stared wearily out at the party, at the men and women gyrating jerkily, caught in a limbo state between drunk enough to dance but not drunk enough to dance well. Others stood on the side, laughing at their "crazy" co-workers. A woman cut in on a group of guys by grabbing one of their behinds before breaking away in blushing laughter. Three women in identical pencil skirts and a variety of bangs scowled in the corner with crossed arms. One removed a compact from her purse and reapplied her lipstick.

Normally I am very active at parties—dancing, telling jokes, meeting people, inventing games—but I felt so tired right then. I thought about the night before, about Felix turning green on the sofa after we smoked that blunt, about my wet oxford shirt, about the faces of Jess and the girl becoming larger and smaller after I'd gone on stupidly, "These are the rules to Awakenings. . . ."

A suited man a few feet in front of me began twirling his dance partner really fast. She spun and spun and almost fell before he caught her by the waist; they both laughed. The music was loud and the floor was loud, too. When people danced by, it groaned as if it were tired from holding everyone up. I started groaning with it, the way you do when you're home alone sick and you know no one can hear you. I watched everyone and felt almost good that I was feeling bad, that I was allowed as a result to sit out this round. I took out my phone to see if Jess had texted.

A man with blonde hair came over and insisted I dance with him. He had an accent. "I am from Sweden," he explained. He was very handsome: chiseled jaw, blue eyes, possessed of that rare yet conventional beauty that requires no special beholder. I refused him three or four times. I never say no to dancing but I was feeling so bad. He confused my saying no with my playing hard to get, and so he came on stronger. Finally I agreed just to get him off my back.

He held me in his arms and told me all sorts of things about his career and life, most of which I don't remember. I found him boring and my head felt so hot. He complimented me on my rosy cheeks.

We danced and danced. He threw me back and forth and I grew irritated because I thought he was breathing more than necessary; I didn't care for the sound. He said I was very beautiful, which made me feel sad instead of happy. I tried to right myself and store his compliment in the appropriate part of my brain, but couldn't. I felt so odd. Like all my emotions were outside of me, clustered in different parts of the room. And as he threw me this way and that—now I was dancing in happiness, now melancholy, now dread—none of it felt at all real, because I knew we were only going to move again. What would any of it matter after we left that part of the room, after we left that part of the night? The Swedish man came on stronger. He begged to know what I was thinking.

Finally, I told him: "Look, I like you. I'm just not in the mood, okay?"

He told me he wanted to take me ice-skating tomorrow in Central Park. He told me he wanted to take me to the Museum of Natural History. He laid out all the dates you plan when you're about to start a big romance, a new relationship in the beginning of winter or the end of fall depending on how you see things. He described the things you do with another person when you are less sure of your feelings than of your desire to feel them. He suggested dates that are so romantic in themselves that you don't even have to be. Perfect moments in which you might feel nothing, but it doesn't matter, because at a well-lit restaurant you can order a fish, because he can just dance you over to the part of the room where love is, and there, together, you can sway for a while and at the end of it, go home.

I said goodbye, and he grabbed me around the waist. He said, "Don't leave like this. I want to see you again." He looked into my eyes, and I nearly laughed—who was he looking at?

The Bastard crashed on my couch again that night. The dry spell had followed him to the party and he'd left empty-handed. He found me waiting for him in the hallway, my face burning, my throat scratchy. "I think I'm getting sick," I said.

On the subway, Felix didn't say much. I went quiet as well. I thought about the shape of my heart and pondered its many unseen sides. I thought about it like an old carousel, like the one in Bryant Park already closed for winter, with people all the time getting on and off. All these people whom you expect will always be in your life— Martin, May—go away, while some guy you met in the bathroom of a dorm party, some guy who made a joint disappear into thin air, turns up years later and takes up residence on your couch. He's the one you talk to.

I felt like my heart was spinning in my chest, like it was going so fast that there was no time for anyone to get on or off anymore, like all I could do was hold on tight so I didn't fly off, too. "I don't want a relationship either," I'd told Jess as we slow danced. "I was with someone for a very long time and now I just want to have fun. This, this is just fun."

At home, I went to my bedroom and shut the door leaving Felix alone in the living room at the computer. I changed into my pajamas and lay in bed with the phone on the pillow next to me. I thought of Martin, about our movie. Perhaps it would end with us meeting as friends, me looking at him over a cup of coffee, saying how it was hard at first, the first few months after our breakup, how for a long time, I wasn't ready, but now I am. "I'm ready to get back out there, I think, ready to try dating again. You know anyone who might be right for me?"

And then, as if it were the furthest thing from our minds, I'd notice him and he'd notice me. We'd look at each other with surprise and delight, with the expression one wears while tripping on destiny in a romantic comedy. We'd look at each other as if we were the freshest idea and simultaneously the obvious answer, as if audiences everywhere had never stopped rooting for us.

And then I got an idea for an experiment. The kind of thing that was just too funny not to do. The kind of thing I absolutely had to do "for science." I opened my phone and typed in the dark. "So I hear you're single again. . . ." I paused for a second and then sent it to Jess. I'll email May about all of this tomorrow, I thought. She'll think it's hilarious.

Then, tired from all the falling in love, I shut my eyes and tried to fall asleep instead. Felix was still up puttering around in the next room. I could hear him tapping softly at the computer, probably answering another email from another girl who rides the subway every day, some lonely girl who saw his post on Missed Connections, a complete stranger who "felt it too."

CHAPTER 2
THE CAPTAIN

He was so earnest that she was surprised and impressed. Evidently he had deep-seated ambitions, for he seemed to speak with actual emotion of these despised things, which were so far beneath his planning for the future. She had a vague, momentary vision of Pitt, at twenty-one, prime minister of England; and she spoke, involuntary in a lowered voice, with deference:

"What do you want to be?" she asked.

George answered promptly.

"A yachtsman," he said.

BOOTH TARKINGTON, *THE MAGNIFICENT AMBERSONS*

ON HEARING OF my plan to sell the T-shirts via eBay, The Bastard became excited and suggested that the shelf once emptied could be *his* room. "It's practically a crawl space!" Felix shouted, motioning toward the boxes and bags still filling it. "My own place," he dreamed aloud, "I could bring girls back here. . . ."

I became excited, too. In selling the shirts, not only might I make a little money, but I'd be performing a good deed by providing a home for The Bastard. With this in mind, The Captain came over with his digital camera yesterday.

We began by spreading a sheet from my bed across the bedroom door to affect a professional backdrop. We had to hang it a few different ways before we could find an area without blood stains.

"Get off my back!" I yelled at The Captain after he made another crack about it.

"I'm not on your back," The Captain said lethargically. The Captain's always lethargic. And pale.

"Yes, you are. You're right on it. And you can get right off! I'm a woman. We bleed. It's a sign of my fertility. I'd be very turned on right now if I were you."

The Captain—tall; pale, like the deck of a ship bleached by sun, salt, and air; and lethargic—looked at me and suppressed a smile. Or perhaps he was actually trying to smile but could only muster a crease. It's hard to tell with him. I went into the bedroom to change into my first shirt and underwear set.

A few nights ago over drinks, he promised to help me set up an eBay store where I could sell my shirts. "It's really easy," he said. "I can help you with it, if you want. We'll just need to take some pictures."

The plan was that I'd model each shirt, and then we'd crop my face out afterwards. I confess I was excited to resume my modeling career.

"I was a foot model back in high school," I yelled from the bedroom. You should see my instep! I was the envy of all my classmates in ballet school," I went on, and then added that it was my dream to be a plus-size model.

"I thought you wanted to be a writer."

I re-emerged from behind the door. "That's my other dream. Hand me a cookie."

He looked around. "I don't think you're big enough to be a plus-size model."

My face fell.

The Captain rushed to soothe me. "You're too skinny, I mean."

I pointed to the Mint Milanos next to a pile of dirty dishes on the kitchen counter. The Captain reached in the bag and handed me one as if it were a single rose.

I took a bite. "Just look at all this gristle," I said, chewing and pinching my thighs as if they were Salisbury steaks.

"You could be a 'skinny but flabby' model. Is that a category?"

"Skinny but flabby, yeah. . . ." I considered, before wiping away the crumbs that had fallen onto my navy blue "Second Base" T-shirt.

The Captain snapped a few shots while I held in my stomach. "Tell me when you're going to take the picture so I can hold my breath."

The windows in my apartment are pretty large, and for a second we both looked out, wondering what the people across the street would think. I'd bought a set of blinds a while back but never bought a drill with which to install them, so I did the next best thing, which was to lay the rolled-up blinds on the floor beneath the window. They're pretty nice blinds. I tried to get the ones James Stewart has in *Rear Window*. I'm a big fan of most if not all of Hitchcock's window treatments.

"It kinda looks like we're shooting amateur porn," The Captain said. "Especially because you have all those weird bruises."

"They're decorative!" I said defensively, regarding a big one on the back of my thigh—from a party last weekend. I kept going in and out a window to smoke on the fire escape and got all banged up. "It's amazing that it's left such a mark," I said, examining it. "It didn't hurt at all at the time. Do you think I might have that disease where you can't feel pain?"

"Alcoholism?"

"No. I think it's called something else. Hold on, the sheet is slipping. Maybe we should tape it. . . . Captain, hand me the tape."

After securing the backdrop, we moved on to the underwear, a black cotton bikini bottom. "Turn around so I can get the words on the back."

I turned around so that my butt, covered by a swatch of black fabric with hot pink letters that read, "Bad Ass," was facing him. "How's that?" I said, straining to look over my shoulder.

"Hmmm," he said, positioning the camera at various angles, searching for a flattering angle of my backside. For the shirts I'd been able to suck in, but we were a little stumped as to what to do about my sagging rear. "Hmmmm," he said again.

"Maybe I can, like, tape it or something."

I'd heard celebrities use tape for photo shoots, so I tried to improvise with a role of scotch tape from my drawing table. It didn't work. After a couple minutes I just had a bunch of tape hanging off my butt.

"It looks like you've sprained your ass," he said.

We troubled over this for a long time. "I don't want people to take the phrase "Bad Ass" literally," I worried aloud. "Like Bad—out-of-shape—Ass. No one's going to want to buy that."

"Your ass is not bad."

"But it's not good, either. No one's going to want to buy these if they think it's going to make them look like me," I said, poking at one of my sad cheeks. "Sad Ass," I mumbled, considering a new design.

Then The Captain had an idea. He suggested we do a shot with the underwear around my ankles.

"I have great ankles!" I said, trying to recover my confidence, which is very important for a model. So I put on my Ocean Pacific swimming trunks with the pictures of blowfish and seaweed on them and lowered my Bad Ass underwear to my ankles, which is when we encountered the next problem.

I hadn't shaved my legs in a while. I hate shaving my legs; it always makes me pensive. I'll be in the shower lathering up and think, if time and space are infinite, my existence will recur an infinite number of times, which means I'll be shaving forever. . . .

"Should I shave them right now?"

"No, it's alright. I can just fix it in Photoshop later. Same as the bruises," he said, fiddling with the camera.

The Captain snapped a few shots of the underwear around my ankles, but the pictures were still not coming out quite right. "Let's take a break," I said and repaired to the kitchen. "I'll be right there. I'm just going to heat up some dinner," I called out before setting the microwave.

"What's that crackling?" The Captain said.

"The silver lining on your dinner. I don't have any microwave-safe dishes. But these only have one or two trimmings of silver, so it just crackles—harmless optimism," I said, waving my hand and then jumped with excitement upon the microwave's last beep.

"Mmm, this is an old family recipe," I lied, bringing out a bowl of raw carrots, paprika, a keychain with a wooden tropical fish dangling from it that a taxi driver sent me in a handwritten letter following a long drunken ride, a few marbles, and a pair of purple sparkly shoe-laces in a soup of warm milk.

The Captain watched as I set the bowl down on my coffee table. "Do you think it needs pepper?" I asked, worried I under-seasoned it.

"What is it?" he said, suppressing a sneer, or trying to sneer. Again, not sure.

"It's my own recipe. Take a photo! I want to make a whole cook-book. I have about five recipes so far. My favorite is grilled lampshade drizzled with Tic Tacs in a balsamic vinaigrette over a bed of pencil shavings. I haven't made it yet, I just wrote down the idea. I'll make it for you next time. We can do the book together if you want. We can wear fake mustaches in our author photos. Or," I said, standing up, "dress up as gorillas." I always stand when I get excited. I was excited, imagining us as gorillas.

The Captain took a quick shot of me, and then another of my dish.

I repositioned myself in front of the backdrop and posed.

After about an hour, we were finished. We still had a few shirts left to photograph but decided to save them for another time, to just start with a few for now. I took a couple of beers from the fridge and gave one to The Captain and then sat on the couch and lit a cigarette. Then I got up and went to the stereo and tried to find something good to play.

"I can't understand it. I have tons of music, but there's never a thing I want to hear. What *is* all this stuff?" I said, motioning to the mess of records without their jackets, loose CDs, and tangled tape spill-ing out from a pile of broken cassettes. I decided on *Felix's Cool Hits Volume IV* finally, because it was already in the stereo. Daft Punk's "One More Time" came on and I sat down, feeling suddenly sedate. It was the song. I'd heard it so many times, always falling for Felix's reasonable plea. "Come on, just 'one more time'?" Felix would say when I'd suggest he turn it off.

We sipped our beers and listened to the music in silence. "Would you like to have dinner with me?" The Captain asked.

"I'd love to!" I said, standing.

I went into the bedroom to get dressed. I put on a yellow long-sleeve floor-length evening gown with some kind of bamboo shoot print on it that I like because I think it makes me look like Phyllis Diller, and a pair of fake-diamond clip-on earrings that used to belong to my grandmother.

"How do I look?" I said, coming out of the bedroom.

"You look great," he responded, lethargic again.

"So do you!" I said excitedly. The Captain was wearing jeans and a blue Friendster T-shirt that his older sister, my friend Caroline, had given him. She'd started working there after she moved back to San Francisco to live with her older brother whom I hadn't met. "He's sort of the black sheep of the family," Caroline told me. "He's a lawyer."

We decided to go all the way to the restaurant downstairs, which I like a lot because they let me bring my backgammon board when the place is not too crowded and because, during the winter, I can get really dressed up and don't have to worry about walking in the cold but just treat their dining room as an extension of my living room.

The restaurant had a two-for-one martini special, which I took as a sign that it wouldn't be around much longer. In the brief time I'd been living there, three separate restaurants had opened and closed in the same space. This restaurant had an elaborate menu of specialty martinis. We started with two each. Then we ordered a bottle of wine, because one mustn't drink hard liquor during dinner—it's coarse—and waited until after dinner to order our second and then third pairs.

We ate and he told me about his current job search and how he was thinking of maybe going to college after all. He was only twenty-two. I'd forgotten. Then he told me all about www.spaghetti-dog.com, a webpage he'd created, which was just a picture of a dog covered in spaghetti that his aunt had sent him. The Captain had shown it to me earlier. "She's single," he said, as if that explained it. It was getting thousands of hits every day.

I sipped my wine and told him I was very excited to be dining with such an illustrious figure.

He shrugged. "It's just for fun. For Christmas I built her a template, so she can upload additional spaghetti-dog photos whenever she wants. She's decided to start a greeting card company," he said, perking up so much that he almost looked alive. Then he told me about his erratic sleep habits and how that's why he's so pale.

"Like a wampire!" I said, pronouncing *wampire* with a *w* a few more times. "Wampire . . . wampire."

Then he told me about Diane Sawyer coming to see his grandmother's duplex where he'd been living for the last six months on the Upper West Side. How she might buy it.

The Captain went on about Diane Sawyer's visit, and my attention went in and out as I tried to gauge whether or not he liked me. We had been seeing an awful lot of each other lately, and he did offer to help me with my website. But then, he'd never really made a move. Or had he? Perhaps he had and I was just too drunk to remember.

We had already slept together a bunch of times, though all we did was sleep. When we arrived back from Atlantic City a few weeks ago and he was too tired to get the train all the way uptown, I let him crash at my place, on my bed, with me. But it had been perfectly chaste. We were still drunk and slept in our clothes on top of the blankets. When we woke up we took off our shoes, ordered food from the diner around the corner, and watched *Attack of the Killer Tomatoes* on my bedroom TV. I have it on VHS.

I'd been at Lex's '80s party with The Captain the night before, and after Lex had finished deejaying, in a fit of old times' sake we decided to go to Atlantic City. The Captain had never been and taking him seemed a good enough reason to go so we left straight from the club, me riding shotgun in Lex's 1972 Buick Riviera and The Captain listless as ever in the backseat.

We picked up a six-pack on the way out of the city but it wasn't enough and by the time we got there, my drunkenness had plateaued. I sat with Lex at the roulette table the way I like to, let the scantily dressed waitresses bring me screwdrivers, and tried to recharge. I was having a great time until one of the guards poked me on the shoulder and said I couldn't sleep at the table. Apparently, I'd dozed off.

The Captain was hanging out by the slot machines, so after dozing off a few more times and being poked awake, I made my way over to him. The Captain sat me on the chair beside him and put my hand on the slot machine lever to steady me before I nodded off again and got yelled at again.

We decided we should go for a walk in order to oxygenate my blood, while Lex finished his banking. I called the casino Lex's bank because he routinely returns to either withdraw money or deposit his most recent earnings.

The Captain and I swam through the ringing bells and flashing lights, the sounds of our footsteps absorbed by the carpeted floor. "I love casinos!" I said excitedly, awake again. I know it must seem like

I'm always saying things excitedly, but the fact is, excitement is the emotion I experience most frequently. Excitement and shame.

"Can you smell that?" I said, inhaling deeply. "The smell of failed romance, of desperation, the city that never was!" I said, looking around and quoting from that Burt Lancaster film. "I love Burt Lancaster. He has the weirdest ears."

We exited the gambling area and began walking through a large atrium with a great fountain in the center. We took seats along the ledge and were talking about something or other when I fell down. The Captain started to laugh. "I lost my balance," I explained from the floor.

"But you weren't even moving. You were sitting down!"

"The rotation of the Earth," I said, getting up. "It caught me off guard." I resettled myself, then fell again. "Damn! You didn't feel that?"

Driving back from Atlantic City, Lex hugged the large wheel of his Buick, The Captain slept in the backseat, and I played with the stereo, searching among Lex's cassettes for Christopher Croft. The sun kept rising higher and higher, and then we stopped at Burger King for breakfast.

Lex was tired but in a good mood because he'd won. Being with him when he lost was much different, and I was grateful for his good fortune. Lex dropped us both off at my place, now just a few doors down from his, before checking his car in a parking garage.

The Captain and I piled onto my bed with all our clothes still on and slept through the afternoon. It was hot, the start of summer, and my apartment was blazing. When we woke up, we watched the movie—the tomatoes rolling devilishly toward their prey, cars exploding, helicopters crashing, sauce. . . . The Captain complained of the heat, and I suggested we strip down to our underwear. I wouldn't look at him if he didn't look at me, I promised, and then I got some ice trays from the freezer and emptied them over him.

"What are you doing!"

"It's only water! Don't be such a baby! It will evaporate after it melts." Then I lay down beside him, and we floated on top of the bed of ice like fresh lobsters until the end of the movie.

"Do you think your sister would be upset if she knew how much we've been hanging out?" I asked over our after-dinner martinis.

"I don't know," he said and shrugged lethargically.

"You have a way with words," I said, taking another sip.

The Captain never says much. A life at sea humbles you, I suppose. That's what I was thinking, but then I remembered he'd never been to sea, that I'd only started calling him The Captain because he wore a captain's hat during a game of gin rummy at his grandmother's apartment one time while she was out of town. And also, because when I invited him to this Halloween party I was throwing on Reggie's roof and asked him what he would come dressed as, he said, "a yachtsman."

It was a barbeque and the night was cold and windy though still pretty warm for October 31st. May was in town for the week and we were exhausted, having gone out every night since she'd arrived, and in full costume the last three. On Friday I was Angela Bower from TV's *Who's the Boss*; May was my mother Mona. Saturday, I was Hamlet alongside my friend Jacob who was Ophelia; May was a sexy hoagie. And then Sunday, the big finish: May and I half-heartedly got into our Cheech and Chong costumes while really wanting only to go to sleep.

Taking on so many roles can really do it to you. Though May gets tired all the time and has been known to take naps right in the middle of conversation, sometimes with a drink still in her hand, I've only been tired a few times in my life. Like I said, mostly I'm excited. But this was one of those few times. I was so burnt out that on our walk over to Reggie's—the two of us, bearded and mustachioed—I wondered aloud if we shouldn't just turn around, just not show up to the party at all.

"We have to go," May reminded me, "Reggie doesn't know any of your guests."

I sighed. It would be too cruel to ditch the party after I'd insisted he let me throw it. "I know, I know. . . . "

Trying to rally, I sucked down a beer and smoked some weed as soon as we arrived. Despite my valiant efforts, however, I was soon overtaken by sleep. After a mini-nap in Reggie's living room I did finally make it up to the roof, to the party, which was then in full swing.

Reggie, dressed as Lou Diamond Phillips in *Stand and Deliver*, was manning the grill. May was off in the corner talking to a guy named Terrence who was dressed as Roy of Siegfried & Roy, post-attack. He had a stuffed white tiger attached to him and blood everywhere.

I caught sight of The Captain standing by himself at the northeast corner of the roof, looking off into the distance as if he were standing at the prow. He was wearing a turtleneck shirt and his captain's hat. And his face was steeled against the wind as he stared out, eyeing icebergs presumably. I went over and told him about my favorite part of Booth Tarkington's *The Magnificent Ambersons*, when the spoiled George Amberson says he wants to be a yachtsman when he grows up.

The Captain nodded stoically and said, "Arggh." He'd been considering a career move, he explained. "I think I might enjoy plundering." He'd recently gotten pretty big into pirate culture, and for the last few weeks, instead of regular chips, had been eating only cheese puffs, buying one brand in particular called Pirate's Booty. He preferred chips, he said, but had made the switch out of loyalty to his brethren. He also bought a plastic hook from a novelty shop, which, for now, he was using mainly at home.

I met The Captain in my last year of college. He was seventeen or eighteen and in from California to visit his older sister Caroline. She'd called and asked if I'd take her brother out for the evening because she had a date, said he'd come by my apartment to pick me up. Naturally it was a Thursday. It's almost always Thursday, I find. Every one out of the seven days, at least.

I don't remember what we spoke about while at my place. I probably did most of the talking. I often do, especially when I'm nervous, flitting from one topic to the next, pausing occasionally for one of my dance demonstrations—"I call this 'the slow-motion electrocution.' Watch!" We drank a sufficient amount, and then I took him downtown to Lex's '80s party.

I saw The Captain again a few more times after that, whenever he was in town to visit Caroline. And then Caroline decided to move back to California and The Captain decided to move to New York.

For the last year now, The Captain's been living with his grandmother in a duplex on the Upper West Side, Sixty-third Street near Central Park. It's just until he finds a job or goes to college or figures out which of these things he wants to do. He didn't go to college because he got a well-paying tech job while still in high school, right before the dot-com bubble burst, and so he figured there was no reason to. He could always go to college later, he figured, and so, now, later, he's been figuring again.

It's ironic that both The Captain and Caroline have such a weak regard for higher education considering their family's history. Their parents are both professors. Well, their dad's an art history professor with a focus on outsider art, and their mom went to school with their dad, but dropped out before completing her dissertation to become an artist herself—"She paints objects that don't exist," Caroline explained to me. "Like surrealist type stuff?" "No, like, she'll go to a house that doesn't actually exist and film herself painting it."

Also, their grandfather, with whom The Captain briefly lived on Sixty-third Street, founded Fruitlands School, a small progressive school in upstate New York where the students farm the land instead of playing team sports, a school Caroline briefly attended—she majored in math and cultivated gourds—before getting expelled for drug use. I met Caroline in Manhattan shortly after her release from her second and final stint at rehab. From the first, she'd escaped by window.

I don't remember exactly how we met, only that it was a Wednesday and I was at my weekly karaoke party. I'd just ordered another scotch and was watching the stage where the lead singer of the B-52s was taking the microphone from some guy belting out "Love Shack," when I pinked-out—what I call blackouts, because I'm a girl.

The following week Caroline approached me early in the night while I was still relatively sober, and filled me in on our having made friends the week before.

"I'm sorry, I don't remember," I said, playing aloof, as if my forgetting were a consequence of fame as opposed to rampant pink-outs.

"I complimented you on your song."

"What did I sing?"

"I Can't Get No Satisfaction," she said, and began laughing. "But instead of satisfaction, you sang 'cock.' You stretched it out. 'Coooock,' you said."

"Really?" I shrugged. "That's weird."

I confess: I'm pretty shy when I'm not unconscious, so this method of meeting people I've already met really works for me. While we're on the subject, that's why I sleep around. I don't actually have sex, mind you, I just sort of pick a guy I like and then try and pass out next to him. It's so much less awkward having your first kiss in the morning, after you wake up next to a guy, than having to go through all that awful leaning-in stuff while you're still standing, nerve-wracked and fully aware of the vast distance between your mouths. Because your face is already right next to his on the pillow, and because your brain is too much crippled by a mind-numbing hangover to register any anxiety, everything flows pretty naturally. Lying like that in someone's arms, it would be much more awkward *not* to kiss.

And so it was with Caroline and me. Seeing as we had made friends already, all I had to do was continue to be. This was a good thing because I liked Caroline a lot. She was smart and funny and sportingly depressed. We'd lie on the bed of her East Village studio, watch one-hour teen dramas, and during the commercials try to one-up each other with our despair. "I tried to slit my wrists with a sketchpad yesterday," she'd say flatly. "I'm pretty sure my mom thinks I'm a loser," I'd counter.

It was hard to believe that just a few months earlier she'd been living in a halfway house. To me she seemed so together, so mature in certain ways—she had a job working as a personal assistant to a music executive—but then immature in others—she spent almost all her free time at a record store where she'd fallen in love with a clerk whom she'd never spoken to.

"Which one is he?" I asked, peaking through the window. We were standing in the cold outside the shop one night in January.

"The tall, skinny guy with all the piercings. He's 6'7"," she said, lighting up. "He's a monster!"

It was strange to remember that I was actually older than Caroline. When we met she was twenty and I was twenty-one, which is a pretty big difference when you're that age, a year being a full five percent of your life. It was strange because my addictions were only then coming into bloom, while hers had already been clipped.

During the quieter times that came later, I asked her what her drug of choice had been.

"Spanish Fly," she told me with a straight face. And then later, "heroin," she confessed.

Because Caroline was always sober while I was always drunk, most of our friends were baffled by our affinity—"You have nothing in common!" May said, standing very close to us. If you looked at us from far away though, it was clear that our only real difference was time; though Caroline and I were roughly the same age, we were moving through it quite differently and so had found ourselves, if temporarily, on opposite ends of the same continuum. I was before and she was after.

But I'm rather prone to this kind of long-view. Alas, seeing the big picture is sort of my tragic flaw. I mean, if you're really in the moment, you shouldn't be able to see life so clearly the way I do. Which brings me to what I like most about drinking. It makes you a little blind. And action requires a certain amount of blindness after all. Take Oedipus. Blind to his very identity, he was welcomed to Thebes as a hero, hailed "a man of action," and named king because of it. Sure, his blindness was the cause of his subsequent downfall, led to the whole kingdom falling under plague, and resulted in the accidental killing-his-father-having-sex-with-his-mother situation, but his blindness was also the source of his strength.

My point is, things happen when you drink, not all of them good, but at least *something* is happening. And sure, there's the downside—

regularly losing my wallet and gloves, collecting bruises from renegade lampposts, suffering the occasional loss of dignity. But there's an upshot, too—being brave and fabulous for the while I'm still standing, being hailed a woman of action before I fall down.

The Greeks defined tragedy as the keen irony of a situation in which the good cannot be extricated from the bad. If you were Oedipus, for example, what would you have done differently? In the glorious despair-filled aftermath of a night out, I often ask myself this very question. Might things have turned out better if I hadn't drunk so much? But then, who am I to question fate? Some people are just built for tragedy.

I still don't know why Caroline chose me, of all the people we met back then, to hang on to. She since claims it was my legwarmers and the way I sang The Rolling Stones that first night, just before I passed out—I'd charmed her. But who knows? Perhaps she was just vicariously enjoying my drunkenness the way I was vicariously enjoying her sobriety. Whatever the reason, we became pretty close pretty quick. And then she moved away.

Six months ago her grandfather died. There was a big memorial service at the school, for which Caroline flew in. And then a week later, her grandmother decided to sell the duplex. It was too big for her to live there alone.

A few weeks ago The Captain called me because, he said, he needed help cleaning out the liquor cabinet. They were showing the apartment the next day and there was a lot of work to do since, naturally, his grandmother wouldn't be moving the bottles to her new place.

"You did the right thing by calling me," I told him solemnly. "I'll be right over."

I'd been to the apartment before, visiting Caroline when she'd stayed there between apartments of her own. We'd sat by the window in her grandfather's office, while Caroline Googled this fat comedian from SNL on whom I'd developed a crush. He was part of our circle and at the last karaoke party, Caroline told me, he had joked about wanting to fist her. She was disgusted and didn't find him funny at all.

"Why didn't he say that to me?" I said jealously. "I would have said something witty like, 'Hey, no, don't fist me. That's gross! Ahhhh,'" I trailed off miserably. It is my curse to lose any sense of humor I might have whenever I'm around someone I like.

"A zinger," she said. "Anyway, it wasn't funny!"

I lowered my head.

"Not you. Him! He was trying to be funny, but it was just gross. He was completely wasted, too."

"He must have to drink so much to get drunk," I said dreamily. "He's huge!" I sighed, impressed by his alcoholism. "What commitment!"

"He laughs at his own jokes and they're not even funny. Look," she said, typing a new search.

I looked, as if into a crystal ball. The Internet was bewildering to me then. Even though I was finishing college and we were in the midst of the dot-com boom, I had managed to remain wholly ignorant of it all. I'd only just started emailing and did it but once a week, sending chatty notes to Emily, my former boss from *The New Yorker*. I'd stop at the NYU computer lab between classes and email her about my dating adventures, telling her how I'd run into Field—a handsome, preppie twenty-five-year-old with floppy hair who worked at *The New Yorker*—how I'd started "playing the Field."

We'd only gone on two dates actually: Both times he took me to dinner at the Afghan Kebab House and asked me if I wanted to have children. After dinner, both times, I took him to a local dive bar where I happened to know all the regulars. "Teeth," one of the old drunks, decided to sit down and share a pitcher with us, both times—had it been only the one time it might have been charming, but I think the second time clinched it for Field and made him not call me for a third kebab. "Though I'm not toothless myself, I have a lot of toothless friends, so I think the general impression I gave was of toothlessness all the same," I'd typed in an email to Emily. "By the way, I ran into Gibb at the Union Square Barnes & Noble the other day. Did he tell you? He told me about your new intern and I asked if Jed had started dating her, too. He said he didn't know Jed and I broke up and I said, 'I like to think of him as just part of the job.' Anyway, how's your love life? Any new developments since I left?"

"Look! There are all these message boards about how bad a comedian he is," Caroline went on.

"Well, *I* think he's funny. And anyway, it's not about his talent. It's about his body! If there were any justice, he'd win *People*'s sexiest-man-alive contest. We should campaign for him. He's romantic, too, you know. He bought me five dozen roses from that rose seller in the diner after karaoke last week. He just said, 'how much for all of them?'"

Caroline laughed, and I began singing the theme song to *The Love Boat*, replacing the title phrase with "The Love Barge." "Do you think he likes me?" I asked her again, feeling simultaneously excited and miserable.

Their grandparents' apartment was in one of those fine old buildings with a manual wood and brass elevator and a man employed full time just to operate it. Thirty-five minutes after The Captain called request-ing my help with the liquor, I was sitting on an embroidered, cush-ioned bench at the back of that little wooden box as the uniformed elevator man took me up.

"Captain!" I said, kissing his check when he opened the door. He was wearing his captain's hat again. I handed him my coat and, rolling up my sleeves, said, "Take me to the patient."

He led me to the full liquor cabinet next to the dining room.

"This looks pretty serious," I said. "I'll have to get started right away. Glasses!" I commanded, like a doctor needing forceps.

I fixed whiskeys for both of us, and he cued up some music on his computer. The apartment was bright, with windows on both sides, a vaulted ceiling in the living room, and a beautiful staircase with a carved wooden banister that led to a second-floor balcony that wrapped around and overlooked the living room. Large oil portraits of family members covered the walls; The Captain's grandmother had painted them. One was an eleven-year-old Caroline in an Easter dress. We took our drinks into the library, which was extensive, and I happily browsed his grandparents' collection, pointing out some of my favorites, "Cheever and Maxwell and Barthelme—my big loves."

"I never read," The Captain said. "I just can't get into it," he told me, and I told him he probably just hadn't found the right book yet, that reading is a lot like falling in love, that timing is everything. "The right book at the right time is paramount." The Captain said he'd never been in love. I suggested *Catch-22*, and we drank some more.

Then, for lack of anything better to do, I suggested we read aloud to each other. He chose some poems at random, some Ogden Nash verses, and we brought our drinks and cigarettes over to one of the windows. When it was my turn, I chose a short story of Raymond Carver's called, "Nobody Said Anything." We drank more.

"Can you play the piano?" I asked, motioning toward the grand in the next room. He couldn't, and I couldn't, which I said made us perfectly suited to play together. I couldn't believe he didn't at least know "Heart and Soul," so I taught him the notes and we practiced for a while, switching back and forth on the upper and lower registers. We drank more.

Then we went upstairs to sit on the second-floor gallery. Our drinks in hand, we sat on the carpeted floor with our backs against the banister and faced the window that began a foot above our heads. The sky was an implacable white. We talked about his feelings about college. Like maybe he was missing out. How the applications were too long though. He quoted lines he liked from the Carver story I'd read—"George is an asshole," he laughed. He told me about how he was tired all the time, how he'd just woken up when I arrived actually, how he'd gotten in the habit of staying awake all night and sleeping through most of the day. How his grandmother said it wasn't good for him. How the doorman called him a vampire. We drank more.

I made fun of his captain's hat. He shrugged and said he liked it. Then he told me that the sea was a difficult mistress and an ambivalent lover. That she might destroy you if you didn't respect her. That she offered great gifts along with great peril. That an experienced seaman had to be vigilant and keen. He said he'd heard about it in a song. "It's called, 'Brandy, You're a Fine Girl.' I think you have it on *Felix's Cool Hits Volume IV*," he said.

I swished and spun around the upper floor balcony and down the steps to refill our drinks—ice, scotch—and then I swished back. The Captain went to one bathroom, I went to another. He cued up some songs on his computer. "What's the name of that song that goes, Shalalala?" I danced to show him what I meant. He made a few guesses, and we went upstairs again.

We sat Indian style facing each other, and I told him I was worried, that I wanted so badly to write something really great. That my parents were getting older. That I can't seem to finish anything. That I'm running out of time. I turned to rest my back against the banister and cried because the view from the window was so beautiful. The tops of the buildings across the street, the gilded cornices, the terrible sky! I told him how I felt about Mallarmé and Baudelaire. About his description of a man weeping at the foot of a statue in a public park. We drank some more.

He agreed that the sky was beautiful. I noted how it had gone white as if it were concealing something, "as if it were saying, 'This is not for you; turn your eyes upon something else!'" The clouds were so many that you couldn't even tell they were clouds anymore. I apologized for my tears. "I guess it's the booze," I said.

"What are you going to do?" I asked him.

"What are you going to do?" he asked me.

"I have class in an hour," I said. I was drunk. I stood up and hugged him and said I had to go.

A few weeks ago Caroline was in town visiting from Geneva—she's moved again—when she decided to throw a birthday dinner for her grandmother. Caroline and The Captain invited five of their friends including Caroline's new suitor, an Englishman living in New York whom she's been chatting with online, who also likes The Smiths. I bought a fancy cake from a bakery near my house and felt very grown-up to be buying a cake and attending a dinner party.

Caroline had cooked dinner, and we all sat around the large wooden dining room table and drank wine, except for Caroline who drank Coca-Cola. Their grandmother smiled and said very little except for how lovely the dinner and cake was. We were having a great time, all of us. Then I suggested The Captain and I play the piano for everyone. Their grandmother expressed surprise. She didn't know The Captain could play.

"I taught him," I said proudly. "Let's show them, Captain!"

We went over to the piano and played our song. After, I scolded The Captain for not practicing more regularly. "You promised you'd practice!" I told him. The Englishman came over and took my place to play alongside The Captain, and then we all retired to the living room for brandy and Coca-Cola. Their grandmother fell asleep in an exquisitely carved chair, and Caroline's Internet boyfriend brought out a pack of cards. In the kitchen, we began gambling peanut shells and drinking whiskey, before finally we wrapped that up, too, and took off downtown to go to Lex's '80s party, which always seems to be happening whenever we get together—Thursday, wouldn't you know. Then it was 4:00 AM, and old times' sake hit us again, so Caroline, The Captain, Lex, and I—the Englishman had disappeared—piled into Lex's Buick and drove down to Atlantic City.

Sometimes I wonder how it is that we can be so young and yet find so many occasions to dedicate to old times?

We sipped our after-dinner martinis and The Captain said, "I love this song," and then I asked The Captain if he was gay. He asked why I thought he was gay, and I explained my theory that "all men are gay and that the only reason they have sex with women is to make more men. It's scientific! Also, you haven't tried to have sex with me."

"I did try!" he said. "Last week, and you said no!"

"I was sleeping."

"So how does that make me gay?" he countered.

"Well, don't get all bent out of shape about it," I said. "I was just theorizing."

Last week we almost had sex. It was late—he'd come back to my place after Lex's party—and we'd run out of beer. I began insisting that he go to the deli and get some, but he didn't want to. Then I said we should have sex. Because it was normal for two people to do that if they were sleeping in the same bed, and anyway, didn't he like me?

He said he did like me, but that he didn't have any condoms. I reminded him that the deli had condoms and also six-packs, and some bacon while you're there—"I'm starving!" I gave him my keys to let himself back in, but by the time he returned I'd fallen asleep, and when he woke me up I told him the mood had passed. "Let's just go to sleep, Captain," I said.

The next morning he complained of my sending him out to buy condoms and then being too tired. I complained that I shouldn't have had to talk him into having sex with me in the first place, and then I pretended I was insulted until he apologized. After we made up, we went to breakfast and ate French toast and eggs Benedict. Then The Captain came back to my apartment and took a nap on my couch while I sat at my computer and tried to write a short story.

I worked a bit on the story and then got stuck and decided to update my blog instead:

"The cradle rocks above an abyss, and common sense tells us that our existence is but a brief crack of light between two eternities of darkness." So begins Nabokov's, *Speak, Memory*. My own mornings begin similarly. The light streaks through my window; I come to. Immediately, my thoughts return to last night. I am like Nabokov peering into the dark recesses of time. Peering into my blackout, I invoke the muse—"Speak, Memory!" How did I get home last night? Was my karaoke performance received well? Did I leave my credit card at the bar, and if so, which bar? Shall I call the bar or the credit card company first?

Posted by Iris at 1:47 pm, 0 comments

When The Captain woke up, I told him he looked creepy when he slept, that his eyes stayed open a little, like a snake's, and then I asked him if he wanted to hear what I was working on. I told him I was writing a short story about him. It took me a second to open the document. Then I read:

The Captain was called The Captain because he wore a captain's hat during a game of gin rummy at his grandmother's house.

"No one's ever written a story about me before," he said. "What's it about?"

"I'm not sure. That's all I have so far." I looked at the lines for a while, added a comma, then deleted a comma, and then saved the document and filed it away in a folder with five or six other stories I'd started and abandoned. "I'm going to call it, "The Bored and Feckless," I said. "It's an homage to Fitzgerald's *The Beautiful and Damned*."

He shrugged, "I don't know it," and I continued thinking carefully about my story while setting up the backgammon board.

We played a few rounds and then went to the liquor store to buy a new jug of wine, this really cheap Chablis, which tastes pretty horrible but is not so bad if you drink it with a lot of ice. Then we started playing backgammon again and before we knew it, it was dark and time to go out. I tried on a few different outfits and asked him what he thought of each.

He played with his cigarettes, shrugged and said, "I don't know."

Then we went to Lex's '80s party because it was Thursday again, which was weird because it was Thursday only the night before.

You ever notice how most of your childhood memories seem all to have occurred at around the same time? Like in every story you tell about your childhood, when asked to recall how old you were, you find you were almost always ten years old? I feel that way about my twenties, like for the whole of it so far, it's almost always been Thursday night.

When we got back to my place at the end of *that* Thursday, I offered to give The Captain a haircut. He'd been saying earlier that he needed one, and so I said that I ought to be the one to do it. At first he wouldn't let me—"Absolutely not!" he said. But eventually—it took a half hour to convince him I knew what I was doing even though I didn't—I wore him down.

I was straddling him on the couch, clipping at one side just above his ear with a pair of large kitchen shears, when I started laughing and he made me stop.

"Alright, that's enough."

"I'm laughing because it looks so good!" I said, laying the clippings carefully on the bookcase next to us.

Then the Captain said he was hungry, so I hopped off and went to the kitchen and made him a snack that he refused to eat.

"Grilled Cheese with light bulb," I said, setting the plate down on my coffee table.

Then we decided to practice our kissing awhile. We wouldn't really be kissing, I explained. We would be "kissing in quotes. Like when actors have love scenes in movies," I said. "It doesn't count as second base when they go to second base on film, because they're just acting," I told him authoritatively. I wanted to experiment with some new techniques, I said, like I'd been doing lately with my cooking.

So we started practicing. I had names for all my kisses. "The windmill!" I'd say, introducing each. And then he'd rate them. "The tractor!" "The warped mirror!" "This one's called 'the discarded pizza topping.' You'll see why!"

"Captain?" I said, looking at him over our second round of after-dinner martinis.

"Yes, Iris," he said lethargically, pale as ever.

I didn't actually have anything to say. I was just having one of those bottle-neck moments when you feel a lot or think a lot and want to express a lot, but don't know what any of that lot is, so you just say whatever pops into your head first. "Do you know any good jokes?"

"No," he said. "Do you?"

I shook my head.

He looked at me and blinked. I wanted to ask him what he was thinking but you can't ask that and expect a real answer, so I just stared at him for a moment and twirled my hair and wondered.

"Have you ever counted your freckles?" I asked.

"Should I?" he said, blushing, his freckles blending together across the bridge of his nose.

"I would think that's something one might want to know about oneself, Captain." Then, all of a sudden, I felt exhausted, one of the few times. "Captain?" I began.

"Yes, Iris."

"I'm so bored of myself." I looked down and held my breath, hoping to shape it into something meaningful before letting it go again. "Do you ever feel that way?"

"Yes."

"Are you starting to hate me?" I asked, feeling so sick of myself, feeling even more sick of myself for having asked him that, feeling sure that he must be sick of me too, of my trying to be cute all the time, of my never stopping. But how can you get away from yourself is the thing? How not to keep getting worse?

"No," he said. "I like you."

I cringed. I wanted to sink into the ground. He had to be lying, or else he wasn't lying, and then what? He was just wrong and he'd eventually figure that out, maybe any second now.

"And you're going to be rich," he added. "Once we get your eBay store going, you'll be able to support me." He paused. "Iris?" he said, imitating the way I bat my eyelashes, giving more energy to his impression of me than to what he gave to being himself.

"Yes, Captain," I said, lethargically.

"Do you want me to hate you?"

I looked up from the table of martinis and found his eyes right on mine, looking at me, I swear, as if I were the open sea.

I changed the subject by thanking him again for all the help with the photos. He said he would work on them overnight and give them back to me all spruced up, sans bruises, in the next few days. And then he'd help me create a store on eBay and maybe a website to go with it.

We tried to think if we knew anyone with a nicer ass than mine to model the underwear, before concocting a scheme to put an ad for models on Craigslist.

"Those pictures we took in the underwear won't do. It doesn't look right around the ankles either," I said. "I guess I'm getting older. My behind used to be much different, you know. Anyway, you should see my feet."

"I have," he said. "They're amazing—"

"They're amazing," I said.

I picked up my backgammon board to put it on the floor, and all the pieces inside made a loud crashing noise. "When I dance," I said, "I make that same noise. I'm like a maraca." I raised my eyebrows.

The table was covered with a paper tablecloth, and I used one of the crayons the restaurant put out to begin composing a want ad for models.

"Are you ready to enter the glamorous world of high-fashion modeling?" I read aloud, as I wrote.

The Captain crossed my words out with his crayon and added some new words, which I crossed out, too, before adding some others, until we had a whole mess of scribbled lines surrounding the few on which we finally agreed: "Model wanted. No pay."

"Do you think it will work?" I said, leaning on my hand and looking up into his eyes. I began twirling my hair like I always do when I'm trying to work something out in my head, but then let it go in order to twirl his. I was trying to twirl the uneven section I'd cut above his ear last Thursday, but the hair wasn't long enough, so I just made circles with my finger beside his temple as if he were crazy.

The Captain didn't answer but had that faraway look again, as if he were calculating weather conditions up ahead. Then, catching sight of something in the distance, he signaled to the waiter for another round.

CHAPTER 3
AUTUMN IN NEW YORK

How far away the stars seem, and how far
Is our first kiss, and ah, how old my heart!

WILLIAM BUTLER YEATS, "EPHEMERA"

THE CAROUSEL IN Bryant Park will soon stop spinning.

A poster at Lincoln Center says *La Traviata* is coming in November. Outside the Met, flags have been unfurled to announce two new exhibits: Kirchner's Berlin Street Scenes, Van Gogh's "Night." Things to do in cooler temperatures.

It's Sunday. Sheep Meadow is locked, and your wiffle bat has begun its seasonal drift toward the back of your closet. Instead of going out, you prepare hot drinks at home. Amid the sprawl of the *Times* and scattered sesame seeds from the morning's bagels, you practice laziness, your pet art. The window is open and drifts of sweet cold float in, inspiring your girlfriend to borrow your extra-large sweater. She wears it rolled at the sleeves, then sits Indian style on the hardwood floor and puzzles over 3-Down. You look over her shoulder and offer a guess: "Possibly."

Go outside. A student film crew is set up in one corner of Washington Square Park. Three NYU sophomores are about to capture in 16 mm that ineffable feeling that is autumn in New York. If only they could stop arguing about that next shot. A young man with scanty sideburns fiddles with his camera while bickering with a purple-haired girl over where to hold the light reflector. A policeman settles everything when he asks them to produce a permit before forcing them to disband.

Later on, you bicycle across town on Tenth Street, a chilly breeze pushes your hair from your face, nibbles your earlobes, and teases you with winter. Will you stop home to retrieve another sweater before you meet your friends for billiards, for bowling, for basketball at the Hudson River courts? The wind swells and the leaves say, "Yes!"

Underground, at the Union Square subway station, notice the stylish couple causing a scene across the platform. She's crying and he's yelling, and they've nearly got it right, are almost ready to return to their acting class at the Lee Strasberg Institute a few blocks over where fall session has just gotten under way. The pretty girl wipes her tears, fixes her makeup, looks in a compact mirror, and ad-libs distress. You catch her eye, and she smiles back slyly. You don't know it yet, but soon she will be famous.

In a park of concrete and metal on Fifty-seventh and Ninth, a young woman is on her lunch break. She's shivering in open-toe shoes and a thin sleeveless blouse, and when the wind rises, she folds her arms across her chest. She might have put on something warmer this morning, but she is unwilling to relinquish the summer so soon; it's only October. Beside her, another lady sweats inside a rust-colored sweater paired with tall leather boots, too thrilled by her new wardrobe to delay by one more hour her personal parade of the fall's newest fashions. Sipping her hot coffee, she dabs the sweat from her brow and happily considers what she'll wear tomorrow—it's already October.

Crowds pour into the Angelika movie house on Houston, excited to see the latest shaky-camera take on the discontents of urban intellectuals at family gatherings on Connecticut estates. Someone's sister is getting married—how bourgeois! Further west is a matinee of *Breakfast at Tiffany's*, and at Film Forum or Anthology Film Archives or somewhere else west or east of here, Woody Allen's *Manhattan* is playing, has just played, or is about to play. Yes, it is autumn in New York. And there are so many wonderful things to do!

But I prefer the other things.

If you'd like to join me, we can film an homage to a New York classic on your camera phone. *Breakfast at The Container Store,* starring ME! I'll buy some vodka, and you'll hold the phone while I stand in my crumpled evening gown outside the shop window on Sixth Avenue. Be sure to catch the light just so, as I look longingly at the lush display of filing cabinets and accordion folders. Between slugs from my flask, I'll say wistfully, "The Container Store is where I go when I'm hungover. Nothing very bad could ever happen to you there." You'll remark about the store's impact on Cold War foreign policy, and I'll point out a handsome bureau inside which we might contain communism.

Next we'll visit the Sharper Image on Fifty-seventh Street to test-run the massage chairs. A store clerk will begin selling you hard and I will interrupt, eyelashes batting furiously, like butterflies bursting from cocoons, asking that he fetch me the foot massager. "Would you please?" I'll say, still in Hepburn mode. We'll stay as long as we want or until my flask runs dry and I start to shake while imagining bats clawing through the walls, like Don Birnam in *Lost Weekend*. I'll cry out in terror, before you press power on the foot massager, tie my shoelaces for me, and suggest I take deep breaths. And then, grabbing my hand, you'll whisk me gallantly off to the liquor store, where you'll buy a fifth of vodka to pour into a cardboard container of orange juice.

You'll put the straw between my trembling lips.

I'll squeeze your hand and ask, "Tropicana with calcium?"

"I'd give you all the calcium in the world if I could," you'll say. And I'll explain how too much calcium is actually bad for you. "It says right here on the label that this will suffice for a daily serving." I'll kiss you on both cheeks alternating thirty-four times, the way they do in Foreignia, where I spent a semester abroad. You'll graciously wait for me to turn my eyes before you wipe away the alcoholic sting of my saliva. "Poor jellyfish," you'll think, regarding the blue veins that decorate my eyelids, while I look sheepishly at the ground.

Hungry? Let's visit the Olive Garden upstairs of Times Square for a *tête-à-tête amoureux* featuring their "all you can eat bread sticks and salad," as advertised on TV. After we've exhausted their supply, you'll excuse yourself to the men's room and on your way tell our waiter a lie about it being my birthday. It's a lie because neither of us will ever get old. After he clears the empty basket from the sixth serving of bread-sticks, three of which now decorate your jacket in place of a pocket square, he'll reemerge from the kitchen with our free cake ablaze, and the wait-staff trailing after him singing their approach. With the cake before me and my eyes pressed shut, I'll pause to draft my wish.

And after a deep breath, I'll begin to blow, steady and full like the change of seasons, as if I were the autumn wind and the candles were old trees—I'll wish we were Russian spies and had fancy gadgets like poison umbrellas, or cufflinks that are tiny cameras, or pens filled with disappearing ink with which we might sign our names to great love letters. I'll wish the day would never end.

You'll pick up the check. I'll steal a dessert spoon, lace it through my hair like a flower. And we'll run out screaming with laughter. We'll laugh until we cry, and then you'll brush a tear from my eye and say with sudden gravity, "You have something in your teeth. Right there. No, you still didn't get it."

Tired but unwilling to stop the fun just yet, we'll take the subway all the way down to Manhattan's bottom lip and go fishing off the stern of the Staten Island Ferry for shoes and discarded hearing aids and whatever other unexpected treasures attach to our hooks. You'll hold my hair back when I lean over the railing, sick, and then catch the dessert spoon just before it falls overboard.

I'll smoke a cigarette after that and attempt to spell my name in the air with it, the way I used to with sparklers in the backyards of Long Island every Fourth of July. After remarking on the fleeting nature of the seasons, of you and me, too, I'll observe the lapping water below, cast a quick eye up at nothing and then look over at Manhattan where windows are starting to twinkle instead of stars. I'll feel sick and start to wish I hadn't drunk all that vodka. "What's wrong?" you'll ask, and I'll say nothing, and then, smiling, I'll say, "It's fall." I'll suggest we stop at the liquor store as soon as we dock.

As the sun dips lower, we'll disembark. Our mood darkening with the sky, our pace slowing, we'll walk uptown arm in arm, our steps sounding a near minuet. I won't tell you what I'm up to, but I'll be stepping as hard as I can, trying to leave my footprint in the pavement beside the older impressions of curse words and pairs of initials enclosed in hasty hearts, until we arrive at the public library just a few blocks from my apartment.

In the back of a darkened reading room, we'll canoodle as they show a free movie starring a young Matt Dillon—"Yes, *The Flamingo Kid*!"—using a loud projector with an even louder fan, the whole thing so much louder than any of the characters' voices. A confused elderly lady will stand for a long time in front of it, complaining about the darkened figure obscuring the picture. Then, letting go of my hand, you'll find her, offer your arm, and lead her to a seat where she will have, you tell her, "the perfect vista."

Stepping behind you down the marble steps after, I'll look up at the sky, almost black, and then out over the street, so bright. You'll say, "It's late already, we're up to our chins in night." I'll say, "Should we go to Grand Central then, for a drink among the transients, give a toast to old-what's-his-name and tell stories about something or other?" You'll pause and look uptown toward the greatness of midtown, and then look downtown toward me, scaffolded again by whirling rings of cigarette smoke. Frightened of arriving at the end of the night, feeling my heart crash inside my chest like a dropped bag of metal parts, I'll bite my lip nervously and wait for your answer.

"No," you'll announce firmly. "We'll go home instead!" And with a quick look both ways, you'll tug at my hand and we'll launch the wrong way down a one-way street before entering the all-night Food Emporium, whose doors open upon our arrival as if our presence on their threshold were the answer to a timeless riddle. Once inside, we'll redeem coupons for Jell-O and soda crackers, buy Slime for fifty cents, our last purchase arriving in a tiny plastic globe and falling from the bottom of a coin-operated dispenser, like a wish.

One block over and three flights up, in the warmth of my one-bedroom apartment, while we wait for the Jell-O to congeal and the sun to rise, we'll tell each other secrets: "I've never read *Ulysses*." "I don't want to kill mice, but just capture and rehabilitate them." "I'm worried I'm losing my hair." "I don't care for Sting; I find The Police's whole oeuvre repetitive, actually." "I ran for president of my high school class and lost." "I gave my cat a dog's name." "I think I'm losing my hair." "I'm lonely." "Are you?"

In the brilliant cool autumn morning, the light, terrible and bright, will streak through my apartment. And we will awake, stiff and uncomfortable where we passed out on the floor, covered in the crumbs of last night's soda crackers, sheltered by the majestic fort we built with our own hands, what looks in the morning like just a pile of pillows. "Get up! Get up! It's autumn in New York; there are wonderful things to do!" says the light as it hits you in the eyes, causing you to shrink back. "Start with an aspirin!"

Unhinging our knees and elbows, stretching the arms up and over, we'll tie hasty knots to close the bags of clanging metal inside our chests. We'll compose our faces and fasten our top shirt buttons. And then, still a bit drunk off the romance of yesterday, the romance waiting for us today and again tomorrow, and the jug of wine now empty in the corner, we'll trot downstairs to lose ourselves once more in Manhattan's surging throngs as we make our way to brunch, to White Castle, just opened up on Sixth—it's time we sample their delicious sliders! Or else, if we're too broke, if we spent almost all our money at the coin-operated wish machine last night, lose ourselves instead in the surging throngs on our way to the nearby Gristedes; it's closer than White Castle and they also sell beer. We can just as well buy frozen sliders, which, transformed by the warm sixty-second embrace of my microwave, taste delicious.

"It's autumn in New York," you'll say, regarding the sweet bite of cold air drifting in through the broken windows of my one-bedroom apartment, inspiring you to borrow my sweater that will be way too small. Then, sitting on the floor among the sprawl of pencil shavings and blank paper, devising questions for a crossword puzzle you're writing yourself, you'll catch my ankle as I pass barefoot on my way to the kitchenette and insist that you toast your can of Natural Light to mine. Motioning to 3-Down, you'll read, "Are we making a mistake?" You'll look at me expectantly before the microwave, in time with our hearts, begins to beep its finale, telling us, rhythmically, another sixty seconds has passed.

BOOK II

CHAPTER 4
DISPATCHES FROM MY OFFICE

He raised his brawny lumberman's arms in the starlit night: "And then, the fundamental fact is that *there's no such thing as a grown-up person* . . ."

ANDRÉ MALRAUX, *ANTI-MEMOIRS*

7:04 AM

I wait on line to buy a cup of coffee at the stand on the main floor of the Humanities building. I consider buying a scone even though I don't like scones. Maybe I can learn to like scones. They're everywhere and if I liked them, it would be a coup in terms of my lifestyle. I handle the shrink-wrapped scone and look at it from various angles until the lady asks me if I'm going to buy it. I say, "No, just the coffee," and then count out exact change. Giving exact change is a coup.

I pull an extra bundle of napkins from the dispenser and place them on top of the coffee lid, which, as I make my way up the escalator, leaks until the napkins are soaked. In my office, I throw the wet napkins in the garbage, turn on the computer, and discover an email from a student asking what she missed in last week's class. I begin to boil and write back, "The reward for being absent is not a private tutorial with the instructor." I pause before hitting *Send*. I press *Delete* and decide to handle it later.

I close my email and Google "Hell." I discover a site featuring a quiz that can determine to which level of Dante's hell I'll be banished when I die. I check my watch to see how much time I have and then spend ten minutes answering a series of questions with this result:

You have been banished to the Second Level of Hell!

You have come to a place mute of all light, where the wind bellows as the sea does in a tempest. This is the realm where the lustful spend eternity. Here, sinners are blown around endlessly by the unforgiving winds of unquenchable desire as punishment for their transgressions. The infernal hurricane that never rests hurtles the spirits onward in its rapine, whirling them round, and smiting, it molests them. You have betrayed reason at the behest of

your appetite for pleasure, and so here you are doomed to remain.
Cleopatra and Helen of Troy are two that share in your fate.

8:00 AM

I walk into class and greet everyone with a cheerful, "Good morning! I trust you've enjoyed a long weekend of fascinating reading and can hardly wait for our discussion to begin." A few students giggle. A few yawn. Most say nothing. One says, "Ms. Smyles, you crazy." I look to see where the voice is coming from. It's the girl who wrote the email.

I smile as if it were a well-tailored but frayed passion of mine to discuss Dante with twenty teenagers on a Monday morning in upper Manhattan. I offer this weary smile throughout my lecture. It suggests I know a lot more than I am telling. It suggests that my knowledge is rich and varied, that I might just be a Dante scholar but only have time in this class to skim along the text's surface. This is my Hemingway trick. I show only the tip of the iceberg. Beneath the surface, however, is not more iceberg, but CliffsNotes and Wikipedia articles.

What do I know about Dante? I read *The Inferno* once back in college and barely paid attention when I did, the way my students barely pay attention now. And then I read it once more after I was assigned to teach it along with a bunch of other epics for World Humanities I. I get around what I don't know by organizing the class according to questions I have for *them*, a teaching technique I've adapted from my relationships with men. I try to answer all questions with more questions: "Where was I?" "Well, where were you?" "Why is Virgil Dante's guide through hell?" "Excellent question. Class? Why is Virgil Dante's guide through hell? Let's write on that for five minutes and then we'll have open discussion."

Mostly no one does the readings, so I don't have to worry too much about their asking me questions, and when they do, if I don't know the answer, I just go mum and disapproving, as if they would know the answer themselves if they looked closer at the text, or else I suggest they do some supplementary research for an extra credit project. I take a moment to wax lyrical about the joys of research and correct citation format as dictated by either the MLA or *Chicago Manual of Style*.

I begin calling roll—this is where you go after you complete a Master's and before you earn a PhD; this is where you pause, indefinitely—then I write a few questions on the board and ask them to free-write. While they write, I review my to-do list:

1. Shave legs
2. Floss
3. Wash face and moisturize
4. Pay Con Ed bill
5. Alphabetize magazine mailing list and email list to Janice
6. Call Mom
7. Grade last week's quizzes
8. Review student portfolios and enter final grades for Monday class
9. Proofread short story, write cover letter and submit to *BOMB* magazine
10. Do dishes
11. Pick up clothes in bedroom

I begin my lecture but am almost immediately interrupted by a hand. It's Juan in the front row. He has a question about the final paper due next session. About citations. I explain that the author's name must be written, "last name comma first name." I write on the board: "Last name, first name." He responds, "So, Alighieri, Dante." I say, "No. In that case, it's just Dante." He stares at me along with the rest of the class and waits for an explanation. I oblige: "Dante dropped Alighieri like Madonna dropped Ciccone." I shrug. "Let's move on. We've a lot to cover. . . ."

9:30 AM

On my way out of the classroom, I open my phone in order to look busy and avoid talking to my students in the hallway. It says I have fourteen messages. All accumulated in the last week. I'm too bored to listen to them, so I check the missed call log instead. Most of the calls are from Janice, who always calls back anyway.

The phone rings while I'm still holding it. Janice. I pick up. "What's up?" "Did you get my message?" she asks. I say, "Yes, but I haven't had a chance to listen to it yet." I arrive back at my office and go inside, shutting the door behind me. I ask her what she said in her message and she says she just said it was Janice, stated the time, and then asked me to call her back. I tell her that the call log tells me what time she's called, and that it was she that called, and so she doesn't need to state her name and the time when she calls. She says, "but then I'd have nothing to say on voicemail." I don't say anything. Then I ask her, "So what's up?" and she says, "Nothing." Then she tells me she's thinking about texting my friend Jacob whom she slept with a week ago and who hasn't called her since.

I ask her what she wants to text him and she says, "'What's up?'" I suggest she make it more specific. I suggest she text him, "Shit Fuck Rat Cock." "Won't that be weird?" she asks. "Yes. It would be weird, which is why it will up the chances of his replying, maybe even calling you back. He'll want to know what the hell's the matter with you. He'll be intrigued." She is silent for a second. "I don't know," she says. I say, "Think about it for an hour and see how you feel. Type the words into your phone just to see how they look on the screen, to see if you're comfortable with them. If not, delete." "Okay," she says. "Okay," I say. "Good luck. Now I have to go. Tons of papers to grade."

I get off the phone and stare at the wall. At a conference poster featuring an image of the Irish countryside that one of the other adjuncts hung up.

9:54 AM

My phone rings again. I've set the ring to a soft spooky whistle so that whenever it rings in public places like a supermarket or bookstore, people around me become frightened. They look around, and I can tell they're wondering if they are the only ones that hear it, if maybe they are being haunted for something terrible they did earlier that day that they thought no one knew about.

I look at the phone to see who's calling, hoping it's a telemarketer or maybe someone I don't know who fell in love with me while I wasn't paying attention. It's Janice again. I debate whether or not to answer and then finally pick up, fearing she'll leave a fifteenth message.

"What's up?" I say. She says, "Not much." "Oh," I say. She says, "I'm just calling to remind you about emailing me the mailing list." "Yeah, I'm on that," I say. She sighs. I wait. She sighs again. "Just tell me if you're not going to do it," she says. "I'm going to do it," I say. "Okay, good," she says, "because I'm swamped. And honestly . . ." I brace myself. She always says "honestly" right before she complains. "Honestly, I just feel like I end up doing most of the work." "So stop,"

I say, while pulling at a hangnail. "But then nothing would get done!" she says. I don't say anything. I decide I need a nail clipper. I should carry one in my purse. "Can you go to Staples later and get Post-its?" "Fine," I answer.

Janice is still angry at me for losing a batch of manuscripts last week, so I agree to go to Staples even though we don't need Post-its and all the "work" she supposedly ends up doing herself, she creates out of boredom. Like now. Because Jacob hasn't called her, she's decided to make mailing labels—"And get more labels," she adds. "We're nearly out." I don't mention the fact that we have not yet mailed anything to anyone. I just say, "Okay."

About last Friday: Janice invited me to meet her at a bar in my neighborhood, and when I showed up, she ambushed me with a pile of submissions to the magazine we're starting, "official documents" she wanted me to take home. If anyone has a right to be angry, it's me. Who brings important stuff to a bar on a Friday night?

She was having drinks with a few girlfriends from her Teach for America days. When I got there they were talking about their rewarding but difficult work and drinking very slowly. I ordered a shot and texted the guy I'd planned to meet up with later—a novelist/memoirist in his early forties who's written extensively about his battles with alcoholism. For our first official date, he suggested we meet for drinks. "Just come now," I texted.

Janice and I had both met him the previous weekend, first at the Brooklyn Book Festival and then again at the Corduroy Appreciation Club Meeting where I made him promise to contribute something to our magazine. "Even if it's just a urine sample," Janice added.

He and I immediately hit it off. He'd recently fallen off the wagon, so we ended up having a swell time smoking pot in a lavatory (he was doing cocaine, too, but I declined) and getting sloshed at three different bars (I on the whiskeys that he bought for me, and he on the fruity cocktails that I bought for him), followed by forties on an LES stoop—and then an even more swell time over the phone the next day trying to piece together what exactly had happened the night before. It was a great place to start things, and I was already fantasizing about the long romantic days of wine and roses we might share before his next bout of recovery.

We weren't supposed to get together for another hour but I told him, "Just come now" because the conversation among the girls had moved to Hurricane Katrina and whether or not they all shouldn't just quit their teaching jobs and move to Louisiana to help with the relief effort. It was a tough decision and for a moment they fiddled with their Live Strong bracelets in silence. Who needed them more, their poor students or those poor hurricane victims?

As he and I were leaving, Janice kept saying about the batch of manuscripts she'd brought, "Don't forget the bag, don't forget the bag," like she knew I was going to forget the bag. So I left with the guy and with or without the bag, I forget, and we went to a bunch of bars and did what we did, and then she called me in the morning all curious to see how it went with the guy and also the bag. "What bag?" I asked, still in bed and in the middle of my ritual early-morning reproach. The guy had already gone.

Janice sighed. "You're kidding right?" "I'm sorry," I said. She was silent. "Are we still on for the meeting later?" she asked. "Of course," I said, trying to pretend I knew all about the meeting. "Just tell me where and when." "It's at your place," she answered.

"It's not fair that you get to come up with all the ideas while I'm stuck doing all the work," she told me in my apartment. It was an "executive meeting," which meant the two of us sitting on the floor looking at manuscripts, complaining about men, and waiting for her pot dealer to call us back. "Well, no one's stopping you from coming up with an idea," I said. "When I do, you shoot it down!" "Because all your ideas are bad. Do you want me to say yes and put out a shitty magazine, just so you can feel good?" "No, but it's the way you do it. It makes it hard for me to be creative. We should collaborate more. Anyway, I don't have time to come up with good ideas because I'm too busy doing all the work while you're having fun brainstorming." "Okay, so do you want me to come up with fewer ideas, or just not tell you about them?" "Just shoulder some of the work!" "I do!" "No, you don't!" "Fine. I'm sorry. Tell me what you want me to do and I'll do it."

She looked down at the agenda she brought over and then reached into the bag of new supplies she got from Staples. She placed a gold star next to one item. "Here," she said. "We need to alphabetize our mailing list. It's a total mess." She handed me the agenda. I handed her a beer. Then she told me what a jerk my friend Jacob is, how he called her up last night, "at like two in the morning," and came over and how she had sex with him. "You showed him!" I said and chugged my beer.

10:01 AM

I take out the stack of quizzes I gave last week, which I've yet to grade.

"The daily quizzes should be easy," I told my students at the beginning of the semester. They will consist of one or two straightforward questions that serve only to verify that you've done the reading. It's nothing to worry about," I said, brushing off their concern, "provided you've done the reading."

I look at the one on top.

QUESTION: What does Oedipus do after he finds out he has killed his father and married his mother?

ANSWER: He is sad.*

I draw an X next to the answer and then put the whole pile in a drawer.

10:02 AM

I go online. I email a guy I've been leading on for just over two months; I don't feel guilty because he seems to enjoy it. We met at a reading in January when I was at my most irresistible due to the fact that I was crying all the time. I was haunting the drinks table when this well-scrubbed Asian guy in an oversized hockey jersey asked me my name. He told me his and then claimed, very quickly, that he wasn't on speed but worked in finance. He's since asked me out ten or fifteen times, both personally for drinks and via mass emails for cocktail-hour events, which are addressed back to himself with my address bcc'd, though I suspect I am the only one he's inviting. I think it's a trick where I'm supposed to think I'm showing up to a party, but find upon my arrival that it's just him and me. This actually makes me like him more. Still, invariably, I tell him I'm busy. Usually he'll email and then I'll email back. But the other day he called, so I'm emailing him back. I write:

Sorry, I didn't call you back the other day. I had to return a pair of khakis to the Gap after having fallen victim to their latest and

---

* The answer I am looking for is that he puts out his eyes with Jocasta's dress pins. He puts out his eyes or he blinds himself is also acceptable.

most insidious ad campaign yet, the one in which khakis feature prominently as a winter wardrobe essential. In the commercial everyone is dancing and looking great, so I got the khakis, tried them on at home, and found that standing still, they have the fit of a paper bag. I tried dancing in them for a few minutes in front of the bathroom mirror, and it's true, they do look good this way. But then, most of the places one wants to wear khakis don't encourage dancing—work, for example. So dancing can't be relied upon to bring the pants to life, and if I do go out dancing, I probably won't want to wear khakis but a dress or a skirt and heels or something more flashy—puzzling. So I decided to bring them back. This took some time.

And then I was about to call you yesterday morning when I realized I'd forgotten the toast in the toaster oven, again! It wasn't burned, just cold, so I had to make another toast, and then I got caught up with that until I was rushing out of my apartment to get to work. I was going to call you on the way in, but before I knew it I was underground and had no reception, and then when I got out of the subway I had my mittens on and it was too difficult to take them off and carry my bags and dial all at the same time, so I just figured I'd wait until I got inside. And then by the time I got my mittens off, I was at my office in a rush with my keys because I was worried I might run into the professor in the office next to mine who keeps asking me how I am.

"How are you?" he pries, every time he sees me, and then I've got to stand there and think about it. Anyway, he must have heard me wrestling with my keys because he poked his head out the door *just before I got right with mine. I improvised: "Fine, how are you?" And then I had to talk to him awhile about how he was—he claimed he was fine, too, though I have my doubts—which is why I couldn't call you back right then.*

And then after I dropped my stuff off, I had to get to class. I put some notes on the board, and then everyone arrived, and then we had to talk about The Inferno. *I was rushing out of the room after that, removing my phone from my purse, excited finally to use the opportunity to call you back when I ran into a co-worker who asked about calling me later to meet up for drinks. I told him I was swamped with work and that the first free moment I had was going to be spent with this speedy Asian guy I've been meaning to call for ages, but then accidentally threw in that I'd call him later— it's what people say—but not until I call you first!*

And then I was downtown again at home about to wash my hair because I didn't have time to wash it this morning, what with the toast debacle, and then by the time I got out of the shower it was already so late; I could hardly call you at that hour. So I figured I'd just write you instead the next morning, which is what I'm doing now. Anyway, thanks for the invitation. It sounded like a lot of fun and I'm very sorry I had to miss it. Let's have drinks soon though. I really want to.

10:16 AM

I receive a mass email Janice has just sent to all of our literary magazine contributors asking them to send a two- or three-line bio for our author's page. "Like this:" she writes, and then proceeds to write a fake bio for Jacob, whose poem we are publishing. "Jacob is a self-absorbed jerk who eats his own shit and doesn't respect women."

I try to calm down.

I write an email back to her about what an idiot she is and then press *Delete*. I decide to call her instead. The phone rings and when she answers, "What's up?" I tell her calmly that her email was very "unprofessional." "What are you talking about?" she mumbles, the way she always does when she's lying. I read the email aloud to her. She says, "I didn't write that." I say, "I'm looking at it right now." She says, "Come on, it was a joke." She laughs.

"It's not funny. You've insulted one of our contributors for all the rest to see. They don't know us, Janice, and think, unless we give them adequate reason not to, that we are running a serious magazine. And besides, what you wrote is gross." "I thought it was funny," she says. "It's not funny, it's retarded." "Don't say retarded, my cousin's retarded." "Fine. It's stupid and not funny." "Don't tell me what's funny!" she says.

At a party a couple of weeks ago, Janice railed all night against a friend of mine who'd made the mistake of telling her, "Women aren't funny." It was an impromptu Zombie Roof Party, and I was leading everyone in the "Thriller" dance when she called me over and said, "James here doesn't think women can be funny." I shrugged. "That's hilarious," I said, seeing they expected me to say something.

They went on arguing about humor for the rest of the night and at no time, so far as I could tell, did either of them say anything remotely amusing. But then, I didn't stay for the whole conversation. I went back over to the other side of the roof to apply zombie makeup to new guests who'd shown up without costumes. Janice pointed everyone my way when they came up unadorned. "Iris is going to put special-effects makeup on you," Janice said. "She's really good at it, because she's so great at everything," she sniggered.

And here's another thing: Janice thinks that anything related to the act of shitting or the word "poop" is automatically sidesplitting. I tell her, "There is nothing inherently funny about shit, yours or anyone else's, unless you're five years old." "Caca," she responds, as if no further explanation is required. "I disagree," I sigh. She peppers our website with references to excrement, and I chase after her with the delete key like the owner of a dog that's not yet been housebroken.

When she suggested a farting noise accompany all visits to our homepage, I decided to try a new approach: "What if Harold Bloom looked at the site and saw that? He wouldn't say, 'How refreshing! Finally a literary magazine that addresses what *I'm* interested in.' He'd think the editors were disturbed."

"I don't think we should censor ourselves to suit the tastes of one man," she reprimanded me. "I'm just saying we shouldn't post any material that would disgust those we admire." "Well, I think that's really elitist." "It's a literary magazine! Of course it's elitist! We want to showcase the best and appeal to the best!" "Well, that's not what I want." "Okay, what do you want then?" "I want a really broad readership—I'm thinking soccer moms, doctors, frat boys, mimes, teachers, plumbers . . . everyone." "And you propose to unify these diverse groups through short story, poetry, and crap." "It's what's going to make our magazine special," she said, resting her case. "Don't say special. Your cousin's retarded."

10:30 AM

My phone rings. I don't recognize the number, so I pick up, hopeful. "Hello?" It's a customer service representative from the Wine of the

Month Club asking me why I stopped my subscription last year and if I would like to restart it. I stopped my subscription because I can't afford the Wine of the Month Club. The only reason I started it in the first place was the same reason I started the Tie of the Month Club—I was deeply hungover at my computer and temporarily insane. I canceled both memberships a few months after, though significant damage had already been done. My closet is filled with men's ties that I've taken to wearing as belts and headdresses—I must use them for something!

I can't tell him that though. So I tell him, "I quit drinking. I just started AA so I can't really have wine around the house."

"Oh," he pauses. "I see," he says uncomfortably. Then he stammers, "Well, are you sure you don't want to try drinking for just one more month?"

"I'm an alcoholic," I say. "It's a disease. I'm trying to put my life back together!"

"Of course, of course," he says and thanks me for my time.

I hang up the phone and feel terrible. I hope he's not crying. I've decided that this is his first job out of college and it's not going at all well. I've decided he went to Wesleyan and majored in archaeology and he doesn't know what he's doing with his life now that he's graduated and ended up as a telemarketer. I want to call him back and console him, tell him it's going to be okay even though it's not, invite him out for a pitcher of margaritas—but I can't. Instead, I open a drawer and remove a warm can of beer before swallowing as much as I can without gagging. Poor guy, I think. How guilty he must feel, trying to push wine on a recovering alcoholic. Then I become angry and tell myself every man is responsible for his own actions and his were really quite objectionable. I alternate between outrage, sympathy, and despair until the can is empty.

10:55 AM

I smooth my hair into a bun, pull a lint brush from my desk and run it over my sport jacket. I like to dress conservatively these days; one can conceal a lot more in professional attire, I find. I start down the hall, my modest brown pumps punctuating my stride like gentle commas separating items on the long list I've just posted to my blog*.

At The Leonard T. Gertz Room, named for its benefactor and decorated with his forbidding oil portrait, I make my way immediately toward the drinks. Because the English department is rife with political unrest—when not teaching, the senior faculty devote themselves to loftier pursuits, like getting their colleagues' Distinguished Professorships revoked—parties are often scheduled in the middle of the day. If they weren't, no one would show.

I'm uncorking a bottle of Yellow Tail—the standard fair, as it's the cheapest—when Veronica, a teaching assistant with short black hair, a lip ring, and a large tattoo that says "VEGAN" (encircling her neck where a string of fake pearls decorates mine), appears beside me. I look up from the bottle and freeze as if caught.

"I didn't eat breakfast," she says, her eyes fixed ravenously on a tray of assorted cheeses.

"Me neither," I say, motioning to the wine.

She spears a cube.

"Such a waste," Veronica says, holding up a purple, cellophane-tipped toothpick. "Think of how many trees we could save if everyone brought their own forks." She goes on about her new magazine, which

---

* Names of Women Jack and Larry Met at The Regal Beagle: Olga, Diane, Tanya, Shelly, Sheila, Audrey, Kate, Sally, Francesca, Linda, Agnes, Lauren, Lucy, Lydia, Betty, Beatrice, Marsha, Mandy, Sandy, Lucia, Allison, Henrietta, Shannon, Sharon, Beatrice, Claudine, Christine, Sherri, Simone, Cynthia, Susan, Madeline, Meghan, Felecia, Charlotte, Jennifer, Leigh, Samantha, Terry, Clarice, Dana, Carrie, Karen, Anna, Jane, Beth, Lulu.

she's going to call *Fork*. "It'll be like nothing else. We're going to publish fiction, nonfiction, and poetry."

"In the future," I announce, "everyone will edit a magazine for fifteen minutes."

"How's yours going? Are you and Janice going to do a print issue?"

A thunderous burst of laughter breaks nearby—a professor from the speech department.

I refill my cup, casting an eye right and left like a thief. Though drinking in the English department is not uncommon, only those with tenure do so openly. Because I'm an adjunct, when I bring a six-pack into the building, I can't throw the cans in my own trash, but must dismember the six-pack in the style of a mob killing and scatter the empties in bins throughout the building.

I move over to the fruit plate and run into Howard, sixty-eight years old, with flames of white hair. Howard has been the on/off Creative Writing Chair since the department's inception in the mid-'70s. He has "ink for blood," he likes to say, and regularly transfuses it into the pages of his once prominent literary magazine.

Filling close to one-third of every issue, his fiction catalogues the sexual fantasies of an aging writer/professor who, like Howard, has not published a book in almost twenty years. In his most recent story, which he modeled on *The Inferno*, Howard's alter ego "Professor Moshe Blum" is a modern-day Dante who believes salvation lies in the penetration of Beatrice's fiery vagina—Beatrice is a redhead undergraduate in Blum's creative writing seminar.

I like Howard. He drinks too much, frequently devolves into tears, and has a form of Shakespearean Tourette's that makes him explode into occasional soliloquy. Mostly I like him because he seems to like me.

"Again with the beret."

"It's my look!" he answers.

Howard wears berets. At the last party, a bit drunk off Yellow Tail, I plucked one from his head and, poking him in the chest, told him, "You can't just go around wearing a beret, Howard!" "I'll give you a beret," he slurred, grabbing my finger. Later, when his back was turned, I snuck down to the mailroom and hid it in the English department microwave.

I ask him if he knows how to erase a Google memory queue. "Every time I type something beginning with *f*, 'free porn' pops up." I tell him about an article on pornography I've just read in a new scholarly journal/lit-mag hybrid. "What kind of pornography do *you* like, Howard?"

"*The Collected Musil*," he pronounces carefully.

An attractive brunette in her thirties joins us and says something that sounds like, "My book is made of porcupines and I find myself often shiny about this." I've no idea what she's talking about and after making a few requests for her to repeat herself, I nod as if in agreement. Howard remarks on her exotic accent and asks where she's from. "School of Ed," she answers.

Howard launches into a speech about his "ink for blood" before Jerry, another adjunct, interrupts. Jerry is upset because he suspects one of his students of having plagiarized. He rings his hands and asks us all what he should do.

"Count your blessings," I answer. "I *wish* my students would plagiarize. It would certainly make for better reading. Unless a student actually hands me the book from which he's copied with the page dogeared and the exact words underlined, what do I care? I'm just happy to be able to give out an A."

I plop down in an armchair and cross and uncross my legs impatiently. A woman across the room wonders aloud if she's hearing cicadas. Howard stares. Our circle widens to include a female Melville scholar (the White Whale as feminist icon against which Ahab's wood is impotent, etc.) and a gay black Gender Studies professor. I knock back what's left of my Yellow Tail, feel myself becoming intolerably charming, and rise up. "Duty calls!" I say to Howard.

"'Reflection is the business of man,'" Howard booms, "'a sense of his state is his first duty: But who remembereth himself in joy? Is it not in mercy then that sorrow is allotted unto us?'"

I tap my watch. "Class in five."

12:20 PM

"The book opens in a dark wood, with Dante confessing he's lost his way. A poet in exile, Dante despairs. Then, seeing a light up ahead, a mountaintop offering sanctuary, he begins toward it only to encounter three beasts blocking his path. Dejected, he turns back and there meets the ghost of Virgil, his favorite writer. Virgil tells Dante of another path to the heavenly hilltop, but warns that before they can ascend, they must first pass through the place of eternal punishment, and then purgatory, a place of lesser punishment.

Traveling through nine torturous circles, Dante meets hell's resident sinners—both strangers and those he once knew in life: former teachers, friends, enemies, politicians, and mythological heroes, all being punished by God. Inspired by their suffering, Dante begins an investigation into his own troubled soul, the subject of the book that will redeem him. As much fiction as it is memoir, *The Comedia* is an allegory of 'quarter-life crisis'—what each of you will go through when you finish college, can't find a job, and start seriously considering graduate school."

A hand shoots up in the front row.

"Wasn't Dante thirty-five in *The Inferno*?"

"Yes. But the people of the Middle Ages believed thirty-five to be the new twenty-five." I look at my watch. "I'm afraid we're out of time."

I wave a book of CliffsNotes, which I've begun recommending officially on the syllabus. "Remember, there is no shame in supplementing your reading with a study guide. And one more thing: When referring to a book's plot, it is customary to use the present tense. 'Odysseus is *trying* to get home.' 'Dante is *going* through hell.' Please remember that when writing your papers this weekend."

12:55 PM

I drop another stack of quizzes on the desk and immediately shut the door lest a student actually stop in for "office hours." I light a cigarette, turn on the computer, and check the stat counter on my website, www.PhilipHasASmallPenisBlog.com. There is a recurring visitor with an IP address from a west side office which I decide is Philip, whom I haven't seen or spoken to in months. Back in December, he wrote, asking to see me, telling me he had a Christmas gift. I told him to mail it. He didn't mail it, probably because he didn't actually have one. I wasn't surprised.

I go to Philip's Flickr page and look at the album he's labeled, "Breakfast." In each photo I see my bare knees and feet sticking out from under his glass coffee table. My knees under his plate of egg whites. My feet and his feet under a plate of sausages. My hands and his knees under two bagels and lox, under two bowls of cereal. . . .

Then I look at the photos from when he visited me in Greece over the summer, at the album he's labeled, "My trip to Greece." There are almost no pictures of us together. There are many photos of my parents' house, however, with each room labeled. "Chez Smyles living room," "Chez Smyles bedroom," "Chez Smyles marble bath and chrome Kohler fixtures." They look like real estate photos. There are quite a few views, too, which Philip has labeled, "Sunset over Pelion," "Sunset over Volos. . . ."

Eventually, I come across a single photograph of us, standing on a mountainside, the sunset at our backs. It was taken right after another couple asked Philip to take *their* picture. After, the guy said, "Now you two," and motioned for us to pose. Philip shrugged and handed him his camera, as if he were doing him another favor on top of the first. The photo is labeled, "Sunset over Kala Nera," as if the sunset were the focus and the two of us had gotten in the way.

I look back at one of the pictures he took of my parents' living room and pretend I'm Philip looking at it. Then I think about what I'd tell him if I saw him again. "You're a bad thief. If you had any brains, you might have stolen much more and it is for this reason, above all others, that I despise you so. . . ."

A half hour passes this way, with me delivering a scathing speech to him in my head. I craft each line meticulously as if it were the Gettysburg Address. I insult him as an American flag waves thunderously at my back, and I revise my insults again and again until they are perfect, until they are glittering jewels inlaid into the handle of a musket, until they are multi-colored fireworks, bombs bursting in air, until I am a revolutionary insulting him for a cause. I choose each word carefully, with the kind of precision I've never been able to muster in my writing. And I destroy him. I destroy him. Then I remember the last time we had sex.

1:04 PM

My phone rings again. Janice. I don't answer.

1:05 PM

I update my other blog, www.IrisHasFreeTime.com, and refresh the page thirty times in thirty minutes to see if any comments have been left. A comment finally shows up. It's from a guy in Texas who calls himself "Chessman." He's my most faithful reader. Sometimes he writes more in his comments than I have in my actual post. He checks back even more than I update and complains that I need to update more often. His dedication to my blog is creepy and stalkerish, so says Caroline, who only very occasionally reads my blog herself.

On my last post, Caroline left a comment after his five, saying, "Hey, Iris, who's the lunatic that keeps commenting on your blog?" But then, he seems to care more about what's going on with me than any of my friends do and routinely tells me I should be writing for *The New Yorker,* that my writing is lyrical and funny and brilliant and beautiful, so I don't think he's so bad and frankly, I'm a little bit annoyed with Caroline for insulting my fan.

In his comment, he says he was in New York City last week. He visited the Marshall Chess Club downtown and imagined all the girls he saw walking in the village were me. I'm pretty sure most of the people I actually know don't look for me in the faces of strangers. I know this because whenever I run into friends and acquaintances, they always look surprised, as if their view of the world hadn't included me and now they must make room, as if I had shown up very late and unexpected to a dinner party, and they had to shuffle for an extra chair and place setting. They look almost annoyed, like there might not be enough dessert. But here is this stranger, my fan, thinking of me, wondering about me. For a while, I feel wonderful.

My friends don't read anything I write. Not even Reggie. Not even Reggie, whom I regularly pass out next to when I don't feel like springing for a cab late at night. Not even Reggie who is basically in love with me. His irritating courtship strategy seems, literally, to wait until he is the last man on Earth, to wait until the zombie apocalypse eliminates all possible alternatives, causing me to one day turn to him and say, "Okay, Reggie. Now it's your turn." I find his patience both reassuring and disgusting. On the one hand, I don't have to worry about dying alone. On the other, dying alone seems preferable.

You would think someone so in love might be a little more *interested* in me, might read my blog or something, seeing as I want to be a writer. But not Reggie. He'd rather just moon around and wonder why I'm not into him. What bothers me most is that he lies to me about it. I'll stop him and say, "Look, Reggie, it's okay. I know you don't read my blog." And he'll say, "But I do, Iris. I've read them all!" And then he'll start to chew on his tongue, a nervous tick. So I'll say, "Okay, fine," and proceed to ask him a simple question about my last post, just to get him to cut the crap and stop lying to me already. He'll squirm through an answer the same way my students squirm through their daily quizzes.

> ME: "Well, if you read it, then you should have no problem telling me what I did after I found out I accidentally killed my father and married my mother."
>
> REGGIE: "You were sad."

1:19 PM

I stare directly at the fluorescent light fixture.

1:45 PM

I write an email.

Subject: Hubris and Lust

Hello, everyone!

Here is a link to the site I told you about in class today: "The Dante's Inferno Hell Test." OMG! I have been banished to the Second Level of Hell—it's hot. Don't forget, final paper proposals are due next week. See you in Hell if I don't see you Monday!

—Ms. Smyles

I go to www.Sceenz.com to see what people are doing at the intersection next to my apartment. There is a camera hidden above the building housing the Christopher Street Smoke Shop, which casts a live feed to this website, *Sceenz*. Sometimes I look in to see what I'm missing while at work.

People are crossing the street again. What else would they be doing? I watch as a cluster of tourists waits for the WALK sign. The DON'T WALK sign begins flashing and they wait. I wait. The light changes. Now they're walking.

I send another email, this time to all my contacts:

Subject: Who wants to know what I'm wearing?

Three pairs of underwear because I LIKE panty lines and don't want to give the wrong impression, like I'm not wearing any underwear. One brassiere (white). An oxford shirt (blue), a cable-knit crewneck sweater (gray), a corduroy skirt (brown), high-heeled penny loafers (also brown), a Band-Aid on my bloodied knee (was driven off the road on my bike the other day by a school bus), and tights (black). Otherwise, I'm completely naked. Wait, I'm putting on my jacket (brown, tweed). I'm procrastinating. . . . Who thinks I should renew my internet porn subscription?

—*Iris*

I get an idea for a fiction blog called, *Hellen Gimbel, Editorial Assistant!* It will chronicle the adventures of Hellen Gimbel, woman-about-town/editorial assistant/plant lover/detective. I will update it daily until I have amassed a whole novel. I quickly register the domain name, choose from a few ready-made blog templates, and am ready to go!

I can think of nothing to write.

I decide to add an FAQ section to *Iris Has Free Time* instead.

FAQ

RE: THE BIG BANG

QUESTION: If the universe is expanding, are we—my boyfriend and I—doomed to grow apart?

ANSWER: Cooling is inevitable on a scale both cosmic and personal. But so is death. My advice? Try not to think about it. My advice? Go get your hair done.

RE: COSMETOLOGY

QUESTION: Why do I always feel sad after having my hair cut no matter how well it comes out?

ANSWER: Human hair grows from the root, making that last inch of hair at the very end the oldest. If you have long, shoulder-length hair say, you will be losing a ten or fifteen-year-old piece of yourself. Naturally, this will feel traumatic.

In today's busy, modern world, however, a haircut is a loss for which we occasion no ceremony. If it's really getting you down, though, on your next visit to the salon bring a decorative urn in which to gather up the clippings. Then, you can either place the urn on your mantle at home, or say your goodbyes while spreading its contents over your favorite body of water.

RE: HISTORICAL ERRORS

QUESTION: What is the difference between a *mistake* and an *error*?

ANSWER: A *mistake* you make once. It's an accident, like a typo. An *error* you make repeatedly. It's a misjudgment, like youth. Hence the popular expression, "Oh my god! You're [getting married/moving/enrolling in graduate school/dying your hair back to its natural color]. It's 'the end of an error'!"

RE: CROWDS

QUESTION: Why am I lonely at parties?

ANSWER: Because everyone in the room is eventually going to die and what the party is really celebrating is the accidental fact that none of you are dead yet. Because the universe is expanding and you and your boyfriend have grown apart. Because your hair is short. Because from the distance of a few feet, all conversations sound the same.

Because the din of oblivion is the sound of silverware on crystal, of toasts made to dinner party hosts, of pleas for coat-check girls to distinguish among identical umbrellas, of inquiries with cater waiters regarding a mix-up with your specially requested vegetarian plate. And because nobody really talks about anything interesting. Because there is usually no one very handsome to talk to anyway. Because the food is frequently not very good. And even if it were, did you attend the party for the food?

RE: LINGUISTICS:

QUESTION: Why can't you make the word *red* into an adverb? Like, "He stared *redly*?"

ANSWER: But of coursely, you can. You can make anything into an adverb by just adding "ly." Start nowly!

RE: SPONTANEOUS HUMAN COMBUSTION

QUESTION: Is it possible?

ANSWER: Spontaneous Human Combustion was once believed to be an outcome of excessive drink. Today, "SHC," as it is called in the scientific community, is a source of much contention, though I can't see why. People blush, don't they? Some more than others turn redly when embarrassed. Could SHC not then result from a deeply humiliating experience?

The next time you spill a glass of red wine at a dinner party where you've already grown morose, and feel your skin begin to tingle with shame as everyone stares, give yourself a break. Stop beating yourself up. Put things in perspective by imagining the greater mess you might still make were you to burst suddenly into flames.

RE: TIME

QUESTION: The other day I was in the subway when suddenly, out of nowhere, I felt as if I were looking back in time, as if the present were already a faraway memory, and I felt an overwhelming desire to return to it, to get it all back even though I was still standing there, even though I'd not yet left. I got off at Fourteenth Street, but why did this happen?

ANSWER: What you felt was an earthquake in your brain (brainquake), and so you briefly experienced time in a nonlinear fashion with past, present, and future occurring all at once. This happens more often as one gets older. Like a trick hip, your mind is now something you'll just have to be careful with.

Crossword puzzles may help, or try this: Imagine you are in a dark room with a single spotlight shining a path through it. Now imagine the same room, but with many spotlights turned on all at once and shining in every possible direction, illuminating the whole space so that instead of a single path, you see a vast room without any paths at all. You see space where you previously saw only direction. You see emptiness, which makes you sad, but also, you see possibility. This is most likely what happened to you on the subway. But don't worry. Many people are subject to such flashes of brilliance. Quit your job and become an artist or don't.

Posted by Iris at 2:21 pm, 0 comments

2:22 PM

I decide to stop fooling around and get to work. But first I must use the bathroom. I lock my office door and start down the hall, grabbing a sheet of paper before I leave, just in case I run into Howard. I try always to carry some vague document with me so I can use the excuse that I am on my way to deliver it and therefore don't have time to stop and sit in Howard's office and have one of those long conversations where he just stares and doesn't say anything.

At the university, a walk down the hall can take all day if you're not careful, or if you want it to take all day. Most of the professors keep their office doors open, so that when I or someone else walks by they can call out, "Hey!" and "Come in!" and offer me or whomever a bit from the blender they have installed in their office to make smoothies and life a bit more comfortable. These occasions are something I both hope for and dread. On one hand, I appreciate the break from the day's dreary monotony, and on the other, once I'm sitting there talking with whomever, I find myself longing to be returned to the day's dreary monotony.

I pass Albert's office and he spots me. Albert teaches a class called, "Reading *Tootsie*: American Phalofeminism After the War," and seems to like me. In his mid-forties, he is younger than the rest of the professors and by university standards quite handsome. He obviously works out and wears very tight wool sweaters to show off his muscles, so that he often looks shrink-wrapped, or like a muscular sheep that got trapped in a clothes dryer. He has a motorcycle and long thick straight gray hair that he ties in a ponytail—a popular style among the female academics—and a very large head, as if he were a caricature of himself.

He stands up from his desk and invites me in. I linger in the doorway and think. "Umm, okay, but just for a second." I wave the piece of paper in my hand to show my pressing business and step inside, feeling an immediate difference. Albert does not use the building's fluorescent overhead lights but has lit the room with a variety of soft lamps from Pier 1 Imports. He invites me to sit on his plush leather couch, and I do. "A nice little oasis, you have here," I say. Then I notice a pile of smooth stones on the rug beside a filing cabinet. I offer to help him clean up, but he says they're supposed to be like that. "Feng shui," he explains. I nod knowingly.

He attends to the small bar arranged above one of his bookcases— a decanter of amber liquor surrounded by four highball glasses decorated with Mondrian paintings. He offers me whiskey. I accept. He pours out a few fingers full, hands me the glass, and sits back down behind his desk.

"Aren't you going to have any?" He says no, he can't, and then looks at me as if sizing me up, but faster than there is actually time to, so that it's more the suggestion of sizing me up. He says, "I have Hep C, so I'm not supposed to drink." Making conversation, I say, "Gee, how'd you get that?" and he tells me you can get it from sex or sharing needles and then looks at me flirtatiously, like he's dangerous and not like the other professors. "I read your blog," he adds quickly. "It's very interesting."

"I'm glad you like it," I say, sipping my drink uncomfortably, wondering if I can catch anything from the glass.

"You know, you look a bit like my decanter," Albert says, motioning to the bottle's Mondrian reproduction.

"I get that a lot," I shrug. "Albert," I say, with formal enthusiasm, "I love what you've done with your office. This couch is just—"

"—sumptuous."

"That's the word. You know, you must have the nicest office on campus."

"Not as nice as the president's," he sniffs. "We're friends, you know."

"Oh, is that why you were at the president's dinner?"

Colin Powell, an alumnus, had been the guest of honor, and Barbara Walters had introduced him. This to say, it was a very posh event at Chelsea Piers where I hardly belonged. I was there as the guest of one of the college's new donors in whose name I had recently won a writing award. I submitted a novella about a young woman who loses her grip on reality as more and more people in her life stop using the subjunctive mood. The story ends in a psych ward, where she's been admitted following an arrest—copyediting street signs in her nightgown, she is picked up for vandalism. There, a young nurse tries to give her some advice, prefacing it with the phrase, "If I was you," which causes my protagonist to begin screaming, "Were! Were!" while futilely beating her fists into the wall until an orderly quiets her with an injection. For her, all hope is lost, the reader understands; the hospital will never release her now. The whole thing takes place in the 1960s, and the changes in men's hat etiquette is used as a foil.

I was very nervous the whole time I was there, as I was weighted with the twin goals of trying not to drink too much so as not to upset the donors who kept talking to me about my thanking them when I eventually win the Pulitzer, while trying still to get sufficiently bombed so that the night would not be a total bust.

I excused myself to the bathroom numerous times. I wanted to cry, but I just stared at myself in the mirror and mouthed, "Who are you who are you who are you?" A new habit. I did not mean it metaphysically but practically. What I meant was: Who are you trying to fool, them in there, or you in here? "Figure out what you want and then go for it!" says every self-help book. I like to dip into self-help books when I'm at the bookstore. It's a great way to fill the dull hours during which one is doing nothing to improve one's life. So I told myself, "both," and walked back to the table with renewed confidence.

At the table they had these delicious chocolate desserts, which I decided to try not to eat as a fresh alternative to trying not to drink, when I spotted Albert across the room, his thick gray hair pulled back into his standard ponytail, his head too large for his body, his wacky proportions accentuated by his tiny suit: a capri suit, cropped at the wrists and ankles, and finished with a short tie. He looked like an auctioneer. I was surprised to see him because most of the professors from the English department had not been invited. I thought he saw me too, but then when I waved, he looked away.

"The president likes me for some reason," he goes on, watching me intently. "He's a writer, you know. Like you."

"I'm not a writer," I rush to correct him, too embarrassed to own up to my aspirations which, in the last eight years I've come no closer to achieving, around which I've settled into a kind of permanent orbit.

"Sure you are!" he says.

"I could just as well call myself a shitter," I tell Albert. "I shit every day, too, and get paid the same amount for it." I cringe almost immediately after the words leave my mouth. It reminds me of something Janice might say. What's happening to me?

Albert looks at me and composes his face into one of his two expressions: the Greek mask of happy (comedy) and the Greek mask of sad (tragedy). He does happy and nods. "Well, you're already famous around here," he says. "Everyone's always talking about what a great writer you are."

"I doubt that's what they're talking about. Anyway, this place is hardly a reliable barometer for success. Half the staff is self-publishing and hoping their students will hook them up with *their* agents. Don't tell anyone I said that!" I add quickly, realizing my mistake too late.

"You're very beautiful," he says, narrowing his eyes.

"So are you."

A blonde T.A. with oversized dangling earrings pokes her head into the room and says, "Still at it?" Greek mask of happy. They exchange a few words, what seems like a continuation from a previous conversation. I put my glass back on the bar beside the bouquet of colored glass swizzle sticks.

"Listen," I say, turning to them. "I'm going to go. Have to get back to work." I wave my sheet of paper like a hall pass. "Thanks for the drink, Albert."

He makes his Greek mask face at me—Greek-mask-sad that I'm leaving, followed by Greek-mask-happy that we've conversed. "Any time!" he says, still smiling. "Hey, Shell Levine, this is Iris Smyles. The two best writers on campus!" "Oh, come on," she says, waving his comment away. "Seriously, you're famous! Everyone's always talking about what a great writer you are." I interrupt to shake her hand and say, "Nice to meet you, Shell," and then squeeze by her through the door.

I float down the hall on barely a buzz and review my conversation with Albert. "Drinking is orbit," I say to myself, and think again about how I should stop. And then I think about how I should really get back to work and try to calculate in my head how many quizzes I need to grade before I can take a break. Then I squeeze my waist to see if my love handles are still there, vaguely hoping they might disappear on their own without my having to do anything. I poke at my sides absentmindedly, as if checking the number on a lottery ticket I buy every day.

3:31 PM

I stop into the mailroom to see if I have any notifications in my mailbox. Next to the copy machine, I spot a pile of free copies of last month's Associated Writing Programs magazine. I scan the names and titles listed on the front: an essay on memoir writing, an essay on small press publication, an essay called, "Poetry and Self." The women writers, pictured in small boxes on the cover, have university hair—long, frizzy, gray, brushed straight and pulled back into a clip. They smile as if they were perfectly content to be featured in the magazine of losers who've found a way to make losing work.

Their essays are always about "the craft" and the importance of "showing up for the work." What they neglect to mention is that their showing up is only important to them. No one else cares if they don't show up. The *AWP* bears an eerie similarity to self-help manuals. One of the features about memoir writing is called, "Writing to Save Your Life!" Because I love self-help manuals, I pick up a copy.

I take the magazine back to my office. Settled in, I immediately turn to the back and circle a bunch of calls from literary magazines I decide to submit to but never will. I do this every month. They have names like *Salamander* and *Natural Bridge*. One wants stories about Southeastern women who've been battered. Another, *Trout Magazine,* wants only stories about trout fishing, specifically about trout and transcendence. I think about trying to write something about trout fishing. I think about trying to adapt a love story I've already written by adding a scene with a trout. "Write what you know," goes the classic advice, but there are never any calls for stories about what I know. I feel hopeless. If only someone would take me fishing and then batter me.

I get an idea for a surrealist story in which a woman wakes up as a chicken cutlet and is worried because how is she supposed to get to work on time and continue to support her parents and her brother's violin lessons? I rush to write the idea down in my notebook. Then I think of another idea for a realist novel and jot down, "Story about a woman who is just like me but better. Everyone loves her. She drinks and never gets hangovers. She solves crimes and is impeccably dressed. She hasn't gone to college or grad school or a second grad school and has never for even a moment thought about working as an adjunct in the Humanities department. Instead, she makes a lot of money stuffing envelopes at home—it turns out it's not a scam!"

I close my notebook and pick up the stack of final portfolios from Monday's class. I've asked each student to do a self-evaluation, to collect all their work from the beginning of the semester to now, and then attach a cover sheet with a brief paragraph assessing their work, along with the grade they think they deserve. "The reason for this," I told them, "is that *I* am not *giving* you a grade. *You* have already earned it. My role is simply to assess. There should be no surprise on your part, and no difference between the grade I think you should receive and what you think you should receive." The real reason, of course, is to save myself the effort.

I skim through each portfolio and record the grades exactly as they've written them. Then I stare at the door for a while. It's beige.

4:05 PM

One of the adjuncts who shares my office arrives with a student trailing her. I offer to step out for a half hour so she might use the space for a meeting, and then I go sit in the back stairwell. It's rarely accessed, so I can count on a few minutes of solitude. I decide to pass the time by finally listening to my fourteen voicemail messages. One message is from B, a guy I've been seeing, and it makes me smile. I've already heard the message. He left it yesterday, but I haven't called him back yet, because once I call him back, then it will be his turn to call me back, and I just want to feel good for a while, like I'm not waiting for someone to call me back all the time. But then, I don't want him to think I don't like him either. I debate what to do. I decide to text him later on tonight. I type into my phone, "shit fuck rat cock," just to see how it looks and then erase it. Then I type, "I'm thinking about you right now. Can you tell?" I press *Send* and immediately revert to feeling unloved. I distract myself by erasing all the messages from Janice.

When I return to my office twenty minutes later, the other adjunct is alone and packing up to leave. She says she has to rush downtown for a doctor's appointment, but that students will be dropping by all afternoon to leave their final projects—will I be here to receive them? I say, "Yes, I will be here to receive them," and she thanks me profusely. After she's gone I close the door, and when I hear footsteps or knocking I try not to move or even press the keypad because it's one of those old keypads and can be quite loud.

"I guess she's not here," one female voice says to another. "Should we just leave it?" No answer. Pause. Another knock on the door. Silence. The sound of footsteps receding.

I crack open one of the beers I've hidden in my desk and light up a cigarette. I use the antique ashtray, presumably the property of the tenured professor whose office I've been assigned to. She's on sabbatical. Before she left, she posted a little sign over the bookshelf that reads, "Do not remove books!" and put clear tape over the bookshelves as a deterrent. Dexterously, as if I were playing a game of Jenga, I slip out a volume of Barthelme and start reading a story about porcupines invading a college campus but quickly find myself bored. I'm bored of reading. I'm bored of words. I'm bored of myself.

Barthelme used to teach here back in the '70s. I try to imagine running into him in the hallway. I wonder if he'd like me. If he'd ask me out thinking I was one thing, and then leave me waiting by the phone when he found out I was another. Howard says he was a total jerk. That's always happening. All the authors you love are total jerks. I'm about to replace the volume but then decide to put it on a different shelf. An hour later, I have all the books spread out on the floor and am rearranging them at random. There are three other adjuncts who share the office, so I know I won't get caught.

I open the door to use the bathroom. Three dioramas of Shakespeare's Globe Theater are piled up, blocking the door like a fort, and I have to step over and around them to get out. I take the long way, so as not to pass Howard's office. Halfway down the hall, I spot the back of Albert locking his door. I turn and head the other way quickly.

After I wash my hands and water splatters my skirt, so that I actually feel more dirty than before I washed them, I start back and realize that in order to enter my grades into the online database, I'll need to get my pin number from the English office. Everything is high-tech now, except we still have to go in person to get our pin and also a printout with the instructions for how to access the database. They refuse to email the information so that in streamlining the process, they've actually complicated it further. I steel up for the English office.

5:20 PM

The English office is haunted. Pale adjuncts loom in perpetuity, ever at the ready should a portal to the next world open up—"I can teach Fiction Writing if Howard's gonna be on sabbatical. . . ." Because the department heads are always busy trying to out-maneuver their peers, the secretaries have inherited full run of the department; it is they who decide who will teach what and when, they to whom the ghosts voice their wretched appeals.

When I walk in three adjuncts lean lifelessly against the corner filing cabinet. I stand before the desk and wait for a break in the sec-retaries' conversation. They ignore me and continue talking. I shift from foot to foot, holding my tongue politely, smiling like an idiot. Four minutes pass—they look behind me, at the papers on their desk, at each other.

"Excuse me?"

The head secretary looks at me surprised, as if she didn't know I was there, as if I were unconscionably rude. I hang my head in shame. "One second," she says, indignantly. She talks with the other secretary for another two minutes before finally turning to me. "Yes?" she says. "*Now* can I help you?"

I smile and stutter my request for my pin number. I make a big show of thanks after she gives it to me. Humiliated, I head back to my office, ready with the key before I arrive.

My phone rings. Janice. I don't answer.

My phone beeps, alerting me that I have a voicemail.

5:36 PM

Just before I round the corner, Howard spots me as he's coming out of the literary magazine office. "Gotcha!" he says. He says he must talk to me and without waiting for my reply, he turns and begins walking with the expectation that I follow. I don't want to be rude, so I do. He walks briskly in short steps that make his hips seem like tight hinges needing to be oiled, like he is all business and has no time to oil them.

When I get to the door where he is fumbling with his keys, he pushes his briefcase toward me and says, "Hold this." I take the case and say, "Don't tell me what to do!" Then we both go inside.

There are piles of paper everywhere. He clears some paper off a chair directly across from his desk, orders me to sit, and then walks purposefully behind his desk and takes his own seat. This is an act; Howard has been without purpose for twenty years. He stares at me.

Finally, I break the silence. "Is there something you wanted to talk to me about, Howard? Or did you just want to stare at me for a few minutes?"

He stares for another few seconds, then says, "Why don't you like to be looked at?" He leans back behind his desk and flexes an eyebrow, as if he's said something wonderfully provocative. He pulls a caramel candy from his desk drawer and, without offering me one, unwraps it and stuffs it in his mouth as if he were at the movies, as if I am the movie.

I shrug. "I don't mind being looked at. I just think it's rude is all."

He crushes the cellophane into a tiny ball without taking his eyes off me.

I say, "So, what's new?" I look around the room as if something new might present itself.

"I haven't seen you in a while," he says.

"I've been keeping to myself. Working hard."

Silence.

Silence.

"You look tired."

"Thanks."

"Are you alright?"

I tell him I'm broke. That I can't afford to buy a new package of coffee filters until next week. He reaches into his desk drawer and gives me one coffee filter to take home. "It's the wrong shape for my coffee maker," I say, looking at it. "Worse comes to worst, though, I can use it when I run out of toilet paper, which will be soon. Thanks."

"Have a sip of wine with me later," he orders more than asks. His phrasing irritates me, the "sip of wine" part. It sounds cheap and a little gross, like he expects us to share the same glass. Howard is cheap. He makes me pay for my own drinks when I go out with him and sometimes even his. Seeing that he's tenured and roughly forty years my senior, I think he should be the one buying. Instead, he acts like he's this big shot writer whose favor I should court, ignoring the fact that he can't publish outside of his own magazine. I told him once what I thought. I said, "It's not gentlemanly, Howard." To which he explained that he was modern, and then complained that I was too old fashioned. He said, "Get with it, baby!"

I answer, "I can't. Too much work."

He mentions the possibility of public restrooms and their fully stocked toilet paper dispensers. "You could use the bathroom there," he says, "and save a few squares at home."

"You're a temptress, Howard. But why buy the cow when I'm getting the milk for free?" I wave the single coffee filter he's already given me.

"So why don't you like to be stared at?" he asks, reviving his previous line.

I try to stare back but then give up from the awkwardness, realizing Howard actually likes it and could go on like this for hours. I stop to shuffle through some Xeroxes of a short story by Musil that are piled on top of a filing cabinet beside me. I explain, "Actually, I love to be looked at. Being looked at is wonderful! But it's not right if someone insists that you know it while it's happening." I flash him a quick look out of the corner of my eyes to show him that I know. "I prefer to walk by and have no idea someone's looking. I'm told I look very good walking by. But then, some people have no grace, do they Howard, and they insist that you follow them to their office and ask you to sit down and then they don't say anything and just stare and eat caramels."

"You're very sexy when you get angry. You should use that in your writing."

"I'm not angry," I say, "I'm sexy. I'm very angry when I get sexy."

I untie the silk scarf from around my neck and retie it as if I were performing a magic trick. It gets so cold in the building that I always have to wear a scarf to keep warm.

My phone rings. I leave it in my purse and make no move to answer. Its haunting whistle fills the room. I feel guilty for rearranging the professor's books in my office.

Howard asks me if I'm nervous.

I tell him that I'm always nervous, except for when I'm asleep and even then I'm nervous, worried that my dreams don't measure up. I stand. "Let's have a drink now! Dig out one of those beers in the back of your filing cabinet, Howard. I know they're there."

"I can't now," he says, "Later."

I shrug. "I can't later."

Then I tell him I have to get back to work. I motion to the sheet of paper in my hand as if it were a key aspect of the pressing business that's calling me away.

"What's that?" he asks, motioning to the paper.

I look at the sheet, turn it over and shrug. "It's blank," I say, and leave the paper on his desk. "But I still have to go."

Instead of going back to my office, I go downstairs, past the security guards, past the double doors, outside, and across the street. At the crosswalk, I buy a cup of coffee from the lady I buy coffee from every time I go up to the school.

I say, "Hi, how are you?" the way I do every morning, as if I've never asked this before, as if I have suffered some sort of head trauma, rendering me incapable of progressing past this single line, as if I must repeat the same conversations and gestures over and over, every time, as if it were the first time. She responds, "Hi, how are you?" Neither of us gets an answer.

I take my coffee and walk a few paces to sit at the bus stop bench facing the college, at the hulking, relatively new Humanities building obscuring the much more beautiful neo-Gothic buildings of the old campus. The breeze tickles my arms; my jacket's back in my office because I wasn't planning on going outside. Still, it's warmer than it is inside. Office buildings and classrooms, no matter what time of year, are always so cold. When my students ask me about the weather in hell, I tell them that Christian hell is hot, while Homeric hell is cool and damp, making it particularly uncomfortable for the arthritic. Then

I paraphrase Milton—what I've gleaned from the CliffsNotes—and say that the mind is its own heaven or hell, cool or hot depending.

I hold my coffee, feel its warmth in my hands. I squint, and my eyes tear from the brightness of the sky. It's an overcast day and the sky looks as it looked this morning—a dull white sheet—still somehow too bright. I look at my watch. 6:27 PM. I have accomplished nothing on my to-do list and soon it will be dark. The sun will set at 7:36 PM today. Yesterday it set at 7:35 PM. I checked the sunrise and sunset times online.

There are a few others at the bus stop with me. A middle-aged Hispanic woman standing by the curb, clutching a briefcase, looks in the direction of the bus; a young man in baggy pants and oversized headphones sits beside me, bobbing his head; and a young woman in tight jeans stands a few feet in front of the bench, her hip cocked, her face down, as she uses her thumbs to punch something into her cell phone.

The bus arrives and they all get on.

I sit for a few more minutes. And then I go back inside.

CHAPTER 5

CHINESE FINGER CUFFS

I delight in a moat.

HENRY JAMES, *PORTRAIT OF A LADY*

MY NEW ROOMMATE was standing in the doorway when I arrived. "I'm May," she said brightly before hugging my mother, my father, and then me. She had already claimed her side of our dorm room, which she'd decorated with a poster indexing different species of butterflies, a couple more from the Broadway musicals she'd seen with her parents on previous trips to the city, and some charcoal drawings her older sister had made in a college art class. I'd brought few decorations myself. Just a string of fake flowers I'd purchased while shopping for a hamper with my mom at Bed Bath & Beyond and a pile of fake shit from my parents' store.

After unpacking by simply dumping all my clothes onto the plastic dorm-issued mattress—there was no time to fold or hang, my parents said, they needed the suitcase and were double parked—I laced the string of flowers through my new metal headboard and then placed the pile of shit in the shadow, just under the corner of my bed as, partially obscured, the effect is more realistic. I moved it a few times—an inch to the left, an inch to the right—and then stood back as if it were a painting and I were checking to see if it had been hung correctly. May sat on her bed and watched.

I saw nothing strange in this, just as I'd seen nothing strange in bringing "my parents' handcuffs" into second-grade show-and-tell. "They really work and come with a pair of their own keys, too," I announced to the class, before offering to chain my friend Lydia to her desk—my teacher wouldn't let me. "They sell them in their store . . ." I went on. In hindsight, I can see my teacher's first thought was probably not of a party store where one might obtain a witch costume come Halloween, but of some other kind of shop, like those surrounding my current West Village apartment. In addition to being one of the most desirable neighborhoods in Manhattan, the West Village boasts a dominance of sex shops. I've only to step outside to find dildos in every shape and size, flavored lubricants, multi-colored condoms, and, yes, handcuffs.

Growing up, the handcuffs had been one of my favorite toys. Playing alone in the basement, singing softly to myself through vampire dentures, I'd handcuff myself and then un-handcuff myself repeatedly to the coffee table. Eventually, I'd grow bored and wander off into the storage room to "explore." Digging through a box of old novelty items one time, I found a handful of colorful bamboo tubes. Turning them over curiously, I had no idea what they were; naturally, I thrust my fingers inside.

I was stuck.

I yanked and yanked. In a panic, I rushed upstairs, awkwardly working the doorknob with the heels of my hands, and found my mom.

"Pull yourself together," she said, meaning literally to pull my hands together. English is my mother's second language, so sometimes she mixes up words, says "pull" when she means "push," etc.

I blinked. Losing her patience, she grabbed my hands and pushed my fingers toward each other, freeing me with very little ceremony, and sending me back into the basement to continue my games.

I staggered away, marveling at the finger cuffs and my newly freed hands. Only a minute ago, I'd been trapped, was figuring my dad would have to use the pliers he'd used to extract my baby teeth. And what if that didn't work? I'd have to learn to eat, write, and play the piano with my feet, like that kid on TV. My whole horrible future had begun to unfold, when suddenly, it was over. Amazing, I thought, regarding the cuffs. A mind game. A trick. You have to push instead of pull, go toward to go away.

Though my parents closed the party store years ago, its remnants still suffuse our house. Sometimes on visits home, I'll poke around my parents' junk drawer, "exploring" like I used to as a kid, searching for lost treasure—among paper clips, I'll find a finger puppet, a rubber pencil, a whoopee cushion, an unopened box of New Kids on the Block paper plates—and when I spot something particularly wonderful, I'll ask my mom if I can take it home with me. The New Kids on the Block paper plate I've hung in my kitchen, the way my mom hangs real ceramic plates with hand-painted flowers in hers.

Every year, though, there is less treasure left. The house, for the most part, has been plundered. So I take great delight in stopping in novelty shops in Manhattan now and then. There is one party store, lonely among the sex shops, just a block from my apartment. Last fall I bought a jug o' blood there and portions of Philip's Halloween costume.

■ ■ ■

After we broke up, Philip posted a picture of himself in his Halloween costume on his Friendster page—with me cropped out. I had dressed as Virginia Clemm, Edgar Allen Poe's real-life consumptive child-bride on whom he based his poem, "Annabel Lee." Since Philip didn't have a costume idea, I asked him to be Edgar Allen Poe. We had a big fight about it. He said no one would get it; Edgar Allen Poe was too remote a figure. So I said, fine, he could dress as whatever he wanted and asked him what he wanted. He went silent and began to mope around the costume shop, pensively picking up a package of hillbilly teeth before putting it down again. He handled a blue punk wig, then spent another ten minutes studying a package of clown makeup. At last we bought a plastic yellow bird.

At my apartment, we painted it black and then attached it to his shoulder using high-powered magnets, which I sewed into his jacket—"The Raven." I tied a white scarf around his neck and he shaved parts of his beard to match Poe's. I wore an old-fashioned lace dress and painted on a pallid, deathly complexion. I blended dark circles under my eyes and made my lips slightly blue with just a trace of blood trickling from one corner. Philip set the timer on his camera and we took photographs together as Edgar Allan Poe and Virginia Clemm. We had to take a lot of them because in each one Philip was smiling. I kept having to tell him, "Stop smiling! I'm dying! Doesn't that make you sad?"

We went uptown to the Cathedral of St. John the Divine to see the original *Nosferatu* with the church organ playing in the background. Afterward, there was a procession of ghouls, and some puppeteers made these giant papier mâché skeletons dance. Every now and then, I'd reach into my purse and pull out my handkerchief, a lacy white cloth I'd doused with fake blood, and cough into it tragically.

On the subway after, a homeless man called across the car. "Excuse me, Miss, but I think you're bleeding." He pointed toward his mouth, to the spot where I'd painted a thin trickle of blood on mine. I smiled proudly and explained it was part of my costume. He laughed and examined both of us. "Let me guess," he said, and began quoting lines from "The Raven." "I love Poe," he told Philip. And then he looked at me and recited, "My love and my life, my Annabel Lee in a kingdom by the sea." I looked at Philip and smiled because here was one more reason for him to love me, because I was building such a strong case.

By the end of the night, Philip acknowledged that it had been a good costume. And by the time we got back to his place and were taking off our clothes to prepare for bed, he even began saying that his costume was better than mine. I was in the bathroom wiping off my pallid complexion and looked out to where he was sitting on the couch, picking lint off his black sport jacket. "But it can't be," I said. "It's *our* costume. Mine *is* yours!" But he kept insisting his was better.

We went to bed after that. We had sex, and then he turned over on his side to face the wall. I lay awake awhile longer, staring at the dusty stuffed animals his ex had given him when they were sophomores in college—"It's an inside joke," he'd told me when I asked about them—still artfully arranged on his windowsill.

On his Friendster profile, he's labeled his photo, the one with me cropped out, "Edgar Allen Poe." It's one of the many photos in which he was smiling because I was dying. In the bottom corner, the lacy shoulder of my costume is just visible. "Single," it says under "Relationship Status."

■ ■ ■

Through the novelty shop window, a dusty Monica Lewinsky mask stares back. I have a few minutes to kill and debate whether or not to go inside. I look past the mask display toward the multi-colored streamers, shiny greens and blues dangling down from the ceiling, and then go around front to the entrance. A bell rings as I enter.

The place is packed solid with fake cobwebs and plastic vomit and hand buzzers and wax lips and masks and streamers and confetti in every color. I wander up and down the aisles, past a unicorn costume in sizes small and medium, past balloons organized by color, past capes and plastic swords, daggers and police badges. The room is quiet and smells faintly of the baby powder in which new whoopee cushions are stored. The scent, like church incense, is calming and familiar. I run my hand over a three-dimensional paper pineapple, try on a witch nose, a mask of Zorro. On my way out, I stop to buy a pack of gum and impulsively grab a handful of Chinese finger cuffs from a large jar next to the register.

I get to the restaurant a few minutes late. Philip is already there, standing out front and looking toward West Fourth Street. He has one hand in his pocket; with the other, he smoothes his hair. Why do I always see him first?

"Hi," I say, and he turns as if surprised, as if he hadn't been expecting me. "Hi," I repeat, "Sorry I'm late." I smile and then feel my heart clench into a fist. I rescind my apology, tell him that I owe him nothing, certainly not "sorry," and proceed to end things once and for all once again, right there beside the stop sign. I lean against the stop sign and stare hard across the street. He watches me lean. Then we go inside and order a bottle of wine.

We've been secretly seeing each other for almost a month. It started when I ran into him at Reggie's birthday party and has been going on almost every day since. We're not back together. We only see each other to break up, to discuss how we won't be seeing each other again. Then, when we've said all we have to say, we have sex.

The menu has few choices. I keep my eyes on it, reading the description of each dish carefully, giving Philip ample time to study my indifference to him. The waiter arrives and I order a pasta. I watch Philip order. I watch his mouth move. I watch his lips, cruel.

After the waiter has gone, I say, "Henry James wrote that in every woman's life there is a man with a mustache."

"What's that mean?"

"That every woman at some point has or will date a villain."

"A villain?"

"Usually he is very handsome. Usually he has a mustache."

"I don't get it," he says.

"He doesn't love her!" I say a bit too loud.

The waiter brings a bottle of wine, uncorks it silently, and pours a little into Philip's glass. Philip goes through the ceremony of swirling, sniffing, and sipping, before setting the glass back on the table and nodding.

"I have great news!" I continue after the waiter has gone.

"Oh?"

"I realized something today."

Philip takes a sip, sets his glass down. "What's that?"

"I don't love you," I say, smiling brightly. I raise my glass for a toast. "As a matter of fact, I don't even like you!"

This is how I do it. I tell him I hate him, that he disgusts me. I text him, "You're filth!" and then reluctantly agree to meet him just one more time. Over dinner or drinks, I break up with him because he doesn't love me, and then he pursues me, because when I'm leaving, he thinks he does. Pavlov trained his dog to salivate with a bell, and I am training Philip to love me with goodbye.

I catch sight of the waiter on the other side of the room. "Water," I mouth, as if I were crawling through the desert. Philip unfolds his napkin and spreads it across his lap. The waiter approaches with a pitcher and two glasses. He begins pouring, and after just a dribble I motion for him to stop. I pick up the glass, swirl, sniff, and swallow before setting the glass down and nodding. Then I motion for him to pour the rest. When the waiter leaves, Philip says I'm rude.

"He knew I was kidding. You're just upset because he and I were laughing at you."

"He laughed," Philip says, "because he wants a good tip, but he was obviously uncomfortable. You're completely oblivious to the feelings of the working class."

"I find it very interesting how sensitive you can be to the waiter's feelings, indeed, to the feelings of an entire class, yet when it comes to mine, you remain conveniently in a fog."

He takes my hand where it's resting on the table. I leave it there a moment and then pull it away.

I sip my wine. "I went to see that Woody Allen movie, *Match Point*."

"I saw it, too. Did you like it?"

"The main character, the murderer, reminded me of you. He's just a little more ambitious is all. With him, there is a more exciting mix of good and bad qualities, while with you, it's all bad, which is why there is no movie about you. It would get bad reviews."

"How many stars?"

"No stars. Zero stars," I smile.

The waiter brings our food and asks if we'd like another bottle of wine. I say that another bottle would be a "catastrophic success." Philip agrees on my motion to "surge," and nods for him to bring a second.

I decide it's time and open my mouth to tell him we're through.

"I think," Philip says before I begin, "that I'm in love with you."

I stare at him stonily. "You *think* you're in love with me. You *think* so, but you're not sure?"

He looks at me looking at him. "No," he says after a long pause.

"Well, thank you so much for telling me that, Philip. I *think* I don't give a damn what you *think*."

He looks down. His eyes glisten in the candlelight. He looks out the window and I look at him. Then I remember myself and look out the window, too.

The waiter takes our ruined plates.

"I Googled "sadomasochism" the other day at work. I think I have it," I say, alluding to the turn our sex life has taken recently.

It's become increasingly fetishistic. Last week, we rented porn and then stopped in one of the sex shops in my neighborhood to buy sex toys. I felt shy and didn't know what to get, and so I told Philip I'd leave it for him to decide. Philip proceeded to buy a cock ring and some other stuff that would enhance only his pleasure and then flirted with the woman behind the register when she rang us up.

"You can't *have it*. It's not a disease," he answers.

"Well, however I caught it, I think I'm a masochist or something. On Wikipedia it says there are two kinds of masochism, the normal kind, which involves restraints and physical punishments, and then another very rare form where the person gets turned on by being emotionally humiliated. Leave it to me to catch the unhealthy type of masochism. *You* probably gave it to me," I say accusingly.

The waiter refills our wine glasses.

Philip tells me how much he enjoys my blog and then proceeds to critique the writing in some of my more recent posts, saying which posts are good and which posts need work. He goes on about how interesting it is to read about himself.

"Why do you assume everything is about you?"

He shrugs. "I thought *Philip Has A Small Penis Blog* was about me."

"Well it's not. It's about me. Some things are about me, you know. God! Being with you is like an exercise in feeling unimportant."

"Yes, I read that on your blog."

I sip my drink.

"So then, why are you with me?"

"I'm not. I only came here tonight to give you the courtesy of telling you in person."

He pays the bill and we leave. He walks me to my door and then says he wants to talk a bit more about the breakup. He says he isn't ready yet to say goodbye. He looks at me longingly. He begs. I concede. "Fine, but only for a minute."

He enters first. I lock the door behind us and follow him into my bedroom where he's already standing at the foot of the bed. He says, "I'm going to humiliate you now like your disease demands."

He tells me to take off my clothes and I do.

He tells me to lie on the bed and I do.

He says, "I'm going to tie you up."

He looks around for something to tie me with. I look around and spot my purse.

"Here," I say, producing the Chinese fingers cuffs. "We can use these." I reach my hands behind me through the headboard and secure my fingers inside the cuffs. I pull my hands apart to show him that I'm trapped.

He tests my restraints by pulling at my wrists. Satisfied, he gets up and stands at the foot of the bed. Methodically, he takes off his clothes and folds them. For a few seconds, he stands there naked and watches me. I turn my head to the side. Then he takes my ankles and pulls me roughly toward him, stretching my body across the bed. He spreads my legs wide and says, "Wait here."

He closes the door to the bathroom. I hear the shower running. After fifteen minutes he returns with wet hair and looks at me lying exactly as he left me. He kneels on the bed between my legs and lifts my hips. He says, "I'm going to fuck you now, Iris."

He says my name over and over. He says my name until he comes and I come and I push my fingers together and I free myself from the cuffs and I wrap my arms around him and I pull him into me and let out, "I love you, Philip."

He rolls off.

"I mean, no, I don't! That was a mistake. I said that by mistake. I don't love you. I don't love you."

BOOK III

CHAPTER 6
EUROPE

There is always some specific moment when we become aware that our youth is gone; but, years after, we know it was much later.

MIGNON MCLAUGHLIN

MARTIN WAS TWENTY-FOUR when we met and had been working for two years as a paralegal at a large firm in Manhattan. He opened his letter of acceptance to law school before our third date, and told me in a cab stalled in traffic crossing Central Park that he'd be starting in the fall. He was a year older than me, born and raised on the Upper East Side, had asthma since childhood and an unexpectedly muscular build. He was passionate about ideas, paradoxes, and also efficiency; he lectured me on escalator etiquette—"the right lane is for standing, the left for passing"—and on making trash as compact as possible by crushing orange juice and milk containers to reduce volume. "You're throwing away air!" he complained, holding a carton I'd just discarded. He blushed easily, always told the truth, and wore glasses that required constant adjusting. "Life," he told me, adjusting them, "is about learning." He taught me tennis (or tried), the correct way to eat sushi, and how to open a bottle of beer with a plastic lighter. He played piano, read philosophy, enjoyed basketball, *The Simpsons,* and getting stoned. He was six-foot-two and had to lean down, removing his glasses first, to kiss me.

We met on a Thursday, at an '80s party in the beginning of spring, after standing for a while side by side at the crowded bar. Four days later he called me from an unused conference room at work. I was standing in the middle of my living room, staring at all my T-shirts.

"Who?"

"Martin. It's Martin from the other night."

He asked me what I was doing. I confessed I'd always had problems answering that question as "observation alters the outcome of the experiment." I'd just finished heating a Hot Pocket and didn't want him to know. He said he found my honesty refreshing and called me Schrödinger's Cat. I got touchy and said I was no one's cat. Then he described a few of his favorite paradoxes and invited me out for a drink.

We went out that Friday and the Sunday following, and then a few days later, and then all the time. It was a few weeks after our first date when he came to my apartment in Hell's Kitchen and we walked over to the Hudson River and watched the sun set over a BMW car dealership. "This is my favorite spot," I said, and showed him to the top of a metal garbage bin outside an old warehouse overlooking the West Side Highway. "I come here a lot by myself."

He sat upright, and I lay on my side resting my head on his lap. He ran his fingers through my hair and the cars whizzed by and the sun made the river pink and silvery as it dipped below the BMW sign. Then Martin explained to me what he thought about love, what he believed it meant in concrete philosophical terms. He'd never had a serious girlfriend before, he confessed, but he had ideas. He said he loved me.

I

1

"Where are we?" I asked, when I finally came to.

Martin stared out the train window, at the overgrown shrubbery obscuring the view.

"Where are we?" I repeated and leaned over to kiss him. "What's wrong?"

"Other than the fact that my pants are still wet?"

I yawned. "Why are your pants wet?"

There is a curse on Thebes because the previous king was murdered and the still-unidentified killer has gone unpunished. Oedipus, the current king, has vowed to protect the city by finding the murderer and bringing him to justice. For most of *Oedipus Rex,* Oedipus chats with the blind seer Tiresius about who could have done it, while Tiresius repeatedly warns him, "you don't wanna know." Instead of taking the hint, however, Oedipus goes on declaring he *does* want to know, that he will uncover the truth no matter what the cost. And so the audience watches nervously, for we know what Oedipus doesn't, which is that Oedipus himself is/was the murderer and that in pursuing justice for the kingdom, he is pursuing his own downfall.

This is what it's like when you get drunk, black out, and wake up on a train heading toward Patras and ask your boyfriend what's wrong. You have two choices: Pursue the truth and restore order to the kingdom by accepting whatever consequence comes from knowing, or go on accursed, wondering why your boyfriend has wet pants and pulls away when you try to kiss him. Confront fate and save Thebes? Or hide and keep running from the disasters that will inevitably plague all your future affairs? The previous king was dead, and Oedipus didn't know who killed him. Martin's pants were wet, and I didn't know why. I steeled up and asked him a second time.

The truth is revealed. Shocked, horrified, Oedipus puts out his eyes (using the dress pins of his wife/mother who's already hung herself in their bedroom), thereby exchanging physical sight, which has steered him wrong, for "insight," as possessed by the blind seer Tiresius. Like looking directly at the sun, the complete truth, Sophocles implies, is potentially blinding.

I blinked at Martin and then looked away as if from a blinding glare.

2

We'd known each other only two months when we decided to take the trip. Martin's parents drove us to the airport. We took backpacks instead of luggage, two novels, and Wittgenstein's *Blue Book*. Martin's father unloaded our bags from the trunk, while his mother took her time kissing us both goodbye, telling us to be sure and take plenty of pictures. "It's wonderful to have pictures from your twenties," she said wistfully.

Our plan was to fly to Rome, then make our way south to Brindisi, where we would board a ferry to Greece, visiting Corfu, then Santorini, and perhaps another island, before wending our way north to a village on the Aegean coast where my parents have their summer home.

On our first day in Rome, we went for a walk and then sat for a while at the edge of a large piazza. Night was falling. I looked up to where the building tops meet the sky and watched the evening darken and the city lights come up. Young people filled the square—chatting, laughing, the boys flirting with the girls. I thought about my upcoming job as a teacher and wondered if I looked like one. Martin was a few steps away, practicing his Italian with the Roman teenagers he'd befriended after asking if any of them knew where he could buy weed.

He followed one around the corner and returned moments later with a block of hash. "This is my girlfriend," Martin said, introducing me. "*Sofisticata*," his new friend said, kissing my hand. I was wearing a knee-length red summer dress, preoccupied as I'd become with dressing my age. I was twenty-two, a woman, and women didn't wear miniskirts. We shared a joint, and then they invited us to the opening of a nightclub up the street.

Outside the club, a sign in English read, "Blue Cheese."

Martin laughed. "In America, the same club would be called, 'Fromage Bleu.'"

One of the Italians regarded us curiously and then, smiling, ushered me in first. "The lady," he said, as I passed.

It was an open-air club and, because we'd arrived early, still relatively empty. Disco lights swirled against the white concrete walls and potted trees evenly spaced along the gravel floor. I was having a great time, sitting on the edge of an empty stage with my legs dangling off, feeling the wind blow through my hair and smiling at Martin as I danced with just my arms, raising them high above me, a beer in one hand, the other floating free and in time with the music. . . .

The next morning, Martin and I went to see the Coliseum. Silently, we climbed through the ruins before stopping at a nearby tourist trap, an outdoor café with the Coliseum in view. I collapsed into a seat and held my head in my hands. The sun was high and the air, still. I felt nauseous. My head was pounding.

"You feel sick?" Martin asked.

It was the first thing he'd said to me since our argument earlier that morning. I'd woken up alone and found him sleeping on the floor.

"What are you doing over there?"

"You don't remember?"

I shook my head, climbed out of bed and lay down next to him.

His sophisticated girlfriend had gotten so drunk that nightclub security had asked her to leave. When she refused, they called the police. Martin apologized profusely, promised to take her home right away while she went on spitting, "Come on, you pigs! You hobby-bobbies! You flat-foots! Come and get me!" Her knee-length dress rode up sloppily around her thighs. The Italians had to hold her back. At the hotel, he helped her to bed, removing each of her shoes as she told him his cowardice disgusted her, and swore up and down that she'd rather die than share his bed.

"I'm sorry," I said, and began to cry again.

Martin watched me silently, kicking lightly at the gravel floor. Near our table, a large soda machine hummed loudly. Martin stared off toward the top of the Coliseum, just visible behind the shack at the back of the café.

"It must be 90 degrees," he said after a while, mopping his brow with a waxy napkin. Then he turned to me. "Why are you crying, Iris?"

I hiccupped and tried to catch my breath. "Because I love you and now I've ruined it. Everything is ruined!"

He watched me for a few seconds and then looked around. "You can't blame yourself," he said softly, a hesitant smile breaking across his face. "It was ruined when we got here. Just look at it." He motioned to the Coliseum. "Ruined!"

"You know what I mean," I said, looking down at the fresh scrape on my right knee—from falling down, I guessed. "I didn't mean to drink so much. I don't know what happens to me."

Martin came closer, lifted my chin and kissed my tears. "It's not ruined," he said slowly, circling me in his arms. "It's going to take a lot more than that to ruin us."

3

There were no sleeper cabins available on the overnight ferry from Brindisi to Corfu, so we purchased tickets for the deck and decided to stay up all night. The ship had three coach decks, one open to the air and two inside the ship's belly with rows of chairs all facing the same direction. We claimed two seats in one of the indoor decks, and then I went to the bathroom to fix my hair and apply some lip-gloss while Martin went upstairs to buy a bottle of Johnny Walker.

We met up top a few minutes later. Martin had heroically gotten hold of some plastic cups and poured us each two inches. I pointed to the early moon dangling above us like a paper lantern. Martin said it looked too perfect to be real. "Just a stage moon." Then, in a gesture half-honeymoon/half-frat-party, we toasted our cups and began the night.

Two inches later, we were sharing our whiskey with a young couple from Norway, and two inches after that, we all decided to find the social deck: an empty dance floor lit with spinning multi-colored lights and flanked by a long deserted bar. We took turns performing joke-moves for each other and then, after a few more drinks, a good song came on and without really deciding, we began dancing for real.

We drank past dinner and met more people—a cluster of English college students, all male; two seventeen-year-old Dutch girls; and a Greek guy named Costas. We brought our cups together for another toast.

At around two or three in the morning, Martin's girlfriend began to fade. Seeing her eyes close, Martin led her downstairs and helped her to her seat. Not tired himself, he returned to the deck to take in the view, the paper moon, and some fresh air. When he returned, she was slumped and snoring at the end of the row. Quietly, he maneuvered past a few sleeping passengers before settling into the seat next to hers and accidentally knocking her elbow off the armrest; Iris stirred.

"Then you muttered something, stood up, pulled your pants down, and sat on my lap."

"Why didn't you stop me?"

"I tried to. But you weren't responding, and I couldn't raise my voice for fear of making a scene. That's when you started to pee. . . ."

Most people become uncomfortable when I talk about blacking out. You're not supposed to do that; it's dangerous, frightening, a telltale sign that you're out of control. All of this is true. And yet, as a method of last resort, is there really anything better? If we are powerless to change the past, I mean, isn't the next best thing just to forget it?

The body is a pretty good custodian of itself, I find, and blacking out is one of its more effective systems. It's the brain's gag reflex, jumping into action whenever a memory proves too noxious to keep. It's my mind's way of telling me, just like Tiresius tells Oedipus, "You don't want to know."

The way turtles have protective shells, porcupines are covered in needles, and skunks emit a terrible smell, alcoholics forget. Sure, the needles of a porcupine prevent you from cuddling with it. Sure, there's a downside—that Oedipus thing again, where the source of your strength is also the source of your weakness—but that's just part of life's great irony and not my fault. What can I do besides accept it and try to navigate as best I can among life's strange paradoxes? Blackouts are just one of nature's many peculiar blessings and should thus be counted. Sitting before Martin then—his pants still wet as he angrily related the events of the previous night—I struggled to assign this particular episode its proper number. Blackout blessing #144?

"The splashing was pretty loud," Martin continued, "and everyone started to wake up. Then the boat hit some swells and the puddle began to stream down the aisle, forming a kind of river, which this little old widow traced back to us. Standing on her seat to get out of its way, she screamed and then pointed. Everyone started yelling, babies were crying, a priest spit at us, and then everyone began collecting their things and rushed to exit the cabin." Martin sighed. "You peed for a very a long time."

"My God! What did you do?"

"I smiled and tried to act natural."

4

You know when you look back on your childhood, how it's almost like watching a movie about someone else? How you know it was you that was kissed behind the church in Greece that summer when you were fourteen, but also, you know that it's not you anymore? You look back and watch: There you are pressed up against the building. Only, instead of seeing what you actually saw out of your own eyes—which were closed—you see the whole scene objectively, as would a stranger happening by. You see the trees in the background, the leaves rustling against the sky, you see the way the light reflected off the brick, the geometry of your bodies, his hand on the small of your back. It's as if your memory were a photograph someone else took, a postcard from the past arriving perfect, complete, in the mind of your future self.

As a result of my blackout, I felt as if a long time had passed since the events Martin was describing. The previous night was a distant memory, so distant in fact that I could recall none of it. So distant that when Martin filled me in when I woke up on the train the following morning, I was able to see the whole thing rather objectively, as if I were watching a movie. I was receiving the postcard when I should have only been sending it.

There was Martin trying to "act natural" while his unconscious girlfriend sat on his lap, mistaking him for a toilet. And all around them, mayhem. Men and women yelling, children running away. I began to laugh. Like Oedipus, I couldn't help but see the situation's comedy.

At the close of *Oedipus Rex*, Oedipus beholds the truth. Horrified, he blinds himself and sets out to wander the earth in self-imposed exile for the rest of his days. In the sequel, *Oedipus at Colonus*, Oedipus is an old man, who, after years of suffering finally accepts the fate he's run from all his life and with that, finds peace. He dies, a white light surrounds him, and his body is snatched away by the gods. But before that, just before, he looks back on all that's happened and he laughs. "Comedy equals tragedy plus time," he tells the audience.

"You're going to laugh about this some day," I told Martin, exhibiting the calm, mirthful perspective one has of events relegated to the distant past. I smiled and invited him to join me in the future.

"No, I won't," he said angrily and yanked me right back into the present. And with that, whatever humor I'd glimpsed disappeared. If anything could put out the flame of our love, I was sure pissing on it was it. I let out another jagged little laugh, not because I found anything funny anymore, but because I so desperately wanted to.

"It's not funny," Martin snapped. "When we disembarked, one of the shipmates threatened me. 'I remember your face. You no come again. I see you, I call police!' You should have seen the way he looked at me."

"I see," I whispered.

"Do you?"

"Martin, I'm sorry."

Martin took a breath and said he couldn't possibly consider accepting my apology until his pants had dried. "As long as they are wet, I am still living the nightmare."

"You're so dramatic!"

"Yeah, I'm dramatic. *That's* it."

"Yes. Yes you are," I said, and turned to the window so as not to show my tears.

II

The dining car was just like the other cars, but with a few booths rather than regular seats, and a snack bar in the corner where you could buy a Fanta and potato chips or a prepackaged croissant filled with chocolate. It was the middle of August. All the windows had been opened in hope of a breeze, but since the train was moving so slowly, there was none. The air was hot and still, so still you felt compelled to move, to touch your hair or shift in your seat, if only to remind your soul that your body still lived, lest it get confused and try to climb out.

Bored and uncomfortable, Martin asked if I wanted to play cards. I smiled, thinking his anger had passed.

"For my sake, not yours," he clarified with a scowl.

We weren't playing five minutes before the conductor appeared, waving his arms and yelling, "No Play! No Play!"

"Why not?" Martin asked.

"No play!" the conductor repeated, taking the cards from our hands and laying them on the table.

"He must think we're gambling." I tried explaining that we were only passing the time, that there was no money involved, but it was hard because he spoke no English and I didn't know the Greek word for *gamble*.

"No Play!" he insisted, until we put the cards away.

We took our books out and decided to read instead. I was reading Sartre's *Nausea* because Martin said it was his favorite novel. Though I liked the detail of the self-taught man reading his way through the library alphabetically, I found the book surprisingly lackluster. I stopped reading to examine the cover again. "Does he ever actually throw up?" I asked Martin, "Or is he just queasy the entire time?"

Martin ignored me.

"Queasiness," I said aloud, half to myself, thinking of alternate translations and finding the word funny. "Life makes him queasy," I went on mumbling. "Simone De Beauvoir was his main quease."

Martin shot me a dirty look. He was reading Céline's *Journey to the End of the Night*, one of my favorites; I'd given it to him at the start of our trip. A mistake I'm always making with men. I give them great works of literature about callous, self-centered misogynists. In my freshman year of college, I gave *Tropic of Cancer* to Donald, a boy from New Jersey with whom I'd accidentally fallen in love, the one I'd later see inside the *Maxim* Man costume. Having read it the summer before college, I was struck by the novelty of its plotless narrative and immediately took to the idea that I, too, might one day live plotlessly.

Donald of the gold chain and white tank tops that came in packs of three became, for a few years, my destiny. My crush on him, like almost everything that's deeply important to me, had started out as a joke. Wouldn't it be funny, I thought, eyeing him in the dining hall one afternoon, if I liked *that* guy? Wouldn't it just be hilarious? Martin had an expression for this phenomenon.

"Joke, joke . . . normal," Martin told me, describing how he'd come to love beef jerky. He repeated this aphorism all the time. At a house party thrown by a friend of a friend of a friend, pointing toward a hipster wearing a trucker hat, Martin offered this assessment: "One minute you're wearing a trucker hat as a joke, because trucker hats are so *un*cool. Then the next thing you know you've forgotten all about the joke and can't leave home without your hat. And there you are, a guy who wears trucker hats." He shook his head pityingly. "Joke, joke . . . normal."

"That's so true!" I said. "Perhaps the whole world started out as just a joke." I poured some of his drink into my own plastic cup. "And on the seventh day, God laughed."

"You need to calm down now," Martin answered.

Back in college, in the dining hall, I pointed Donald out to all my friends and made joke after joke about how I was falling in love. I'm not sure when it stopped being funny and began feeling real, I just remember one minute laughing and the next lying alone on my dorm bed, listening to music in the dark, waiting. He'd said he'd come by my room but never showed.

Hopelessly infatuated by Valentine's Day, I'd left the book, *Tropic of Cancer*, in front of his room, with a flower as a bookmark—I still cringe thinking about it—an iris of all things. What was I thinking? That he'd read, "Paris is a whore," bring the iris to his nose and fall in love with me?

The train rumbled along. We might have made better time by getting out and walking alongside it. For a few minutes, I considered doing just that but then decided the weight of our bags would slow us down. The train shook from side to side, exacerbating my already formidable nausea—physical not existential. Too hungover to focus on the page, after a short interval we both gave up. One at a time, we closed our books and sat quietly, gazing out the window, at the view— a sliver of sky above a bank of close-set trees and parched no-name bushes. There was nothing at all to look at, so we stared.

We grew older. Just slightly. But age is cumulative and every second counts. How else do you pass a year or ten if not one second at a time? I wasn't wearing a watch but I knew that Martin and I had gotten older by at least an hour, and so, arriving at this newfound maturity, we looked around. Seeing as we were the only ones left in the dining car, we brought out our pack of cards and split the deck. What one isn't allowed as a child, one often is permitted as an adult. Perhaps time enough had passed to allow us an adult round of Spit?

"I don't want to brag," Martin began bragging, "but I was the reigning Spit champion in my fourth-grade class."

"We'll see about that," I said, and we began seeing about it.

Martin dealt. We played three or four hands in a fast silence. Then the door to the next car opened, and in came the conductor. Without any new lines on his face, as if a whole hour had not also passed in his life, he stormed toward us, waving his hands. "No play!" he yelled wildly. "No Play! No Play!"

"Why won't he let us play?" Martin wailed, sulkily returning the deck to his bag.

"Because he wants to make the trip as long and as miserable as possible, and he's worried that a card game might reduce our suffering. He's punishing us."

"This is the train ride from hell," Martin grumbled.

The Overseer of Punishments took a seat in the booth across from ours and directed his gaze out the opposite window. He took a crumpled pack of cigarettes from his breast pocket, lit a new one with the old one and flung it out the window into the brush. I imagined bright orange flames exploding in our wake. Was this our penance for being bad tourists?

I took a deep breath to keep from throwing up. I thought of Camus' suggestion to imagine Sisyphus enjoying his curse—his actually being happy to roll the same rock up the same hill for all eternity—and did my best to enjoy mine. Miserable, I started to laugh.

Martin caught my eye and smiled. Then, lifting his index finger from where his hand was resting on the table, he pointed at me—a familiar gesture. It meant, "You. You're the one, and you know it and I know it." If we were at a party and ended up on opposite sides of the room, he'd catch my eye and raise his finger just like this, so that only I'd see. Sometimes I'd blush and mouth, "What?" And he'd mouth, "You know." Or else he wouldn't say anything but just keep pointing silently, resolutely, and it felt like we were tied to each other by an invisible string, connected no matter how crowded the room got, no matter how far apart we grew—then he remembered he was still angry and stopped. After a moment, he shut his eyes.

We'd been dozing for some time when suddenly there was a great buzzing, like a muted chainsaw or a swarm of locusts, interrupted now and then by a loud thud. I blinked wearily and looked around. Surveying the car, my eyes fell upon a hideous insect. It was the size of a tennis ball and its body, furry and stout, was flanked by horrible wings. More beast than bug, outside the movies, I'd seen nothing like it. Silently, I rose up. The sound grew louder. It was coming toward me. I screamed.

Martin opened his eyes. "What the hell is that?"

"A dragon!" I squealed.

Quickly, Martin took my hand. We ran through the car.

"Duck!" he yelled, as it zoomed over our heads.

We zigzagged toward the other end. It zigzagged after us.

The Overseer stood up and motioned for us to be still. Obediently, we froze, our backs against the far wall, watching as the beast came at us once more. Then, throwing his arms over my head, Martin pulled me into him before the bug crashed into the wall behind us and fell heavily to the ground.

Disoriented, its buzz intermittent, it bounced weakly at our feet.

Calmly, the Overseer approached, reached down, grasped it firmly by one of its wings and, looking toward the half-open window, flung it out.

The car was quiet but for the chugging of the train. The Overseer looked at us—wild eyed, breathless—and let out a laugh. He returned to his seat, then turned to us and added, "*Ella Katse.*" He pointed to our booth. "Is okay," he said. "Is okay now."

Tentatively, Martin and I sat down.

"That was crazy! What *was* that?" he whispered frantically.

"A chimera!" I said excitedly, leaning across the table. "Did you see it up close? It had the body of a goat and the head of Pat Sajak!"

For the next three hours, we were besieged by Pat Sajak bugs. "They must be local to the area," Martin said, as the Overseer calmly removed another that had landed, this time, on the table exactly between us.

The train chugged along in the hellish heat. The sky rained monsters. And as conditions around us worsened, things between us got a little better. United against the terrifying perils of the underworld, we were able to forget for a little while about our argument. And slowly, perhaps exactly at the speed of a train inching its way toward Patras, the previous night receded into the past.

"You know, the ancient Greeks believed the Chimera to be a harbinger, a sign that a storm was coming or a volcano was about to erupt. It foretold all kinds of natural disasters," I said.

"Falling in love chief among them," Martin answered. Then, reaching his hand across the table, he laughed. "You're a catastrophe," he said. My eyes filled with tears. "My catastrophe," he added and squeezed my hand. Martin stood up and came round to my side of the table. He sat down beside me and found my hand again. I started to apologize, but he cut me off. "Let's just forget it," he said and fixed his gaze on our window, on the non-view we shared. We stayed that way for the next few hours. And like that, with a promise to forget, we began a relationship that would last three years.

III

1

Sometimes I wonder if we hadn't gone to Europe that summer, would we have broken up sooner? Urinating on him in New York, for example, might easily have been a deal-breaker. He'd wake up in his apartment the next morning, find his pants hanging in the shower where he'd left them to dry, and think, "No, perhaps I won't ask her for another date after all."

Waking up somewhere in the middle of Greece though, in the middle of a month-long vacation with me passed out beside him, what choice did he have but to find a way to forgive me? Then again, if we'd stayed in New York, I might never have drunk that much whiskey to begin with, and so might never have pissed on him at all. If Oedipus hadn't left home, if his birth mother hadn't sent him away. . . . Was his fate inevitable? Was this relationship our destiny?

For the rest of our time in Greece, Martin and I visited a combination of sunny beaches and historical ruins. Our running joke was to feign surprise at finding everything ruined by the time we got there. "Ruined!" we said upon first sight of the Parthenon, before stepping in front of it to get a photo of us together: twenty-two and twenty-four, new statues with our arms around each other.

At the Parthenon we read how archaeologists and engineers were working to restore the ruins by installing new phantom pieces to fill the gaps left by lost parts. When they finished, tourists would be able to see the Parthenon as it once looked to Socrates and Plato and all those who walked through the roped-off structure we now circle. I told Martin about all my visits to the Parthenon as a kid, how my parents toted me around to see ruins all over Greece, how I hated it. "I don't see why we had to come all this way to see a bunch of rocks," I'd complained, kicking at the dirt.

Back in New York, I told Martin's parents the same story over dinner, my cute anecdote about ruins striking me as "a bunch of rocks." "I didn't appreciate history then the way I do now, now that I'm grown," I said, my voice suddenly childish. Asked about our trip, Martin and I talked about our sightseeing, about the oppressive heat on the steps of the Acropolis, about the bargain Martin had negotiated with an owner of a wonderful pension in Positano, about the argument Martin had won while trying to rent a moped on the island of Folegandros—his resorting to the demonstration of a logic puzzle as a way of proving why his American driver's license should suffice for an international one—about a long afternoon on Santorini's black pebbled beach, which had soothed Martin's feet but hurt mine, so he carried me.

We skipped right over the more interesting story of my pissing on him and our being summarily banned from a fleet of Mediterranean ships, and reprised instead our favorite new joke. Passing around our glossy photos, Martin began, "Iris was so excited to see the Coliseum, but when we got there, it was ruined!" We savored this, recited it whenever possible, precisely because it wasn't very funny. It struck us as the kind of humor that adults might exult in, and by aping adult behavior, we thought we might grow up ourselves—Joke, joke . . . normal.

That summer together in Europe was to be our last as kids.

2

September. 5:00 AM. The alarm clock sounds. I shower and dress in the dark, then walk seven blocks to catch the 6, before transferring to the

4, and heading uptown into the Bronx where I catch a bus and then another bus and then walk six blocks to Community School 4.

"Ms. Smyles! Ms. Smyles!" my students yell. "Raise your hand," I respond, imitating the woman they think they are addressing. I'm an adult, I remind myself, standing before the room. I'm in charge of thirty-six children. If I am still a child, then what are they?

On the bus after school, my ears ring with my new name. I shut my eyes, hoping to sleep a little before night school. In a café, I prepare my homework, then walk over and up two flights to another classroom for a Teaching English course, followed by another hour and a half commute home, to eat, to sleep, to do it all again in the morning.

Some nights I go home, grab a quick change of clothes, and catch a bus up to Martin's on the Upper East Side. With a briefcase full of lesson plans, I look out onto Madison Avenue, into the glittering store windows filled with party clothes I've no occasion to wear. Responsible young adults, Martin and I rarely "go out" anymore. We go to dinner.

I buy a Zagat guide. Martin subscribes online. We argue over which rating is more important. He insists "food" while I prefer "ambience" and consider food, provided it's not terrible, incidental. We gain weight. I learn to cook. On a Saturday, we argue over my roast chicken. He complains I use too much lemon. I cry, feeling I've disappointed him.

Our first Halloween together falls on a weekday. Overwhelmed by my new job, I don't notice the approaching holiday until it's already upon us. A friend of his comes over dressed as a Brazilian soccer player.

"This party's going to be great. You guys have to come!" he says, passing the bong back to Martin.

"Can't," Martin answers.

I yawn my agreement.

We tell him of our plan to heat a DiGiorno pizza and watch TV: *The Simpsons' Treehouse of Horror*.

I am asleep before the end of the episode.

Is it supposed to be this hard? We don't talk about it because talking would only make it more difficult, because we're unhappy, because we're ashamed.

Born into a world built in our service, we'd been shepherded to schools (Entire buildings were dedicated to the cultivation of our minds!) and had our lunches prepared (Candy bar companies had made things "fun-size" for us!). Only yesterday we were young, aristocrats rich with time. And the way a snob is proud of the money into which he is born, we had been proud of our youth.

And then we lost it. We graduated. We did our best to grow up, though often our best wasn't very good:

I got drunk at a fundraiser for the private school that hired me a year later. During a dinner auction I placed a bid on airfare to Paris and then at the coat check on the way out, I began hugging a parent who, in a conference one month earlier, had expressed doubts about my syllabus. Two other teachers had to tear me away.

Martin smoked too much pot and then followed it up with too much wine at a fancy Italian restaurant where I'd taken him to celebrate his passing his Tortes exam. Ever decorous, following the first course, he vomited onto his plate.

"Check please!" I said immediately, throwing my cloth napkin over his mess.

"I'm not ready to leave!" he slurred, straightening his back and adjusting his chair. "And even if I were, it's not your place to ask for the check."

"I just thought—"

He dressed me down, explaining that by asking for the check, I was siding with the wait-staff. A regular argument of ours—whether or not I was on his side when it came to disagreements he had with his mother, friends, classmates, and now the wait-staff. Instead of making preparations to leave, we resumed our former squabble.

When the waiter did finally come to collect our plates, Martin announced that he had nothing to hide. Proudly, as if he were a magician about to unveil the new location of his vanished assistant, with a flourish he removed the napkin, revealing a neat little mound of puke. "I'm finished," he declared, his chin in the air.

The way to handle things, he explained to me once outside, was to act as if throwing up on your plate were completely natural. It was they who should be embarrassed for even batting an eyelash. "A good waiter would have known better than to go on staring like that," he said, scowling.

The Park Avenue wind whipped our faces as we walked home. Martin held me roughly. "It's a shame," I lamented half to myself, "that we can't go back there. I really liked that place. The décor was perfect and the maître d' so charming in the beginning." "The food was a three," Martin sniffed. "Anyway, we could still go back if you'd only just followed along! No one told you to go and make a scene!" he scoffed, as we turned a stone corner and hurried through the December cold.

IV

In the first months our relationship, Martin had given me a tour of his New York, the city of his youth, in ruins all around us. The pizza place he went to every day after school, a favorite bar that didn't card, a corner of the park where he and his friends used to smoke pot. Walking down Broadway from West Seventy-eighth Street, he laughed while confessing membership in "the pervert club," what his middle school friends called themselves after spending too many lunch periods prowling the sidewalks for women.

On a weekday evening, following a walk in Central Park, we stopped in a deli and he remembered: "I was buying potato chips right here. It was, like, two in the morning and this lunatic came in and picked a fight with me out of nowhere. We were fighting up and down the aisles. It was like a movie. There were crushed Cheetos everywhere! Eventually the cops came. . . ."

And while visiting his friend Zach at Zach's parents' place on Park Avenue, Martin recalled getting caught. We were in the study and Zach was fixing us drinks from a bar hidden theatrically behind a false bookcase next to a real one decorated with family photos, one of a great-grandfather receiving the Nobel Prize. "For something or other," Zach answered me, before launching enthusiastically into a story about when his mother nearly discovered them smoking pot in this very room. "You should have seen Zach's face when he heard her coming. 'Zach!'" Martin imitated her.

Imagining Martin as a kid, I felt a peculiar pang. We lose people to the future all the time. And we grieve; we expect to. So why shouldn't we also grieve for what the past takes? Before is no different than after really, so if you can miss someone looking forward, you can just as easily miss someone looking back. I saw pictures of Martin—a boy I'd not yet met, would never get to meet—and nearly wept. I missed him so much.

We went for a walk in Battery Park. He bought me a bracelet from a street vendor, a silver chain that looked like monsters holding hands. The day rushed by, was over in just a few hours. The ocean, the sky, the grass roped off, the buildings heaped up against the Southern Bank. The Statue of Liberty, the whole city at our backs. His face close to mine, his mouth, his cold hands. How fleeting is an afternoon, when compared to its memory? The scary stories have it backwards, I think. It is we the living who are the ghosts of this world, we who haunt the past. And the present—Martin's cold hands touching mine—is just a vapor.

Dining out, visiting museums, kissing on street corners . . . Martin and I soon made new memories. Climbing a fence to play basketball at night, bringing gin and ice to mix cocktails between plays, I blocked too aggressively, too drunkenly, and showing off bumped into a fence, giving myself a fat lip, which Martin kissed.

I was standing at the corner of Eighty-second and Madison when I saw Martin approach on rollerblades. He was coming from the park where he'd been playing hockey with his friends. The sunlight broke through the trees dappling his figure as he sped closer, before he stopped, just in front of me, and took me in his arms.

We rode the Seventy-ninth Street cross-town bus a certain way. I liked to sit in the middle of the extra-long buses with the accordion center. And as it bent back and forth on its way through the park, we'd pretend it was a rollercoaster and raise our hands up over our heads. We were a blur of motion, a changing shape. Together, rushing ahead, claiming the future in the name of the past.

V

It was probably a Tuesday. For most of our relationship it was very often a Tuesday, Tuesday being the most nondescript day of the seven, Tuesday being like the middle of the bread—what my father shapes into dice.

When I was a kid, during summer vacations in Greece, after dinner while my mother chatted with the rest of the family, my father and I took turns rolling his bread dice against the table, arbitrarily trying for double sixes and snake eyes. My mother would pause to voice annoyance, while I would pause to marvel at my father's wondrous talent. How my father could make something out of nothing, dice out of bread—that was magic! For a few years, Martin and I were, too. For a few years, we made life out of Tuesday.

We'd just finished dinner and were sitting in the dark on an antique chaise-and-sofa set his parents had given him. We'd ordered Chinese takeout and were opening our fortune cookies by the light of the TV. Martin read his aloud: "You are happy."

He scowled. "What a rip-off! A fortune is supposed to tell your future, not your present. I hate when I get this kind." He crumpled the strip of paper and began packing some weed into a glass bowl his friend Zach had given him for his birthday.

"Maybe it is about the future," I said, still opening mine. "Maybe later on, years from now, you will look back on this moment and see that you were happy even though you didn't think you were at the time, even though at the time you thought you were unhappy because you figured you'd gotten a lousy fortune that told you nothing at all about your future, though it actually did, does."

Martin shrugged. "I don't think so. What's yours say?"

"'Life is a tragedy for those who feel and a comedy for those who think.'"

"You got the better one."

"Mine's less personal. More Western Philosophy than a fortune. You know the fortune cookie was invented in California?"

Martin took a big hit, expanded his chest to accommodate the smoke, and exhaled. Then he had an idea for Western Philosophy fortune cookies and began talking again about Heidegger and the Nazis, the misuses of philosophy, logic traps, and Zeno's paradox.

He passed me the bowl. I declined. I sipped my gin and tonic and suggested we broaden the line of cookies to include peach-flavored gummy candies shaped like busts of Friedrich Nietzsche. "They'd be small, come four or five to a pack, and we could call them, 'Peachy Nietzsches.'"

"Existential Chewing Gum," Martin added. "It would lose its flavor after only a minute, which is to be expected in a godless world. And yet, one must continue to chew. To find meaning in it, even pleasure. 'Sisyphicous.' 'Sisyphusilicious,'" he tried again slowly, puzzling over the pronunciation.

"Your dessert depresses me," I said. "You are happy," I reminded him.

I slipped my fortune into my wallet where it remained until my whole purse—with my fortune in it—was stolen off the back of my chair at a cafe a few years later, after Martin and I had broken up.

VI

"Imagine you have a heap of sand before you."

"Okay."

"Are you imagining it?"

"Yes," I said into the phone.

"I don't believe you. Where is the heap?"

"It's on my living room table. I'm looking at it right now."

"Okay, good," Martin said. "Now, imagine yourself removing one grain of sand at a time."

"Wait, I accidentally got two. It's hard to separate them."

"That's okay. Just keep going." He paused. "Now, is it still a heap when only one grain is left?"

"Umm . . ."

"If not, then when did it go from being a heap to a non-heap?"

"I don't know."

"Exactly. That's the heap paradox. Sorites paradox is its official name, but—"

"I'm sorry, what? I couldn't hear you."

"I said, 'Sorites paradox is its official name.' I can't talk any louder because I'm at work—I'm a paralegal. The conference room was empty, so I figured I'd try you. . . . I should get back though. But, um, I was wondering if you'd want to get a drink later?"

VII

We promised to remain friends, but after a few tearful attempts decided it would be best not to see each other for a while. We continued to call each other on birthdays and major holidays, and now and then we exchanged emails: One regarding the launch of my new literary magazine. Another announcing the death of his parents' dog. I sent my condolences. He sent his congratulations. And then . . . a heap.

Last week, we met for dinner at a restaurant in the West Village.

He looked assured, handsome . . . grown-up.

"You mean old," he said with a laugh.

I picked up my menu and hid behind it.

"You haven't changed," he added, referring to my hiding.

Whenever we spent any time apart, even if it were only a weekend, I'd react this way. With two days worth of facial hair, he'd greet me in the doorway. He'd come very close, reach his arms around me, and I'd squirm away, flitting off into the kitchen or the bathroom or anyplace where I could watch him at a distance until I got used to him again. "You're like a cat," he'd say, when eventually I'd come closer, sitting across from him first, then brushing up along his side, until finally winding up in his lap.

"You've changed," I'd say suspiciously, touching his beard. "I have to get to know you again." It became our routine. Martin would laugh. And I would laugh with him, knowing how silly I sounded. But hadn't he changed? Wasn't his beard proof? Time had passed, and when he'd bring his face close to mine, I'd feel all the intervening hours between us.

I put the menu down after only a few seconds. Whereas a weekend apart had once left me feeling distant, years apart had left me feeling paradoxically close. We talked about movies, the weather, our current lives, and then about the past, as if it had nothing to do with us anymore, as if we were tourists.

Martin had gotten a job at a new firm. A lawyer at last. Why, just yesterday he'd used some of the philosophy from his college thesis in one of his closing arguments. I mentioned my writing. He said he enjoyed the piece I'd recently published in the *New York Press*—"An Open Letter to My Date of Last Friday."

I reddened, worried what he'd think of me now, writing trashy dating stories for a free newspaper. "It's basically fiction," I said defensively. "I actually wrote the piece a few years ago. I've been trying to submit my writing more, trying to work on my follow-through, 'go the distance' and all that. Been watching a lot of *Rocky* . . ." I trailed off.

"It was good. I told everyone I know to pick up a copy."

I cringed. "Really?"

"I told everyone it was fiction, of course."

"Of course." I looked down. "So I got an email last week from this editor who's starting a web-magazine. He read my piece and wants me to write their sex column."

"You're going to write a sex column?"

"Well, no," I backtracked. "It wouldn't be a sex column, exactly. More of a 'single girl's column.' I'd write about my life, about dating and work, what I'm thinking about. . . ."

Martin chewed. "What are you going to call it?"

"I'm trying to decide between 'Rue the Day' and 'Second Base.' I like 'Second Base' for the obvious Homeric echoes, the island of Calypso being second base and all that—did I tell you my theory about baseball being based on *The Odyssey*? Think about it: You leave home.

You try to return home. There are a series of islands—bases—along the way, and outside forces try to strike you out or help you along, just like the gods."

"I like 'Rue the Day.' I don't know if people are going to get the reference to Homer. They might just think you mean 'up the shirt.'"

"Well, that too."

Martin poured some more water into my glass.

"The site's aimed at young people who don't buy newspapers, who've grown up doing all their reading online. That's what the editor said. Everyone writing for it is, like, just out of college; I think he thinks I'm younger than I am."

"Perhaps you *are* younger than you are."

"I have the résumé of a much younger woman, that's true."

Martin put his glass down. "So, what's the first piece going to be about?"

"I'm not sure yet. I have all all these things I started writing in my early twenties. So I'm thinking to start by just finishing those. Rewrite each as if it were all happening right now. This way I don't have to actually go on any dates. I can just stay home in my bathrobe, transcribing old sex stories, like a, like a sex-monk. You know?"

"Sex. Monk."

"It's a real job, Martin. He's going to pay me."

Martin raised his glass. "You're a writer!"

"Hardly." I blushed. "But it's a start."

Then Martin brought up the night on the ferry.

I stiffened.

With glee he recalled the widow and her disapproving look, how the other passengers collected their luggage and hurried away from us, the color of the shipmate's face as we disembarked and he made his threat, banning us from the ferry forever. "My god!" Martin laughed. "There are actually parts of Greece from which I am forbidden!"

After dinner we walked awhile, laughing about all the things we once fought over. It was the beginning of spring. The sidewalks were crowded with young people. The air was mild and filled with the promise of summer. And then, as we rounded Bleecker Street, I pointed.

"Right there. Remember?"

It was only a month after we met. A Saturday before it all became Tuesday. The sun was shining and I'd come downtown to the Village, having agreed to help him search for a new chessboard and bong—his twin passions at that time, chess and pot. Because all our previous dates had been at night, I'd always worn heels. Walking beside him in flats then, I mentioned feeling short.

Without warning, Martin took hold of my waist and hoisted me up onto his shoulders. With our considerable heights combined, his six-foot-two and my five-foot-nine, the sight must have been horrific. It was the kind of thing that would have thoroughly irritated the both of us had we seen anyone else carrying on like that—Martin had once described his ideal protocol for sidewalk traffic: "The left lane is for passing and the right for standing or strolling, though strolling is thoroughly discouraged"—and yet, we walked like that for two full blocks, laughing carelessly, an exception to our own rule. I hadn't thought of it in years, had forgotten all about it until then, until, with uncanny clarity, the whole image—complete—like a postcard, rushed back. And I saw us vividly, the way others must have seen us: Bounding down Bleecker, the blue sky behind us, a monstrous totem of youth.

CHAPTER 7

"IRIS'S MOVIE CORNER"

This week Iris reviews The X-Files: I Want to Believe, *starring David Duchovny and Gillian Anderson. Directed by Chris Carter, and written by Chris Carter and Frank Spotnitz.*

"I'm working on lying less."

"You lie often?"

"No," he said. "I mean, no more than anyone else."

"*I* don't lie," I lied, being sure to make eye contact.

"What I meant was, I am working on being more honest with myself." He looked at the menu.

We'd just seen *The X-Files: I Want to Believe*, which I didn't think was very good, so in the spirit of honesty, I told him.

"I liked the movie," Glen answered. "But I was expecting there to be aliens."

"Exactly! *The X-Files* is always about aliens! Why did they make the sequel about stem cell research controversy instead?"

Glen ignored my question and tucked into the menu as if he were reading a very good book. We'd already ordered. I tightened the caps on the salt and pepper shakers. I was nervous, having decided earlier that I was going to have sex with him.

"Truffle Oil!" Glen boomed, slamming his fist on the table. He looked up from the menu, lightning in his eyes. Glen's an actor and sees drama everywhere. He told me so on our first date. "Iris, look around you. Everything's a script. You and me, but 'poor players.' Take that choking hazard sign—" I looked over at the illustration of a man doubled over with a blue face, holding his throat. "That's Shakespeare."

Glen licked his index finger and turned a page, moving his mouth mutely as he perused the side dishes.

"I'm having a great time," Glen said at last. He folded the menu and popped an olive into his mouth. "Aren't you?"

"Of course!" I said, but I wasn't really sure. I was too excited to call it a bad time, but it wasn't exactly a good time either. Also, since I'd already decided to sleep with him, having a bad time was out of the question. I was determined to have sex and wasn't about to let a little thing like his personality stand in my way.

"It's just nerves," he said, sensing my discomfort. "Because we're still getting to know each other. It will get easier."

I nodded, not really sure that I agreed. It was more that I wanted to agree.

After dinner, we went back to his place and he tickled me for a while on the couch. I'm not actually ticklish, but it would have been too uncomfortable to just sit still and stare at him while he pinched me all over, so I writhed and giggled as if it were a wonderful torture. Seeing what a success the tickling was, Glen kept at it, surprising me every ten minutes of our kissing with tickle attacks. It was exhausting. Wishing he would stop, I thought about telling him I'd been miraculously cured, or else actually confessing the truth, but that seemed too hard.

One lie begets another, inevitably. And so, after another minute, when I could stand it no more, I grabbed his crazed hands and looked into his eyes. "Listen, Glen!" I said. And then I told him I was frightened because he was clearly more sexually experienced than I.

He relaxed and asked me how many men I'd been with.

I made my eyes wide. "I can't tell you. It's too embarrassing." I turned my face away.

"Why?" he asked gently.

"It's so few."

"That's okay. I don't want to be with someone who's been around the block. You can tell me."

"How many women have you been with?" I asked.

"You really want to know? It's not a little."

"Of course. You're so charming and handsome. What's it, like, fifty?"

"Something like that," he said, apologetically. He lifted my chin and looked into my eyes. "I'm sorry I've been with so many women, Iris. But if we're together, I promise I won't be with anyone else." He brushed the hair from my eyes and for a second I worried he was going to tickle me again, but instead he asked, "So how about you?"

I thought for a moment and began blushing—the result of my planning to outright lie to him. I tried to think of the smallest number plausible for a single woman my age, a number large enough not to overburden him with too much innocence, yet small enough to suggest virtue and catalyze his wish to protect thus making for a warmer post-coital experience. "Three," I said, twirling my hair and looking up to see if he was buying it.

His eyes flashed like he'd just found money in an old pair of pants. "That's okay," he said and kissed me gently on the forehead.

We made out for another half hour (one-third the length of *The X-Files: I Want to Believe*, which was, in my opinion, a little too long). Glen moved his tongue around the inside of my mouth as if he were searching for something, which naturally compelled me to try to hide it. What this something was, I didn't know, but I was sure he mustn't be allowed to find it.

While we kissed, my mind wandered back to the movie. *The X-Files* is traditionally about aliens—how Mulder believes in them and Scully is skeptical. And then there's the unfulfilled sexual tension between them. But *I Want to Believe* had no aliens and skipped right past sex to a scene in which the two of them are lying side by side in pajamas, suggesting a committed relationship from which the sex has long since gone. Could the movie actually be an allegory for a long-term relationship? A relationship in which you continue to say, "I love you," but what you really mean is you *want to love*, just like Mulder "wants to believe" in aliens, though they're completely absent from the script. A loveless relationship . . . An alien-less *X-Files* . . .

Glen tongued my ear, making a sloshy noise in my head. "I love kissing you," he breathed, before reapplying his saliva to my mouth. Did he really love it, or did he just want to love it?

He suggested we move into the bedroom and I made my eyes fearfully wide again, as he seemed to like it the first few times.

"If you feel like things are moving too fast we can just sleep, or if you feel uncomfortable with that, too, I can put you in a cab. Though I hope you'll stay."

"It is pretty late," I said, pretending to think it over.

"It would be great to wake up next to you," he said.

"It would probably be difficult to find a cab at this hour," I said, over the sound of car horns and running meters coming through the window.

He sat me on his bed and removed my sport jacket, then my sweater, button by button he removed my shirt, then my undershirt, then my camisole (I like to layer). Then my skirt and slip, my stockings . . . until I was all at once naked beneath his hands—naked but for the remaining layers of bra and underwear, of course.

Then, he took off his own shirt, revealing a hairy chest. Then he stood up and took off his pants, revealing a pair of even hairier legs.

When he was finished, he kneeled down on the bed and hid a condom beneath the pillow behind me.

He offed my bra, and we were both naked: Him, but for his boxer shorts and body hair. Me, but for my panties, which are large and sexy (I like full coverage—over the waist and down the top of the leg, with a little extra room in the seat). When a man undresses me and finds me in these, he gets the feeling that what he's about to do has never been done as, were I accustomed to casual sex, I would never wear such hideous under-things. My underwear thus creates an atmosphere of uncommon vulnerability, zero guile, the headiness of which triggers erections of unusual fierceness!

Overcome by my disarming sexuality, Glen stood up to examine me. Frantically, he removed his boxer shorts when suddenly, it was revealed: He was completely hairless in the area surrounding his penis. I shrieked and pulled back. "What happened to you?"

"What do you mean?"

"Your hair!" I said. "Someone stole it!"

"It's there, it's just shorter than the rest. See?" he said, inviting me to take a closer look.

I picked up the penis between my thumb and forefinger and moved it to the side. He was right. The hair lay flat, hugging his pelvis like a crop circle. Still investigating, I asked him more questions.

Did he shave it? I asked.

No.

Nair?

No. He was not into hair removal, he said.

Had his penis recently suffered a scare of some kind, which might have caused the hair to fall out?

He told me that would only make it turn white, and No.

I asked him if he'd waxed.

Of course not, he sniffed, as if appalled by the idea.

Electrolyzed.

No.

Alopecia?

No.

Might his penis have eaten the surrounding hair?

He looked at me incredulously.

I thought for another moment. "The shock of recognition!" I cried. "Perhaps you recently read a novel that was very good?"

"I haven't read a book in years," he said emphatically, and I believed him.

With his head propped up on his hand, and his penis still exposed but flaccid against his stomach, he said that he was just naturally hairless down there. "Just lucky, I guess," were his exact words, which seemed an odd way to describe his hideous condition. His penis looked so vulnerable, like Bambi's mother in the forest clearing, so available to the aim of gun-toting hunters. The sight of it filled me with a robust sense of melancholy.

I concluded that such a thing could not possibly occur in nature. He was lying. I was sure of it.

"I'm just not a very hairy person," he insisted, running a hand through the thicket obscuring his chest.

"Listen, Glen. It's okay. Even I primp a little." I took off my underwear to show him my own pubic hair, which had been gathered smartly into a side ponytail.

"I'm all natural," he swore again. "I like yours though. That's really cute. I've never seen anyone style theirs like that."

I shrugged. "Thanks."

"The pink scrunchy's a nice touch."

"Well . . ." I blushed and, leaning over, gave him a kiss on the forehead.

I was relieved by his approval. Preparing for our date, I'd switched the pony tail back and forth, trying it on the right side and then on the left side five or six times, unable to decide which way it looked best. I'm forever worrying about my pubic hair being out of fashion and so, getting intimate with a new man makes me feel doubly vulnerable. Is mine different than other girls'?

Glen removed the scrunchy and began kissing me again. At last, we did it.

I woke an hour later to the sound of Glen's heavy breathing, to his arms draped over me, which I slunk out from under. I turned over and watched him in the dark, wondered what all this tenderness meant. I had wanted only sex from him, but now that I had gotten it another desire began to stir in me. The way the joints of the arthritic can predict a coming storm, I felt the dreadful swelling in my chest that always prefigures a monogamous relationship.

Glen isn't so bad, I thought, listening to him snore softly. He's kind and well-intentioned if not exactly brilliant. And isn't caring and tenderness ultimately all that matters? But can he be trusted?

I peeled back the covers to investigate his private area again. I couldn't shake the idea that he'd been lying to me. Though I had been with men before who had done some clipping in the area, none had ever shaved it completely. What had come over him? Also, the others had never denied it. They just liked to keep things neat, they said, and wasn't everyone doing it these days?

The look was especially weird on Glen though, as he had a considerable amount of hair everywhere else. Why only remove it there?

Why not at least try to blend the edges? Surely, no one would do this on purpose? He must be telling the truth, I concluded. And yet, while I believed Glen's assertion that he was not responsible, I also knew that nature could never produce so aberrant a feature. There was only one possible explanation.

It was done by aliens under cover of night; the design above Glen's balls was a communiqué from beyond. I stared at his flaccid penis again, so vulnerable in the field of shorn hair. The moon came through the window and shone on the design of shorter hairs as they lay like crop circles around his penis. What were they trying to tell us, I wondered, looking through the window and up into the night sky?

I stayed up for hours puzzling over his penis, ready to catch the aliens in the act of marking him with their hieroglyphs. Then, at some point during my stakeout of Glen's genitals I must have nodded off because the next thing I knew, light was pouring through the window and Glen's face was floating over mine.

"French toast!" he boomed, reading a takeout menu he'd glued to the wall, "Or not to be!" He'd already put his boxer shorts on and was squatting beside the mattress where I lay.

I groaned and pulled him back into bed with me. He kissed me with my eyes and mouth still closed. I mumbled my reluctance to kiss back as I hadn't yet brushed my teeth. "Don't worry, neither have I," he said, though his lips were cool and minty.

Things started up again and before I knew it he was pulling off my underwear. "You are so cute," he said, stopping at the site of my pubic hair, arranged neatly into two braids. I arrange it this way when I sleep, so it doesn't get too tangled. "Do you know how sexy you are?"

I gave him what had become my trademark frightened/sexy look. He took my hand and placed it over his boxer shorts. I pulled off his underwear and felt him again, smooth to the touch, like a frog's belly, ready to be dissected of its secrets.

He mirrored my gesture with his own hand and then, silently, one at a time, he began untying my braids. How we complimented each other, how he was hairless where I had hair, how we fit like a lock and key—was this what the aliens were trying to tell us?

"I think I'm falling in love with you, Iris."

"No, you're not," I said skeptically. "You're just saying that. I'm sure you say that to all the girls."

"There are no other girls," Glen said, making eye contact.

He kissed my neck, and I ran my fingers over the flat, stubble-like formation where the aliens had gotten to him—the proof—and wondered what mysteries the universe had in store for us. Beyond this morning in bed, after we went out for breakfast, after we kissed good-bye on the street, was it too far-fetched to think it might be love?

"Oh, Glen," I cried, "I want to believe!"

The X-Files: I Want to Believe *will be available on DVD and Blu-ray December 2, 2009.*

CHAPTER 8

SCIENCE FICTION

If we placed a living organism in a box . . . one could arrange that the organism, after any arbitrary lengthy flight, could be returned to its original spot in a scarcely altered condition, while corresponding organisms which had remained in their original positions had already long since given way to new generations. For the moving organism the lengthy time of the journey was a mere instant, provided the motion took place with approximately the speed of light.

ALBERT EINSTEIN

Seldom, very seldom does complete truth belong to any human disclosure; seldom can it happen that something is not a little disguised, or a little mistaken; but where, as in this case, though the conduct is mistaken, the feelings are not, it may not be very material.

JANE AUSTEN, *EMMA*

A cat is penned up in a steel chamber, along with the following device (which must be secured against direct interference by the cat): in a Geiger counter, there is a tiny bit of radioactive substance, so small that perhaps in the course of the hour, one of the atoms decays, but also, with equal probability, perhaps none; if it happens, the counter tube discharges, and through a relay releases a hammer that shatters a small flask of hydrocyanic acid. If one has left this entire system to itself for an hour, one would say that the cat still lives if meanwhile no atom has decayed. The psi-function of the entire system would express this by having in it the living and dead cat (pardon the expression) mixed or smeared out in equal parts. It is typical of these cases that an indeterminacy originally restricted to the atomic domain becomes transformed into macroscopic indeterminacy, which can then be resolved by direct observation.

ERWIN SCHRÖDINGER

Too late, too late!

THOMAS HARDY, *TESS OF THE D'URBERVILLES*

DRUNKS HAVE A funny relationship to time. Though alcohol accelerates your aging physically, it retards you psychologically. For the while you are drunk you are suspended, preserved in the moment of your first sip, so that when your bender is over, a week may have passed for everyone else, but for you it's just the morning after a very long night. A number of benders becomes a few years. And before you know it, you wake up the same age you were when you started drinking, but with your body strangely ravaged by time, as if during the night, during some practical joke, you were quietly bundled and jettisoned into the future. You wake up nineteen, but it's your twenty-ninth birthday. Alcoholics are time travelers. That's why they're always so confused. That's why they sway and stumble like seamen when they leave a bar. That's why their rhythms are slow and different from everyone else's, and why they're always laughing—they see life from a great ironic distance even while it's happening. That's why they're so sad. Time travelers are notoriously lonely.

■ ■ ■

It was a Thursday night and I was having dinner with Glen at a restaurant on the Lower East Side. We'd just finished eating and Glen was in the bathroom, doing whatever he does. I was waiting at the table, checking the TV guide on my phone to see what time *Law & Order* would be on and if I'd be lucky enough to catch two episodes in a row. I've been watching a lot of *Law & Order* lately. So much that the percussion sound [*Gungh, Gungh*] the show uses to denote scene changes has gotten stuck in my head. I was disappointed to find that night's episode was not only a repeat, but one I'd seen already. Twice. I could hardly watch it a third time. Could I? I looked up from my phone to see if Glen was coming. [*Gungh, Gungh*] There was no sign of him.

Glen regularly disappears into the bathroom following dinner for ten, sometimes fifteen minutes. I don't know what he does. I think he gels his hair or something because he usually comes back looking extra shiny, though when I ask him, he says, "What do you mean?" and stares at me vacantly.

I began searching the upper channels to see what I could be watching if I ordered cable—a reoccurring fantasy. The upper channels: additional airings of *Law & Order*. I never used to watch much TV, but I've been staying home a lot the past few months in order to write, which means that I've been watching a lot of TV and thinking about how I should be writing and taking lots of naps in between television shows, exhausted from the stress and guilt of not having written anything for all those hours spent watching TV. I watch *Law & Order* because it's almost always on, and also *Masterpiece Theater* on Sunday nights because my mom watches it and we discuss the show when she calls.

Aside from flesh and blood, my mom and I have very little in common, so when she calls, after we discuss the weather, we've still plenty of time to fill. She's of a more practical nature than I am and doesn't read much, if at all, so we can't talk about books. I gave her *The Bridges of Madison County*, trying to excite her interest in literature, but she couldn't be bothered. I chose to give her *The Bridges of Madison County* because I'd seen the movie and had heard the book was really good, and also because it only cost a quarter at a library sale. The book is ubiquitous on sale racks; it's the literary equivalent of *Law & Order*. To be fair I haven't read it either, though I own three copies. At that price? I'd be losing money if I didn't snap them up while I had the chance.

My mom likes the show *Survivor* and *The Amazing Race* and sometimes talks to me about them, but I'm not a fan of those shows and have little to contribute. Watching *Masterpiece Theater*, which airs film adaptations of classic books, allows us to meet halfway. My mom loves period pieces because, like me, she's old fashioned and the themes of purity, honor, love, and the making of a profitable marriage are always on her mind.

Last week, they showed Thomas Hardy's *Tess of the d'Urbervilles*, which I read in college. When I called her later in the week, after we swapped dew points and information regarding a cold front approaching from the Southwest, we debated over whether or not the story had any true villain, and whether or not Tess could really be considered pure.

I insisted Tess was *morally* pure and the least corrupt of all the characters though the most put upon, too. I suggested Hardy's aim was to point out moral hypocrisy in the supposedly devout and respectable and proposed that society had made her into a murderer, and Angel, her true love, recognized this in the end, which is why he didn't give her up to the police after she brutally murdered her wealthy husband.

"I guess that's why it was so controversial," my mother added, referring to the show's introduction, in which the host remarked about the book's reception in 1891, the scandal caused by its subtitle, *A Pure Woman Faithfully Presented*.

Last month my mom called to remind me to watch the last episode in the Jane Austen Collection. I'm not much for Jane Austen personally, but she's my mother's favorite author-adapted-to-film, probably because all the novels end with a wedding and my mom is feeling wedding deficient. The last episode was not an adaptation of one of her novels but a biographical film about the authoress herself. It was called, *Miss Austen Regrets*, and was all about Jane Austen not marrying but pursuing a career as a writer instead.

Watching it alone in my apartment that night, I knew my mother was seeing me as the Jane Austen figure, but in a happy way, as if I had a great destiny like Ms. Austen, as if it were because of my mission to write that I remain, to this day, single. When I spoke to her the following evening her tone confirmed this, and I was touched by her optimism, her choosing to ignore the fact that so far I have only approximated Austen's failings without coming close to any of her successes. Like Austen, I am approaching thirty without a fiancé. Unlike Austen, I've not published a single novel.

In the film, Jane gets drunk on a lawn with her young niece whom she is advising about whom to marry. A couple of hours later—film hours are like dog years—Jane Austen dies at forty-two. But single women died young in those days, at least according to the novels. If heartbreak didn't kill you sooner, loneliness got you later.

After perusing the TV guide with no luck, I decided to go to the movies and made a quick check of the local listings. *Marley and Me* was starting in ten minutes on Second Avenue. I had just enough time to get there if I rushed. That's what I was thinking when Glen, shinier than ever, returned to the table looking befuddled. He's been looking befuddled more and more lately. Or else I've been noticing it more and more.

"I'm going to go see *Marley and Me*," I announced as he sat down. I'd already told Glen I couldn't sleep over; my column was due Monday morning and, still not knowing what I was going to write about, I felt I needed to wake up in my own bed.

"What's that?"

"It's the new heartwarming comedy starring Jennifer Aniston and Owen Wilson that promises scene after scene of adorable canine high jinks," I explained wearily. Lately I find myself speaking in movie blurbs. When Janice asked me about my relationship with Glen, I shrugged and told her it was a "non-stop thrill ride." I think I might be depressed. Either that or I'm very happy. It's hard to tell.

"Oh, yeah," Glen said. "The dog dies at the end."

I glared at him and made another mental note to break up with him later. "I just told you I was going to see it, so why would you tell me how it ends?" I said through my teeth. "I make a point of not reading reviews so as to avoid spoilers, and then you go ahead and in less than one second say, 'By the way, everyone dies at the end.' Thanks a lot, Glen!"

"I lied. He doesn't die." Glen blushed and bit his fingernails.

"It's too late now. You already said it!" I said shrilly, and then felt immediately bad for yelling at him. My dad says I have a short fuse and that I have a tendency to get fixed. That I probably make it difficult for any man trying to date me, and that I should, "Try cutting people some slack, Iris." "I do, Dad!" I told him last weekend, "You have no idea all the things I think but don't say!"

"Anyway, it looks stupid," Glen continued.

"You look stupid."

He paused. "I thought you were going home because you had work to do tomorrow."

"I do. I just think a movie will relax me and help me sleep better. Anyway, I don't care if the movie is stupid. I just want to go to the movies."

"Can I come?"

"No."

"Why?"

"You just said the movie was stupid! Now you want to come?"

He didn't say anything.

"You talk too much and make noises and I just want to be alone so I can relax."

"Fine, go without me," he said petulantly. "I don't want to go anyway."

On the street outside the restaurant, Glen kissed me goodnight and made me promise to call him later. I'm not sure why since we'd been silent through most of dinner.

You know the death-march scene at the end of *Empire of the Sun*? The part when they pass a field decorated with a few mansions' worth of luxury English furniture, and the woman who has become a kind of mother figure to Christian Bale's character takes a seat on a plush divan and tells Christian Bale to go on without her before she dies from thirst and exhaustion right there in that beautiful chair? And at the same time that she's dying, Bale's character sees an atom bomb explode in the distance and mistakes it for her soul rising to heaven? Sometimes I feel like that when I'm with Glen. Like I'm on a death march and I want to say to him, "No, Glen, go on without me. I'll stay here among the exquisite armchairs and silver tea settings. . . ."

But I didn't say that then. I just looked at him and said, "Yes, I'll call you when I get home." You see, Dad? I do cut people slack!

I got to the theater just in time and clomped in with my laptop bouncing on my side—I had been working at a coffee shop earlier that day. Ostensibly working. Mostly I checked my email, read *Gawker*, and deleted people from my Facebook account. I also made a to-do list of all the things I would need to do later that I wasn't doing then. 1. Brainstorm column 2. Write column 3. Edit column 4. Wash face 5. Brush teeth 6. Shave legs—I like to throw in some basic tasks related to hygiene that are relatively easy to complete so that when I cross them off, I feel accomplished and emboldened to forge ahead with the rest of the list.

The column should be easy enough to write, but I always make it unnecessarily complicated. I'm supposed to be a sex columnist and just write about my dates, but once I start writing, I find myself wanting to do more than just spill the beans about penis size; I find myself thinking of Horace and his notion of literature's higher purpose, which is "to delight and instruct!" And so I end up waxing scientific, introducing rare brain disorders and new developments in quantum physics to bear upon my quest for love. Or else I wax lyrical, describing Glen's penis as if it were Proust's Madeleine about to unlock the floodgates of memory and with my first taste of it bring to mind my lost childhood among the garden paths of my parents' backyard in suburban Long Island. I don't know what's the matter with me.

The lights had already gone down and I searched in the dark for the perfect middle seat. The room was large and cool, empty but for one person off to the side and near the back. I eased into the chair as if into a very still lake.

Going to the movies alone is one of my very favorite things to do. Where else in New York City can one enjoy so much space? Most apartments are tiny and cluttered, and on the street you're always brushing by people. In shops there are crowds. Even at the library, someone inevitably answers a cell phone just next to you, or a homeless man decides to talk to himself at your reading table. At the gym girls stretch in pairs, talking about their jobs and their boyfriends and their words—"like like like"—whiz past you like machine gun fire. But if you go to the movies alone at the right time, for two hours—two whole hours—this huge dark room is yours.

I like to lose myself at the movies, to be completely swept up into the dream. If I'm with someone, though, this won't happen. If I'm with someone, I'll start to wonder what he thinks of the movie, if he is having a good time. Or else I'll worry that he might talk at the wrong moment and break the mood, which breaks the mood. Movies are just not conducive to sharing. That's what I've always thought anyway, though recently I've started to wonder if this kind of thinking isn't symptomatic of a larger problem.

When my ex-boyfriend Philip visited me in Greece two years ago, for example, he commented regularly on the beauty of the sunsets. We'd be sitting on the beach, side by side, and he'd be looking out to sea and I'd be looking at him. I was glad the sunset was beautiful, for his sake, but I couldn't pay any attention to it myself, not while he was there. It was one or the other. Philip or the sunset. By the end of his visit, I was actually eager for him to leave so I could finally enjoy the sunset, too.

I'm not sure why I couldn't do what he did, what others seem to do with relative ease—to have my own thoughts alongside someone else's. Instead, when I'm with a guy, everything but him goes right out of my head. We'll walk somewhere and I'll have no idea how we got there. The sun will go down and I'll have no idea evening has begun. The whole sky, every star, every tree, every street, every room will fall away and I'll see nothing but him, his face filling the world, a world from which I too have disappeared. One minute I'm there and then suddenly—eclipse. I end most of my relationships for this reason. Because after a while I become tired of living a life so reduced. But I'm the one that did it. No one blindfolded me or said I couldn't look at the sunset, too.

I've been thinking a lot about this lately, worrying that I can't share things, like views or spaces or movies. Say I get married, will the whole world fall away forever? Will I fall away with it? Which brings me to what I like most about Glen, which is that I don't actually like him very much. This makes it much easier for me to stand apart, for me to know where he ends and I begin.

The coming attractions started. More romantic comedies, more fabulous clothes, more scenes of female coworkers gathered around the watercooler to talk about love, more plots featuring hapless men who turn out to be the one, while the ones originally thought to be the one turn out to be hapless despite their great abs. I thought about Glen and wondered if the thirty-sixth or thirty-seventh one could still be the one. I thought about the phrase "the one" and wondered if it could be short for something. "The one that got away." "The one I eventually settled for." "The one that irritated me the least. . . ."

My parents took me to the movies every weekend when I was a kid. Mostly we saw grown-up films that I couldn't follow or didn't want to follow. Two hours to a child is like a summer to an adult; you might even be taller when you leave the theater. Bored, I'd turn in my chair to watch the light stream out from the projector, watching it spray out from a tiny point in the back. Staring into it, I imagined I was looking back in time, to the origin of all things, certainly the origin of all things on screen anyway. I'd watch the dust dancing above the audience in a long light beam expanding toward the screen. And I'd watch the faces of the other moviegoers behind me, wondering what they were watching, wondering what so engrossed them, wondering what they felt. Everyone was under the same spell. Everyone but me.

I felt fantastically alone then. Like the time traveler in movies who can stop time for everyone but himself, who can walk through a room where a party is being thrown and see the confetti stuck, suspended in midair, and see sound as if it were a physical, measurable thing—the laughter of party guests dangling half in and half out of their mouths—see someone just about to tap someone else on the shoulder, see potential, just before it is activated. The privileged time traveler who is able to appreciate the moment more keenly for his being outside of it, but who also, paradoxically, lives in exile as a result. As a kid, staring the wrong way in the movie theater, at the projector and at the faces of the audience lit up by the screen, I felt like that—an exile—like I was looking back in time while everyone else was looking forward, watching the moments pass and everyone around me pass with them. Everyone's eyes were on the sunset, while I watched them watch.

The opening credits began and the lights dimmed further until the room was completely black. I was not expecting *Marley and Me* to be extraordinary. I was expecting it to be well-produced and easy to watch, with a few round laughs along the way. Because my expectations were so reasonable, it was unlikely that I would be disappointed, which is what I like most about big Hollywood movies and Glen.

Marley and Me was as delightful as I'd hoped. It's about a columnist—like me!—who writes about his life; his wife, their dog Marley, their three kids and how their lives change. And, yes, as Glen said, the dog eventually dies. It was a very sweet story, and during many parts I cried.

But I cry easily at the movies, so that's no way to rate the quality of a picture. I cry somewhat reliably, for example, during any scene involving flight; perhaps I was a low-flying bird in my past life. In my dreams, flying is my primary mode of transportation. It's not a big deal when I fly, but just how I get around. For a few years after college, while I was teaching middle school and dating Martin, I stopped flying in my dreams all together which scared me; I was afraid something inside me had died. After I broke up with Martin and went back to school full time, I started flying again little by little, but then I started drinking a lot and stopped remembering my dreams, so I don't know now whether or not I'm still flying.

Marley and Me had no flying in it, but it still moved me. Perhaps because Marley looks so much like my stuffed animal, Herbert, which made me think again about getting a dog and naming him George Foreman after my grill. I've never had a dog, only Dan, the peacock I had as a kid, and when I was very young, a guinea pig named Spud. Also, this one time I bonded with a box turtle that wandered into our backyard in Long Island. I had to let him go though.

They were free beings, my father told me, and "if you love something, you must set it free." He was paraphrasing a line from my favorite *Smurfs* episode. "If you smurf something, let it smurf," Papa-Smurf tells Handy, regarding his mermaid sweetheart who cannot stay with him on land. Handy built her a special bathtub but it wasn't enough. I cried, but did as I was told, too, and set the turtle free among my mother's bed of impatiens. Is this what men are thinking when they don't call you after a one-night stand? Having "loved" you, must they now set you free? I brought out my pen and notebook and scribbled, "Possible idea for column. . . ."

Absorbed in the film once more, I began to draw "unfair comparisons" between myself and the columnist in the movie. I picked up the phrase "unfair comparisons" from my friend Jacob who's been in therapy his whole life. "You're not supposed to compare yourself to anyone else," Jacob told me. "It's unhealthy because you will always lose." I'm not sure if he meant me specifically or "you" in general. Either way, I'm not supposed to do it, but that's what I was doing.

In the movie, the main character's column is full of charming anecdotes about life with Marley. In one scene, his whole family gathers in the kitchen to reread his old clippings. Warm and happy together, they are delighted to find their shared memories evoked in print. Why can't I write a column like that? I wondered. I tried to imagine my future husband rereading *my* columns. "Ha," he'd say looking up, as I caught him in the kitchen, poring over a binder full of them.

"What you got there, hon'?" I'd say, laying an affectionate hand on his shoulder.

"I love this one about you blowing your obese ex-boyfriend and this one, too, about you vomiting in front of your rebound flame. Son, get in here!" he'd call into the family room, to our eldest playing Yahtzee with his little brother on the rug before the fireplace. Two small boys with matching bowl haircuts would gather round, eager to hear Dad share Mommy's writing. "Letting my upchuck burst into full flower . . ." he'd read aloud, before beaming at me proudly with that same look Jennifer Aniston gives Owen Wilson in the movie. The one that says, "How'd I get so lucky to get a woman like you to be my wife?"

If I got a dog, I could write about him instead . . . I could give up sex writing . . . I could send my parents my articles. . . .

When an essay of mine was recently published on *Nerve*, I felt so proud—my story was featured on the home page beneath a large photo and ads!—naturally, I sent my parents a link. When I spoke to my mother on the phone a few days later though, and asked excitedly if she received it, she said, "Yes. But don't mention it to your father. I'm afraid it will upset him. It's a little dirty; you know how conservative we are," she said gently.

"It's fiction!" I said quickly, burning with shame. "It's only fiction, Mom!" It's fiction, despite the fact that another "character" says my name within the piece, despite the fact that the other "character," "Glen," removes my underwear before exclaiming, "I think I'm falling in love with you, Iris." I use this "fiction" excuse for everything. If I ever committed a crime, robbed a bank say, and were caught in the act, I'd probably scream out, "Don't arrest me! It's fiction!"

To be honest, though, Glen never said he was falling in love with me, so it is sort of fiction. What Glen actually said was, "Iris, I think I'm falling off the bed." He was all the way at the edge. Also, I never actually went to see *The X-Files* with him. I went alone, in the middle of a very hot day in Southwest Florida where I was visiting my parents for a week. The parking lot was huge and hot and empty, and I was alone in the multiplex and alone on the drive back to my parents' condo. I just wanted to write about Glen's weird genitals and saw the movie as an opportunity.

The piece was published under the title, "The Truth is Out There." It wasn't my title; my editor changed it. I had wanted to call it, "Iris's Movie Corner," as I was hoping to break into movie reviewing.

I could get a dog . . . change my ways . . . write about my dog instead of my boyfriends and repent for all that I've written so far. . . .

I watched the giant faces of Owen Wilson and Jennifer Aniston and considered the possibilities. But then the same questions arose that always do. What do I know about caring for an animal? And what about travel? If I go to Greece in the summer, would I leave the animal with The Bastard, or stow him in baggage and bring him with me? Both solutions seemed a bit cruel. And what if I were irresponsible and forgot to feed him for a few days and he felt hungry and it was my fault? What if he were unhappy? What if he stopped flying in his dreams?

I got the column a few months ago after reading an announcement for a competition to be the next sex columnist for *New York Press*, a free weekly newspaper I pick up regularly for the cartoons. It was the first time in my life that I'd read a want ad and didn't feel immediately that I wasn't up to the job. Instead I thought, I could do this! Most of the sex columns they'd been running had been first-person reports about the nightmare dates each writer had endured. My angle was that *I'd* be the nightmare date. The only question was which nightmare would I document? I had terrorized so many.

"An Open Letter to My Date of Last Friday" was accepted and ran, and they even paid me. I didn't win. Nobody did. The competition was so popular that the newspaper decided to keep the column open. But then, a few weeks later, an editor from a new online magazine who'd read my piece contacted me about a job. And just like that, the purpose of all my failed relationships was revealed to me: I was to write about them. On my back and on the backs of all my ex-boyfriends, I would commence my writing career!

For some time before that, I'd been feeling like I was ruining my life, not to mention my health, and often, if I could sleep at all, I'd wake up terrified. Then, hungover and shaking one morning, at twenty-eight years old, I got this column, and it seemed like everything might finally click into place. It was nice to think, regardless of whether or not it was true, that all this ruining was actually in the service of something, that perhaps I had been on a path after all, that maybe I wasn't getting more lost everyday but just pursuing my own special destiny, that this was me, following years of heroic suffering and wandering, ascending to Mount Olympus where I would remain for all eternity, happily writing my "sexploits."

Suddenly, it looked as if it hadn't all been for nothing. Instead of trying to bury the memory of every past affair, I could redeem them, like coupons for my future. Each shameful act, I discovered, was a paying article. By the way, I lied. I was twenty-nine when this happened, not twenty-eight.

When I turned twenty-nine then, I decided to begin lying about my age as a way of making the lie I was planning to tell when I turned thirty more believable—two years would be too much to shave off all at once, but if I shaved one now and then just kept it off on my next birthday, I might more easily blend. It wasn't about vanity. I just felt I hadn't earned my age. Though twenty-nine, I was still a child in most respects, still so dependent on my parents, still without any accomplishments beyond my quite excellent SAT scores (800 Math! 780 Verbal!). And now, not even finished with my quarter-life crisis, I was embarking on a midlife one.

Since my life was pretty boring when I got the column—I had cut down on drinking a few months earlier in an effort to get serious about writing before I turned thirty and with that had all but retired from my social life, rarely seeing friends and even more rarely dating—my first few pieces were about things that had happened to me before, which I wrote as if they were happening to me just then.

I decided to call my column "Second Base," for the ambiguity appealed to me. Second Base meant "up the shirt," but it also meant the island of Calypso in *The Odyssey*. Odysseus's second stop where he is stalled for seven years on his journey home, just like I've been stalled for seven years since my graduation from college.

There are some drawbacks to writing a sex column. Since starting the column, for example, I've developed a weird habit of relating sexual anecdotes in casual conversation with near strangers. Like the other day when I met my editor in person for the first time and he told me he sang in a Prince cover band and that they would be performing the entire *Purple Rain* album at an upcoming party—would I like to come? I said I might come, that I also love Prince, and that I actually lost my virginity while a record of *Purple Rain*, which I had borrowed from my local library in high school, was on the stereo. He said, "Oh," and then I wondered why I was so indiscreet and eager to share.

Aside from worrying about what my parents think, I also worry that publishing these stories might make me unmarriageable—the worst possible fate for a Greek girl, and most especially for one so principally incompetent ("Single women have a dreadful propensity for being poor. Which is one very strong argument in favor of matrimony."—Jane Austen). This columnist gig might give men the wrong impression of me, might make them think I'm fast. And I'm not. Really. I'm not that kind of girl! I'm not at all callous when it comes to sex, nor flippant about whom I have it with. I want to fall in love and, to me, sex has everything to do with that. It's a very big deal. So big a deal, as a matter of fact, that I seem to be chained by it to Glen. So much for my notion of remaining distinct from him; I'm pretty much eclipsed.

And though I enjoyed the show *Sex and the City*, about a sex columnist like me, I was always mystified by how the four women could have sex with a man and after discard him so easily. My column is much less *Sex and the City* and much more *Tess of the d'Urbervilles* in that respect. *Tess of the d'Urbervilles* minus the rape and murder, but otherwise, nearly identical. *Tess and the City* would be the name of my TV show if I had one, and it would be subtitled *The Adventures of a Pure Woman in Manhattan Faithfully Rendered*. Because I'm just like Hardy's Tess, a pure woman corrupted by society. Remember that, future husband, when you read my binder full of clippings!

Marley and Me ended and I stayed to watch the credits, figuring I'd be on the street again soon enough, floating among the honking horns and city lights, sharing the sidewalk with everyone else. Finally, the lights came up and I stood up to put on my coat. Looking around for the first time since I came in, I noticed the other man in the theater was still there. [*Gungh, Gungh*] He was looking right at me.

Who is this guy and why is he looking at me? Quickly, I looked toward the projector to see if there was anyone there to witness a crime should one be about to occur. We were all alone.

The man, middle-aged, was closer to the aisle than I was and I would have to pass him in order to exit the theater. Stalling, I remained in place, pretending to fiddle with the buttons of my coat, pretending to adjust my scarf. I tried to think of what I might use to defend myself were he to come at me, and gripped my keys in my pocket. He began walking toward me. I began to sweat.

Only a few feet away now, the man, perhaps in his fifties, stopped, smiled, and in an Italian accent said, "You know, I like it so much, the movie. I had a dog just like the Marley, and it remind me my own family."

"Oh," I said, frozen stiff. *Your family, sure, before you killed them. If there ever was such a family! Where are they now, huh? Why are you here at the movies alone on a Thursday night, you creep, you criminal, you rapist?*

He smiled warmly and motioning to the screen, said, "It was very good. It made me cry."

"Yes," I said rigidly, smiling politely despite my fear, not wanting to appear rude. At last, he turned and left.

After the door closed behind him, I followed and exited the theater, too. I was eager to get home. The *Law & Order* percussion sounded in my ears again. I thought of my home address.

189 West Tenth Street

On the street, I thought about the man from the theater and felt bad. Perhaps he wasn't trying to brutally rape and murder me, but just wanted to connect. Instead of reacting the way I had, I might have offered my own feelings about the movie: "I too could identify. I just got a Roomba—a robot vacuum cleaner—and he eats up all the dust just as Marley ate up all the furniture. What's that? My Roomba's name? I'm still deciding, but I've narrowed it down to Charles, Knuckles, or Saul. I had originally wanted to call him Oonchaka, but the name already belongs to an ex-boyfriend's penis." We might have shared a laugh had I not reacted so defensively. After all, wasn't I also suspiciously alone at the movies on a Thursday night? Wasn't I also a creep?

I arrived home and greeted my plant Epstein, my Roomba _____, and my stuffed animal Herbert. I was safe. Alone and safe. I studied my to-do list. I still had to wash my face, brush my teeth, and shave my legs, but I decided instead to write my column right then and there. I took out my computer and set it down on my desk.

Second Base
By Iris Smyles

Wave or particle? Quantum physics has it that light and in fact all matter is both, or rather, exhibits both properties depending on how it is observed, though, when it *is* observed, it can only be one or the other.

I think about this a lot when I'm having sex with Glen. Sometimes, I imagine him as a wave and other times a particle. "Wave or particle! Wave or particle! Yes! Yes!" I'll cry, near the end of our double-slit experiments, before, like a wavefunction, he collapses on top of me.

According to the Copenhagen interpretation, it's impossible for me to know exactly when and where Glen's going to come—electrons have been known to turn up in the most unusual places!—but using probability statistics, I can guess to pretty near accuracy whether it will be after ten minutes and on my chest, leg, or back, or more Newtonianally speaking, within the confines of the condom.

For a full minute after testing my theory, Glen lies sprawled on top of me, his breath slowing. Finally I ask him to move so I can record the results in the Chemistry ledger I keep next to the bed. With a pencil, I write the date and time and then, "thigh," before curling up next to him.

Glen says I think too much, that I should stop trying to put him in a box. That he doesn't care about Schrödinger's equation. "You need to open yourself to life's great mysteries and stop obsessing over explanations." Then, in the same breath, he tells me he's got me all figured out.

"You know what your problem is? You're not a romantic," he told me yesterday. "That's the difference between you and me; you've never been in love."

"How do *you* know where I've been?"

He laughed and said, "I know. Your wild past, right? Reading novels by David Rukowski and Hunter P. Farmson. Drinking wine coolers and staying up late with your girlfriends." He dismissed me with a wink.

Heisenberg's Uncertainty Principle postulates that one can never know exactly where a particle will turn up, though we can narrow our guesses by studying the statistics of where they've turned up in the past. A wave-function is basically the sum of such probabilities, like a map of every possible outcome, which collapses once an observer takes a measurement. That's how Schrödinger could have an equal probability of a live and dead cat in a box at the same time.

Once you look inside the box though, probabilities don't matter anymore. All possibilities but the one observed disappear and what you've got is a cat, alive or dead, not both. You've got the thing itself, a particle not a wave. But before anyone checked, everything was true. Before you locate the electron, the thing could be anywhere. Like the way I could be anywhere, but instead I'm here with Glen, who, let's face it, is kind of an asshole.

"I am, too, romantic! I just don't think romance should hinge on shutting your brain off." I should have told Glen that. I should have said, "Glen, you don't think enough! That's your problem. *And* you're slightly overweight!"

Lately, I find myself acting subatomically and I have no idea what to do about it. I mean that all the laws I used to obey just don't seem to correspond to my present life or what I'm doing with it, or what I'm doing with Glen. What *am* I doing with Glen?

Glen and I fight all the time and I think it has everything to do with special relativity. The fact that we each believe ourselves to be the fixed point in our experiments, the objective observer—which, as Einstein noted, is an illusion just like love—is a constant source of conflict. I tried explaining special relativity to Glen the other day as a way of bolstering my side of the argument, but he's a more forceful arguer than I am and wouldn't have it.

The argument: He keeps insisting I don't move around enough in bed. I told him I was trying to compensate for our age difference by moving very slowly; Glen's six years older than me. I told him that by lying very still while he moved around at a speed approaching that of light—"Faster!" were my exact words—we might make time dilate, with the effect that he would grow younger and I would grow older and theoretically we might climax at the exact same age, and how much fun would that be! Sweating all over me, Glen said, "Don't tell me what to do!"

I still dream of a Grand Unifying Theory, especially when Glen takes me out to dinner or says something funny and I laugh and we seem to be getting along so well. But more and more I doubt the possibility of my ever finding it, or more specifically, of my ever finding it with Glen. What would a wedding prove?

Regardless of whether or not time exists, regardless of gravity and so much space, and the confusing wave-particle duality of love itself, regardless of the ever-increasing probability of my ending up alone, perhaps it's time this experiment comes to an end.

After a couple hours of writing, with a first draft before me, I stopped to brainstorm a title. "Iris's Science Corner," I typed up at the top, just under "Second Base," thinking perhaps this piece might help me break into science writing. Imagine my name in the *Scientific American*! My dad would be thrilled.

Before closing my computer, I checked my email: a message from Glen. "How was the movie? Sorry I couldn't go with you," he wrote, as if I'd even asked him to. He is always doing this, revising past events according to how he would prefer them to have happened. As if I don't have my own memory, too.

But then, I often revise things about him to include in my column. I suppose everyone does this to a greater or lesser degree, whether they are writing or just talking to their friends. For example, I wasn't in Florida visiting my parents when I saw *The X-Files* sequel. I lied. I was in Florida, but I was there alone. My parents were in Greece for the summer, and instead of visiting them there, I went to their place in Florida to spend four months by myself during hurricane season. Having just turned thirty—yes, I lied about that too—and having just stopped drinking, not cut down—that too—I went there "to finish my novel" (a phrase I've been using for the last seven years in a more or less unwitting lie) in isolation and to continue writing the column I'd been hired to write five months *after* I got sober, the column that would detail my sex life as a binge drinking twenty-eight-year-old Manhattan girl-about-town.

Einstein's theory of special relativity is often explained with an anecdote about time-traveling twins. One twin is sent into space, traveling at the speed of light. (If you could travel faster than the speed of light, physicists say, you could, theoretically, travel through time.) When he returns to Earth, he finds his twin brother much aged while he has not aged at all because for him, time had slowed. Einstein tested his theory by measuring the ticking of a clock in motion compared to the ticking of a stationary clock, proving that a clock in motion ticks slower than a stationary clock. The heart is a clock, too.

This is what it's like when you write about yourself: You split yourself in two. There is the you who is traveling—not precisely at the speed of light but at the speed of memory, which is even faster—and the you moving through time normally whom you can visit at any age. The two of you live at different speeds and occupy different dimensions. "Iris" has free time. I don't anymore.

So it wasn't exactly a lie, my saying I was twenty-eight, for one version of me was. And when I insisted *The X-Files* piece was fiction, I had been telling my mother the truth, too. Unobserved and by myself in Florida, watching storm warnings on TV and writing stories about the alien assault on Glen's pubic hair, I was like Schrödinger's cat before you look inside the box, paradoxically alive and dead at the same time. Twenty-eight and thirty. Drunk and sober. Ruining my life, trying to save it.

Just before I went to Florida, I was dating the Glen I've written about and often talked to him about my column, hoping he might read it but unable to come right out and ask him to. I felt conflicted since writing about sex is sort of shameful and low, and yet, it was the first thing I'd done since college of which I was proud. I wanted him to see me and felt I was somehow more there, in my stories, than here, right in front of him. So, I'd drop hints and say things like, "I have to go home and work on my column," or, "I got into an argument with my editor about the title of last week's column." But he didn't seem at all interested. He pretended he was interested, but I'm pretty sure he was just making his actor's listening face and nodding his head.

I hadn't started writing about *him* yet because I was still catching up on older stories. But when I did eventually write about him later, after we'd broken up, I wondered, if he were to read this—Are you there, Glen? This is you!—would he recognize himself? In my column's comment section, a reader asked how Glen felt about my writing, if the column was affecting our relationship—if my observations had influenced the outcome of the experiment.

My findings are as follows: When I write, I feel as I did when I was a kid at the movies with my parents, when everyone was facing forward and I was facing back. When I write, it's like I can go anywhere in time and stop everything for a moment, just freeze the scene. I can walk around everybody, walk around Glen, see him stuck in mid-action, about to kiss me goodnight, about to walk away after a tiff outside of a restaurant, about to exit the bathroom shiny and return to the table where I've been waiting for the last fifteen minutes, reading the TV guide on my phone.

I step outside the moment, and everything in it becomes clear. I see him, but I can also see myself finally, too, my eyes fixed on him as usual, fixed on his eyes and where they are looking, concerned again too much with what he's seeing, with what he's thinking. It's one of those moments during which I felt myself in full eclipse, one of those moments when I thought I had disappeared. But there I am in plain sight. There I am. The cat is alive.

CHAPTER 9

SMYLES' GAMES

A COMPLETE HANDBOOK CONTAINING ALL
THE GAMES PLAYED IN THIS BOOK, WITH THEIR
RULES, REGULATIONS, TECHNICALITIES, ETC.

It were indeed to be wished that less time was killed. . . .

"A LETTER FROM A GENTLEMAN AT BATH," *HOYLE'S COMPLETE HANDBOOK OF GAMES*

AWAKENINGS

PLAYER ONE: You

PLAYER TWO: The Bastard Felix

After smoking some very strong pot, notice Player Two hasn't spoken or moved in quite some time. Instead of saying, "[Player Two], are you alright?" Pick up the Beanie Baby your mother gave you for Christmas, the one resting on your bookcase that you don't know what to do with. What's a grown woman of twenty-five supposed to do with an adorable small stuffed dog? Throw the adorable small stuffed dog at Player Two and watch his arm shoot up suddenly, just like the catatonic patients' arms in that sad movie, starring Robert De Niro and Robin Williams, about that hospital where people fell asleep for twenty years. Say, "Felix! Felix! I have an idea for a game!" Sit down and feign catatonia. Say to Player Two, "Now me!"

DRINKING GAME #1

PLAYER ONE: You

PLAYER TWO: Your college roommate May

PLAYER THREE AND FOUR: Two girls from your dorm

Meet Players Two through Four at a bar where you accidentally have one too many. Discover how witty you are after three. Discover your heretofore untapped leaning capabilities. Take up smoking.

Talk about boys in the dining hall with the other Players the next morning. Refer to them as "men." Say something wicked, then leave the table to get more fro-yo. Return with a smart remark about the "man" who got your phone number last night.

Go out for drinks with the other Players again. Have one too many on purpose. Discover how witty you are after four, five, and then six. Discover older men who find you fascinating. Discover you have this in common with them; you find you fascinating, too! Catch sight of yourself flirting with one in the mirror behind the bar. There's something about you, isn't there?

Notice he's not too attractive. Humor him and give him your number anyway. Humor him and agree to go out with him when he calls. Humor him and meet him for drinks during the week. Humor him and let him kiss you. Humor him and go home with him that night. Humor him over eggs in the morning. Prepare to humor him when he calls. Wait for him to call.

In laying out crib, consider your hand, also whom the crib belongs to, and the state of the game, because what might be prudent in one situation would be less prudent in another.

"MAXIMS FOR PLAYING THE CRIB CARDS," CRIBBAGE, HOYLE'S GAMES

HIDE AND SEEK

PLAYER ONE: You
PLAYER TWO: Your friend Caroline's brother, The Captain

At the studio apartment of Player Two's sister who is out of town, count to five with your eyes closed. Now yell from the bed where you're sitting, "You can run, but you can't hide!" Open your eyes. Spot Player Two crouching nervously between the refrigerator and the dresser. Run a few steps and touch him on the shoulder, then say, "Tag, you're it!" Look around as he counts to five. Scan the 275 square feet frantically as your time runs out. Now make yourself small inside the bathtub in the kitchen.

> The cards being shuffled and cut, a certain stake, from a cent to five dollars, is deposited by the dealer, who gives three cards to each of the company. The elder hand, and the others after him, having examined their hands, either 'pass,' which is signified by laying down their cards, or 'brag,' in which case the dealer's stake is to be answered by all who brag.
>
> "MODE OF PLAYING," BRAG, HOYLE'S GAMES

SCARY ROOMMATE

PLAYER ONE: You
PLAYER TWO: Your college roommate May

When Player Two is studying, stand partially obscured by the door to the living room, so that one eye is visible and the other is blocked. Wait patiently for Player Two to look up and see you. Laugh when she starts screaming. Return to your own homework. Scream later when you're watching TV and are startled by Player Two's one creepy eye staring out at you from the closet.

DRINKING GAME #2, ROXANNE/RED LIGHT

PLAYER ONE: You
PLAYER TWO: Your boyfriend Martin
PLAYER THREE: Rachel, a girl Martin knew in high school
PLAYER FOUR: A plump girl in a pink cashmere cable-knit

PLAYER FIVE THROUGH PLAYER NINE: Five twenty-four-year-olds in an East
Hampton mansion

Turn your head from right to left in order to take in the enormity of
the "house" you've just pulled up to. Hop out of Player Two's jeep.
Ask Player Two, "Whose house is this again?" "[Player Three's], a girl
I knew in high school." Nod. You met Player Three before at Player
Two's friend's rock show in the city (Player Two's friend is the son of
the world's most famous concert violinist); they all grew up together.
That night, at the show, you could tell Player Three liked Player Two,
but you weren't worried because Player Two was *your* boyfriend,
because you knew he liked you and not her, and because you were
wearing such cute vintage pumps.

Feel your used pumps sink into the gravel driveway as you
approach the large forbidding front door. Notice Player Three's bare,
perfectly pedicured feet when she greets you. Take in the pearly ease
of her smile. Reciprocate awkwardly when she gives you a kiss on the
cheek. (You and your friends don't kiss on the cheek.) Follow her long
legs from room to glorious room as she makes some joke about her
and Player Two being "Jewish WASPs," a joke they both laugh at,
which you don't quite get.

Arrive in the dining room where six Players surround a long ban-
quet table with a small CD player placed purposefully in the middle.
Offer your name. Accept a beer. Take a seat. Don't be shy.

Ask in your friendliest voice, "What are we playing?" Listen to a
plump girl in a pink cashmere cable-knit summer sweater (Player Four)
count out the players on Team One and Team Two. "You're Team
Two," Player Four tells you last. "Team One has to drink every time

Sting sings 'Roxanne.' And Team Two, every time he sings, 'red light.' Also, 'Ra' counts, Team One!"

"Could you?" Player Four asks, before you realize you're closest to the CD player.

Nod. Reach over. Press Play.

The game consists in moving your men from point to point, so as to bring them round into your own inner table and then moving or bearing them off the board. The player who first clears off his men wins.

BACKGAMMON, HOYLE'S GAMES

PS4 STRATEGO

PLAYER ONE: You

PLAYER TWO: Mario, a fourteen-year-old boy in your sixth-grade class in the South Bronx

PLAYER THREE: Jade, a twelve-year-old girl in your sixth-grade class in the South Bronx

PLAYER FOUR: Mario's father

When Player Two refuses to sit down, get your gradebook and write a zero next to his name. Stand in the center of the room while you do this and wait for him to notice. Write very slowly and deliberately. After Player Three says, "Yo, Mario, she givin' you a zero!" look up from your gradebook. Stare Player Two down as he ambles slowly toward his desk, then sits *on* the desk instead of *in* the chair. Say, "You want another zero, [Player Two]?" Don't say anything when he responds, "I'm sittin', aren't I?"

After school, pull out your roll book and find Player Two's home phone number. Go to the teachers' lounge and dial the big beige phone. Wait for Player Four to pick up. "Hello, Mr. Mojica? This is Miss Smyles, Mario's teacher. I'm calling to talk with you about Mario's behavior in class today." Listen for a few seconds to a string of Spanish words you don't understand, some yelling in the background, a long call: "Marioooo!"

Listen to another voice say, "Hello?"

Repeat, "Hello, this is Miss Smyles, Mario's teacher—"

"Hi, Miss Smyles, this is Mario. My father don't speak no English, but you can talk to me and I'll translate."

Clear your throat. Say to Player Two, "Mario, I was calling to talk with your father about your disruptive behavior in class today."

"A'ight. I'll tell 'im."

"Thank you Mario."

"See you tomorrow, Miss Smyles."

Now hang up. You lost.

'Assisting' is where your partner is the dealer, and, with the help of the card he has turned trump, you deem your hand sufficient to take three tricks. In other words, suppose the Ace of Hearts to be turned, and you hold the Left Bower and King; you say to your partner, "I assist," and then he is obliged to take up the Ace turned and discard the same as though he had taken it up voluntarily.

"ON ASSISTING," EUCHRE, HOYLE'S GAMES

THE LAUGHING GAME

PLAYER ONE: You

PLAYER TWO: Your college roommate May

PLAYER THREE: Your college boyfriend

PLAYER FOUR: Your boyfriend's roommate

When your freshman dormitory closes for June, invite Player Two to spend two weeks with you at your parents' house in Long Island in order to audition for Broadway musicals. Between making home movies in your backyard starring the two of you as you talk about boys, pick up a copy of *Backstage* and discover an open call for *The Scarlet Pimpernel* happening in the city tomorrow!

Take the Long Island Rail Road into the city with your tap shoes.

Hand over your headshot and résumé, take a number, and learn the routine. Get cut the first round and say to Player Two, "So, what do you want to do now?"

Go to lunch with Player Two at The Cottage near Union Square, a Chinese restaurant you've heard serves unlimited free wine with lunch. High-five after the waiter takes your order and does not ask for ID. Surprise the whole staff as you request yet another and yet another full carafe. Stumble out of the restaurant three hours later.

3:00 PM. June. The sun in full fire. Walk. Hold up Player Two as she sways beside you. Walk. Trail after her as she spots Victoria's Secret on Fifth Avenue, runs inside, yelling and excited. In the cool fragrant store, see the shop girls coming toward you with assorted lace, saying, "sale sale sale," their faces floating in a black void. Say, "okay okay okay," and hand over your parents' credit card.

Outside, with your shopping bag full of assorted thongs, which you don't wear but bought as a joke, nod when Player Two says she feels sick. Say, "Don't worry. I'll call a cab. We'll go right to [Player Three's]."

Rush hour. Watch the cabs fly by. Turn your back on Player Two to hail more aggressively. Turn around again and find her lying on the pavement, asleep. Try to pull her up as a car stops short of running her down. Try to pull her up as she says, "I need to sleep, Iris. Just let me lie here for a while." Drag her down the block until a female police officer sees you both, hails a cab for you, and gives you stern warnings about all the things you've done that you must never do again.

Give the driver Player Three's address in Hell's Kitchen—"Fifty-third and Ninth!" Try to roll down the window before it's too late. Tell the driver you'll pay for the mess. Tell the driver to just stop yelling already. Pay. Pull Player Two out of the car. Prop her up on Player Three's stoop and ring the bell. When there is no answer, sit down beside Player Two and feel the sun hot against your skin. Shut your eyes and fall briefly asleep.

Wake up when a young man taps you on the shoulder, says you're pretty and asks for your phone number. Say, "I can't give you my phone number. I don't even know you. I'll give you my mailing address and you can write me a long letter stating your intentions." Argue with him for a while about the best way to reach you. Drift back to sleep.

Smile when Player Four comes home and finds you and Player Two dozing on his stoop. Smile when he says, "What a surprise!" Say, "I know you weren't expecting us until tonight, but [Player Two] got sick, and I didn't know where else to go." Turn to Player Two, peaceful now, covered in vomit. Help Player Four bring her inside.

Take your shoes off. Feel the linoleum tile of Player Four's kitchen, cool and sticky against your feet. Drink Coca-Cola and talk with Player Four while Player Two takes a shower. Give Player Three a smile when he walks in, after Player Four says, "Look what I found." Kiss Player Three.

Retire to Player Three's room for a nap. Before you do, call your mother and say, "[Player Two] and I are going to stay the night at our friend Marcy's."

In Player Three's bed, which he's separated from the rest of the room with police tape, beneath a small poster of The Wu-Tang Clan and another of Harvey Keitel, beside the bureau where an E. T. puppet sits lifelessly, kiss Player Three. Turn your face modestly as Player Two and Player Four pass through the room on their way to Player Four's bedroom in the back.

In the kitchen, two hours later, with the linoleum sticking to your bare feet again, pass the bong to Player Two, who's just announced, "I'm not drunk anymore," who says, "Sorry for throwing up on your jacket, Iris," who's saying now, "Let's play a game!"

Listen as Player Four gives the instructions: "It's harder than you think. The object of the laughing game is to make your opponents laugh against their will. You're it, until you can make someone else laugh; then they're it. Got it?"

Let "rock, paper, scissors" determine that Player Three is "it." Sit on the floor of the living room beside the dark TV. Watch the silent straight faces of Player Two and Player Four as they watch Player Three in eager anticipation. Watch Player Three disappear into his bedroom and reappear a few seconds later, confidently holding the E. T. puppet from his bureau. Watch as E. T. begins an impersonation of Robert De Niro, before Player Two bursts out laughing. Watch as Player Three says to her, "Now you're it."

Watch Player Two stand up and begin to make farting noises with her hands and her face, and then begin to turn red from the silence with which she is received. Watch as she yells, "blooby blabby!" and pulls her cheeks away from her face with her fingers and shakes her head pathetically. Cringe as you witness her humiliation. Have mercy, stage a rescue, force a laugh.

"Ha!" she says triumphantly, pointing at you now. "You're it!"

Stand up and walk around the room. Think. You've always been funny. You make people laugh all the time. Try to say something witty about the nature of games in general. Feel the words crumble as you say them. Try something else. Again, something else. Feel your throat run dry. Laugh nervously. Think.

Look around the room, at Player Two, Player Three, and Player Four; silent, stone faced, and sadistically smiling, respectively. Look directly at Player Two, recite an inside joke, a line that always makes her laugh when you're alone. Say in your best Scottish accent, "I discovered the cure for the plague of the twentieth century and now I've lost it!" Watch her face register nothing as she leaves you squirming in the spotlight.

DRINKING GAME #3

PLAYER ONE: You

PLAYER TWO: Your boyfriend Martin

Get drunk with Player Two and his law school friends in the middle of the week. Go to work the next day hungover. When your sixth-grade students notice the scent of whiskey issuing from your pores and wonder aloud about the odor, tell them to "spell it." When they ask, "What do you mean spell it, spell what?" Tell them to "identify the variable." When they ask you what *variable* means, tell them to "look it up." When they find out what variable means and ask you to repeat the assignment, tell them to "rewrite the equation." When they ask you what an equation is, tell them to "spell it." Hold your head in your hands and rub your temples.

When they ask why you decided to become a teacher, tell them to "look it up." When they ask you if you want to have kids of your own one day, tell them to "spell it." When they ask you how they're doing in your class, tell them to "identify the variable." When they start screaming because Mario and Peter are fighting again and Mario's gotten hold of a chair, tell them to remain seated until the end of June. Wrestle the chair away from Mario. Tell Peter to sit down. Quit your job and apply to graduate school.

If you play at either Two- or Three-handed Put, the best put-card deals. Having shuffled the cards, the adversary cuts them; then the dealer deals one to his antagonist, and another to himself, till they have three a-piece: five up, or Put is commonly the game.

PUT, HOYLE'S GAMES

SOLITAIRE

PLAYER ONE: You

After you graduate from college, begin lingering in bookstores, searching for the one book that will tell you all you need to know. Decide you can't find it because it doesn't exist. Decide you must write it. Think about what you must write on the subway. Think about what you must write on walks by the Hudson River. Think about what you must write when you meet up with friends who tell you stories about their day—about the argument Jacob had with his roommate regarding whether or not to hang their pots and pans on the wall in the kitchen, how he hung them without asking her, how she took them down while he was out. Sit down at your desk and wonder how to begin.

Write a short story about a dog whose owner is unhappy with his recent dental work, how his dentist makes perfunctory fillings and how the effects of the dentist's bad work trickle down, affecting the owner's sloppy care of his dog. End the story with each character looking through a different window but finding that through each, the trees outside are all barren. Have the dog start when he sees a squirrel but then give up before even setting out, recognizing the futility. Look away from your computer screen. Wonder if you haven't taken a wrong turn in your writing. If this is really what you wanted to say. Rewrite the story this time from the dog's perspective.

Enroll in a creative writing course for adults at the School of Continuing Ed. Raise your hand and ask the instructor a question about how to get published. Concentrate really hard when he answers, "Look up the address of some literary magazines and send your stories to them. Include a self-addressed stamped envelope." Write down, "self-addressed stamped envelope" in your notebook while mouthing the words.

Go home and rewrite your story again, this time from the perspective of one of the perfunctory fillings. Compose a cover letter to a literary journal you have no interest in reading. Lick the envelope. Stare at it. Think about the things you must write, the things you must say. Email your instructor. Tell him you're considering various graduate programs in creative writing. Would he recommend you?

POSTAL POWWOW

PLAYER ONE: You

PLAYER TWO, PLAYER THREE, PLAYER FOUR. . . : Everyone in line at the post office
at midnight

Familiarize yourself with the taste of envelope glue as you prepare to send applications to twenty different graduate schools scattered across the nation. Make a chart listing the deadline for each. Wait until the end of the very last day to mail them, and then race to the twenty-four-hour post office on Thirty-fourth Street. Rush up the giant stone steps, past the large Greek columns and, once on line, tap your foot nervously. Watch the clock, the minute hand racing you slowly to midnight. Think: You must get that postmark!

Walk across town on Thirty-fourth Street after, imagining your future in Minnesota should you be accepted. Notice the garbage on the sidewalk, the dim storefronts, the street lights lit as if only for you.

See the same faces at the post office again next week. And again the week after. Start to enjoy it, the panic, the urgency, the desperation of others like you, trying to escape their lives through an application to Iowa or Missouri or San Francisco. Read a biography of Fitzgerald while you wait on the long line for Window Three. Remember how you embarrassed yourself at a party last weekend when you got too drunk. Read of a depressed Fitzgerald crouching in a window at the Princeton club, joking pathetically that he would jump. Think: Well, at least I didn't do that! Imagine meeting Fitzgerald at a party today. Imagine him snubbing you. Look up. It's your turn at Window Three.

PIÑATA

PLAYER ONE: You

Open your mailbox. Open it again. Open it again. Now watch as the confetti of rejection letters rains out.

Pretend you're not ashamed when your parents ask if you've heard back. Tell them your work is modern, experimental really, and as a result, easily misunderstood. Say, no, it's not a sign you should do something else. Write a short story about the post office at midnight. Write a short story about the School of Continuing Ed. Make notes for a whole bunch of new short stories you have in mind. Get a new idea for a novel! Watch TV and cry inexplicably during a commercial for Dannon yogurt.

Take a nap.

Wake up and work on your cover letter to the magazine you've decided to send the dog/dentist story to. After reading a Faulkner novel, you've rewritten it to include five different perspectives, one being a retarded character named Benji. It's completely incomprehensible now, which pleases you, because how can anyone tell if it's bad? You're sure your story will be accepted this time, and published, provided you get the cover letter just right, which is why you've been working on the cover letter for months.

"Best wishes?" or "Best regards?" Your closing line will make all the difference. You've read as much in back issues of *Writers' Market* and *Poets and Writers,* magazines you pore over at the Mid-Manhattan Library. Decide you need a break. Walk to the Mid-Manhattan Library and read another issue of *Writers' Market.* Then borrow twenty-nine VHS recordings of movies you've been meaning to see. Put *McCabe and Mrs. Miller* back when you are told the limit is twenty-eight. Go home with your hands full.

Take another nap.

Go downstairs, collect your mail, and find a letter of acceptance to a Master's program in Humanities from your alma mater. Call your parents and tell them, "Great news!" you're going back to school. Decide to do it all differently this time—join a club, learn a foreign language or two, purchase a college sweatshirt, and write a novel on the side.

> The players being all ranged round the table, two of them take the two packs of cards, and as it is of no importance who deals, as there is no advantage in being eldest or youngest, the cards are commonly presented in compliment to some two of the players.
>
> LOTTERY, HOYLE'S GAMES

THE LET'S-THROW-MAGIC-MARKERS-AT-MY-CEILING-FAN GAME!

PLAYER ONE: You
PLAYER TWO: Pedro the bongo player
PLAYER THREE: Alice the xylophone player, possibly Pedro's girlfriend
PLAYER FOUR: Guy with a long braid that he calls a "rat's tail"
PLAYER FIVE: Girlfriend of Guy with the long braid he calls a "rat's tail"
PLAYER SIX: Your friend Jacob
PLAYER SEVEN: Creepy guy called Ben whom it turns out nobody knows

Buy another drink before last call, then invite whomever's left in the bar back to your place. Pick up a few six packs on the way. At your place, while Player Two rolls a joint and Player Three sets up her xylophone and Player Five sits on the floor behind Player Four and unties his "rat's tail" and Player Six prepares a peanut butter and jelly sandwich with the crusts cut off and eats it without asking anyone if they want a bite, which causes controversy among your guests, and Player Seven discovers the hiding place of your pornographic playing cards and begins shuffling the deck declaring, "Double Penetration is wild!" give each player a magic marker. Flick the switch to activate your ceiling fan. Say, "Now everyone, throw the magic markers at the fan!" Laugh and cover your eyes when they spin out wildly in your direction.

HOKEY POKEY

PLAYER ONE: You
PLAYER TWO: The Bastard Felix

When Player Two discovers your collection of children's party records and says, "Sweet! Let's do the Hokey Pokey!" stand up and reluctantly comply with the song's demands: Put your right foot in. Put your right foot out. Put your right foot in and shake it all about. Do the Hokey Pokey and you turn yourself around. Now stop dancing and ask yourself: What is it all about?

DRINKING GAME #4

PLAYER ONE: You
PLAYER TWO: Your friend Janice whom you met at Graduate School

While media outlets are all abuzz over the impending "death of print," decide to start a print-only literary magazine with Player Two. Bicker about the contents. Seethe over the layout. Try to hide your relief when, shortly before the release of the first issue, Player Two informs you she's decided to move to Israel in order to live on a Kibbutz and reevaluate her life choices. Stay behind and devote yourself fully to your new magazine.

Print one thousand copies. Sell fifty at your much-anticipated launch party. Smile brightly when greeting people at the door. Speak enthusiastically about your "vision," leaving out the detail of having founded the magazine in a blackout. Fidget in the corner and furrow your brow when you think no one is looking.

Discover someone was looking when you are emailed photos of the event in which you are fidgeting in the corner, furrowing your brow, thinking no one is looking. Stare at the photos for a long minute before checking the rest of your email. Wonder how you ended up editing a literary magazine—you don't even read literary magazines—in much the same way you wondered how you ended up in bed with that poet after the launch party—you don't even read poetry, not much, not anymore.

When you can't sell the magazines, mail free issues to various colleges, give more away at nearby bookstores, put free copies in the doorways of hip cafés, burrito shops . . . laundromats. Use a few to pack some delicate plates when your friend Reggie asks you to help him move, and store the remaining 750 at your parents' house in Long Island.

When you run into old acquaintances and they ask you, "Whatever became of [Player Two]?" shrug as if the thought had never occurred to you. Say, "[Player] Who?" Cringe when they ask you if you're still "doing the magazine."

PILLOW DIVING

PLAYER ONE: You

PLAYER TWO: Your friend Reggie

PLAYER THREE THROUGH PLAYER SIX: Assorted friends gathered at Reggie's
apartment on Avenue C to watch the game.

Go over to Player Two's to watch the Super Bowl. Have a beer. Have some chips. Have some more beer. Have some more beer. Fall asleep. Wake up and have wings. Wash it down with beer. Have a few more beers. Cheer when everyone else cheers. Then, struck suddenly by the indescribable beauty of a Sunday afternoon, the way it briefly catches your life in mid-blur, like a photograph of someone running, get up off the couch where the other players all sit with their eyes glued to the TV. Get up and go to the window to smoke a cigarette. Sit by yourself and look out. Shiver a little as the cold spills into the room. Turn. Make eye contact with Player Two ten feet away. Put out your cigarette. Look out the window again expecting to see something more than you do—just a few people bundled and rushing. Close the window.

Dance back over to everyone else. Notice your beer can is empty. Dance over to the refrigerator. Console Player Two when his team loses. Find him a bit more handsome than usual. Look into his eyes; suggest he help you take the sofa cushions off the couch in order to arrange them in a line on the floor. Volunteer to go first.

Begin running from the far side of the apartment, from inside the bathroom in order that you have runway enough to build adequate speed. As you approach the pillow landing, prepare for lift off. Now jump! Now dive! Get up and say, "Who's next?"

Should your partner announce that he will play alone, you cannot supersede him and play alone yourself, but must place your cards upon the table, face downwards, no matter how strong your hand may be.

"ON THE LONE HAND" EUCHRE, HOYLE'S GAMES

DRINKING GAME #5

PLAYER ONE: You

PLAYER TWO: Your new boyfriend Philip

Saturday, 2:00 PM. Buy a bottle of vodka and a quart of orange juice and return to your apartment. Pour the vodka and the orange juice into two glasses, giving one to Player Two. Repeat until the bottle is empty.

Walk over to Hudson River Park, remarking on the beautiful day but for those clouds over there, gathering in the distance.

Get caught in a sudden downpour and take shelter beneath a deserted jungle gym. Kiss. When Player Two lies on top of you, unzip his pants, spread your legs, let him push your shorts to the side. Kiss. Wrap your arms around him as he collapses into you.

When the rain stops, suggest walking out to the edge of the pier to take in the view. Forget your sunglasses on the grass beneath the jungle gym. Stop short when a policeman taps Player Two on the shoulder. Wait as the cop writes you each a ticket.

Get into a fight with Player Two the next day. Wait for him to call so that he'll realize you've stopped taking his calls. In the meantime, take the subway down to City Hall to pay the ticket you received for "accessing a children's playground without a child." Squint without your sunglasses as you search for the address.

LIMBO

PLAYER ONE: You

PLAYER TWO, PLAYER THREE, PLAYER FOUR. . . : the other adjuncts at the college
    where you've been hired to teach World Humanities

All the players should line up outside the English office and take turns reminding the secretary to the chair that you're interested in teaching an elective.

> An elder hand composed of the king, nine, and eight of hearts; queen, seven, and five of diamonds; knave, eight, and seven of spades; ace and nine of clubs; with this hand it is most probable you will lose the party. . . .
>
> "HINTS TOWARD PLAYING," REVERSIS, HOYLE'S GAMES

DRINKING GAME #6

ANYONE CAN PLAY!

Go out Monday for drinks with friends. Go out Tuesday for drinks with friends. Look down on people who watch TV, people who watch *Friends* instead of having them and going out with them the way you do. Now go out for drinks with friends on a Wednesday, but do not drink because you are on antibiotics for a sinus infection. Wonder what everyone else is laughing at. Wonder: Who are these assholes you call your friends?

Come to after a week-long bender. Buy a ticket to a movie matinee—a romantic comedy about a woman your age. Bring an oversized bottle of water to rehydrate. Notice the characters in the film don't drink the way you do. Realize you've not gone more than a week without drinking since you were eighteen years old. Wonder if you could have a drinking problem. Decide to test yourself with a month of sobriety. Make that two weeks. Make that a week.

Go out that night with your friends and do not drink. Wonder again what everyone is laughing at. Discover again that you can't stand any of these people. Wonder if it's not a drinking problem you have, but a friend problem. Consider your options:

1. Resume drinking and continue to see your friends.
2. Drink alone in front of your television set—*Law & Order* is almost always on—or by the windowsill looking out into the street, or in front of the computer while you work on your fiction, i.e. upload a new profile photo to your Facebook page.
3. Stop drinking and make new friends.

Put off choosing for as long as possible. Wonder: When did all these games stop being fun?

DRINKING GAME #7

PLAYER ONE: You
PLAYER TWO: Does it matter?

Develop an impressive alcoholic threshold through tireless practice and unerring commitment to the game. Get older. In quieter moments between hangovers and drinking binges, recognize you have a drinking problem and begin to worry about if and when you must quit.

Remember how you used to say, "I'm an alcoholic!" precisely because it wasn't true. Notice how you now say, "I'm not an alcoholic!" for fear that it is. Blush when you reach for the wine bottle at a dinner party. Hope no one notices how quickly you refill your glass.

Catch yourself saying at a cocktail party on a Wednesday evening, "Oh my, I think I'm a bit tipsy," and act surprised by the powerful effects of alcohol on your small frame, as you're sipping only your second drink—aren't you so careful at a cocktail party on a Wednesday night—the second drink, that is, if you don't count the bottle of wine you finished at home while getting dressed, the tepid can of beer in the shower.

On Thursday morning, lie in bed and review the events of Wednesday night. Tell yourself: You didn't do anything so embarrassing so far as you can tell, so why are you so ashamed? Stop beating yourself up! Decide you need to get out of your apartment. Call Player Two and remind her of the two-for-one margarita special at that great Mexican place down the street.

Say, "Sorry I'm late," and arrange your coat on the back of the chair so that the bottom hem drags on the floor. Sit down and say, "Tell me everything," then look around until you find the waiter. Nod. Say, "Look. You can do better." After the third round, laugh loudly at whatever she says before drifting off into a brief silent melancholy. Notice the way the lamplight reflects off the wooden bar in the middle of the room. Notice the perfect dusk receding from the window where you're seated with Player Two. Notice the winter. Feel yourself on the brink of a revelation, feel the world boiling down to now. Tell a joke and back away from *now* slowly. Signal to the waiter. Suggest you do shots.

CHAPTER 10
OUT OF HELL'S KITCHEN

With a changed voice now, and with changed fleece,
I will return a poet, and at the font
Of my baptism I will take the laurel crown.

DANTE, *COMMEDIA: PARADISO*

The only paradise is paradise lost.

MARCEL PROUST, *IN SEARCH OF LOST TIME*

V

7

I had a couch in Hell's Kitchen at the foot of West Fifty-seventh Street. I had a roommate, too.

We were matched up two years before the couch, in a freshman dormitory on Fifth Avenue, just above Washington Square Park. May was standing in the doorway when I arrived. "Are you Iris?" She smiled and came toward me, her arms opening for a hug; I cordially offered my hand. My parents were a few steps behind; handshakes were exchanged all around. Then my father reminded my mother that they were double-parked.

We barely spoke that first night, only when she came out of the bathroom and, finding me already in my bed, asked if it was okay to turn out the lights. For a full week I avoided her—on the second night, I fell asleep in the student lounge; on the third, I crashed on the floor of some guy's room, a transfer student I'd met in the dining hall who'd kissed me on a bench in Washington Square and lay on the floor beside me at two in the morning, leaving his own bed empty; on the fourth, where did I go, who was I with? And the fifth?—until, too tired to stay away any longer, I returned.

It was a Sunday afternoon. May, a musical theater major, sat on her bed, perusing some sheet music, while I, a drama major, sat on mine, updating "the books"—the charts and graphs I kept in the back of my journal organizing my sexual exploits into statistical data. Names were listed along the Y-axis, maneuvers on the X.

I looked up. "How many boys have you kissed?"

May began counting on her fingers some number between three and four. "One of the kisses was iffy," she explained.

"I'm up to thirty!" I said proudly, rounding up.

"Wow," May answered, her eyes wide. "I don't even know that many boys."

Most of my kisses had occurred during my summers in Greece. I'd had French "boyfriends" and German "boyfriends" and Dutch "boyfriends" and Serbian "boyfriends." I showed May the graph I'd made, which resembled a page torn from the immigration records at Ellis Island. Belying the statistics, I wasn't very experienced, however. I'd had sex with just one person, my boyfriend of two years with whom I'd broken up before coming to NYU.

"Who's this?" May asked, referring to the blank spot next to which I'd written, "Patchy."

"I don't remember his name. I kissed him at this discotheque in Volos behind the WC. He had an eye patch." I shrugged.

May had spent almost all of her summers at theater camp where generally the boys didn't go further than stage kissing, she confessed. Then she got out her own journal and decided to make a graph, too. "For science," we agreed.

This first conversation set the tone for our relationship. I would be the scientist, rushing headlong into the unknown, and May, my faithful assistant, her lab coat flapping, as she hurried after.

6

After that Sunday, we were inseparable. Thanksgivings were spent together with my family in Long Island, and spring breaks with hers in Alabama. For a few weeks after our sophomore year, instead of going home, May came to stay with me in Long Island, and the following year, she joined me in Greece.

We were more than friends; we were a duo, a team, a stage act—Iris and May! Exaggerating our differences, we defined ourselves in relief of one another. May, a technical virgin when she arrived in New York, became the petite, wide-eyed, innocent Southern Belle, while I, nominally more experienced, became the tall, jaded, fast-talking New Yorker. More accurately, we were both just kids from the suburbs.

In 1998, at the end of our sophomore year, we decided to get our own place and rented the first and only apartment we saw. If we didn't take it on the spot, the realtor warned us, as we stood a few feet away, huddled in nervous deliberation, someone else would surely scoop us on "this exceptional deal." It was a one-bedroom railroad on the first floor of an old tenement on West Fifty-seventh Street close to Tenth Avenue, a no-man's-land between Hell's Kitchen and the Upper West Side, which I later dubbed, "Hell's Kitchenette."

The apartment had mice and bugs and a deeply slanted wood floor broken up near the radiator where they came and went freely. It had three windows, one in the bedroom that opened onto a narrow airshaft with a view into the neighbor's kitchen, and the other two, eye level with the garbage dump out front and extending all the way up to the ceiling.

"The twelve foot ceilings really add to the spaciousness," the realtor said. The floor of the apartment totaled 425 square feet. "These French doors are brand new," she added, opening and closing the slatted balsa-wood partition that separated the "bedroom" from "the living room." "And it's walking distance from the subway." Three long avenues, it couldn't be much further. But we didn't see any of its flaws then; we saw "brand new French doors," we saw high ceilings, we saw potential. We couldn't believe our luck.

For furniture, we shopped exclusively at the Salvation Army. We bought four red and white rolling chairs—"We'll have everything on wheels!"—and a large glass dining room table, which made May nervous. She was accident-prone and thought the glass frighteningly fragile. She suggested we might do better with something wooden. I brushed off her fears. "How can you possibly break it?" I asked, knocking on its sturdy surface.

And then there was the couch, our favorite piece—a charming striped thing about to buckle beneath our weight. We'd buttress it with magazines, course books, and photographs that we took of each other in our Halloween costumes, in wigs that we donned even when it wasn't Halloween but just a Thursday, and architectural drawings of the fort we built one night by piling all our furniture into two towers and throwing a blanket over the top; we photographed that, too. We took tons of pictures back then, and we'd store them all usefully beneath the cushions of our collapsing couch.

We claimed our respective sides, naming mine "San Juan" and hers "San Sebastian." The couch was an island, we said, surrounded by the flotsam of empty liquor bottles, splayed alternative weeklies, crayon drawings, broken cigarettes, and the occasional renegade Jenga piece, toy soldier, or mix tape. We were Robinson Crusoes of the West Side and engineered the whole apartment to fit our late-adolescent idea of civilization. To get off the island, one had to alight to one of the rolling chairs— our dinghies. We made a game of it—as the floor was on an incline, rolling toward the kitchen was a delightful adventure, but getting back out to the living room, a harrowing ordeal—we made up games for everything.

Peeking down from my pirate's lookout ten feet up—over the edge of my loft bed—I'd call down to May through a megaphone I'd crafted out of colored construction paper: "Who's that on the phone?"

"It's your idiot boyfriend," she'd say, putting him on hold.

"You talk to him." I'd wave my hand. "Pretend you're me."

This was one of our favorite "science experiments." My boyfriends would call and she'd pretend to be me, while I waited to see if and when they would catch on. We conducted lots of "experiments"—the all-Baby-Ruth-and-Diet-Dr-Pepper diet, the "let's-call-all-our-friends-and-tell-them-we're-in-jail-to-see-who-offers-to-bail-us-out" hypothesis, or the time we attempted to package smoke. I took a long hit off a freshly rolled joint, exhaled into an empty Diet Dr Pepper bottle, and spun the cap quickly. We would stop the smoke from diffusing, save it to breathe in again later. Peering through the clear plastic, had we done it? Would we find a little white cloud floating inside tomorrow?

The apartment, like our couch, fell apart almost immediately. Or rather, it had been a wreck to begin with and its flaws just began to show. In the three years we stayed, the paint peeled from the heating pipes; the roof leaked in the bathroom—regularly in a steady drip that increased in urgency every day, sometimes so much it seemed as if it were raining—mice moved in, we could hear them scratching in the walls at night; and the small kitchenette on the far end of the apartment, connected to the bedroom by a long narrow hallway, became crowded with dirty dishes we could not clean fast enough.

And then the light high above the sink blew out. Unable to change it without calling the super, we left it dark. Did we need a kitchen anyway? Blocking it from our minds, we abandoned the room to time. The kitchenette became a frightening unlit cave downstream of our island, filled with culinary relics and crustaceans—worldly cockroaches who'd been living in the apartment long before May and I arrived and would continue to live there long after we left—that we'd venture into only sparingly and always on tiptoe.

Even the glass table exploded. One night, after taking her nightly sleeping pills—May's father, a doctor, mailed them to her regularly—May stood on one of the rolling chairs to close the top window shutter, slipped, and crashed through the table behind her. I wasn't home at the time, but staying the night at my "idiot boyfriend's." At 1:00 AM, the phone rang.

"I'm sorry, Iris. I broke the table," May said groggily.

We rushed over and found a pile of broken glass where the table had been and May, resting in her silk nightgown, on the island nearby. She was bleeding from a small cut on her leg. Miraculously, she'd only a scratch. "I was so worried about you—" I said. "I was so worried," she interrupted, not hearing me through her haze, "that you'd be mad about the table. I know how much you loved it." My boyfriend and I began to clean up. "I made such a mess," she said, as she climbed up to her bed.

The next day, using the legs from the broken table, I made a new table using a large magnetic backgammon board I'd brought back from Greece. May was amazed at my engineering, which involved opening the board which folded in the middle and laying it perpendicular to the parallel lines of the two sets of table legs. "Voila!" I said, "a new table/gaming center!"

We began playing a lot of backgammon after that, and then, growing bored, invented a new game based simply on the set's magnetic properties—if you faced the pieces one direction, they'd stick together, while placing them in opposition caused them to fly apart. Laughing, we'd chase each other all over the board, the winner declared after she'd driven all her opponent's pieces out. We called the game "War."

Your first apartment— a milestone in your journey toward adulthood. We called ours "the clubhouse." Sharing a bedroom, we installed two loft beds, one of seven feet and the other, "the castle," rising a majestic ten feet off the ground—a nice auxiliary for the weighty questions that plagued us in those days. "Should we get high or really high?" I'd ask May, before rolling a joint and alighting with her to one of our beds.

"The castle" had to be specially made. "We don't build 'em higher than seven feet," the man at the loft store told me. I drew a picture of what I wanted. "But you won't have enough room above you!" he insisted. "Let me worry about that," I said. To stabilize it, the structure had to be attached to the wall, and a safety partition added to the side to keep me from rolling over and falling to my death. "It's magnificent," I said when it was finished. I then set about covering it with white Christmas lights, which I attached to The Clapper, so that every morning it glowed with May's applause.

Turning the radio on, we'd climb up to May's bed and sit with our legs dangling over the edge and look through the airshaft at our neighbors looking back. I passed May the joint. "Sitting on the edge of my bed . . ." May sang when "Dock of the Bay" came on, "watchin' the time roll ahead. Watchin' our neighbors walk in, and then we watch them walk away again. We're just sittin' on the top of my bed, wastin' time. . . ." I'd whistle, exhale a long plume, and then hatch an idea for our next home improvement project—"a lifeguard chair next to the window! We keep the top shudders open so we can look out on the street, and the bottom shutters closed to maintain our privacy!"

Today, when people see photographs of us from that time, thinking we were perhaps ten or twelve years old, they are shocked when I tell them we were nearing twenty-one, for even our expressions during that period had become vaguely childlike.

For decoration, I covered the inside of our apartment door with my steadily growing collection of black-and-white postcards, among which I hid two black-and-white photos of May and me. May: looking glamorous at a masquerade ball we'd thrown at our Soho dorm for my last birthday. Me: in a vintage swimsuit, half submerged in the kiddie pool we'd installed in our dorm-room for the "pool party" we'd thrown before that—we'd moved all our furniture, including our beds, into the hall.

In the corner, where the glass table had been, we placed a mini-trampoline we'd rescued from a dumpster. We were always on the look-out for great new pieces, so when we spotted a twelve-foot-long cardboard candy cane lying on the curb among the trash, we immediately knew we needed it. Spilling out from a loft party in Soho at 4:00 AM, I saw it first. Our only thought was of how to transport it; the thing was so large, so unwieldy. We ended up holding it against the outside of a cab, our arms looped around it through the open windows.

Four in the morning. May riding shotgun. Me in the back passenger seat. The cab driver yelling when I drop my end, again, onto the road. He stops the car short and I wake with a start before opening the back door to fetch my end. The driver lays into me. May rushes to my defense, telling him indignantly, "Stop yelling! Can't you see she's tired?"

When we did finally get the thing home, it was much too large for our small apartment. It would fit neither upright nor sideways, and so we had to place it on a diagonal, a candy cane hypotenuse bisecting the living room, extending from top right corner to lower left. Accessing the bathroom from that day forward required an impromptu round of limbo—another game!

Winter nights, lying aloft in our skyscraper beds, unable to sleep, we'd speculate about our futures. Blinking in the dark, I'd imagine a husband for May, describing various scenarios in which her husband, a concert pianist who'd grown unhappy and jealous of May's tambourine playing (I'd given her a tambourine for her birthday), wished, midlife, to switch to the tuba. "The tuba won't pay the bills!" May would protest. He'd be alcoholic and would hide his schnapps in the large horn, which May would find and drink herself, resulting in more terrible fights.

Then she'd do the same for me: My husband would be a very wealthy businessman whom I'd despise and who would give me a gaggle of children who'd also irritate me. Regularly, I'd lock myself in the parlor where I'd remain all day drunk, playing with an electric train set and maniacally working a Hula-Hoop to keep svelte. I'd give explicit instructions to the servants to keep the children out of the west wing. My hair would grow wild, my nails long and curling.

Sometimes we'd remark on the oddness of our being twenty years old and sharing a bedroom. "Do you think our husbands will mind the sleeping arrangements?" May asked, giggling through the dark, having just described a future in which, despite all the changes time would bring, the condition of our shared bedroom, with its twin loft beds soaring high into the night, would remain. I laughed. "They'll just have to get used to it, I guess."

5

Fall, winter, spring. And in summer we'd separate, leaving the apartment to boil without us. May would return to her family in Alabama and I'd visit mine in Greece where I'd update "the books."

"An influx of Germans," I reported upon my return, summarizing my amorous adventures to May.

For all the privileges of summer, however, we couldn't wait to get back, to resume the duo, to resume our experiments. And so, in the August before our senior year, we returned two weeks early. May would use the time to go on auditions, she told her parents, while I, having already changed majors, told mine I'd need to prepare for my upcoming internship at *The New Yorker*.

It was the summer of 1999 and the city was hot. The buildings themselves seemed almost to be melting. Every day brought reports of record highs. A weatherman fried an egg on the sidewalk. The mayor reminded us, "Drink water to prevent dehydration, check on neighbors, the elderly, and seek out the city's air-conditioned cooling centers." Surviving the heat became the first priority of every New Yorker. May and I had no air conditioner but had set up a circuit of fans to ameliorate the blaze, to blow the hot air into our loft beds and all around the apartment, across the trampoline, under the candy cane, over the island, and through to the next room—a trade wind you could follow on one of our rolling chairs.

Submitting to the heat and its command to do as little as possible, we forsook our previous plans and spent the days lounging on our island, sipping cold beer and waiting for our pot dealer to arrive. We'd turn up the radio—always oldies, always CBS FM—and May, growing impatient, would bounce on the mini-trampoline, a full-body alternative to waving a paper fan. I told her this would only make her hotter, but she persisted, up and down, singing along to her favorite song— "Big Girls Don't Cry"—resting only to rehydrate during weather and traffic updates.

With my bare feet dangling over the shores of our couch, I was busy with my hobbies—drawing more Naked Woman cartoons, rendering crayon outlines of my face onto construction paper, or clipping the occasional article from the *Weekly World News:* "Alien Endorses Bush for Presidency—the same alien that endorsed Clinton in 1996!" I taped it to the wall next to the calendar where I wrote my itinerary for the month: "Prepare a list of demands and sell to bank robbers," "Decide to change tomorrow," "Decide to change tomorrow," "Entry into martyrdom. . . ."

In anticipation of our delivery, sometimes I'd design a new pot-smoking device. Since my visit to Amsterdam three summers before ("field research" I'd called it, showing May photographs of the Dutchmen I'd kissed), I'd developed my own style of joint-rolling, which involved colored construction paper, numerous double-wide rolling papers and index cards. "I'm the Jeff Koons of marijuana para-phernalia!" I announced, holding up my latest creation. Atop exagger-ated sculptural filters—bulbous cones and chimerical, animal-shaped hollows—I'd poke a small hole where I'd attach the joint. "I can't wait for your retrospective," May marveled.

Like this, lost in our respective delights, we'd wait for a bike mes-senger to buzz our door, and then, beer cans in hand, we'd receive him with flirtatious smiles and an offer to share a blunt with us, if we thought he was at all cute.

That same August, "drunk and delirious from the heat," so I claimed, I tongue-kissed a few strangers and was renamed "Hurricane" at a local bar, while May met a Frenchman and began to doubt roman-tic love. It was during that August, after the Frenchman had disap-peared, that May, still a virgin, announced her decision to have sex.

All our friends were aware of and had discussed often the fact of May's virginity, so much so that her virginity began to seem less a function of time and more a permanent characteristic, like the shape of one's nose or the landscape of lower Manhattan. Her decision to change it thus, seemed drastic. It was as if she'd announced the leveling of a historic building with a subsequent plan to put up a condo in its place. Our reactions, naturally, were mixed. We were all in favor of progress, sure, and yet, shouldn't May be preserved as she was? Couldn't we keep her virginal, declare her a landmark, and convert her into a library or something? Her decision shocked everyone, a feat that, up until then, had been *my* specialty.

4

In the waning blaze of August, we descended upon the Coliseum bookstore. Sweating, high, and ever studious, we bought *Hot Sex: How to Do It*; *Sex Tips for A Straight Girl from a Gay Man*; *The Good Girls Guide to Great Sex;* and the more romantic *How to Make Love to a Man*, which cited *The Best of Neil Diamond* as the ultimate sex soundtrack.

Drinking through the afternoons we read intently, copying notes for perplexing maneuvers on index cards, which we'd compare over lunch. May was a wizard in the kitchenette and sometimes (before we abandoned the room completely), I'd stand beside her, stoned, watching as she performed her magic on a box of Kraft macaroni and cheese. Red-eyed, nodding, "Miraculous!" I'd say, after she let me taste a bit.

Back on the couch with our bowls, May asked me about "the up and over" hand-job technique she'd read about earlier that morning, if I'd ever done it. "I *may* have done it once accidentally. But I'm not sure I could repeat it is the thing." For dessert, we'd have Rice Krispies Treats laced with pot—expediently done so by simply placing a green sprig on top of an opened "Fun Size" package.

Pen in hand, I informed May of my goal to write a self-help book called, *How to Be the Worst Sex of His Life!* "It's an unfilled niche in the marketplace. I'm reading to find out what *not* to do." I had lots of goals back then—actress, cartoonist, novelist, gentleman farmer, reverse-stripper (I would begin naked and, one article at a time, get dressed. This would take a while as I like to layer—underwear to overcoat, then gloves, scarf, and hat—and then I'd walk off stage, out into the audience, out the front door and into the cold winter night!). Self-help author was but one more.

May's goal was sex itself. "Do you want to fall in love and then have sex? Or fall in sex and then have love?" She wasn't sure, she told me. It was more the fear of the buildup that had inspired her to build down. "Disarmament," I interjected, "got it." "I just don't want to be a virgin anymore," she answered.

Unsure of how to proceed or with whom, May continued to prepare for sex as if for nuclear attack. "Up and over!" I yelled now and then, calling a drill.

Then, as the summer cooled into fall, May met someone. Felix took her on a whirlwind date of free events in Central Park, made her laugh while she ate a hot dog, told her she was beautiful when she laughed with her mouth full, held her hand, and kissed her up against a very old tree, she told me happily, before he didn't call again for a full week.

Lying aloft, unable to sleep on the third night of his silence, May began making fun of his ugly face, cursing his ridiculous hair, and related something stupid he'd said about rowboats. She'd laughed out of pity; it wasn't funny at all. I agreed that she could do much better and told her so over and over again. "He's a fool," I repeated, until she fell asleep.

A few days later, arriving home from an adventure at the drugstore's makeup aisle, our answering machine blinked with a message from Felix. I cheered and suggested we conduct "an experiment." May didn't laugh or agree, but just quietly found his number and took the phone with her into the bathroom.

After that, they began seeing each other pretty regularly. Then, one day in October, just as the weather was really beginning to change and the wind had begun to sing through the leaves the way it always does in early fall, I arrived home, slightly drunk after a long day of "work" at *The New Yorker,* and found May sitting by herself on the couch, her face serious. She'd been waiting for me, she said. She had something to tell me, she said, her face breaking into a horrible smile. "I did it, Iris!"

We went out that night—Felix had to return to L. A., she explained, so he'd gone to his parents' place upstate to pack, which is why he wouldn't be coming along. On our way to the bar, we stopped at the drugstore to buy a new disposable camera. "To capture my post-sex glow," she said cheerfully.

At the bar, I told her I knew how she felt, thinking one moment that it meant nothing and the next, that it meant everything. She said that wasn't it and looking over her shoulder at the camera, shot a sultry expression. All night she studied her reflection, in the mirror behind the bar, in the bathroom, in her makeup compact, in shop windows on our way home. "Do I look different?" she asked me.

When we got the pictures back the next day, she was disappointed. Instead of looking sexy, worldly, and knowing, she looked uncertain, as if all night she'd been asking the camera, "What now?" Following a brief perusal and handoff to me, she took all the photos and filed them under the couch. Then, taking her place on the cushions above, she asked if we shouldn't call the dealer. I shrugged and got out the number.

With the approach of Halloween, May grew nervous and every day more distracted. During our costume-planning session, I'd had to ask repeatedly if she would be able to get hold of red swimming trunks by October 31st; we were going to be "Siamese Superheroes." I was sitting on the floor, sewing two T-shirts together to make one with two neck holes. We'd share the cape. "May? Are you listening?" Felix was still in L. A. and not sure when he'd be back.

"He said he missed me," she said later through the dark. He'd called that afternoon; she'd taken the phone into the bathroom again. "I mean, I don't expect him not to see other girls or anything," she said from her bed. I just wanted to do it, you know?"

"I know."

"He probably thinks I'm in love with him or something."

When Felix finally returned to New York a month later, she began seeing him as often as possible, wanting, I figured, to stay close to that part of herself she'd lost, what he had somehow gained. Or perhaps it was her heart, not her virginity she wanted back. Or perhaps I'm completely wrong, and she wasn't trying to get it back at all. Perhaps she had given it.

3

That fall, I underwent a change myself, slowing down so much with men that I became nearly impossible, telling one as he leaned in for a kiss, that "a long calm must precede the storm."

"I need time to sort my findings," I told May, after returning early from a date one night. I'd always felt compelled to supply an explanation, especially now when I didn't really have one. "I'm still organizing data," I said, alighting onto the island where she was sipping a beer and watching TV.

Felix spent most of that winter in L. A., picking up small parts in films and extra work when he could get it, and now and then returning to New York for short visits. When he was in New York, he stayed with us, sharing May's loft bed across the room from mine. In the morning, he'd roll a joint, which they'd smoke in the living room while reading *Backstage,* before taking off together to see about an open call.

Wishing to get a head start on her career, May graduated a semester early, so in January, instead of commuting downtown to classes with me, she found a waitressing position at a restaurant in our neighborhood. She was given an apron and immediately went out to buy some sensible shoes and a memo pad. A day later, she began waiting tables as if it were the most natural thing. Then, with the money she saved from her first few paychecks, she purchased a new couch for our apartment. A large blue sofa bed, so that when Felix came to visit, he'd have a place to sleep.

I finished my internship at *The New Yorker* and my relationship with one of its editorial assistants that December. In January, while May worked, I focused on my studies, specifically on my thesis, "Melancholy and Mania in the Creative Tradition," and watched as May rushed toward the ringing phone, as she locked herself in the bathroom to speak in hushed tones, as she borrowed my colored construction paper to prepare a valentine for Felix.

On graduation day, Felix happened to be in town. And since he'd forgotten to return his cap and gown after his own graduation two years earlier, he decided to come with us and graduate a second time. The three of us exited the subway on Eighth Street and began walking toward Washington Square Park where commencement was being held. On a bench outside the school's fitness center, we stopped and sat down. Felix, decked out in his wrinkled purple robe, rolled a joint— "Our last one as college students!" he announced.

The park was blooming with purple gowns, hundreds of faces I'd never seen before. A stage had been erected in the center, above the fountain, far away. Felix cheered histrionically during the speeches. Some students nearby asked him to knock it off. "Hey, it's my graduation, too!" he yelled back. After they introduced "the Class of 2000," Felix stood up and clapped louder than everyone else. "Come on, Iris. Stand up!" Felix shouted. I stood up and screamed a little, too, not sure if something was beginning or ending, if it all added up to a loss or a gain.

Afterwards, Felix had an audition and, kissing May goodbye, disappeared uptown. May and I walked over to Broadway to meet our parents. Though I had spent a lot of time with May's family, and she with mine, this was the first time our families met each other. Conservatives, for the most part our fathers got on well, though my dad leaned toward libertarianism while May's toward Christian republicanism. They dealt with their differences fairly easily, however, by ignoring them and moving on to a conversation about us, their bright and talented girls who'd both ordered the lobster.

There is a photograph my father took that day of May and me. We are walking up ahead of everyone on our way to lunch. We are side by side, a stretch of sidewalk at our backs. We are walking purposefully, as if we know exactly where we are going, though it took us no less than a half hour to settle on a restaurant, no less than a half hour of our trying and failing to recall the exact location of that really nice place we'd gone to once together, the one with the beautiful garden.

2

I made arrangements to leave for Greece immediately following commencement. I didn't have a job, but I wasn't worried. I was confident about the future the way one is confident of the contents of a package before you open it, before you realize the coffee maker you ordered off the TV is missing a part, or the closet organizer that's going to revolutionize the way you store your clothes needs first to be put together.

At the same time, May got a lead role in a touring company. "I'm going to be Peter Pan!" she squealed, watching me pack. "We'll be traveling around the country all summer and part of fall, so I guess we'll get back around the same time," she said. She climbed up to her bed and sat with her legs dangling over the edge. "Felix says he'll visit me on the road."

I stayed in Greece for four months, longer than I ever had before, writing letters to May and to a handful of ex-boyfriends, using our correspondence as an opportunity to hone my prose style. I was particularly weak when it came to botanical descriptions and if I were going to be a writer, I considered, I'd most certainly need to learn the names of more trees.

When I wasn't writing letters describing the wind through the poplars, I worked on my novel about all the drunks I'd gotten to know in the hallway bars of my Hell's Kitchen neighborhood, about one in particular, the fictional Hank, a twenty-seven-year-old alcoholic looking for redemption in his glass. Twenty-seven seemed so far away, and I had to work hard to imagine what that might be like. Trying to imitate hard-earned wisdom, I wrote metaphors for each drink: "Whisky is an accomplice," I scribbled in my notebook, before taking off on my bike to weave back and forth through the olive groves. I'd ride and dream about the characters in my book, squinting my eyes to see them, wondering what they might do next, in a way that I had not yet wondered about myself.

1

I returned to New York in October with four spiral notebooks containing my novel, ready to put my party girl days behind me and begin my new life as an author. It was late evening when I arrived and fit my key into the lock. May wasn't home, but there were candles that had recently been lit and an overpowering smell of gas. I went into the kitchen, which was bright—the light bulb had been replaced—found the open nozzle on the stove and turned it off.

I returned to the living room, which was a mess—piles of discarded clothes I didn't recognize. It was a mess nearly identical to the one I'd left, except none of it was mine. The relatively new sofabed was opened and covered by a tangle of sheets. It took up most of the room and I had to turn sideways to get around it, to make my way to the window to let in some air.

May arrived later on that night, with Felix in tow. They each gave me a hug. May handed me a beer and then, saying she hadn't realized I was arriving today, apologized for the mess. "Sit down," she said, motioning to the now closed sofabed.

She'd quit the show, she said. It was a lousy production and she missed Felix. Somewhere in Indiana, at a Hooter's restaurant where the whole cast had gone as a joke—she showed me the cool T-shirt she bought there—she'd begun crying and told the director right then she had to quit.

She asked me about my trip, about this summer's crop of boy-friends, about "the books." Felix sat beside her, listening. I said that

I'd had a fine time, that I'd tell her all about it later, but that I was tired now from traveling. I left my beer half-full on the coffee table and went into the next room.

She thought I was coming back tomorrow, she repeated, apologizing again as I climbed up into my bed. That's why it was so messy. She'd clean it all up tomorrow.

May turned on the assortment of fans and closed the doors to the living room where she and Felix unfolded the sofa. For a while I lay awake, noticing the shorter loft bed of May's empty and listening to the muffled voices coming from the next room.

IV

5

My future plan, hatched on the plane ride home, was to take a night job. I imagined myself a librarian, serving the graveyard shift at the big building on Forty-second Street. In luxurious silence I'd wander the stacks, pausing occasionally to shelve something. I would be lonely, weary, but comforted by my great mission to complete my first novel.

When I went to the library to apply, however, I was shocked to discover that there *was* no night shift. It was closed in the evenings just like every other library. I asked the librarian for an application anyway, and then, with a stack of forms that I barely looked at, I wandered around the building, realizing only then that I'd never actually been inside.

There was something hateful about the place, I decided, as I skipped down the front steps after. Something awful about its solemnity, its large hollows, its people who went steadily about their work. The way no one had looked up when I came in, had acknowledged my arrival, the way no one had recognized me. Outside, the autumn air was brisk and cool, the large stone lions implacable in their gaze. I walked home.

I spent the next days and weeks perusing the want ads of newspapers I'd never read before, while May and Felix smoked pot and blasted classic rock—Pink Floyd and Led Zeppelin tapes I'd brought back from Long Island but never listened to. Searching for songs on Napster, the two of them sat in front of my computer, Felix marveling at how fast a Van Halen track was downloading, especially compared to the Beatles song that had required three separate tries and forty-five minutes.

Unable to find any office job for which I was qualified—When was I supposed to have learned PowerPoint and Excel?—I took a temporary job at Barnes & Noble in Union Square. It was the holiday season and they needed extra hands, they said at the information desk, after I'd ordered *The Beautiful and Damned* (there were no copies left) and, spur-of-the-moment, asked if they were hiring. It was the next best thing to a library, I figured.

My primary responsibility was re-shelving the books customers left on the ground, in the bathroom, on the magazine rack, or in the café on the second floor. But I spent most of the time trying to read all the books I hadn't in college, going from aisle to aisle in order to avoid the undercover store security guard, whose constant staring caused me to reread the same lines again and again so that I never got passed, "Stately, plump . . ."

I ended up spending as much money as I made, buying the books I'd started at work, thinking I'd finish them at home, but then, once home, finding it even more difficult to concentrate. "I had a farm in Africa, at the foot of the Ngong hills," I read, before May and Felix turned on the TV. "The Giants are 'bout to tear it up!" Felix howled.

"For a long time I used to go to bed early. Sometimes, when I had put out my candle, my eyes would close so quickly that I had not even time to say, 'I am falling asleep.' And half an hour later the thought that it was time to go to sleep would awaken me; I would make as if to put away the book which, I imagined, was still in my hands, and to blow out the light. . . ." I read at 2:00 AM, before the locks began to click and May and Felix stumbled in.

"Beer and bacon!" Felix sang, pushing his way through the bedroom below on his way to the kitchen. Marcel Proust had been a dilettante, I read in the book's introduction. Then at thirty years old, after years of constant partying, he quit that life and took to bed where he wrote his masterpiece. Peels of laughter in the next room, Felix saying, "I'm comin' to getcha!" I lay in bed ten feet in the air, trying to imagine a manuscript in loose pages all around me.

Some evenings the store would host readings on the fourth floor, and I'd hope to be assigned there so I might watch. On a Sunday, George Plimpton read from *Pet Peeves*, his new book for pet lovers. I took out my notebook and wrote, "If I ever get a dog, name him 'Peeve.'"

No one came. It was a cold December evening and through the windows you could see Union Square, lit up with festive lights as shoppers teemed in and out of the outdoor holiday market. The room from where I looked out was almost empty. There was a small platform set up before the window and one hundred or so chairs, as if they were anticipating a large audience. Among the one hundred, eight or nine seats were occupied, four filled by the homeless who hung around the store all day, and another handful by those who'd sat down to read a magazine or book they didn't plan to buy.

The store manager made a brief introduction. A few people applauded, mostly staff. I stopped what I was doing—reading *How to Write a Movie in 21 Days* (I'd been assigned to Film and TV that afternoon)—and watched Mr. Plimpton, a white-haired man in his seventies, ascend to the podium, tripping on the second step.

Adjusting the microphone, he made a joke about the turnout and then chuckled softly to himself. "The audience" did not respond. No one, it seemed, had any idea who he was, only that he was old and had written a very thin book marketed to pet enthusiasts. After a moment, those who'd turned to listen went on browsing. I was behind the information desk when a New School student, Dave, who'd been working there a full year, stood beside me and said, "That's George Plimpton. He's like a legend and now look at him."

I nodded. "What's he a legend for?"

Dave shrugged. "You know, writing or whatever."

The image of Mr. Plimpton tripping as he made his way up to the podium stayed with me the whole thirty-block walk home. He seemed so embarrassed—he'd blushed—though hardly anyone had seen it happen.

I was horrified to find out that no matter what job I took, the one at the bookstore, or the other I got a few months later as a restaurant hostess at a sports bar in Greenwich Village, I'd be required to work. "I just want to *have* the job, I don't want to *do* the job," I told May at home, trying to make light of it. In truth, I wouldn't have minded doing any job, had I not been so bad at every one I tried.

Wondering about the future now, I felt frightened. It didn't seem to be up ahead of me anymore but suddenly at my back, as if my potential, all my time, was spent.

I lay awake in bed every night, trying to ignore the muffled sounds coming from the next room. The clicking of channels. The light from the TV flickering through the slats of our "brand new French doors." Carefree giggles broken by coughs, as May and Felix passed a joint back and forth.

In my dreams, I saw myself standing alone in a clear plastic forest, surrounded by a dense fog. I'd raise my hand before my eyes but the fog was so thick, without beginning or end; I was trapped in a cloud that would not disperse. And I could not find my hand. I could not find myself.

4

While I floundered, May flourished. Felix had moved back to New York unofficially and was now staying with May—with us. They stopped bothering to refold the sofa-bed, and so it remained splayed out all day long, filling the living room and making it difficult for me to get to my desk. Finally, I said something.

"Of course!" May said and began apologizing profusely.

"I'm sorry to mention it, it's just—"

"No, it's my fault!" she snapped, as if I were trying to take something from her.

"Well, thank you. Also, I hate to be a pest, but it would help if you could tell Felix not to leave food on my desk. I kind of need some clear space to work."

"Absolutely." She nodded vigorously and smiled. "Anything else?"

Around this time, May began tending bar at The Village Idiot, a dive famous for its jukebox full of country music, a mounted boar's head covered in the bras of past patrons, and its dancing. Dressed in half-tops and Daisy Dukes, the lady bartenders would climb on the bar to perform a two-step, pausing now and then to pour directly from the bottle into a customer's open mouth. Drinks were cheap, making it a hotspot for bikers, truck drivers, and editorial assistants. I'd wound up there myself after a few *New Yorker* parties.

"It's so cool," she told Felix and me, after her first shift. "They actually *want* us to drink on the job." Though she disliked the half-tops, she liked the money and the days off it afforded, she told me—she and Felix could follow up on auditions, or else fill in as extras on the film shoots Felix often heard about. Plus, once or twice a week she was assigned a day shift, which, if less profitable, was more enjoyable because Felix could come in and stay the afternoon.

While May served the regulars, Felix sat at the end of the bar. She'd rig the jukebox so he could play his classic rock selections for free and slip him free beers of whatever was on tap. Then, when her shift was over, they'd come home and reopen the sofa-bed I'd closed.

3

Morning. Felix in the living room, in his underwear, rolling a joint, before heading purposefully into the kitchenette to make breakfast. He had restored the light bulb and dug out the dishes. "It's cheaper to eat in," he told May.

Putting some classic rock on the stereo and settling down to eat in front of the muted TV, they enjoy a leisurely breakfast while consulting *Backstage* for help in deciding what to do next. May doesn't have work today, so they can "decide" for hours.

Removing a half-eaten apple Felix has left on my desk, I ask, sheepishly, about their plans.

"You wanna come to the park with us?" May answers charitably.

"No, thank you. I was just wondering what your plans were, so I could try to plan mine around them; I thought I might do some work," I say nervously, fingering the slim stack of notebooks I brought back from Greece.

"Oh sure," they answer together. "We'll get out of your way." Three or four hours later, they keep their promise.

Alone at last, the sun disappearing, I sit, frozen in front of my computer, with one of my notebooks opened in my lap.

Monday . . . Felix rolling a joint . . . Tuesday . . . Felix in the kitchen making breakfast . . . Wednesday . . . May and Felix on the couch next to me . . . Thursday . . . Bugs Bunny on the TV saying,

"If you can't beat 'em, join 'em" . . . Friday . . . May laughing as Felix tickles her . . . I exhale a long plume of smoke and say I'm going out.

I began going out as often as possible, avoiding the apartment as I'd avoided our dorm the first week of school, except now, because I was twenty-two, I went to bars. "Research," I told myself, "for my novel." I brought a little notebook with me to write down my ideas.

And then, one day, too exhausted to stay away any longer and feeling I'd accumulated more than enough "source material," I came home, pushed the door open—it was unlocked—and came upon May and Felix having sex on the couch. When I returned a half hour later, I announced my decision to move.

That weekend I visited my parents in Long Island, who explained that moving was something one did *after* one found a job.

"I can't afford to make any changes until I find a job," I told May and Felix when I returned, as if it were my decision, "so I'm going to stay after all."

2

If May and I had been a duo in college, she, the virginal lab-assistant and I, the worldly scientist, who were we now? Who was she if she wasn't hurrying after me, and who was I if I was no longer forging ahead? Moreover, who were we to each other?

"Felix has been here every night this week."

"It's my apartment, too, and if I want to have my boyfriend over, that's my right."

"I'm paying *half* the rent, not a third."

"If you were the one with the boyfriend, we wouldn't even be having this discussion."

"You're right; I wouldn't make my relationship your problem."

Just as we dreaded parting ways all those summers prior, now, though we would never say so, we couldn't stand to be in the same room together.

"I'm an intruder in my own home!" I complained to Caroline, to The Captain, to Jacob, to Lex, even to Reggie, whom I'd started dating in part just to avoid going home.

"I never liked her," Caroline said, putting her cigarettes on the bar.

"I don't get it. If she wants to live with her boyfriend, why doesn't she just move?" asked The Captain.

"I think I have a lamp fetish," said Jacob, fondling the price tag on a reading-light at Crate and Barrel.

"Here's what you say: 'Fuck you both. Now get the fuck out!'" said Lex, before stealing one of my fries. "I like your shirt by the way. Did you make it?"

"But she's still my friend," I told Reggie when he came out of the bathroom and found me in his bed, my "Second Base" T-shirt crumpled on the floor.

"It's not her, but the situation," I told all of them, eventually coming to her defense. "It'll pass," I said wearily, trying to focus on the big picture, a perspective on which I had tutored May back in college. When faced with the decision of whether to go out on a Tuesday night or stay home and study, we'd weigh the pros and cons, and then I'd tip the scales by announcing, "Big Picture!" Life was about living, I reminded her. "Big Picture!" she'd agree at the bar an hour later, laughing as she raised her glass to mine.

What was important, I reminded myself now, was our friendship, for if I had achieved anything of lasting value while at college, it was this relationship with May. May, with whom I shared everything. May, whom my father sometimes accidentally called my sister. May and I would eventually leave this apartment, and then, a bit more grown up, our friendship would resume its natural course, I told myself, kept telling myself.

Since I'd announced my decision to stay though, conditions at home only worsened. Every time I walked in the door, May would abruptly stop speaking—while I had retreated inward after gradua- tion, May had become more social, having new friends over to the apartment almost every day—and I was certain it was because she had been talking about me. Silently, I'd pass through the living room, feel- ing their eyes on me as I took off my coat and inched uncomfortably toward the bedroom, before closing its flimsy "French" partition.

Turning on the fan, I'd climb the ten feet up to my bed to lie down, for it was the only semi-private place in our apartment. With two feet of space between me and the ceiling, what had once been a fun, cre- ative use of space—"just think of all the top halves of apartments that go unused!" I'd told May two years earlier—now felt like a coffin.

1

In April, I was marking time at my hostessing job and planning the rise of my T-shirt empire, when my parents called to remind me that my lease was coming up for renewal.

They were surprised it hadn't arrived in the mail already since the lease was set to expire in just a few days. I said I'd take a look, that "it's probably around here somewhere," underneath Felix's dirty underwear, is what I thought but didn't say.

My mom called to remind me about the lease again the next day, and so, the day after that, I finally got around to asking May if she'd seen the thing. She shrugged, said no, said she'd keep an eye out and tell me when it came. Then she went out. Since there was only one day left before our lease expired and since my parents were on my case, I dug through my desk until I found the landlord's number. I figured it must have gotten lost in the mail and that I'd just ask him to resend it, if not go to his office and pick up a new copy myself.

"I have the signed lease right here," he said when I got him on the phone. "Your roommate dropped it off ten minutes ago." He chuckled awkwardly, the way a person does when nothing funny has happened. "Let me see. I'm looking at it right now. You would be Iris Smyles, the young lady whose name is crossed out?"

"Yes, I'm Iris. But I never received it. I mean that's not legal, is it?"

He paused. "I'll send out another lease today." And then, with a combination of annoyance and pity, he sighed. "Talk to your roommate. Send it back when you've got it sorted out. I take it you'd like to renew?"

May arrived home a half hour later. I was on the couch, waiting for her when she walked in.

"I know what you did."

Her eyes went wide. "I'm sorry," she said immediately.

"If you're sorry, than why'd you do it?" I asked, my mouth splitting into a painful smile.

"I didn't want to. My parents told me to. I told them I didn't want to, but I didn't know what else to do. They want me to stay because it's walking distance from the subway and close to all of my auditions."

I stood up. "You think I want to live with you? I'm not moving because I don't have a job. Because I *can't* move. If you want to live with Felix, that's great! Find a new place! You didn't have to *lie* to me."

"I'm sorry," she repeated and, wiping her tears, she disappeared out the door.

I sat back down and felt sick. I was sitting in the same place an hour later when the phone rang. It was my mother. Well, my mom on one phone and my dad on another.

"May's parents just called us, Iris." My mother paused. "We need to talk to you," my father finished.

I heard sniffling, my mother crying. My father went on softly, "May's father just called," he repeated. "He says you've been drinking a lot, that May can't live with you anymore because of it. He said he became worried on his last visit when he saw you after May's play. He says you're an alcoholic, that you're in trouble, and that we need to take you home."

"May's play was a year ago, Dad. Odd that he should wait until now to voice his *concern*. Odd that he should want to discuss this immediately after they were caught trying to steal the apartment?"

I told them what happened, explained that this was clearly another tactic to get me out.

My parents went silent. "Yeah," my father said at last, "I knew something wasn't right in his voice."

I promised them that I was okay. I promised them that I was okay. I promised them that I was okay. And then I said it again.

"So you're okay?" my mother asked weakly.

"I'm *fine*, Mom. *Please* don't worry."

"I can't understand it," my father mumbled. "She was like a sister to you. Is that lousy little apartment really worth so much?"

It was night when May walked in, drunk, her face stained with tears. She told me that she was sorry again.

"Your parents called," I said, calmly.

"I told them not to."

"Do you know how worried my parents are?"

"I told them not to," she sniffled.

"Why are you crying?" I asked, smiling brightly.

"Because I feel terrible about what happened."

"I suppose I should apologize to you then, since you're feeling so down."

She looked at the ground.

"Poor you," I laughed. "Trapped in an apartment with a dangerous alcoholic. You must be so frightened. Maybe I should call *your* parents and tell them the real reason you want me out? Tell them their sweet Catholic daughter has been shacking up with her freeloading boyfriend, and when she's not working at a tits-and-ass bar downtown, all she does is fuck, drink, and do drugs, and so my presence here really cramps her style. There's a whole lot I could say about you, May. But I wouldn't. I didn't."

"I told them not to call your parents. My father did it on his own!"

"You told them all that stuff about me! *You* did! It was *your* choice! You know what I told my parents about you?

She shook her head.

"Nothing," I shouted, "I didn't tell them anything, because you're my friend!"

III

I don't know how to be angry. This isn't a virtue but a flaw in my character. I forgive people before they've even asked to be forgiven, before they even want to be.

What was I supposed to do? Never speak to her again? All of a sudden treat her differently than I had all five years prior? It seemed so much easier to let go of the events of the day, of the year, than to let go of the last five. I forgave May after only a few minutes, not because I'm magnanimous, but because I'm weak, because forgiving her seemed so much easier than staying angry, because we were still living together, because she was standing right there.

"I'm sorry," she said again, staring at her feet.

I nodded uncomfortably. "I know," I said, looking down at my own.

So then what? What do you do after all is forgiven? May and I, just as we had on the night she lost her virginity, decided to go out and celebrate.

We went to the same bar on Ninth Avenue, ordered a round and raised our glasses, toasting the renewal of our friendship. We laughed and carried on like we hadn't in a long time. We took turns playing songs on the jukebox. "Dock of the Bay," "Big Girls Don't Cry." And then May played, "Back Stabbers," another oldie that aired frequently on CBS FM. When it came on, May said the song was about her, that she was the backstabber.

"No, you're not," I said, rushing to console her, before she could get out another apology.

"Yes, I am," she said tearing up, and I think she hated me a little bit more right then.

A month later May found an apartment. She rented a van for the day and asked all our friends to help her move. On the street, she over-thanked me.

"It's nothing," I said, waving away her gratitude.

There wasn't much. Most of the furniture that we'd bought together, May had fallen through or the mice had gnawed at, so aside from some clothing and books—she left the sex books—all that needed to be moved was the couch, the sofa-bed she'd bought on her own.

May and I didn't bother trying to lift it ourselves. The guys—my "idiot ex-boyfriend," Felix, Jacob, and Reggie—picked up the four corners while May and I guided them up the long narrow stairway. It took them a little over an hour to move, for it was much heavier and bulkier than a regular sofa, and to get it around each corner, they had to maneuver it up onto its narrow side. And then, when they had it up like that, the inside would start to unfold right in midair—the bed splayed open with a tangle of sheets still on it—and they'd have to stop and wait for May and me to stuff it back in before they could move it again.

A few weeks after that, May invited me over for dinner. We remarked on how weird it was that we weren't roommates anymore, how I was her guest. She'd made a whole lemon chicken, a dish much more advanced than any that she'd made while we lived together. She said she was getting into cooking. Then she showed me the door on which she was starting a new collection of black-and-white postcards, like the one I had arranged on the doors of all our former homes—she had amassed only five so far, but was on the lookout, she said. Then she showed me around the rest of the apartment, which Felix, not officially living with her, had clearly decorated. There was a rack of comic books in the bathroom and two or three of his original paintings on the living room wall.

Back at Fifty-seventh Street, I wondered what to do with the second loft bed. And in the living room, in place of the couch, there was now a big empty stretch of floor. In a few months it would be filled with boxes of T-shirts from my fledgling business. And then, some time after that, I would meet Martin and begin to see less of May until I wouldn't see her at all.

The last time was on a double date. Felix and May, and Martin and I, met up at a bar near her new apartment on the Upper West Side. It was, oddly, the day after September 11th, and also, the day after my first day of teaching. All the schools and offices were closed, while the restaurants and bars were overflowing as if it were a holiday.

I'd been at Martin's earlier that morning, watching the news with some of his friends when, one at a time, we began to notice a strange odor. For a moment, we thought we were being gassed and looked at each other, wondering if this wasn't the next part. Then we realized it was smoke from the rubble finally reaching us. That some of the great white cloud, what had been the two towers, was dispersing.

Terrified of the rising death count, terrified of what might happen next in the subways, on the streets, in the sky, I was also terrified of returning to my new job and the thirty-six students suddenly placed in my charge. Yesterday morning, standing before the class, futilely yelling for their attention, begging them to please sit down, sending one after the other to the principal, all I had wanted was to hide, and now, like a child hearing news of snow on the day of a big test, I was relieved.

When another teacher had come into my classroom, had taken me outside to explain that a plane had flown into the Twin Towers, I'd barely understood her. Curtis had just thrown his chair across the room. I had just split up a fight between Mario and Victor. Christian had told me to fuck off, and I was trying not to cry. I nodded dumbly. All I understood was that school was closing early.

Martin's friend Fred, who had recently moved to the financial district, had spent the night. We watched the news until we couldn't anymore, the same image of the towers falling again and again, small black figures falling from the windows. Then May called, told us to come out, to meet her and Felix somewhere in Times Square.

We played laser tag—I'd never played before—at a place called Playland or Mars, I don't remember the name. Martin and I wandered through a dark maze filled with smoke and lit with red and blue lights . . . May and Felix sneaking up behind us . . . Martin and me hiding, running, dipping around corners, before shooting wildly . . . the whole room humming.

Then we went to a bar, and after that, stopped at a diner. We slid into a booth: Felix and May on one side, Martin and me on the other— two duos. Felix and May cracked jokes and laughed loudly. They had drunk more than we had, had been drinking since the morning. May looked at me across the table, her new hoop earrings catching the light. They reminded me of the black patent leather raincoat she'd purchased freshman year, just before winter break.

Preparing for her first visit home to Alabama, we'd gone shopping on Eighth Street to find "something chic and sophisticated," an outfit that would impress all her hometown friends, an outfit that would let them know she'd changed; she was a New Yorker! "Wait 'til they see me in this!" she'd squealed, posing beside her suitcase in front of the dormitory door. I'd snapped a photo.

"Cool earrings," I said. Then Felix pulled her face into his for a kiss.

I went back to Martin's place after and as we got ready for bed, I told him I didn't have a good time. Martin went into the kitchen and filled two glasses with water. He placed one by my side of the bed and then, putting the other down on his side, sat down and began unlacing his shoes.

What was supposed to happen? If things had gone as she'd hoped? Would she have watched as I packed my bags, as my parents waited outside, double-parked? Would she have held the door while I gave her my keys? And after, on her own finally, alone with the bugs and the mice and the leaks, a giant castle, empty, across from her bed, would she feel happy, would she feel she'd won?

"They're kids," I said, standing in my underwear. "Everything is a game to them."

He shrugged. "She's *your* friend."

II

3

Three years later, two apartments later, I'd just moved to West Tenth Street and was planning a birthday party with my friend Jacob. I'd quit my job—I had never *wanted* to be a teacher and didn't know how I ended up one—writing to the headmaster during summer break that I'd been accepted to graduate school and would not be returning in the fall.

I was going to start over. While I studied and wrote papers, which now seemed so easy compared to the dismal work of showing up for students and answering to parents and bosses, I'd write my novel, a new novel that would pave the road to my real life, which still hadn't started, my life as an author. More than a degree, graduate school would give me time.

My idea for the novel? Why, it would be about work, of course, and about not working, too. About young people who were unhappy with their jobs. Two of the characters would be named Jacob, after my friend, and they'd hate each other, thinking there could only be one. The other novel I'd drafted that first summer after college I now put aside, recognizing the complete falseness of my twenty-seven-year-old alcoholic protagonist, my pretending to be Damon Runyon and Henry Miller. My idea, this time, was to pretend to be myself.

I was quite disciplined in the beginning, writing every day, pausing only occasionally for the sake of my studies. But eventually, my schoolwork began to take precedence. It's a difficult project, leading a whole fake life while maintaining the belief that another life, the one you are not actually living, is more real. It's a difficult project being a writer who is not a writer.

When I was young, I wanted to be a famous actress, to own my own dirigible, to win the Nobel Prize for literature! My ambitions were great and I had plenty of time; the future was still far away. At a certain age, however, after you've been living in the future a while, continuing to say what you *want* to do is less laudable than laughable. To say you *want* to be a writer starts to feel embarrassing. Especially when you hold in your hand a book by an author who is younger than you are, younger than you were, younger, younger, younger, receding from you in age. For the adult, the question naturally follows: So, why aren't you then?

It was around this time that a grisly habit took possession of me. In the same way I began studying *The New York Times* wedding announcements after breaking up with Martin, with every book I came across, I began subtracting the author's birthday from the year of his or her first publication in order to see how much time I had left, how much time I had lost.

Too late to be the next Carson McCullers, F. Scott Fitzgerald, or Malcolm Lowry. Too late to be a phenom, but there's still time to be Céline or Henry Miller or, if I get lazy and alcohol takes precedence, there is always Bukowski. . . . Over the next years, I continued to tick authors from my list, until Frank McCourt became a key palliative in my anxiety attacks.

Plenty of time, I told myself. Frank McCourt published his first book in his sixties, after he retired! *Of course, in your sixties no one's asking what you do anymore, because they assume you've already done it. And sixty years is an awful long time to hide out in your fake life, waiting for the real one to begin. And then, of course, I will have missed out on the opportunity to be beautiful and successful and have men want to use me for my status and power, to feel happy and secure in the fact that "the real me" plays no part in their love. I'd be* *too old to enjoy my success, but . . .* and then I'd steer myself toward some easier thought, some vague plan like, *well, I guess I'll just have* *to hurry.*

Nearing twenty-five and about to start over both professionally and personally, I decided to stop telling people I wanted to be a writer and began saying instead, "I'm going to be a professor." But as I said it, I whispered this to myself: What a long road it is to earn a PhD, Iris. How many more cushiony years in which to protect your dreams from the harsh light of reality. How many years for you to continue safely to want, without having to do. You could still become . . . had years to become. . . . My goal, if I'd really been honest with myself, was a life of endless preparation.

2

Because I had only very recently broken up with Martin, I had few friends of my own to invite to my birthday party, so Jacob invited his friends and asked them to invite theirs. "I want to have a wild party!" I told Jacob, feeling myself so old. I must stop dressing so maturely, I decided. And getting ready for the party, I put on a slinky black mini-dress as if dressing were an act of protest, as if my body were a banner raised against time.

Martin called early in the day to wish me a happy birthday, instructing me that I start to get used to it. "Twenty-five is the last good birthday. After twenty-five, instead of growing up, you grow old." I told him he was a downer. I told him I was just grateful to have survived another year without an air conditioner falling on me and insisted that all birthdays were good ones. I lied and told him I was happy. And then I promised myself that this year I would get one year younger, that I would be young again before it was too late.

I invited a few people that I'd reconnected with on Friendster, the new social network that Jacob and I had begun obsessing over—we revised our profiles multiple times a day, endlessly rewriting our "about me" sections as if it were our descriptions and not our lives that needed the work. I invited Reggie, who had friendstered me months earlier, after we'd run into each other online outside the Halloween store. Reggie responded, saying Felix was in town; would I mind if he brought him along?

"I wouldn't mind," I answered prissily, "so long as he behaves." Having spent the last three years trying to be a grown-up—I'd gone to cocktail parties on the Upper East Side, organized parent-teacher meetings, rode the subway during rush hour, and graduated from night school—I didn't want to lose what I'd worked so hard to attain. If I wanted to be young again, it was not to escape adulthood, but to use this second youth to better prepare for it. "Youth is wasted on the young," Shaw wrote, and I didn't want to waste mine twice. "Just make sure he doesn't break anything," I wrote back warily.

Jacob came. Reggie came. Felix came. Some old friends from college came. A lot of people I didn't know came—Jacob and I, worried no one would show, had dispatched a small crew to invite people they met in the bars and streets surrounding my apartment—and then some people they knew came.

Felix danced and played DJ. Everyone drank. Everyone danced. Everyone drank more. We piled into the bathroom and smoked a joint. We all stood on the furniture at once. We decided to put on a talent show and appointed judges. A girl no one knew drummed the bellies of three men, one of them Jacob, who, lying down, had a flower tucked behind his ear. A couple danced to "Disco Mickey Mouse." And a guy ate crackers very fast. And then, at midnight, Felix handed me his phone. "It's May. She wants to wish you happy birthday."

She said she was sorry for everything that happened, for everything she did. She said she'd wanted to call so many times. She said she missed me. We exchanged email addresses, promised to keep in touch, and then I hung up and blew out the candles someone had stuck into some cupcakes a friend had brought over, which everyone ate before I had a chance.

We danced more. We smoked a few more joints. More people came and went and I put on my roller-skates. We talked about the weather, the Super Bowl, irregular French verbs, fortune telling, igloos, the Donner Party, and our favorite discontinued snack cakes. I demonstrated a logic equation I'd learned from Martin, using the red and blue magic markers from my drawing table. We played a game.

And then at some point I must have hit my head on something, because when I woke up there was a big blue bruise near my hairline and a half-dressed Reggie lying beside me. I heard rustling in the next room, and then my bedroom door opened. There was Felix with one of my disposable cameras. "Cheese and crackers!" he said to both of us, before snapping a photo from which we shielded our faces. "Come on, breakfast is ready."

1

She'd been living in L. A. for two years, she wrote in her first email. She and Felix had officially moved in together just before it all fell apart, she wrote in the next one. Now she was by herself, she said over the phone. She'd been doing a lot of commercials, had just landed a Diet Dr Pepper campaign, she told me over drinks; it was Halloween and she'd come for a visit.

We dressed as Cheech and Chong for a party I threw on Reggie's roof. At another party the night before, May was Mona (the oversexed mother of Angela) while I was Angela (the uptight advertising exec) from TV's *Who's the Boss?* All night I kept calling out, "Tony!" as if I were quite exasperated, before The Bastard Felix, who'd been living on my couch before she arrived, appeared, mock-quizzical, holding a dishrag.

I visited her in L. A. the following winter. She picked me up from the airport and once on the road, popped open the glove compartment. Rice Krispies Treats laced with pot: "My pharmacy sells them. They're just like ours," she giggled, "except they actually bake the pot inside. I bought them in honor of your visit!"

It was her birthday and when we arrived back at her apartment, after she showed me to her couch, I presented her with a leather picnic basket that held two martini glasses, shakers, bottles, and olives. We took it to the beach with us that afternoon, toasted our glasses, and shivered in the sand.

4

In Greece this past summer, I saw very little of my friends. Mostly only in passing, in the late morning, as I rushed to the dock to meet Leonidas, my twenty-two-year-old boyfriend whom I met at a beach party at 4:00 AM, after everyone else had gone home. They waved to me and sometimes, reaching a hand into a stroller, helped their babies wave, too.

"Your turn," my mother told me back at the house.

"I've got plenty of time," I said, grabbing my towel. "American women marry later. Not one of my friends back home is married." I zipped up my bag and skipped off to meet my new beau.

Leonidas had his own boat, or his father did. Having just graduated from college, he'd borrowed it for the summer, planning to tool around the islands while he figured out what he wanted to do. The boat wasn't very big, but it had a small cabin underneath where he could sleep and keep his fishing equipment and a cooler of ouzo and beer. Most mornings, I'd say goodbye to my parents and go out on the water with him. Feeling shaky and hungover from the previous night, I was always eager to see him, to share a small bottle of ouzo, to feel the wind and breathe the sea air.

The trick was not to drink too much, but just enough to take the edge off of last night. It was difficult to stop though, and what began as just one often turned into too many, turned into a long afternoon followed by another long night. Sometimes my parents would be asleep when I got home. Other times, they'd be up, waiting.

"It's 6:00 AM!" my mother would yell, opening the door before I could turn the key. I'd dive past them to the stairs, grab the banister and try to steady myself, holding my breath so they wouldn't smell the alcohol on it. "I'm twenty-nine years old. I'm a grown-up!" I'd say defiantly. "Exactly!" my father yelled.

The wind was blowing and the sky was clear, the mountains crisp along the coast as we motored past. Leonidas asked me what I was so worried about. It was noon. I had told my mother I'd be back for lunch and we were nowhere near home.

Earlier, Leonidas had passed unexpectedly in front of my parents' house. He'd cut the motor and let down the ladder. My parents were on shore when I waved to them, before we sped away. We were only going over to the next village, he said. We'd be back within the hour.

But it was noon now, and we'd been gone two hours already and were still at least two hours from home.

"It's summer," Leonidas reminded me. "You have plenty of time."

"Yes, but my parents will worry."

"You're not a child, Iris. You can do whatever you want."

"I don't like to make them worry," I said, looking down at my drink.

He shrugged. "I like my time," he said, leaning back against the boat as it rocked gently beneath us. We'd stopped in a cove for a quick swim. He put his arm around me, his young arm, and said, "What are you so scared of?"

My eyes filled with tears. He wiped one away and smiled. It was a beautiful day. "The sky is clear, the sea is clean, and we are together." He toasted his plastic cup to mine. I took a sip of my ouzo and then another and then another, and with each my heartbeat seemed to slow, with each I smiled a little more. The hurrying thoughts, with every sip, drifted further away. I looked up at the clear blue sky where he'd pointed, and then down at the clean blue sea. Ignoring the horrible ticking in my chest, I jumped in.

I stayed in Greece for all of August and flew home on the first of September. Waiting on line at customs back in New York, I checked my voicemail, having kept my phone off the whole time I was gone.

There was a message from May: "I'm engaged!"

3

At the beginning of *Speak, Memory,* Nabokov describes a friend's anxiety over the thought, inspired by a home movie, of the world before he came into it. The film, shot just before he was born, shows an empty pram, bought in anticipation of his birth, which Nabokov's friend likens to a coffin. It frames his non-existence, he explains. And he fears un-birth the way many more commonly fear death. Nabokov acknowledges the strange truth at the heart of his friend's anxiety by describing every life as book-ended by an abyss, making before and after, birth and death, essentially the same occasion.

I thought about Nabokov while I searched my pockets for a tissue and the customs officer stamped my passport. I thought about my upcoming birthday, my thirtieth. I thought about Martin's phone call on my twenty-fifth four and a half years earlier, about the bitter birthdays he told me to expect. I readdressed the question his warning implied: Is a birthday an occasion for celebration or mourning? I replaced the word birthday with "May's wedding," and found myself staring directly into Nabokov's abyss.

2

The room began to spin, the whole world was spinning, and I realized with a start that it wasn't just beginning, but that I was only now noticing.

"I have plenty of time, Mom."

"The world will wait for us," Leonidas said with a smile, after cutting the engine and handing me a drink.

"The rotation of the Earth," I'd told The Captain, after falling down in front of the fountain in Atlantic City.

He gave me a hand to help me off the floor. "You were sitting still!" he said. "Who loses their balance when they're sitting still?" he laughed.

"The world," I explained, brushing myself off, "moved without me."

Standing before the baggage carousel, I saw May climbing up onto one of our rolling chairs, reaching to close the top window shutter, the wheels slipping beneath her, her eyes going wide as she fell backward . . . crashed through the glass. The carousel turned and turned.

"Congratulations!" I exploded, as soon as she picked up. I'd called from the taxi on my way home from the airport. "Tell me everything!"

She told me how he proposed. She told me the wedding would be in the spring.

"That's so great," I gushed, before stammering to a halt. "So how does your fiancé feel about the sleeping arrangements? About our sharing a bedroom? Have you told him yet, or shall I?"

May laughed and said she'd almost forgotten. Then she gave me his phone number and said, "Pretend you're me."

1

In bed, back in my apartment, I lay awake for a long time.

I blink, straining to see, but the daubs of paint are giant, the branches great arms blocking my eyes. Inside the big picture, it is dark, it is night, I am in a clear plastic forest, the fog is dense, and I am lost. I turn onto my side, onto my back. I pick up where I left off:

Too late to be Hemingway . . . too late to be Capote . . . too late to be Salinger. But I could still be Isak Dinesen . . . I could still be Proust—Proust, the life-long dilettante, deciding one night out of nowhere, to leave the party early. Didn't he also have a lot of catching up to do? What did Dante do when he found himself lost? He wrote about a time that must have been hell for him; he called it a comedy. And once he set it all down—his friends, his enemies, his heroes, his loves—he wrote himself out.

OVERTURE

FOR A LONG time I used to go to bed late. Sometimes I never went to bed at all but just drank until I passed out, my eyes closing so quickly that I had not even time to say to myself: I should take off my shoes. And half an hour later the thought that it was time to go to the bathroom would wake me. I would make as if to put away the bottle which I imagined was still in my hands, and to turn out the light; "I had gone on thinking, while I was asleep, about what I had just been reading, but these thoughts had taken a rather peculiar turn; it seemed to me that I myself was the immediate subject of my book."

It's 10:00 PM in New York. I'm in bed; I'm finally reading *Swann's Way*. Every night I go to sleep early, rising at the hour I used to turn in. Yesterday, at 6:00 AM, I walked over to the Hudson River and saw a cluster of twenty-somethings, drunk, laughing, returning home at the end of their night. They didn't see me though. It was as if I were looking through a two-way mirror; the light shines from one side and looking through you can see the past, but when you try to look from the other, into the future, all you see is yourself reflected in the present. Every morning, I wake early. The days race by and I chase them into the night—there's barely enough time.

In my apartment on Tenth Street, the furnace burns at all hours. Before I go to bed, I open the windows to move the heat around; the blare of horns from the traffic below swirls up. I shut my eyes and for a few minutes, before I fall asleep, I think: I could be anywhere. Am I in bed on West Tenth Street or with Martin on the Upper East Side? Am I in Murray Hill in my apartment over the Midtown Tunnel or ten feet up off the ground in Hell's Kitchen, with May and Felix in the next room, May in the next bed? What is my book about? A song from one of the cars stalled at a traffic light comes through the window, some laughter, the sound of two girls talking, searching for the address of a party. How does it begin? The furnace sputters and clangs all through the rooms, all through the building, and all at once, I am reminded of the old place:

My first apartment, its furniture, how it always rained in the bathroom, how the mice scratched in the walls at night, how the kitchen was a dark continent and our couch, an island bluff. How we sat together the last summer before graduation underlining our instruction manuals, snapping photos of each other in our Thursday costumes as if to catch our lives mid-blur. How our couch was an island like Manhattan, to which we'd both decamped separately at eighteen, and where we found each other, laughing, spinning the cap over a bottle of smoke, half believing that we would always be young, half afraid that we would never grow up. I think about our buckling couch, our youth, and the beach eroding on all sides. I think about the feel of its cushions, held up by so many lost things. Our couch—not an island at all, but just a raft—on top of which, for a few years, we floated.